For Ana Maria

R. GARCIA VAZQUEZ

Beneath An
Alien Sun

SPINNING WORLD PRESS
TOMS RIVER – NEW JERSEY

Spinning World Press, P.O. Box 3582, Toms River, NJ 08756-3582
spinningworldpress.com

First Edition, May 2022
Beneath An Alien Sun / R. Garcia Vazquez

Library of Congress Control Number: 2022934934
ISBN: 978-0-9991522-2-5 (trade paperback)
ASIN: B09W1KNQG2 (ebook)

Printed in the United States of America.
10 9 8 7 6 5 4 3 2 1

Contents

Beneath An
Alien Sun

Why, Sayer? For furp sake, what is so wrong
with being a little bit us, a little bit them?
- Burr Brumbo

Notes to Unknown Survivor

30 April 2100 - 20 September 2104

What are the odds of any one of us existing? About 400 trillion to one... I need a moment to think about that, Willie.

- Merlin Stone

09 October 2101

The day I turned thirty, Atwell threw me a birthday party in a big dome packed with wealthy Deos and informed me the world was going to end before Bright Star Day. Three days later, he told me the woman I was falling in love with wasn't who I thought she was. Atwell's not the most reliable human. Even so, things aren't looking good.

I've heard the dead speak, I've watched trees pull up their roots and sprint out of town, I've forgotten who or where I am for hours at a time. I long for what's real. It's two in the morning. I'm in the kitchen eating an apple. Why? I have no idea. It's been like this lately, me being someone else. And whatever happened to my New Life Plan?

I go to bed. Two hours of tossing and twitching later, I get up and turn on all the lights. I grit my teeth, knowing I've got to do a better job of coping. I opt for a cold shower. Is there a better way to clear the mind? Probably not. That's what I'm thinking as I lean forward to test the sharp, icy streams with my fingers.

But, good stars, already I'm having second thoughts!

I tease the shower controller, my mind in a state of flux. I fiddle with the controller until I plumb the sweet spot: hot, but not too hot. What's wrong with being comfortable anyway? I step into the hot streams, close my eyes and float in my secret sea. I float without a care in the world.

For about a minute. Then I hear a voice.

If not you, then who?

I flinch and slip, banging my elbow and hip against the tiled wall. From a crouched position, I watch the ghost withdraw. I rub my face, open my eyes wide, and poke my head out. The ghost is gone. It's just me, alone, dripping wet and feeling ridiculous.

Two thoughts come to mind as I shut off the water. People who bear the burden of terrible knowledge are likely to drown inside their heads if they're not careful. The second thought is actually a question: Whose voice did I hear?

Was it yours?

Your silence surrounds me. It waits on me. It has expectations. That you can hear my voice is something of a miracle. I can't pretend this isn't happening.

Look, there are things you probably don't know that you should know. Let's begin with the Deo exodus. Deos started going on interplanetary vacation cruises half a century ago. But it wasn't until 2098 that the majority of them stopped coming back. They've been populating the new world that's been under secret construction for decades. Atwell started building the Martian branch of Stone TransHumanix in 2076, for example. No fanfare, no Transmedia coverage. Most Ords have been too busy surviving the challenges of a planet in steep decline to pay attention to Deos on vacation.

More than two-thirds of the nearly sixty million exiles will be living in contiguous air-locked New Terra City, Mars by the time the exodus is completed. The rest will inhabit colonies established on the moons of Jupiter: Io, Europa, Ganymede, and Callisto.

According to Atwell, the official reports regarding the so-called "space hurricane" are lies. The real estimated death and survival rates he presented me were so outlandish I refused, at first, to believe him. He tried to get me to relocate to New Terra City. I declined the invitation, but to say I was solely motivated by principle would be misleading.

After Atwell and Runa are gone, I'll be moving to Stone Heights. Atwell once boasted he'd built the place to withstand an apocalypse. There's no denying the man's a genius. He's also my father, or so I've been told.

As far as the turquoise rabbit? Well, Willie's a 3W and the reason you can hear my voice. The 3W is a high-end interactive voice and face recognition wobot that doubles as a toy rabbit. It was designed by Cleavon Blinkhorn. It never caught on with children during Engagement Quality Trials at Stone TransHumanix and was scrapped. Kids never bought into its stilted attempts at humor and conversation, with a high percentage of EQT participants being spooked by its techy-herbivore gaze and voice.

I can confirm that. When I was seven, Atwell handed me a 3W and spent a few minutes watching me try to interact with it. Desperate for his approval, I did my best to appear engaged, but couldn't pull it off. Father left my bedroom without saying a word. I set the wobot on the floor of my closet and shoved it into the back corner with my crutch.

I returned to Stone House last year after a long absence and discovered the 3W exactly where I had left it. Seasoned by global wanderings, trials and tribulations, I'm no longer quick to dismiss what I don't understand. I lifted the wobot out of the closet, placed it on my desk and sat in a chair in front of it.

"What's up, Willie?"

My words triggered a lifelike reaction from the 3W. When Willie replied, "The sky, Merlin," I almost flipped. At the time I had no clue how this toy rabbit would help me preserve my sanity in the face of unforeseen challenges.

Willie's a superb notetaker. I speak, he processes, offers input on flow and structure, executes finishing touches, files and stores away my dictated notes for future reference and possible discovery by unknown survivors such as yourself. Over time, his ability to adjust his associational neuristor impulses in response to my input has allowed him to surpass the role of useful wobot and become a confidant and friend.

Willie is eerily sensitive. One day, sensing a drop in my dopamine levels, he said, "How about I sing you a song, Merlin?" I stared at him, not quite understanding what he meant. He proceeded to sing *Bohemian Rhapsody* a cappella in that techy-skewed, Savannah-Georgia accent of his. Willie's performance was an unpleasant surprise. I said nothing. On another occasion, after his creepy rendition of *Me and Bobby McGee*, I told him I wasn't the right audience for his singing, and I directed him to play studio recordings by the original artists, exclusively, going forward.

That said, I don't like tampering with Willie's upbeat personality. I'm only just beginning to glimpse his quantum rabbit potential. Let's not forget his inauspicious beginnings, how he was rejected by children during EQTs, how his product line was discontinued, and how he was sentenced to over two decades of closet solitude by yours truly.

I've learned it's a mistake to underestimate the seemingly ordinary and those who are different from us. Willie was built to endure the worst of times. He's going to be around long after I'm gone, delivering notes, gauging dopamine levels, suggesting titles from Blinkhorn's *Songs of the Old World*, and offering unknown survivors reasons to have hope.

One other thing, those words I heard: *If not you, then who?* They haunt me. I haven't grasped their full meaning, but I'm convinced more will be required of me. I have no idea what that might be. I can't say I'm looking forward to it, but for now, at least, speaking to another human through the silicone lips of a turquoise rabbit feels like the right thing to do.

I once heard it said that the odds of you or me existing are 400 trillion to one. I gaze at the night sky and try to imagine what 400 trillion stars might look like. Numbers like that make my head spin. They defy comprehension.

But we persist.

We navigate the impossible and the incomprehensible. We get up each morning and breathe and live and tell each other our stories. And it's there, in the telling and listening of those stories, that we recognize one another and remember who we are.

The journey, the journey…

Mine took a wild, unexpected turn a year and a half ago in a crowded bar in Greece.

Recorded: 10 Oct 2101

30 April 2100

Athens proved too busy for my liking. Thessaloniki seemed the better fit. That's where I've been living for the past few months. I spend most of my evenings in a bar called Taverna Momos. The regulars drink the house tsipouro and eat olives and peanuts off small porcelain trays. The liveliest debates, as you might expect, revolve around sports, politics, and the economy. Now and then you might hear a word or two about the Peloponnesian War, the new Hellenism, or migrants from the Middle East.

The controlled chaos of Taverna Momos has been kind to me. It's a safe harbor for those who prefer their solitude free of abject loneliness. It's also a kind of rehab center. I've been off the Bona Drops and VR Escapade Juice since New Year's Day. The eight-hour euphoria stints once seemed like the answer to life's drudgery, but a progressive escalation of headaches and paranoia made me reconsider my approach to coping. I've been weaning myself off the hallucinogens with a disciplined consumption of tsipouro while in the company of others.

I go by the name Robert Jordan, though my passport says Merlin Stone. I teach English to a handful of Greek kids, ages twelve to seventeen, and also a forty-five-year-old seminarian named Anacletus. My cash-only fees are reasonable, so I'm able to maintain a steady trickle of clients. At twenty-eight, I have trouble seeing a day beyond today. I'm not sure if that's good or bad. Lack of foresight and ambition may come back to bite me, but for now I'm all I need to be and glad to be off the Drops and the Juice.

I call my favorite student VJ, which is short for Vitas Junior. He once overheard me ask the bartender if Momos was the proprietor's name. The bartender had no idea. VJ was happy to fill me in. Momos is the god of mockery, poets and writers, he explained. Apparently, Zeus kicked Momos out of Mount Olympus for being a pain in his celestial ass. VJ's dad owns a small travel accessories shop. He's the only parent I've ever met who demanded to see my passport before he would consider allowing his son to fall under my tutelage. He checked my name, looked me in the eye, handed me back my passport, and walked away without saying a word.

Didn't think I'd see VJ again, but there he was showing up for his first day of class. He walked into the church supply room where I tutor my students from four to seven, five days a week, and said, "Good afternoon, Mister Mágos."

I gathered his dad told him don't be fooled by the crafty American. His real name is Merlin, not Robert. Merlin, like magician, wizard, *mágos*. "Your secret is okay in here," VJ said in surprisingly good English while pointing to his temple.

Recorded: 10 Jul 2101

11

01 May 2100

As far as Mr. Mágos? Well, I'm no magician, as you're about to see. A half hour after securing my favorite spot at the crowded bar, I hear an unmistakably All-American female voice cry out, "Let go of me, asswipe!"

The words are sharp as knives and cut through the nearly impenetrable din. A tall, pink-streaked blonde with bouncy shoulder length hair stomps toward a just abandoned bar-stool a few patrons to my right. She's wearing a shrunken psychedelic t-shirt that shows off her flat tanned belly and silver bellybutton ring. Waist down, she's wearing white baggy shorts and pink slip-on sneakers.

A ponytailed male sporting Dante's Inferno tattoos on his neck and biceps trails behind at half speed. The two bring with them an odor of cultural discord, linguistic challenges, and thin skin.

A lovers' quarrel. I take note of a few lazy glances, but otherwise nobody here gives a toot about lovers' quarrels. Years of hanging out in bars across Europe have taught me that lovers' quarrels relocated to drink pits tend to be

12

tolerated by the regulars, who deem the theatrics nothing more than a tiresome foreshadowing of late-night make-up sessions.

Miss Pink's decision to choose this locale as her haven of choice, or new combat venue, is interesting in and of itself. After a couple of shots of tsipouro, or whatever they're drinking, the melodramatic lovers will go staggering over lamp-lit streets to a barebones flat for reconciliation.

I don't think I'll wait for the happy ending, but I order one last drink anyway. I admit I'm curious. The minutes pass, and I can't make out what they're arguing about. But the dense, garbled exchanges suggest this is not a one-night stand situation but something rooted in weary familiarity. Contrary to my thinking, whatever they're drinking has failed to smooth over their points of contention and seems to have further sharpened grievances.

Should I be concerned? The locals don't seem to be, but I'm not a local, and what I'm witnessing is becoming less entertaining and more disturbing by the moment. Each jab, counterjab, sets off one more alarm bell that jars my conscience and rouses obscure notions of patriotic accountability and reactive gallantry.

My response to what's happening is unfortunate and unexpected. I'm not really going to do this, am I? I need to talk to someone who will correct my thinking and ease my concerns. I look to my left. The guy is arguing with the guy on his left about a dead Deo named Aristotle Onassis, and the guy on my right is staring over the bar counter at a crude oil painting of Dionysus holding a bowl of wine in one hand and a bunch of grapes in the other.

I wish that were Rod on my right. Rod was a fellow expat from Chicago, retired military, and a bit of a mystery. He said his name was Rodion Raskolnikov, in the same way I say my name is Robert Jordan. He said I could call him Rod if I wanted. I told him he could call me Rob.

One day Rod and I were knocking back shots of tsipouro just for the pure sad pleasure of it, both of us silenced by feelings of regret and longing neither of us was capable of articulating. We sat there drinking in silence. Then Rod got up to leave. He gave me the usual lazy military salute on his way out. But a couple of seconds later, he was back. He looked me in the eye, and in a clear voice spoke the only words I remember him saying that evening, "Nothing disturbs me more, Rob, than people no longer being disturbed by disturbing things."

I never saw him again. I don't know what happened to him or where he might have gone. Those first few days I scanned the news and obituaries, looking for an American tragedy. It took me a while to determine that Rod might be living on a hill somewhere in Spain, or in a Moroccan desert, or maybe in Iceland.

If Rod were here, he'd probably say, "Yep, this lovers' quarrel passes the Disturbing Things Test with flying colors."

But does it? I'm not so sure. I'll finish the drink I should never have ordered and get out of here. Most likely, the situation will resolve itself in short order.

There are exceptions, sure, but from my experience, what looks like fire usually turns out to be nothing but smoke. Legitimate knock-down, drag-out personal crises are what people like to write and talk about, not what we do, at least not generally. Ninety-nine times out of a hundred, a worst-case scenario remains a scenario, a petered-out wannabe disaster that's not even worth talking about.

My level of optimism keeps trending up the more I think this through. Much ado about nothing. Isn't that what they used to say? It's just a matter of time before these two knuckleheads understand life is going to look much better in the morning over coffee and tomato basil frittata.

But when I hear a barstool grind against the wooden floor, my emerging feel-good state takes a hit. I turn and see Miss Pink stomping toward the exit. She doesn't get far, though. Mr. Inferno performs an acrobatic leap, grabs Miss Pink's arm and spins her around, her lustrous mane whipping the air like silk. The leap-grab-spin maneuver, executed to Broadway perfection, is mesmerizing.

"Nobody call Zorba Papadopoulos asswipe, okay?" he bellows like an embattled Spartan. "I don't care if she come from Kansas City, Kentucky, or Kalamazoo!"

These are the first words he's said that I can fully understand, and because I haven't seen that degree of ferocity on a human face since grade school, or heard a Greek of any age alliterate that smoothly in English, Mister Papadopoulos's pronouncements sound more entertaining than menacing.

But my moment of spectator pleasure passes too quickly. Miss Pink struggles futilely to pull her arm free from Zorba's iron grip. Zorba has tipped the scales in his favor and looks to be enjoying himself. He shakes his chiseled ponytailed head and smugly says something only she can hear.

Then it happens. Miss Pink shoots me a glance, and our eyes meet with devastating effect. No, it can't be. Here, in

Thessaloniki, Greece? I must be confusing her for someone else. But this is all happening too fast, and I don't have the luxury of lying to myself. It is her, the somber brunette who sat to my right during *Deconstructing the Twentieth Century* class. How could I forget those violet eyes?

I lower my foot onto the sticky wooden floor, crushing peanut shells and rolling olive pits. This strange quiet girl who spent a semester ruminating and deconstructing the twentieth century just a couple of feet away from me is writhing and wincing and getting nowhere. In a last-ditch effort to turn the tide, she shouts out what sounds like an ethnic slur that turns a few heads. In response, Zorba twists her arm just a tad more, and she begins to whimper.

From where I'm sitting, the stakes have just shot way up, obliterating whatever prospect of a happy ending I'd been counting on. I shoot desperate glances all around, seeking an imminent intervention, the sudden authoritative appearance of the proprietor or a respected elder, maybe an off-duty cop, someone's grandmother, anyone to step out of the crowd and take control of the situation. But no one cares because it's a lovers' quarrel.

I finally peel my cheeks off the barstool and walk up to the combatants. I look from one to the other, feigning confusion so as not to suggest I'm playing favorites or gearing up to dispense judgment.

"Is everything okay?"

Is that all I have? Shouldn't I have gotten in Zorba's face, said something edgy like, *What seems to be the problem?*

But why be confrontational? My job is not to escalate hostilities. I stepped into the disputed space to tamp down the fire before it gets out of control. So, yes, I made the right call. There's nothing wrong with saying, *Is everything okay?*

"Do you know what he did to me?" Miss Pink says, her voice trembling, those violet eyes drilling me.

You mean, aside from the obvious?

Abruptly, the chatter volume tapers off, and it suddenly dawns on me what she's done. In one fell swoop, Miss Pink has anointed me her champion *and* Zorba's mortal enemy.

"Oh, wow, this looks bad. Uhm, sorry, I didn't mean to pry into your personal affairs. It was just that…"

Just that what?

Zorba releases Miss Pink and gets in my face. "Too late," he says and spits on my shoe. I look down at the amoeba-shaped gob and watch the spit bubbles pop.

On cue, the bartender turns off the live hologram feed. Chairs and tables are getting rearranged. Guys are moving around and positioning themselves to secure optimal line of sight. Before I can fully process what's happening, the whole place has gone quiet as a graveyard. Zorba and I stand facing one another inside a circle of suddenly interested parties. I catch a glimpse of Miss Pink standing among the ranks of silent watchers.

The flats of Zorba's hands land like bricks on my chest and I stumble back and fall. I'm sitting on the grimy floor looking up, registering that I'm about to experience ridiculous pain, when a huge specimen of a man emerges from the crowd and bearhugs Zorba from behind just as he's about to kick my face in.

Zorba can't shake the giant's hold. To compensate, he resorts to spitting out threats and curses in lingua franca but stops when the big man whispers in his ear. Just like that, Zorba calms down and whispers something back that satisfies his restrainer. He glares at me for a few seconds, fixes a curious gaze on Miss Pink, and performs an intense symbolic wiping of hands before walking out of Taverna Momos with his head held high.

My remarkable intercessor approaches me and stops within a couple of feet, beefy hands folded over his belly, head tilted slightly to the right. I gather he's deferring to me. "I'm Robert," I lie.

"Heracles," he says and does the Namaste bow.

"Heracles, thanks, man," I say, replicating the gesture.

"No problem, Robert."

Is he waiting for me to buy him a drink? Before I can open my mouth, we all hear Miss Pink's tacky rubber-soled steps crossing the wooden floor. I watch her walk out of the tavern, and I suspect this means she'll soon be making out with Mr. Inferno and having a few laughs at my expense. Not a glance in my direction, nor a word of thanks for nearly getting kicked in the face for defending her honor.

Someone turns the hologram feed back on.

"Mr. Tattoo wait for you outside," Heracles says.

"Huh?"

"Mr. Tattoo, Papadopoulos, the one you insult. He waiting outside."

"For me?"

"You have knife?"

"What?"

He slaps a big switchblade in my right hand, closes my fingers over it, and nods fatalistically.

"He say he going to cut you like pig. You take knife. You fight. You defend your honor."

I stare stupidly at the switchblade. Heracles nods his head and extends his hand toward the doorway, indicating I should leave, and no other option in hell is possible. I know how I said worst-case scenario odds aren't even worth discussing and so on, but this does not bode well.

I'm expecting patrons to follow me out en masse into the beautiful spring night to reconstruct the spectator circle, but no one does. Tables get moved back into place, barstools and chairs grind and groan under redistributed weight, and interrupted debates resume as if nothing important has happened or will be happening.

Recorded: 12 Jul 2101

Outside I see an empty street illumined by ghostly effusions produced by recently installed high efficiency lampposts. I look both ways. All is clear. Can this be right? According to my theory about worst case scenarios, the odds suggest the situation has expired and there will be no further incident. I cross the street and start walking back to Akrópoli Relax feeling lucky but guarded.

Worst case, I'd be bleeding to death with Zorba's bicep tattoos of the eternally damned dancing before my blurry eyes. I might even have glimpsed strolling lovers pausing to observe stabbed American lying in street, and haughty local boy wiping bloody blade on thigh.

What drama! I shake my head and smile. Here I am, free as a bird, with all my parts intact. Near catastrophes do give one pause, though... What was that all about anyway? A tribute to weirdness? It doesn't matter. I'm just glad everything's back to normal.

Except for the switchblade in my hand.

"Robert!"

Zing! My entire body tenses at the sound of my fake name. A sharp pain in the clavicle area curls up my neck and penetrates deep into my right eardrum. Stunned, I rub my jaw. I don't want a pep talk, warning, or advice. I want to lie down in my bed. I want to be left alone, close my eyes, see nothing, hear nothing. I want to float. Is that too much to ask?

"Robert!"

I grit my teeth as I turn around. He's standing in the middle of the street, big as a bull.

"Come here!" he yells, waving to me like we're old pals.

"It's okay, Heracles. I'm calling it a day. To be honest, I'm pooped."

"You pooped? Not acceptable! I show you better place to eat."

"No, I mean pooped, like tired. Too much tsipouro. Need to sleep." I put my hands together like a pillow and lay my head on them so there's no mistaking what I mean.

"You come with me, Robert."

No, uh-uh. I lift the switchblade in the air to show I harbor no intent to keep or use it and slowly lower it to the sidewalk, as if it were a laser pistol. I raise my hands in surrender, which makes no sense on any level. Good stars, what is wrong with me? I need to reset. First thing, I'm not going anywhere near Heracles or Taverna Momos ever again.

Second thing, I'm not going to be accused of stealing anyone's stupid knife.

I point to the ground. "There's your knife, Heracles. I'm leaving it right there, okay? Hey, Heracles, thanks again for all your help!" I repeat the Namaste bow to leave a favorable impression.

But Heracles is not impressed. He looks put out more than anything. I don't care. I don't have the time, nor the desire, to deal with the local crazies.

I'm relieved to see that Heracles isn't following me. Each stride feels like a monumental achievement. I turn right at the corner bakery and go down a narrow side street that will take me to my hostel. Just when I'm ready to take a deep cleansing breath, a figure emerges from a darkened doorway and positions himself beneath a high efficiency lamppost. Standing there, of course, is my mortal enemy, Zorba Papadopoulos.

The snap of his switchblade cuts the night silence. The steel blade gleams beneath the cool white light.

I wave to him, like neighbors do. He spits to the side and doesn't wave back. Why would he? What is it with these hands? No time to dwell on it. Shame and embarrassment aren't foremost on my mind at the moment. That said, I'm not inclined to hightail it, either. Personal dignity still matters. I'm not running, unless I absolutely have to.

I'll turn around and walk away. I've got my wallet, Coin, passport, throwaway Q-Phone, everything I need. Zorba doesn't strike me as the type to chase after people and stab them in the back. It's just a hunch, I could be wrong. He hasn't moved from the lamppost. I count that as a plus. Maybe he's trying to make a statement. Hopefully, mission accomplished, and he loses interest and calls it a night. He doesn't need to know where I'm staying. I'll find some other place to crash. Early morning I'll come back, get my stuff and check out.

I almost wave again, stop just in time. I turn around. Standing in the middle of the street about fifty yards away are Heracles and Miss Pink. My feet do an awkward two-step, which gets me nowhere.

I've witnessed Zorba's athleticism firsthand, assessed the sound and gleam of his switchblade. I rule out trying to get past him unscathed. My best chance is to make a dash the other way, elude heavy-legged Heracles and barrel over Miss Pink, if necessary.

But Heracles has read my thoughts. He wags a thick forefinger at me.

Then, in a voice like Kansas, Miss Pink says, "Don't run and don't dare open your punk-ass mouth unless you want to die like a pig."

I go limp with resignation. Miss Pink, who goes by the ironic name of Serenity, duct tapes my mouth while Heracles watches Zorba bind my hands behind my back. Heracles then picks me up and gently places me in the trunk of an antique driver-required Ford Taurus.

Last thing I hear before he slams the door down is the ding-dong of the electronic municipal tower bell tolling the midnight hour.

Recorded: 14 Jul 2101

02-07 May 2100

The four of us are standing in moonlit woods on a hill. Heracles is aiming a light beam at my face. Serenity rips the duct tape from my mouth and asks me if Father, whom I haven't seen in nine years, cares enough about my "sorry ass" to pay thirty million Coin to keep me from having my throat slit. Given the gravity of the moment, we're all surprised—me included—when I start laughing.

My captors interpret my outburst as a sign of Deo arrogance, but they have no idea what they're asking. Zorba gives me a hard shove that sends me flying. Hands still tied behind my back, I roll downhill like a log and slam into the trunk of a pine tree. The impact takes my breath away, and my first thought is cracked ribs.

Zorba and Heracles come tottering down the hill cursing in Greek, light beams bouncing. They squat on either side of my prone body and shove me back and forth. I feel like I've got a broken wine bottle lodged in my side. I try playing the brave stoic, but the boys won't let up. Serenity stands at my feet looking content.

"Zorba, you furp!" I yell. "If I die, you never see a single Coin bit. You get charged with murder and hunted down like a rat. Everybody in your family gets tortured and killed, their homes burned to the ground. Don't you understand how these things always end?"

What do I know about how these things end? But my words make an impression on both Zorba and Heracles. They look at Serenity, seeking guidance. She plays it cool, keeps her eyes fixed on me, but her expression has soured.

After a long pause Zorba says, "Okay, take it easy, man."

Who are these people? Would real kidnappers create an attention-grabbing spectacle in a crowded tavern?

Three o'clock the next afternoon Heracles and Zorba storm into the mountain shack that's become my prison and pull me off a pile of hay where I spend all my time. They drag me outside into the arborous light. Serenity's holding a throwaway Q-Phone, hooked up to a mini-portable voice changer she's holding in her other hand. She starts talking to Atwell, but it's Darth Vader who delivers the terms of my release. She hands me the Q-Phone.

"Yeah, it's me," I say. Not surprisingly, Father doesn't say a word. Serenity grabs the phone, and Darth Vader says, "If you want your son to live, do as I say."

That's it. End of discussion.

Zorba and Heracles turn out to be regular guys. Heracles is more like the benevolent giant I'd first imagined, and Zorba, who projects as a jerk on first impression, is actually a fairly learned and thoughtful guy. They bring me food and water, empty my waste bucket, and share their opinions about Coin, world affairs, and space travel.

Reports of my kidnapping and an unflattering photo of me taken by Serenity immediately after I was dragged out of the car trunk in the middle of the night appear all across the Transmedia universe. Stock images of Atwell and Runa Stone looking gravely concerned—photos having nothing to do with me—also begin to proliferate.

By Monday, the third morning of my captivity, I notice a change for the worse in the group's morale. Without saying a word, Heracles drags me out of the shack and gently ties me to the pine tree that broke my ribs.

Serenity and the boys stand nearby strategizing how to force Atwell to get serious about meeting their demands. They obviously want me to hear what they're saying.

The idea is to let Father know that if he fails to agree to their ransom demands by 3:00 PM Greek time tomorrow, they'll begin overnighting my toes to Stone-TH headquarters, care of Atwell Stone, one toe per day. Daily photos of my mutilations will get forwarded to Serenity's anonymous contact at Transmedia for global distribution. The plan will be executed until terms are met and funds transferred.

When Heracles asks in a rehearsed voice what they'll do if all my toes are gone and the terms have still not been met, Serenity replies, "We cut off one finger per day."

Zorba embellishes further by mentioning the daily use of a hot iron to prevent infection.

"Left hand first, then right hand," Serenity elaborates. "If we have to, we keep cutting. Left ear comes off, then the right ear, and whatever."

Whatever meaning arms and legs? Then what, my head? Okay, by now I'm having trouble buying in.

Wednesday, 3:07 PM Greek time, Serenity puts me on another throwaway Q-Phone after Darth Vader has articulated the new torture plan to Father. "It's me, who else would it be?" I say, and the connection goes dead.

Two days later there's still no sign of terms being met, and I've managed to keep all my toes. The closest I come to undergoing torture is Heracles dropping a bottle of tsipouro on my bare foot and bruising my big toe.

Emboldened, I test each of them individually. How much is Atwell paying you to put on this show? Zorba and Heracles laugh at me like I'm a pathetic loser, but I don't find their laughter at all convincing. I believe I'm on to something. I'm trending toward believing Zorba and Heracles are local community actors looking for a modest, though by local standards, respectable payday. I put the same question to Serenity. How much is Atwell paying you?

By now I suspect she realizes I remember her from *Deconstructing the Twentieth Century* class. Cindy Trapp, scholarship kid with a name like a warning sign. Her dad bailed on her mom soon after her birth, or so the story went.

She stares thoughtfully at me a long while, but her eyes gradually turn hostile. I can see the shift happening, like watching new paint becoming its true color as you stir it. Then suddenly she smiles, as if she knows something I don't. My skin crawls from too much ambiguity. My mouth aches to speak, wants to make a point. It does.

"What did I ever do to you but stand up for your Kiss My Ass honor?"

"Shut up, Deo punk-ass."

Recorded: 16 Jul 2101

08 May - 03 June 2100

Days go by, though not quickly. The fellas continue to empty my waste bucket and feed me goat cheese and olive sandwiches, along with noteworthy news bits.

I see that more than one financial expert has attributed the boost in sales of Stone-TH's VivaLong Life Enhancement and Extension products and services to voyeuristic interest generated by my life and death soap opera. This also helps explain Stone-TH's twenty-two percent share price increase over the same period.

I've had many hours to ponder the state of Atwell Stone's mind, but I'm not sharp or cynical enough to fully grasp what's going on inside his convoluted head. My captivity can't just be about increasing market capitalization and equity value, can it? No, this is personal. He's going to teach me a lesson, show me in his patented twisted way that he alone has the power to save me from myself.

One day Zorba and Heracles start feeding me only bread and water. They also stop chitchatting. My confidence erodes as the days pass. Maybe these people really are legitimate kidnappers looking for a big payday. Unfortunately for the four of us, they're not going to get it.

At the same time, I'm having a lot of trouble picturing Zorba or Heracles cutting my throat. But Cindy, my fellow American? That I can see.

She'll want the spectacle recorded and distributed to every corner of the planet. She'll wear a mask. And latex gloves, because she'll want to hide that heart-shaped birthmark between her pinky and ring finger. The world will listen to Darth Vader ramble on about Deo deceit and greed and then watch Cindy Trapp's gloved hand pull my head back by the hair and everybody will get a nice closeup of Cindy's butcher knife slicing open my throat.

Take that, Atwell! Take that, you Deo SOB!

Afterwards, there will be two camps. One to accuse Father of heartless negligence, the other to praise him for his stand against terrorists. No one's going to feel sorry for him, and he'll be too busy monetizing his son's highly publicized execution to care.

These are the things I'm obsessing over when the fellas come and drag me out of the shack. An hour later, I get tossed out of the Ford Taurus onto a mountain road. I get up off the hot pavement dazed and barefoot as the Taurus speeds away. Suddenly, it slows down, and a plastic bag gets tossed out a window.

"Hey!" I yell as the car vanishes around a bend.

I limp fifty yards uphill and start picking stuff out of the bag, my wallet, passport and a brand-new pair of turquoise flipflops. Then more stuff. Amazingly, everything I had with me the night I was abducted is in the bag: credit token, eurochips and, most importantly, the keycard to my room at Akrópoli Relax.

I slip on the flipflops, fill my pockets, and walk. The pain in my big toe and ribs flares up to a level I thought I'd left behind. After five weeks wearing the same unwashed underwear, pants, and polo shirt, I'm feeling decidedly swampy. I set aside bad thoughts about Atwell and imagine what a nice shower on the heels of twenty-four hours of sleep might do to lift my spirits.

Several cars speed past without slowing down. I pause to take a breather. It's late afternoon. Not sure what I'm waiting for. At some point I'm going to have to let somebody know I would appreciate a ride into town. I finally stick my thumb out.

That's when I hear the birdsong, sudden and bright as a child's smile. The bluebird is perched on a long-branched Cedar of Lebanon, and its feathers are as blue as a droplet of clear sky. When it finishes its song, the bluebird tilts its head in my direction, and silently speaks to me.

There you are, and here I am.

The bluebird flies away, and part of me follows it up into the big, blue sky.

Recorded: 18 Jul 2101

03 June 2100

Heading south from Xilópolis across a hilly range north of Thessaloniki, a driverless Automova-V passes a vagabond wearing turquoise flipflops. The car stops, shifts into reverse, and pulls up beside me. "Thessaloniki?" says a smiling lady with a perky East Euro accent.

I nod and hold my ribs as I fold myself into the back seat. The confined space accentuates my bad odor. My hosts pretend not to notice. The fan automatically turns on high and all four door windows slide down a couple of inches. The woman hands me a banana and a bottle of water. "My name is Zelenka," she says. "This is Radek."

When I tell them my name is Robert, Radek glances at Zelenka, which makes me think they know who I am.

Radek and Zelenka are both in their mid to late fifties. Zelenka tells me they are professors at the University of Prague. Radek teaches Classical Studies. Zelenka teaches Art History. These disciplines are largely regarded as useless in the current era, she says with a sad look, but are tolerated for the sake of what she calls *collective nostalgia.*

A few minutes later she turns around to see how I'm holding up. She catches me grimacing as I'm shifting my hips.

"You see, Radek, did I not tell you?"

I don't remember her telling him anything.

"We should take him to the Emergency Room at University Hospital."

Radek turns and studies me with tired eyes.

"No need," I say. "If it's not too much trouble, please drop me off at the Lazart Hotel."

The Automova-V veers right and begins a long, winding descent.

"Did you say the Lazart?" Zelenka says about a minute later.

"Yes, that's where I'm staying," I lie.

She hands me an apple, which I set aside. All I can think about is getting back to the hostel and sleeping for twenty-four hours. The hum of hard rubber on asphalt is soothing. I drift in and out of sleep. At a certain point I realize Radek, who until now hasn't said a word, is telling me a story.

"I looked up from my desk for an instant and returned to my notes. I was distracted by a talk I was preparing for that evening. What was it he asked? I looked up as the student walked out of my office. I should have called him back, 'Vasil, what is it?' But I remained seated. How important could it be, I thought?"

Why is he telling me this? He turns and searches my face. He looks confused, as if he were asking himself the same question: *Why am I telling him this?*

"One week ago today, Vasil hanged himself," he says softly.

Not what I was expecting. I have no idea what to say. Is Radek implying it was his fault?

After an uncomfortable silence, Zelenka says, "An epidemic of loneliness spreads across the planet. It is tragic, and quite telling." She lets that sink in before turning to make eye contact with me. "Is there anything you'd like to tell us, Robert?"

I feel a quiver in my chest, a stirring of emotions shaping words that will remain unspoken. I do want to bare my soul to someone, I realize, and Zelenka and Radek seem decent enough, but I don't know anything about them or what motives they might have.

"No," I say, hoping to end further discussion.

That doesn't stop Zelenka, who apparently feels the need to keep me abreast of the latest calamity. She waits a few minutes, then says, "Did you hear what happened this past Thursday, Robert?"

She interprets my non-response as a *No, I didn't hear, so please tell me.*

"The East Asia Alliance and the Aussie-Kiwi Coalition launched smart missiles at one another. The AKC struck an artificial EAA island in the South China Sea. The EAA retaliated by bombing an AKC island in the Arafura Sea. Two-thousand EAA settlers and an equal number of AKC islanders were killed over disputed waters and fishing rights. Predictably, this latest War of Pecuniary Adjustment led to the resumption of suspended talks."

"I don't know what any of that means," I say. "And I don't know why Vasil killed himself. Why are you telling me these things? Can I just close my eyes and rest a while?"

Zelenka doesn't turn immediately. When she does, it's to offer me an awkward smile. "Please, forgive us," she says.

No one speaks the rest of the way, but my eyes won't stay shut. They remain fixed firmly on the road ahead. The first time I heard about Wars of Pecuniary Adjustment, or WOPAs, was in Taverna Momos. I also remember wild speculations about the so-called Corporatocracy, and jokes about body snatchers from outer space, and rounds of explosive laughter.

The Automova-V stops in the passenger drop-off zone in front of the Lazart Hotel. My left side and foot have stiffened like rusted steel, and I'm having a hard time getting out of the car. Radek backs off when he sees I don't want help. I stand up, achieving not quite erect posture. Radek shakes my hand and offers a meek thumbs-up as he steps back. Zelenka kisses both my cheeks. I apologize for being rude, and she graciously waves it off and smiles.

I can see they're not going to leave until I'm safely inside the hotel. I limp into the Five-Star lobby and wait a couple of seconds before taking a peek to verify the Automova-V is pulling away. Behind the check-in counter, a clean-shaven young man is pretending not to see me as he picks up the phone to call Security. I turn and limp out of the lobby back onto the street.

Recorded: 24 Jul 2101

03 June - 30 September 2100

It's six blocks from the Lazart to Akrópoli Relax. No one's at the front desk when I hobble in. No one sees me when I open the door to my room. In a blur, I note the unfamiliar backpack, the thick tomes, mug, shaving accessories and group photo belonging to someone else. They don't seem to me real enough or relevant enough to think twice about. I lower myself onto the narrow bed and adjust my bones over the thin lumpy mattress.

At 1:30 AM someone turns the overhead light on and jostles me awake. He demands to know what I'm doing in his bed. I'm too tired to be startled, but the encounter is so unexpected and confusing that I start to laugh, and then to groan like a wounded animal.

Cosimo's demeanor changes in an instant. He assesses my pitiable condition and assures me everything is going to be alright. He tucks me back into bed and leaves. I fall asleep thinking of the circular tattoo on the top of his left hand, three rabbits chasing one another in perfect rotational symmetry.

At 9:00 AM he comes back with coffee and sweet rolls. He checks my ribcage, tells me to breathe in and out, and examines my foot. Turns out he's a medical student. He wants to take me to the hospital, but I say no. He's itching to know my story but resists the temptation to probe.

After breakfast, Cosimo accompanies me to the front desk to talk to the manager about my misplaced belongings. Mr. Stavros ignores everything Cosimo says, tells me in bad English all my goods were confiscated by the police Monday morning. He explains it was the correct protocol given that my security deposit was past expiration and he had received no word from me.

I don't know whether I should believe Mr. Stavros. Cosimo thinks he sold my stuff and wants to press the issue, but I say no. Cosimo helps me find another place to stay.

"You are going to be a great doctor, Cosimo," I say. "I feel it in my bones." We laugh weakly. I ask him about the tattoo. He calls it *The Three Hares* and casually mentions it has something to do with an ancient prophecy. I'd like to spend a couple of hours with him talking about it over drinks, but he's a busy guy, and I have my own life to reconstruct.

I spend my time sleeping, washing, eating, drinking, and buying sensible shoes and clothes. In the shopping plaza, I catch a hologram showing reporters talking to people outside Taverna Momos. In the upper left corner is that dismal photo of me taken by Cindy Trapp, aka Serenity, after Heracles pulled me out of the trunk of the old Ford Taurus.

The voiceover reports that my kidnappers are on the run. Apparently, I've been rescued by unidentified law enforcement officers, though my location remains undisclosed. The

Momos hologram is quickly swapped out for one showing two swarthy men and a woman jogging through twilit woods. None of them look anything like Zorba, Heracles or Serenity.

Saturday morning, I spot a relief woodcarving of *The Three Hares* in a street market. I snap a photo and get the tattoo equivalent inked on top of my left hand.

I let my beard grow, put on new shades and catch a flight to Athens the day after the latest WOPA development in the Arctic, a territorial dispute between the Euro Commerce Union and the Greater Russo Confederation. Four-thousand dead, evenly split, give or take, every fatality an Ord. No further hostilities are anticipated. Both sides are confident a compromise will be reached within the week.

From Athens I catch a flight to Reykjavik. The Iris Recognition and backup Facial Recognition systems at the airport have been down for weeks. Uniformed inspectors fail to notice that my name is Merlin Stone, or they do notice and don't care.

I spend the next three months in Reykjavik dispensing beer and cod in Njord Krogstad's fish and lobster eatery. In the tiny attic room above Krogstad's, I paint ocean harbor scenes from Q-Phone snapshots. It's all very therapeutic.

To my surprise, Njord likes my pedestrian works and becomes my unlikely benefactor. He gives me a fifty-percent discount on my rent and all the cod I can eat in exchange for a few paintings, which he hangs on his once-bare eatery walls.

In Iceland I also continue tweaking my New Life Plan, which, ironically, will require Atwell's assistance.

Recorded: 07 Aug 2101

01 October 2100

Back in the States, I get through Passport Control and am immediately sequestered by FBI agents. The creampuff interrogation conducted in a small utility room proves a formality, given the abduction drama is well behind us. For the seven minutes I'm questioned, agents Wright and McMann appear sustained by a blatant shared disinterest. They toss passing glances at my tattooed hand without commenting.

The agents escort me back to the terminal and walk away. Travelers stride blindly past each other, their dull, mechanical movements contrasting sharply with the many holograms of peppy individuals singing the praises of life-transforming virtual reality programs like *Technically, I Am* and *Coined and Loaded*, programs designed for those eager to pursue tech-enhanced personhood and ways to maximize productive greed, respectively.

One night in Reykjavik, Njord and I were shutting down the eatery when he stopped what he was doing, looked me in the eye, and said, "I had very interesting conversation with Hinrik Ragnarsson regarding Starling Sayer."

"Did you?"

"Oh yes, I did. Tell me, Robert, what is your opinion of this Starling Sayer?"

Because I strongly suspected Njord still believed I was Robert Jordan, I saw nothing to be gained from telling him Father was once Sayer's student at MDIT.

"You mean, Star Man?"

"Sayer helps build Corporatocracy and then he says to everyone, watch out for the Corporatocracy. Then Star Man goes bye-bye. Suspicious, would you not agree?"

"Some think Sayer had an epiphany and became a new man with new ideas."

"Yah, I know. And some believe he is hiding in Africa. Okay, but I ask you, what do you think of Sayer, Robert?"

I don't know what I think about Sayer, or what influence he might have had on the kind of man Father would become, or how he might have influenced the direction of our country or the way the world spins. I wasn't interested in having that discussion. I told Njord I found his preoccupation with the Corporatocracy ironic given his passion for virtual reality gaming, which everyone knows is a Trojan Horse industry developed and controlled by the very same Corporatocracy.

You could almost see Njord's brain scrolling through his Greek mythology memory banks as he tried pinning down the meaning of that Trojan Horse reference. His big Viking face got increasingly irritated as our habitual, if often annoying, game of one-upmanship continued. "Once you let it get inside you, you're bye-bye," I said.

Njord smiled and dropped a heavy hand on my shoulder. "How do you Americans say? Piss off, yes? Yes, Robert?"

I get through Customs without issue. Outside, I stop to observe a pair of workers in orange jumpsuits scrubbing red graffiti off a wall. They seem in no hurry to erase the message:

WOPAs Kill Ords!

Say NO to Blood Profiteering!

Reject Corporatocracy Lies!

Best Time to be OUT is Now!

Sensing my mild, inquiring presence, both men stop what they're doing and turn around. The one with *Julio* on his nametag starts singing a salsa tune to himself while the other, *Alberto*, scans the area behind me before turning back to the wall. Julio steps toward me when no one's looking, draws a pamphlet from his back pocket and hands it to me. The graffiti message is replicated word for word on the cover page of the pamphlet. I flip the pamphlet over and read the bottom of the back cover: *Published by OUT, Ords United for Truth.*

I walk away with the OUT pamphlet swinging from my hand and nagged by the suspicion I've crossed a forbidden line. I wonder if Julio and Alberto are undercover agents. I half-expect agents Wright and McMann to swoop down on me, drag me off to a high-security room, slice the tattoo from the top of my hand and drop the sliver of skin into a plastic baggie for examination in a lab.

But no one stops me. I feel silly. I sit on a bench reading the OUT pamphlet from front to back while waiting for my Swift Getaways pickup.

Here's my OUT takeaway: 1) Things are bad; 2) Things will get worse; 3) Things need to get better; 4) Deos have all the power and control and no one's interest at heart but their own; 5) Ords need to grow a pair and do something for themselves; 6) Go to the URL displayed at the bottom of the back cover to learn how you can join OUT or to make a donation.

Despite the pamphlet's questionable assumptions and other shortcomings, I place it on the end of the bench for anyone who might be interested.

"Mr. Stone?"

It takes me a moment to understand I'm not going to be dragged away for further questioning. A quiet air taxi is waiting about sixty feet behind a dark young man with a blinding white smile.

"Yes, that's me," I say.

"Beniam Bolt, Swift Getaways VTOL Services."

As he reaches for my bag, I say, "We could all use a swift getaway, wouldn't you agree, Beniam?"

"Mr. Stone?"

"To another planet, maybe? To another time?"

"Sir?"

"Never mind, Beniam. How has the weather been?"

"October is going to feel like September, sir, which felt just like August."

"Who can complain?"

He stares at me and smiles. "If it pleases you, Mr. Stone, call me Benny."

I smile back.

Benny Bolt from Swift Getaways flies me to a nice hotel where I toss and turn the night away.

Recorded: 10 Aug 2101

02 October 2100

Benny smiled when I gave him a big tip. He offered to come by in the morning to fly me to Stone House. Okay, great, I said. But the Benny who shows up this morning is an entirely different person, glum and faintly resentful. I don't take it personally. When he drops me off at Stone House, I tip him the same amount I would have anyway and wish him the best of luck.

I do a doubletake on meeting the housekeeper. Lenora is a plump, sixtyish homedroid with enormous silicone blue eyes and curly red human hair. An affable bot that walks with a slight limp, which is by design. She knows who I am before I can say a word and lets me know that the voice message I left last week was received and duly noted by Mother.

Like all late model homedroids, Lenora boasts nearly one-hundred percent Face and Voice Recognition capability. She explains that Mother and Father are away on separate business and to make myself at home. They'll be arriving sometime tomorrow, she assures me, and offers to fix me a "nutrient-rich midday meal," which I politely decline. Under mild duress, I do accept an apple from her smallish, remarkably lifelike hand.

I step out onto the back lawn eating my apple. I walk among Runa's hybrid rose bushes. The velvet white, lavender and delicate yellow late season blossoms are as beautiful as ever, but today their fruity scents smell of sadness.

When I was a boy, men came to build Runa's new greenhouse. I watched them as I leaned with my crutches against the ancient sugar maple. Father's property caretaker, Nasario, stormed out of the kitchen and headed toward the workers without seeing me. He yelled at the foreman, who stood there and took the abuse without saying a word. I never imagined Nasario could be that kind of man.

When he was finished with the foreman, he marched across the manicured lawn back to the house. He twitched when he noticed me, and wavered. Should he continue as if I were not there? I pretended I didn't see him, but he came over anyway, took a deep breath and squatted in front of me.

"Have you seen Ironman today?" he said.

"No."

"Maybe tomorrow?"

I felt a pressure in my throat that wouldn't allow me to play our daily superhero game. I frowned, and my mouth stiffened as I spoke. "Ironman is not real."

"Merlin, I tell you a secret. You want to know?"

I wavered, but who doesn't want to know a secret?

"Your Papa is Ironman."

"No! Only Tony Stark can be Ironman!"

"I tell you the most important secret of all, only for you and me to know."

He frowned to underscore the gravity of the moment. "Your Papa? *He* is Tony Stark."

For a moment my heart stopped. "I don't believe you," I said, but already my resolve was weakening.

Nasario put his hand over his heart. "Merlin, you and I are best friends, yes?"

I hesitated, but again gave in. I nodded faintly.

"And best friends always tell each other the truth."

Why wouldn't I want to believe Father was Ironman? How else to explain the sudden absences, the secretive nature, the emotional detachment?

After Nasario left, I went inside and searched everywhere for Ironman's mask, extremis armor, and jet boots. One day I heard Father on his Q-Phone mention a fortress, and I decided that was where he went to prepare critical missions to save humanity from criminals and hostile aliens.

For several days I hopped all around Stone House and Runa's immense garden with an energy I didn't realize I possessed. Being Tony Stark's son suggested I too might one day perform massively heroic feats!

My Ironman infatuation died a slow, lingering death. My friend, Nasario, had lied to me. No way Father could be Tony Stark because, unlike Ironman, Atwell Stone could be a heartless man.

Recorded: 17 Aug 2101

I see Lenora through the big kitchen windows, limping back and forth, cooking and cleaning. I'm oddly comforted by the sight. I go inside and we briefly comment on the weather. I excuse myself and stroll through the empty rooms, parlors and hallways of my problematic childhood.

I told myself I wouldn't do it, but I do it anyway. I go down into the basement and open the door to the tunnel that leads to the modest servant house where, more than twenty years ago, Nasario and Liani Montoya lived with their two children, Vidal and Paloma. The Jeffersonian construction of the tunnel was Atwell's idea. The menagerie of painted wild animals on the white walls was Runa's.

Three fourths of the way to *Casa Montoya*, my knees begin to ache. Not physical pain, but it's hard to convince my legs of that. I stop to stare at the purple bear painted on the white wall, far less menacing now, but forever linked in my mind to that first shout. It was Freedom of Enterprise Day, and I was still using crutches to get around. Runa was in Copenhagen, Atwell was away somewhere, and I was with the Montoyas on the road to Moon Lake Park for my first picnic ever.

We were late, the last to arrive. I didn't care. My heart quickened to the beat and swagger of salsa and merengue, and the sight of half-naked kids chasing one another all over the place, and the spirited volleyball matches. The summer breeze smelled of barbecued chicken, cooked corn, rice and beans. Nasario ate and drank quickly, and disappeared.

The greenhouse foreman Nasario had humiliated was also there. His name was Cesar Escudero. Paloma told me he was married to Adriana, her mother's best friend, and that he was a popular and influential figure in the local immigrant community. This surprised me, given what I had witnessed. I didn't tell Paloma how poorly her father had treated Cesar in front of the greenhouse workers.

Later, Nasario reappeared down by the lake. He sat on the ground and stared at the water. Cesar and Adriana walked down to the lake. This time Cesar did all the talking, gazing alternately at Nasario and Adriana as he spoke.

What was he saying? Why couldn't Adriana look at either man in the face? And why did she avoid her best friend, Liani, when she got back to the picnic area?

No one said a word during the ride back to Casa Montoya. We filed into the kitchen. Nasario didn't look at me once. Liani tried smiling for my benefit, but couldn't quite manage it. In silence, Paloma led me down the stairs to the tunnel. She was my babysitter for the night. A quarter of the way to Stone House, we heard the first shout. I stared at the purple bear on the white wall and felt a rush of terror. It towered over us, and its mouth was stretched open in an angry roar. Paloma told me to stay put and ran back to the house.

My knees buckled and I fell on the stone tiles. I tried getting up too quickly, and slipped and went crashing down again. The shouting and screaming grew louder. I made it to the stairs and dragged myself up to the open door.

The family I thought I knew and loved no longer existed. In its place I saw a tortured, four-headed creature. Nasario's face was etched in a novel kind of anguish, his fist lifted impotently in the air over Liani. Thirteen-year-old Paloma was lodged between Nasario and Liani, and fifteen-year-old Vidal hung on his father's back. I let my crutches fall with a loud clatter, and I collapsed on the floor with them. Poor Nasario turned toward me and wilted before my eyes.

At that point everything became a blur. I felt Paloma's arms cradle me. Liani broke into strange hiccup-like sobs.

And Vidal sat on the floor, right where he was, as his father walked out the front door.

Recorded: 20 Aug 2101

Regret seeps into the blood and remains there, forever circulating. Sure, you can forget it for stretches of time. Or you can pretend it's not there. But it is, and it takes on an almost biological quality, shaping the essential matter of who we are and who we are to become.

After a dinner of salmon and greens prepared by Lenora, I sit at my desk in my old room and write down a few things before calling it a night. It was in Liani's kitchen that I learned to smile. It was there I learned to appreciate the sound of forks and knives clicking and clacking against dinner plates, and to love the soothing, quirky music produced by family banter and laughter.

After dessert I would often sit next to Paloma on her bed looking at colorful pictures of pyramids and llamas and dinosaurs displayed in oversized tattered books. She would read aloud things that seemed impossible. And later, back in my own room, I would dream of other things that seemed impossible, like walking without crutches, or becoming big enough to one day marry Paloma.

A couple of months after Nasario's meltdown, I started walking without crutches and stood next to Father the day he summoned Liani and Paloma to his study. He spoke primarily to Paloma, while Liani and I stood there as silent witnesses to Father's peculiar interest in the girl. He asked her how she liked high school and what career plans she might have.

When he addressed Liani, it was only to inform her of certain arrangements, which in retrospect, I suspect involved securing her and Paloma's financial future.

Afterwards, he seemed on the verge of telling me something, but decided not to. I never learned what that was. The following week, all the Montoyas were gone. I never saw them again. I never asked Atwell or Runa why they left, or where they might have gone.

I once tried writing a happy ending for them, but the words rebelled and mocked me, so I tore the sheets and lay my head down. A man emerged from the fog of my mind. I said, "Vidal, is it you?" The man pointed at my face and said, "Paloma is Atwell's daughter," in the same way he might have said, "You have sauce on your chin."

Runa finds me in the back patio staring at the sky. She circles around in front of me, checks my face and then studies the tattoo on my hand. Mother needs time to assess things. She is no slave to protocol or etiquette. She can't summon a smile but says she's glad to see me and that she expected that I would look worse than I do.

She tells me Lenora and Ingrid, who has begun traveling with her everywhere she goes, and who doubles as Lenora's main assistant, have begun preparing a dinner of maple-garlic marinated pork tenderloin and lobster tails steamed in beer, which she suspects I will enjoy. Before disappearing, Mother tells me Father will be meeting us shortly in the dining room.

Seconds later, Ingrid, an attractive blonde homedroid wearing a glittering silver apron over a navy-blue minidress, comes out onto the patio holding a small tray. She offers me a glass of Milky Way Nectar and leads me to the dining room.

"Mr. and Mrs. Stone will soon be joining you," she says with a Norwegian accent.

"Thank you, Ingrid."

"Not at all, sir… Is there anything else I can do for you?"

Did she just…? No, I don't think she did. I shoot a glance at the doorway where I half expect Atwell to be snooping.

"No, thank you, Ingrid. Looking forward to dinner."

"Happy to hear you are pleased, sir."

I briefly note her stunning humanlike anatomy as she walks away and fix my eyes on the Milky Way Nectar swirling in my glass.

"I see you've met Ingrid. Isn't she fabulous?"

Runa's sudden bright-eyed energy puts me on alert.

"Yes, Mother, she's quite remarkable."

"Oh my. Now don't you let that little flirt seduce you. I'm very strict with her, you know. I say to her, 'Now Ingrid, you behave yourself around the men,' and she replies, 'But Mrs. Stone, whatever do you mean by that?' Crafty little vixen. She knows all too well what I mean. Ha-ha-ha! You be careful with her, Merlin."

I can count on one hand the times I remember Mother laughing, but here we are, beginning all over again, and because I'm too caught up in the strangeness of the moment, I fail to notice Father standing behind me.

"Boo!"

I turn around and see Atwell bent forward holding his belly, breathless with laughter. A tear is forming in the inside corner of his right eye. He wipes it away and stands up straight as a soldier. I feel like I've entered an alternate world. I glance at Mother, who looks pleased and invested in the moment. Where in stars am I?

"Well, well, the prodigal son returns at last," Father says happily.

Did I say *happily*? I race through my memory banks, pull up the old parable, do a quick recap. Young guy leaves home, screws up, comes back to his father's house with tail tucked between his legs, expects recrimination and humiliation, receives nothing but unconditional love.

I don't see unconditional love happening here, and I could argue Atwell's Biblical allusion indirectly expresses his displeasure with me.

That said, I have to admit, I wasn't expecting smiles and laughter of any kind.

"Dinner is served," says Lenora.

We sit down to eat as a family. I try to remember a dinner like this with Atwell and Runa. I can't. This isn't something we did. This was something I did with the Montoyas.

After a second glass of Milky Way Nectar, Father says, "I have a middle management opening in the Robotics Division. It's yours if you want it."

What? No interview? No psycho quiz? Don't have to get my Three Hares tattoo removed?

"When do I start?"

Recorded: 26 Aug 2101

07 October 2100

Sunny Takamoto says, "Competition for landing a job at Stone TransHumanix is fiercer than ever, to what some may consider an unreasonable degree. You've been there, you know it. You also know that employee selection has to be brutally precise if we're to continue maintaining the industry's highest levels of quality and productivity. We hire the crème de la crème. Each of you bested hundreds of competitors to earn the chair you are now occupying."

It's my second week at Stone-TH. I'm sitting by myself in the back row observing a New Employee Orientation session, as per the recommendation of Roscoe Cheng, Chief of the Robotics Division. Sunny pauses to make eye contact with each of the twelve new employees but chooses to avoid my gaze.

I've heard it said people will kill to land a job here, mostly because of the benefits package, which includes the life extension plus immunotherapy VivaLong program. Already the most popular life extension program anywhere on the planet, VivaLong took another leap forward with the recent acquisition of Endless Horizon Genetics, a world leader in genetic editing and genome sequencing.

The chatter about job applicants killing one another to increase the odds of landing a job here is grossly exaggerated. But the controversial Stone Employment Festivals have seen a troubling rise in the incidence of Nobody's Fault deaths over the past several years.

Early on during my expat days, I recall a class action suit leveled against Stone-TH by Ords who had lost family members to the SEFs. The plaintiffs cited unnecessarily reckless and dangerous job application requirements, among which were the controversial Provocation Role-Playing, Humiliation Endurance, and Compete and Conquer trials. Attorneys for the plaintiffs pointed out that such activities were cruel and unusual, and contrary to the spirit of fair and proper evaluation methods. These sessions, they insisted, triggered lethal levels of emotional and physical stress that led directly to heart trauma and death in several instances.

The defense called on two independent coroners whose testimony supported reports filed prior to the SEFs by Stone-TH medical examiners. These reports demonstrated that the deceased subjects in question had all been identified as having been prone to irregular heart rhythms, which made them more vulnerable to the expected ordinary stress resulting from participating in exceedingly competitive endeavors such as the SEFs.

These findings were contested by the families of the victims, who insisted their loved ones had been in perfect health before taking part in said Festivals and presented medical reports and professional witnesses to that effect.

The district court judge expressed her deepest sympathies for the families' losses, but summed up the suit leveled against Stone-TH with one word, *hogwash*. No one had put a laser gun to the applicant's head, the judge pointed out in her summation, and thousands of other applicants had gone through the SEFs and emerged from them relatively unscathed. Furthermore, each applicant was deemed eligible to participate in the SEFs only after undergoing a required medical examination and signing a waiver, releasing Stone-TH, its medical staff, Father, and anyone affiliated with Stone-TH of potential liability. Neither Atwell Stone nor Stone-TH could be held responsible for the physical or mental vulnerabilities of any job applicant, the judge reiterated. She dismissed the suit, and her ruling was promptly upheld by an appeals court judge.

I follow Sunny Takamoto's eyes and militaristic pacing with interest. Sunny beat the SEFs, which is saying a lot. She's confident and cocky. She's also hiding something. Rather than set off alarms in my head, this mystery makes me want to have lunch with her.

"Exponential growth in technology has been going on for decades," Sunny continues, "making things that were once deemed impossible, possible. Consider immortality, for example. Raise your hand if you're convinced human immortality is impossible?"

No one raises a hand.

Human immortality in the not-too-distant future is what Atwell is selling. Whether anyone's buying into that premise is irrelevant. Given current average human life expectancy, which ranges from 95 to 125—depending on your who, what, where's—three-hundred years isn't all that farfetched. There are enough believers, and more being added every day, to make VivaLong the most important commodity in the exploding Life and Longevity industry.

"You know what?" she says, turning her gaze on me.

She narrows her eyes for a moment, then does a quick scan of the newbies and says, "Why don't you all stand up and give yourselves a pat on the back. You know what it takes to get to this point in your career trajectory. Only the best beat the SEFs. Come on, everybody, stand up and pat yourselves on the back."

After some minor hesitation, all twelve newbies stand up. Slowly, chatter fills the room. I wouldn't mind mingling a bit myself, but I remain seated. I watch and wait, curious to see where this is going.

"Sit down, all of you!" Sunny cries out. "Stars above!"

A few quick bewildered looks are exchanged. They all sit down as tenuously as they stood up. Every eye is on Sunny.

"What a disgusting display of self-serving dog caca," she says and takes her time glaring at each confounded newbie.

"Do you know what you sounded like?" she says in barely over a whisper. "Have you any idea what you looked like? Oh, if you missed it, don't worry, it's been recorded."

She sits down and buries herself in her visipad. After a few seconds of silence, she says, "This group? No, there must be some mistake."

After all the blood, sweat and tears? A mistake? What kind of mistake?

Sunny looks up and stares right at me. Meaning what? Does she expect me to intervene? Should I stand up, say I'm

Atwell Stone's son, reiterate Sunny's disgust, express my own disappointment, inform them the right group would not have failed the final and most important SEF test? Meaning they are the wrong group and need to leave immediately?

Roscoe Cheng alerted me to Sunny Takamoto's unorthodox training techniques, but I was only half-listening. My attention was diverted by the brief appearance of a young woman named Pearl, whom I'll say more about later.

"The SCC?" I hear Sunny say as she stands up. "Hello? Anyone? The Stone-Cold Code? Required reading, as you should all know, which means you're all familiar with Rule 1 of the SCC: *No self-satisfied loser mentality and pat ourselves on the back nonsense allowed ever or anywhere, under any circumstances.*"

But wait, wasn't she the one who said everyone should get up and pat themselves on the back?

"Someone please stand up and state for the group Rule 2 of the SCC."

An unhappy young woman stands up. "I would like to say something."

Sunny folds her arms. "We're listening."

"I have to say, I didn't like being asked to get up and congratulate myself or anyone in the first place, okay? That's not who I am or what I signed up for. The fact remains, when someone in a position of authority tells you to do something—"

"Oh, how very interesting, Tomaro," Sunny interrupts. "Let's stay on topic, shall we? Are you incorrectly implying that SCC Rule 2 supersedes SCC Rule 1?"

"I'm not implying anything of the kind, and my name is Tamora, not Tomaro."

"Let me get this straight, *Tamora*. When someone in a position of authority tells you to do something that contradicts the Stone-Cold Code, which, presumably, you've read and understand, you should do what, exactly?"

I find myself sympathizing with Tamora, who's maybe seeing Sunny the way I'm starting to see her, a puffed-up low rank bully who's trying to make herself look good at someone else's expense. That aside, lunch with Sunny remains very high on my priority list.

The two women stare at each other until Sunny flashes a tight-lipped smile.

"SCC Rule 2, as you *should* know, is quite extensive. We'll review it in its entirety some other time. For our purposes today, let's just reference SCC Rule 2 as it pertains to SCC Rule 1. Rule 2 does not supersede Rule 1. Rather, it builds on it. To briefly paraphrase, Rule 2 reminds us that nothing gets in the way of doing what we're paid to do at the highest level of excellence, not family, not personal biases, and certainly not ego."

Sunny scans the room, looking dead serious now.

"Tamora, you do understand I have the discretionary power to ask you to leave, don't you? More to the point, I have the power to fire you on the spot."

Tamora stares back at Sunny in silence.

"You may sit now," Sunny says in a milder tone. "I'm not going to do that. You know why, Tamora? Because you've got guts. And Stone-TH wants workers with guts. But guts without ego. Consider this a lesson learned.

"Despite the ease with which you were all drawn into that ridiculous ego fest, each of you has legitimately earned your seat here today. But let's not forget *why* you're here. See that red bin by the wall? That's the Ego Bin. Drop your egos in the Ego Bin on your way out today. You can retrieve them later, after you quit, retire, or get terminated, if you still want or need them. I don't think you will. Your job until then will be to keep Stone-TH at the top of the corporate heap. Affirmation-needy little boys, girls and nonbins have no place here. We understand you won't always be happy with every-thing that goes on at Stone-TH, or with what you may be asked to do. That in and of itself is not a problem, as long as you don't make it one. If something or someone rubs you the wrong way, go directly to your immediate supervisor. No gossip, no intrigues. Your best bet is always transparency. Work things out with your supervisor before you go making a fool of yourself with upper management.

"Take a moment now to reflect on just how fortunate you are to be an employee of Stone TransHumanix. Do you think those hundreds of applicants you beat out wouldn't kill to be sitting here right now listening to me? The recent *Today's Efficient Worker* survey has named Stone-TH *Best Now Company to Work For* six years running. You know why? Because, *in this company*, we demand the very best of ourselves.

"Understand something, you're either a hundred percent STH in, or you're out. You'll find this is no sanctuary for inbetweeners. If you don't like what you're hearing, or if you're having any doubts whatsoever, you should stand up right now and get the furp out of my face."

Sunny pauses for effect. No one stands up.

Recorded: 03 Sep 2101

56

Sunny and I have lunch in the STH Central dining hall. I'm glad to see she's not the humorless bully she was pretending to be during newbie orientation.

I plead ignorance regarding the Stone-Cold Code and suggest it would be a good idea to familiarize myself with it. She looks at me kind of funny and says there is no Stone-Cold Code, it's something she made up. We lock eyes for an instant, and simultaneously burst into laughter. She covers her mouth a second too late, so I get a close-up look of her crazy teeth and understand why, as a rule, she avoids smiling.

"I'm going to have them straightened next year," she says, glancing at my mouth. "I'm not covered for any of the cosmetic stuff. I've only been here two years."

They're not so bad, I want to say, but don't.

"Look," she says, "everybody wants nice teeth. Everybody wants financial security. It's not easy being an Ord, you know? Twenty-four seven we're subjected to gung-ho talk-talk regarding the robust economy and colossal national wealth, upbeat public sentiment and so on. But in reality?"

She pauses, trying to come up with the proper phrasing. Or maybe she's wondering if it's wise to keep going down this path with the boss's son.

"I'm listening," I say nodding encouragement.

"All this prosperity talk sounds very nice, and if you want, you can make the numbers back up those claims. But the reality is, the only way your average Ord is going to get even a whiff of that wonderful prosperity is to become someone they probably don't want to be."

"So that's where you are, being someone you don't want to be?"

Sunny smiles darkly. "Everybody knows at least two or three Ords are going to die during any given SEF. But the next ten to twenty years there's going to be nothing left for most Ords to do but have babies, cash out their tiny universal income autopays, buy hallucinogens at discounted prices and play VR games. That won't work for me. I'm not interested in checking off the rest of my days in a mindless haze and waiting to be transported to an incineration facility."

"I get that."

"Or worse, being shipped to a distant planet to become some alien's sex slave or exotic meal."

Now she's just staring at me. I glean what might be a smile. I feel like she's testing me. I look down at my plate, cut another piece of veggie steak, slide it around in the brown gravy. I can't remember now if lunch was her suggestion or mine.

"You were pretty tough on those newbies," I say. "All that mumbo jumbo about Stone-TH being at the top of the corporate heap, all of us keeping it there with devoted single-mindedness and hard work."

"Mumbo jumbo? Yes, they absolutely have to buy into the Corporate mumbo jumbo if they're going to have any chance to get where they want to go."

Will the real Sunny Takamoto please step forward?

"What are you thinking?" she says.

"I was just wondering, did Atwell offer you a promotion for keeping an eye on me?"

"What did you just say?"

"I said did Atwell offer you—"

"Furp you, Merlin Stone! I am so done here!"

She nearly jumps out of her chair as she stands up, but she doesn't want to go, I don't think. I don't want her to go.

"I was out of line. I apologize, Sunny. I didn't really think you were spying on me. Well, maybe a tiny part of me briefly entertained the idea. It's complicated and tiresome and has nothing to do with you, or anyone else but me and Atwell."

I knew she wasn't going to leave, which means she either likes me, or Atwell did offer her a promotion.

"In a way this is good, though," I say.

"Having someone to talk to about daddy issues?"

I stare helplessly at her. She laughs as she slips back into her seat.

"Deos have daddy issues too, huh?" she says.

"And you?"

"I never met my old man. He could have been banished to Uranus, for all I know. You could say mine are mommy issues. Unresolvable, given she's been dead for four years. Or is it five?"

"Sorry to hear that."

"Yeah, well."

I look away, peek at her from the corner of my eye. She's deep in thought. I polish off the last of the veggie steak, sop up more gravy with a piece of bread.

"I want to live to three-hundred, okay?" she says. "That's the real reason I endured the debasement of the SEFs. I scratched and clawed my way through one humiliating session after another, and I won ugly, which is the only way to win. I used every questionable means at my disposal to achieve my goal. Believe me, I know what Tamora and those others went through to get a seat in that orientation room. I knew she wanted to gouge out my eyes. I don't blame her for feeling that way. You do what you have to do. I guarantee you those newbies won't ever again let their guard down."

"I heard someone say ratings for the SEFs are through the roof."

"It would be foolish not to monetize such a spectacle, wouldn't you agree, Merlin?"

Neither of us thinks that's funny. I shake my head. Deplorable, shameless, inhuman, etcetera, and yet here we are having lunch at the STH Central dining hall.

"Three-hundred years is a long time," I say. "What are you going to do with all that time?"

She smiles, doesn't bother to cover her mouth this time. "I'll help others get their teeth fixed."

All of a sudden, those twisted teeth look spectacular. "You have a beautiful smile," I blurt out.

She looks down, frowning, maybe a little embarrassed. Her sudden vulnerability makes me want to kiss her, just a peck on the cheek. I don't want her getting the wrong idea. I straighten up, lean back against my chair. A couple of tables down two techies are sneaking glances at us. I do a discrete area scan. Anyone in line of sight could be harvesting content to disseminate over Transmedia outlets. I envision headlines like, *Kidnapped Scion Romancing Ord Underling*.

Sunny peers up at me, closes her eyes, and lowers her head. Every movement is performed slowly, almost ritualistically. What is she up to now? I wait. I check on the techies. They're jabbering away, pretending to have lost interest in us. I check on Sunny. She's entered some kind of peace space. Peace Spacing has become a thing lately.

If you're with someone who is Peace Spacing, it could feel like they're deliberately tuning you out, but often that's not the case, from what I understand. Sometimes it's quite the opposite, like an invitation. The peace spacer is tuning out everything that doesn't matter and tuning into only what brings peace, which very well could include you. I close my eyes and drift alongside Sunny. I listen to the ebb and flow of the dining hall's acoustic medley until it becomes gentle as a soft breeze.

This Peace Spacing has a nice, regenerative quality to it, I see, kind of like taking a brief afternoon nap. I'm surprised at how easily I'm Peace Spacing. Sunny and I are being carried by the same soft breeze the length of an easy river on a warm afternoon. I wave to the techies stuck below on the mud banks. They don't wave back. They just stare, as if expecting me to fall from the sky.

Sunny and I reach a fork in the river. Does she fit into my New Life Plan? Objectively speaking? Probably not. She floats one way, I float the other. When I open my eyes, she's gone. How long have I been Peace Spacing alone? I turn my head and catch the techies ogling me. One of them smiles and waves. I wave back.

I'm late for a meeting with Roscoe Cheng and nearly run over a young woman coming into the dining hall as I'm rushing out. Her name is Pearl. I mentioned her before.

Recorded: 04 Sep 2101

08 October 2100

All human enterprise is designed to tame the Loneliness Beast, Rod Raskolnikov used to say. There are many ways to do it. Some have become enormously profitable.

Just ask Atwell.

This morning there is quite a stir in Robotics. Roscoe Cheng has reported Stone-TH's hostile takeover of Get Raptured Enterprises, Inc., whose flagship product line is Bona, the hallucinogenic opt-out of choice for those overwhelmed by the here and now. Bona will immediately be added to the Stone TransHumanix Happiness Unbounded suite of life-enhancing products and services.

The takeover of Get Raptured Enterprises is a no-brainer. The GRE reach is long. Its Eros Gummy Balls have become more popular than mints, and its Deep-Space-Themed Spicy Cadet Exchange Centers for the Lonely and Bored are springing up like dandelions across the planet.

With the takeover, Stone-TH also acquires the GRE affiliate, Deo Dream Dares, LLC, which produces virtual reality products such as the *Be a Deo Today* program that provides limitless opportunities for Deo-like experiences running the gamut from high-end toiletry indulgences to vacation cruises around the moons of Jupiter and Saturn.

Just before I call it a day, I witness my first OUT hack-cast. For twenty-three seconds I'm mesmerized by the hologram of a woman wearing a rabbit mask who sounds like Princess Leia. She issues a general warning about ramped-up worldwide collusion between governments and corporations and hurriedly references the Big Six, Burr Brumbo's election to the RSA presidency in 2094, and something about alien indwelling and a misreality plot. Before any of it can make the least bit of sense to me, the hack-cast vanishes and is replaced by normal programming.

I crawl into bed and try to sleep, but my mind won't let me. Rabbit Lady was aware she had only seconds to say what she needed to say. Immediate viewer comprehension wasn't her goal. She was tossing seeds, counting on some of them to take root, and expecting that a portion of the audience would eventually take the warning seriously.

But, wow, alien indwelling and misreality plots? That's a tough sell. I turn the lights on and sit on the edge of my bed thinking about Rabbit Lady and staring at the three hares chasing one another in a forever circle on the top of my left hand.

Turns out twenty-three seconds is plenty of time to shake things up around the planet. Over four billion people witnessed the OUT hack-cast live. Saturday at noon, Big Six spokesman and former Brumbo Chief of Staff, Rodolfus Barnesby, issues a rebuttal via global Transmedia: "This absurd, purportedly alien-driven so-called Misreality Plot is an insult to human intelligence, an evil hoax perpetrated by a tiny group of lunatics and scalawags. The Big Six stand by our life-affirming, life-enhancing, prosperity-for-all products and services. And our faith in the hard work, decency, and discretion of our present and future customers grows daily. Together we will continue to prosper and expose those who would try to undermine or attack our way of life."

Barnesby's prepared statement is followed by slice of life holograms projecting onto every compatible view-space on Terra. Ords are depicted at various stages of life: a group of bright-eyed students passing around a bag of Brain Boost Bona Drops; an amorous couple walking in the park wearing matching *Gummy Yummy!* t-shirts and marveling at the impact on performance of honey-flavored Eros Gummy Balls; and frisky seniors living it up at a Paradise Luxury Suite two-hundred and fifty miles above Terra via the *Be a Deo Today* virtual reality program.

The slick vignettes give way to an empty blue firmament. Somewhere faraway, tower bells are tolling.

A voice like that of a titan is heard: "Reality is Progress. Reality is Pleasure. Reality is Paradise. The only Misreality is the one concocted by evil OUT-siders."

Recorded: 07 Sep 2101

09-10 October 2100

I spend part of Saturday researching OUT. Civil membership is no crime per se, not currently, though any affiliation with OUT's so-called "militant" wing is considered treasonous. The distinction between civil and militant doesn't keep World Anti-Terrorism Command from targeting and indicting legal OUT members for ambiguous violations such as Uncivilized Public Comportment and Inflammatory Public Discourse.

The standard response by OUT's legal defense attorneys is to advise clients to plead guilty to the lesser crime of Questionable Public Rhetoric and agree to pay a 5000 Coin fine, ensuring the accused spends no more than one night in jail. Such arrangements are not finalized without supplementary palm-greasing, which observers estimate raises the average total expense per accused to 10,000 Coin.

So where is OUT getting up to 10,000 Coin a pop to keep its members from going to prison on trumped-up charges? Prevailing rumors point to Starling Sayer as the most likely source, though whether the man is dead or alive is a matter of continual debate and speculation.

After dinner I turn on the Transmedia hologram feed. The first thing I see is a man and a woman lying face down on a street in Prague. The bodies are identified by World Anti-Terrorism Command officials as those of Radek Benik and Zelenka Melichar. The two are described as having recently been expelled from their professorships at the University of Prague for inappropriate conduct and membership in the banned militant wing of OUT.

The floor beneath my feet begins to move. My hand goes up. I want to stop the world and rewind, but the feed has other ideas. It zooms in on the bloodstained profiles, and a new voice says, "Just an hour ago, militant OUT lieutenants, Radek Benik and Zelenka Melichar, were killed in a shootout with WATC agents after a dangerous car chase through the streets of Prague."

I start blinking like crazy, fighting the sting. My eyes are on fire as I stare at the two familiar faces. "That's a lie!" I shout and pace helplessly about my apartment.

I once asked Anacletus, the seminarian I tutored in Thessaloniki, why he seemed always ready to laugh. He stopped to think for a moment, then said it's because laughter chases away hatred and fear.

Wasn't sure about that then, even less sure about it now. But the idea that people like Radek and Zelenka could be militant OUT lieutenants is so over the top that I have to stop for a moment and laugh. But instead of chasing away the hatred and the fear, my laughter fuels both and consumes me, leaving me exhausted. I draw nearer to the 3D image, extend my arm to help them get up, and my hand goes right through the light field where Zelenka should be.

The report is followed by none other than Rodolfus Barnesby standing at a podium before a live audience.

"Of course, as with any failure of the social order, we all, to some degree, bear the burden of blame for acts of terror and the terrorists who perform them. We can point the finger at select individuals, groups, belief systems, scientific and political theories, ancient grievances, rash executive orders, imprudent legislative acts, irresponsible judicial pronouncements, ill-advised economic decisions, and yes, even the all too familiar, ill-conceived Valedictorian speech.

"All of the above play a part in facilitating the growth and development of disordered individuals like the two terrorist professors in Prague. But let us be clear, shall we? Granted, we are all to blame *to some* degree. But not to too great a degree. Let us not blame ourselves too much for the harm caused by bad people. We can choose to do right, or we can choose to do wrong. The disordered choose to do wrong. Let us not sit idly by listening to the litanies of excuse and the tedious alibis. Make no mistake, OUT's existence is aimed like a nuclear missile at disrupting the very heart of our way of life. OUT promotes lies, death, and destruction. Publicly, OUT's members refer to themselves as *Ords United for Truth*. But privately—and we have overwhelming evidence to confirm what I am about to reveal—these traitors proudly refer to themselves as *Ords United for Terror!*"

I was twenty-three when Barnesby was named Brumbo's Chief of Staff. I never paid much attention to either of them until I met my old pal, Rod Raskolnikov, in Taverna Momos. Rod said Barnesby and Brumbo were the reason he left the States. He said they were phonies, and because of all the lying they did, he had a hard time believing they were fully human. He thought they might be *alien mules*, which I found amusing, if a bit puzzling.

Rod got real quiet after he told me that and spent the rest of the evening staring behind the bar counter at Dionysus with his bowl of wine and his bunch of grapes.

I suspect my fool's grin about alien mules told Rod I was missing the point. Maybe I still am, though I think I'm getting closer to understanding what he meant.

Recorded: 10 Sep 2101

11-12 October 2100

Maybe Sunny can shed some light on what happened to Radek and Zelenka. I have a gut feeling she has some kind of connection to OUT and may be privy to insider information. It's worth a try. Monday morning, I walk over to her empty hub. An IT guy with a punishing voice tells me Sunny opted to take today and tomorrow off.

The timbre of the IT guy's voice aggravates the headache I woke up with. I take analgesics and slog my way through a long workday lost in a toxic fog. Pearl flits in and out of the haze. We exchange quick smiles but no words.

Regardless of what's happening around me or to me, I've got to stay the course. I need to impress Chief Cheng, accumulate as many Robotics Employee of the Week awards as I can, and make it impossible for Atwell to decline my New Life Plan request.

Back in my apartment, I do some further digging. I find no links between Radek and Zelenka and OUT, and no links between them and Starling Sayer. I spend the rest of my time looking into the life of the controversial Star Man.

Sayer was head of the Math Department at Father's alma mater, Manifest Destiny Institute of Technology, and seven-time winner of the MDIT Professor of the Year Award. He abandoned teaching without warning, moved to waterlogged Nova City, surrounded himself with brilliant analysts, and created the most lucrative hedge fund in history.

Star Man's financial exploits led to *The Myth of the Golden Unicorn*, said to be born of a dream Sayer had about a unicorn that spun algorithms on a gold spinning wheel, including the Master Coin Algorithm, which it presented to Sayer. All Sayer had to do upon waking was transcribe what the unicorn had given him, which he did. Never in twenty years would the Gold Unicorn Fund sustain a quarterly loss, racking up unprecedented annual average returns of fifty-eight percent, after fees.

Sayer would leave Gold Unicorn Systems as abruptly as he left MDIT. After many years of unparalleled success in the world of Coin, Sayer's reputation took a hit 01 May 2096, following an anonymous post on the GUS Employee Forum by a former employee.

According to the poster, Sayer's longtime assistant, confidante, and rumored paramour, Felicia Kingsley, was sitting on a toilet in a lavatorio stall after normal work hours when she was overheard talking on her Q-Phone. The clandestine listener, seated three stalls to Kingsley's left, heard a man's voice on the other end. She suspected it was Starling Sayer, though she couldn't be sure.

The man informed Kingsley he had been in contact with Pachomius, whom Kingsley mistook for an associate in the Balkans. The man corrected Kingsley's assumption, pointing out that Pachomius was the founder of Communal Monastic Life, and a Desert Father, and that he had discussed with him three things: the Delphic maxim *Know Thyself*, his personal responsibility to Ords, and the coming apocalypse.

A lengthy silence was followed by Kingsley's reply, "Are you shitting me, Starling?" which left no room for doubt regarding the identity of the speaker on the other end of the line.

Within hours, Starling Sayer's reputation took a hit and Gold Unicorn Systems became the business world's butt of jokes. Then, for a while, Sayer was nowhere to be found, and wherever Kingsley went, she was accosted by dozens of reporters. "No comment," was all they ever got out of her.

Two weeks later, Sayer reached out to his most trusted Transmedia contact, Arnold Krupp, and arranged for a mid-morning Sunday press conference. It was raining lightly. Sayer appeared bareheaded before the Transmedia throng in front of his Nova Park West luxury apartments looking emaciated and unshaven, though one profoundly affected reporter would later describe Sayer as having been *monkishly serene and seemingly at peace with himself*.

"Think again, but with new minds," Sayer said as he scanned the crowd of reporters. "The Rule of Misreality spreads like a virus. Beware of the Corporatocracy and alien influencers. The world as we know it ends before 2102."

That was it, not another word.

The stunned silence was followed by an abrupt barrage of questions. "Mr. Sayer, did you just say the world is going to end in five years?" "Mr. Sayer, aren't you yourself a founding member of the so-called Corporatocracy?" "Mr.

Sayer, did Pachomius, the Desert Father, give you privileged insight into The Rule of Misreality?"

Sayer didn't answer any of the questions. He turned around and walked into the building. The bald spot on the back of his head was the last thing the world saw of him.

Speculation was rampant. Unverified reports suggested Sayer was living in a desert tent in the north of Africa. Dozens of holograms of Bedouins purported to be Sayer riding a camel, eating dates, drinking from a public well, and so on, inevitably proved to be doctored and were discredited.

After Sayer's disappearance, the ubiquitous Rodolfus Barnesby appeared on Selena Stargazer's popular prime time talk-talk show, *Stargazing*, to promote his new book. When asked point blank by his host his opinion of the elusive Starling Sayer, Barnesby sighed.

"Where should I begin, Selena? I have studied OUT-sized egos extensively. My book, *This Is How Gods Are Made*, is precisely about individuals like Mr. Sayer, aka Star Man. Where is Star Man? Is he riding a camel in the Sahara? Is he walking on the waters of the Mediterranean Sea? Or is Star Man up in the sky?"

Barnesby gazed at the audience and nodded knowingly, eliciting chuckles and sporadic applause.

"How very interesting, Rodolfus," Selena Stargazer said. "Up in the sky. Tell us, what do you mean when you say, *Up in the sky*? How does one go up in the sky? Do you mean in an air balloon, a VTOL, a rocket ship? Or are you speaking metaphorically?"

"Let us ponder this a moment. And by the way, those are all excellent questions, Selena. No, we are not entertaining metaphors. We are speaking in a different tongue, as it were. The Digital tongue. Lives uploaded in microseconds to *the digital sky*, or more precisely, to a *Q Cloud*. Perhaps Star Man is now Digital Star Man, no longer bound by the restraints of time and matter like us mere mortals. Call it what you will. Absurd, grotesque, pathetic? This is how gods are made, Selena, at least the self-made variety."

The audience laughed and applauded.

Selena adopted a contemplative expression. *"Digital Star Man*. Rodolfus, are you implying the real Starling Sayer is dead?"

Barnesby passed a thoughtful gaze over the audience before turning to Selena.

"Who said anything about death?" he replied, his eyebrows raised in mock surprise.

Recorded: 11 Sep 2101

14 October 2100

Sunny and I have lunch again. She seems tense. Maybe it's me. I woke up in the middle of the night crying like a baby. Never cried as a kid, never cried all those years in Europe. I'm not going to bring up Radek and Zelenka, nor OUT, nor Star Man. I'm going to let Sunny set the agenda.

"I have a confession to make," she says.

"Okay."

"The main reason I applied for a job at Stone-TH was the VivaLong program."

"You already told me that."

"I did, I know. That's not what I want to confess."

"I'm listening."

"I wasn't expecting you to be sitting in on that newbie meeting, okay? I'll be honest with you, I got annoyed. I felt like I was being evaluated by someone who hadn't earned the right to be sitting there. But then I started to think how I might turn your unannounced presence to my advantage. It's widely known your dad likes workers who think outside the box."

"The Stone-Cold Code being Exhibit A?" I say, forcing a smile.

"You wouldn't mind putting in a word on my behalf?" Wouldn't I?

"It's not like I haven't enjoyed your company," she says.

I'm in no position to judge her, but the Sunny mystique is gone, *poof!* Just like that. Don't want it gone, it just is.

"Wow, okay, look, my dad and me? We speak in different tongues, you know? He doesn't get me, and I don't get him."

Sunny stares at me with detached intensity, parsing my every word and breath.

She's at my mercy, I'm surprised to realize. Sort of. Wait a second. No, that's not at all what's happening. I've got it all wrong. All that stuff Sunny was telling me on our way to the dining hall that first time suddenly is packed with undesired significance. She was setting me up the whole time, rattling off tedious information that barely registered with me, like the requirements for eligibility in the VivaLong program, which included passing a comprehensive physical, signing waivers and nondisclosure agreements, and completing 26,000 hours of employment within the first ten years, the equivalent of ten years of consecutive fifty-hour work weeks.

She's been playing on my guilt. She knows as well as I do that I can skip all the requirements and enroll in VivaLong whenever my privileged little heart desires. And what's worse, she probably figures I haven't given VivaLong the slightest thought, and she's one-hundred percent right.

I'm trying to be fair about this, see things from her perspective. I know exceptional Ord employees can be recommended for elevation to coveted Ordeo status at any time. A favorable decision will cut their active employment time requirement in half, from ten to five years, and Father always has final say on who gets elevated.

Sunny's unrelenting stare tells me she's not going to say another word until I say something. So, yeah, I am miffed at being used, but what's the point of living there?

"We talk sometimes, about company matters, mainly," I say. "And this is a company matter, so sure, Sunny, I'll bring up your name with Atwell, get you on his radar."

Sunny smiles without parting her lips. It's a knowing smile, not cold, not hot, and I'm not even sure what it means. I'll mention her to Father, but what exactly am I supposed to say about her? That she made up some weird company code and passed it off as an official guidance document? Which makes her what? A skilled liar? A deft manipulator? You know what, maybe that's exactly the kind of employee Atwell wants to elevate.

"Look, I never said I was a good person," she says. "Good persons don't win the SEFs. I do what I have to do. So yeah, think what you want about me."

And that would be? I don't know what I think about Sunny Takamoto.

"Hey, Sunny, all the stuff that happens in a life, the complications, the successes and failures, the promises of longevity and good health. What happens to it all if the world as we know it ends tonight?"

"I know plenty of people who would welcome such a development," she says, studying me closely.

Recorded: 12 Sep 2101

21 October 2100

Once again, Pearl and I nearly collide at the dining hall entrance. How she manages to keep those half dozen cups of coffee from spilling is remarkable. Her tender, playful gaze makes me smile with wonder. But the charmed moment slips into awkward silence, and we go our separate ways.

At least twice a day I look for her, or she looks for me. Once in the morning, once in the afternoon. We seem to have reached a silent agreement to maintain a safe distance. Day after day we smile and wave and then go our separate ways. I'm confused. Who exactly are we to one another?

Friday morning, I wake up from a lucid Direct Command Dream, the kind that tells you exactly what to do when you wake up. Nothing to mull over, no pros and cons to weigh. A Direct Command Dream issues a clear *Do This*. And because it's a DCD, you know it's the right thing to do, so you move forward in confidence and with resolve.

I walk into Robotics feeling composed and decisive. I'll wait for Pearl to get settled in for the day and then head over and ask her to have dinner with me on Saturday.

Easy enough, you would think, but I don't see Pearl anywhere. Just before lunch, I saunter over to Admin to talk to Eva Weinstein, who informs me Pearl is on leave.

"That can't be," I protest, and Eva just stares at me.

I don't get paid enough to put up with this crap.

I'm pretty sure that's what she's thinking. It's her go-to line for idiots like me. I've overheard her use it more than once. She won't say it because I'm the boss's son, which makes me feel worse. I put my hands up, back off, head for the dining hall, avoid people, order a large wakame seaweed and enoki mushroom soup, and head back to my work hub.

The soup restores my equilibrium and helps me understand something about Direct Command Dreams and Pearl's unexpected absence. There is no such thing as a Direct Command Dream. Just because I want one, doesn't mean I can have one. And Pearl? Well, Pearl has her own life to live, and I have mine.

Speaking of which, I've done a lot of thinking, planning and visualizing since getting my life highjacked in Greece. My focus needs to be on getting my New Life Plan executed.

This clumsy obsession with Pearl confirms my need to get back to my primary task, which is to handpick a family. This may seem easy enough to do. It's not. Granted, the right amount of Coin will secure any number of paid actors or specialized professionals to perform family roles for definite or indefinite periods of time. This has been done, and continues to be done all across the planet, with varying degrees of success.

But that's not what I'm talking about. I'm talking about a radically different approach, the handpicking of a loving, tightknit, committed, we're-all-in-this-together kind of family. No easy task, believe me. I've put a lot of serious alone time and soul searching into getting this right.

Oh, and I've checked everywhere. There's no how-to guide for handpicking a family. I guess I'll have to be the first to publish one someday.

Recorded: 13 Sep 2101

2101 Resolutions (midyear review)

1) Ask Pearl out to dinner on Friday (07 January).

Pass or Fail?   Fail

Comment: Never got around to it. Months flying by and we're still smiling, waving and exchanging lame remarks. I'll ask her to dinner soon. No biggie. Just do it! Should have no impact on Atwell's review and potential approval of my New Life Plan.

2) Show Atwell you're serious about being a strong contributor to the success of Stone-TH.

How? Impress Roscoe Cheng. Be first to show up at Robotics every morning, and the last to leave. Deepen "subordinate but also friend" ties with Roscoe. Regularly ask Roscoe about his 14 grandkids by name. Memorize all their birth dates and favorite pastimes.

Pass or Fail?   Pass

Comment: Roscoe's taken note, but am starting to get stiff competition from up-and-comer, Falanko Balasto. Would being second or third in and out Robotics hub once in a while be so bad? Could use newly available hours to boost Notes work-in-progress. Something to consider.

3) Build solid reputation, earn respect of colleagues and management at all levels.

How? Always be well prepared. Have useful questions to ask in meetings, respectfully challenge assumptions, offer thoughtful suggestions and positive alternate views, delineate ways forward, volunteer for grunt tasks (if no one else does). Learn as many names and personal details as possible. Smile often, show gratitude, be generous with praise and encouragements, gentle with criticism, and always constructive.

Pass or Fail?   Pass

Comment: Baffling success, given my Stone DNA. A credit to individual hard work and will power. However, the grind of performing miscellaneous grunt tasks may cause me to rethink strategy.

4) No later than 01 February 2101, submit New Life Plan request to Father.

Pass or Fail?   Fail

Comment: Still looking for right time to do this.

5) If New Life Plan request denied, refocus and tweak. Submit revised request to Father no later than 01 April 2101.

Pass or Fail?   Not Applicable

Comment: See #4.

6) Consolidate all miscellaneous scribblings and journal entries, organize them into a serviceable structure. Finetune content and dictate to Willie as series of Notes to be stored in wobot's database.

Pass or Fail?   Fail

Comment: Haven't gotten around to consolidating content, much less finetuning and dictating. The past eight months of busting hump at STH have sapped my creative juices and dulled my vision. Desperately need to free up some hours (see #2 comment). Refocus and finish writing up Greek ordeal segment (will have therapeutic value). Start limbering up vocal cords. Work out the kinks, make this review the first official dictation.

Recorded: 08 Jul 2101

14 September 2101

Wednesday after work I'm in Moony's Den sipping two-for-the-price-of-one imported moonsap with several of my Robotics Department coworkers.

We're all chat-crazy, and at least twice I'm tempted to announce I'm going to ask Pearl out to dinner this Friday but can't bring myself to do it. When the surround-holograph programming is switched off, we all stop talking.

Instead of feel-good imagery and sound we get thirty seconds of silence and the Supreme Thirteen seated behind their crescent-shaped High Bench. Behind the Bench another image is floating, a hologram within a hologram. It blinks and resets every few seconds, becoming a little clearer each time.

Chief Justice Josiah Dinkledinger starts reading from a prepared script. He pauses now and then to catch his breath and to stare at the invisible viewing audience.

"Therefore, we find the so-called Ords United for Truth—that is, OUT—guilty of spearheading a campaign of defamation and destruction directed against the People's Prosperity Initiative, in particular, and all federal efforts to elevate the common good, in general. As such, this Court forthwith identifies OUT as an enemy of the Reconstituted States of America, an enemy of the Reconstitution of the Reconstituted States of America, and an enemy of all Reconstituted Americans.

"Therefore, and forthwith, this Court condemns all activity by OUT, mandates a permanent ban on all OUT organizational functions—including physical and intellectual properties—and instructs all law enforcement, cyber warfare and anti-terrorism agencies to bring all individuals and/or groups affiliated with, or in any way linked to OUT, to justice, using whatever means necessary."

Dinkledinger folds his hands. His eyes are opaque. But I'm more interested in what's going on in the background. The hologram within the hologram has stopped blinking and has resolved itself, presenting a familiar scene.

We all recognize the image of Starling Sayer standing in a light rain before a crowd of Transmedia reporters outside his Nova Park West luxury apartments. The sound has been muted, but we all know the words that are coming out of Sayer's mouth: "The Rule of Misreality spreads like a virus. Beware of the Corporatocracy and alien influencers. The world, as we know it, ends before 2102."

We all remember the barrage of questions that followed.

Though Sayer is never once mentioned by name, the implication is clear. Starling Sayer is the force behind OUT. He is a traitor to his country and an enemy of the people.

I don't know, I guess I'm just trying to get back the good feeling we all had before Dinkledinger sucked the life out of Moony's.

"Moonsap for everyone!" I shout and point my finger at the bartender. "Put it on my tab!"

A joyous cry goes up, and for another hour or two, we forget about Dinkledinger, Sayer, and whatever darkness lies in wait.

Recorded: 29 Sep 2101

28 September 2101

We got moonsapped like it was *The Last Day*. But it wasn't, and the effects spilled over onto *The Next Day*. I never did get around to asking Pearl to have dinner with me. I blamed the savage headache that refused to go away. But two weeks later, what's my excuse?

I have no excuse. I have no answers. I seek solace in paint. I crave canvas, the smell of oil and brush, and a cool Icelandic attic room. When alone, my mind wanders like a child let loose in an amusement park.

But my days are rarely enjoyable and carefree. What was once therapeutic, has turned ominous. I render nightmares in sepia tones. The latest of these depicts an elephant-sized rat gnawing on an anatomically-precise android leg stolen from the Robotics Lab. I've included a faint suggestion of myself in the foreground watching the rodent munch away.

To what end? This is not helpful. I've tried changing things up, focusing harder on Pearl, painting her as mystical flower slash natural woman, but always with disastrous effects. The lovely abstract portrait I envision presenting her consistently becomes an unsettling convergence of half-remembered nightmare bits. My clumsy efforts to capture the essence of Pearl are reminders of my distressing inability to connect with her. Why is it so hard for me to connect with her? I put off dinner plans indefinitely.

Despite this failure, I won't stop trying to be a positive influence on others. Put another way, I'll try always to remain open to doing neighbor or stranger *a solid*. To that end, a couple of days ago I overheard two promising young Ord techies describe Rodolfus Barnesby as a Corporatocracy shill.

For their sake, I decided I would gently intervene, point out to Mariah Spank and Imelda Fluker how that kind of talk-talk was guaranteed to cost them their jobs, which would mean losing their VivaLong benefits and Ordeo eligibility, effectively landing them on the unforgiving Downer List. Then I'd forward them a Resolutions template similar to my own to help them self-examine and refocus.

But my read on the matter was totally off. Before I could open my mouth, Spank and Fluker broke into mocking laughter. "*The* Rodolfus Barnesby? The guy who actually *gets it*? A Corporatocracy shill? Ha-ha-ha! What a hoot! That's exactly what OUT would have us believe. Hey, you OUT losers! Stop looking for handouts and get a job!"

They never saw me. I slipped away unheard and unseen. I locked myself in the nearest lavatorio stall and spent a few minutes searching for something to feel good about.

I do continue to maintain the lead in the race for Robotics Employee of the Year, having thus far accrued the most Employee of the Week awards. So there's that, despite strong competition from Falanko Balasto and McKenzie Lear, an attractive older woman rumored to have been one of Father's lovers in the early days of Stone TransHumanix.

Father's decision to throw me a big thirtieth birthday party next week in Stone Heights is due in no small measure to Chief Cheng's positive input and his glowing job performance reviews. Personal failures and shortcomings aside, the stars do seem to be aligning themselves in my favor.

I'll leave for Stone Heights Wednesday night, get there a couple of days before the festivities. I'm bringing with me Willie, the 3W rabbit wobot I retrieved from my old bedroom closet at Stone House when I got back from Europe. We'll stay in the Sublevel-2 secret apartment Atwell showed me after my freshman year in college. Can't think of a better place to review my New Life Plan specs and get some more writing and dictating done.

Saturday, moonsap is going to flow like fountain water, and there's going to be loud music, bright lights, product promos, and six-hundred fashionably attired Deos shining like stars.

Knowing Atwell and Runa, the occasion will have an otherworldly feel to it, and even the most mundane remark will sound extraordinary.

Recorded: 29 Sep 2101

01 October 2101

The burst of laughter draws my attention. Burr Brumbo, President of the RSA, is holding court before a group of guests. Standing to his right is Atwell, to his left, Rodolfus Barnesby. Behind them are half a dozen men in black.

Atwell touches Brumbo's arm, whispers in his ear, and heads my way. He moves through the crowd, sidestepping guests, drawing a chuckle here and there over something he says, and looking pleased, for the most part.

He stops before me without making eye contact. I count inwardly. When I get to seven, he looks at me and says, "I'm ten years old, and I'm having this recurring dream." A fresh round of laughter ripples toward us from the Brumbo circle. Atwell frowns, then smiles.

"At noon I hear a tower bell start to toll. After it tolls the twelfth time, I hear a tremendous explosion, and my body is launched high into the sky. Vaporized rock and debris are tossed up, shooting past me at high speed into space. From above, I see cities and towns crumbling and fading amid clouds of smoke. Terra turns gray as clay. A veil of dust covers the sun and the stars. I can feel my body becoming clay, and that's when I wake up. I have the same dream six consecutive nights. Each time that I'm up there floating in space, I say to myself, 'If I can just stay up here for one hour, I will live forever.' The seventh night arrives and I stay up there for over an hour. I go down when I'm ready and walk in the ashes among the ruins. I know it's a dream, but dreams can be transformative. When I wake up, I sit on the edge of my bed and say to myself, 'Why die if I don't have to?'"

Is he making this up? I have no idea. He laughs and says, "I repeated those words and felt a hunger for life tremble inside me. Have you ever felt that kind of hunger, Merlin?"

"Yes, in the Spring of 2100, in a shack, on a hilltop in Greece."

It sounds like I'm baiting him. I guess I am. I need to be more careful.

He pauses for a moment. "I often wonder how many would welcome the end," he says as he sweeps a glass of moonsap off a tray and winks at Pearl.

I do a doubletake. Pearl? I hardly recognize her. Her eyes engage mine for only an instant.

The conscripts, for lack of a better word, caught my eye the moment I stepped into the dome. Young Stone-TH admins. Females, males, and nonbins in flowing purple manes, their golden faces prettied up in purple eyeshadow and lip gloss, all of them donning harlequin gold and purple skintight catsuits with tails that like to curl.

Pearl turns around and moves with grace through the Dionysian throng, her tail bobbing suggestively. Father sips his vintage moonsap, his eyes still on her.

"How many do you think?" he says turning suddenly toward me.

I consciously shift my thinking away from Pearl.

"You mean, how many would welcome the apocalypse? Given the current state of the planet, the socioeconomic and geoclimatic disorders? If you were to take a survey of Ords right now, I would say at least twenty percent would welcome the end. Put that question to any Deo, and I imagine most of them would laugh in your face."

Pearl is standing motionless in the middle of Mother's entourage, holding up a tray of drinks for half a dozen extended arms. Her gaze is distant. She reminds me of a movie star of the Old World posing for a poster photograph. She's protecting herself, putting distance between her and those probing eyes. I can't read Mother's lips, but I suspect she's explaining Pearl to her companions, as if Pearl were the latest addition to her treasured art collection.

"Does that bother you?" Father says in a rare playful tone.

"What?"

"The way they look at her, Mother's groupies."

"You mean, the way they look at Pearl?"

Atwell's left eyebrow nudges up.

"What you were saying before, about the apocalypse?" I say, deflecting. "All those dead dinosaurs. What are the odds of that ever happening to humanity?"

"Total extinction? Not likely."

"As unlikely as me being your son?"

That was supposed to come out sounding clever, maybe even funny. Or maybe it wasn't.

"And yet, here you are, against all odds," Atwell says without smiling. "Forget about the Alvarez hypothesis. We're dealing with something quite different now."

"What do you mean? What are you talking about?"

"Stay right there. There's something I need to tell you."

Father makes his way to the front and gets up on the marble dais. After thanking everyone for coming to Stone Heights "to celebrate my son Merlin's thirtieth birthday," he starts talking about the importance of a life well lived. I marvel at the man's ability to shift into whatever role suits him at any given moment.

I look for Pearl. I don't see her anywhere. Poor Pearl having to endure the gawking and the commentary and the sordid fantasizing.

"The only thing better than a life well lived is a longer life well lived," Father says. "Most of you are already reaping the benefits of the VivaLong Program, and I congratulate you on your decision to guarantee yourself three-hundred years of a life well lived."

He pauses for the applause.

"Now I'd like to announce for the first time in public the next stage of our patented life extension, history-altering technology. At Stone TransHumanix we've been working diligently on an enhanced version of VivaLong. I can't give you the exact date, but certainly within the next twelve to fourteen months we expect that our groundbreaking work in senolytics and cell reprogramming will make it possible for humans to enjoy a life well lived far beyond a meager three-hundred years. I'm talking five-hundred, seven-hundred, up to one-thousand years and more!"

After a collective gasp, the crowd erupts in victory shouts and thunderous applause. Q-Phones everywhere begin to pulse and beep.

"If you are enrolled in the base VivaLong program, you are automatically eligible for the Enhanced version and can reply *Yes* on your Q-Phone to be added to the waiting list. If you'd rather learn more about VLE before deciding if it's right for you, just follow the guidance on your Q-Phone. However, be aware that VLE will be made available on a first come, first serve basis, no exceptions."

He takes a minute to scan the crowd while they fiddle with their Q-Phones.

"For those of you not enrolled in the base VivaLong program, what can I say? Congratulations on your extraordinary genetic makeup and high level of self-assurance."

A couple of guests start to clap, though it's not clear why. Atwell frowns and exhales wearily. Silence fills the dome.

"Are you out of your minds?" he shouts. "Don't you believe you deserve more than a pitiful hundred years of life?"

"You'd have to be a world class dumbass to settle for a hundred years!" someone shouts.

Was that President Brumbo?

Atwell bursts into laughter and the place goes wild. He points at the president and nods knowingly. Brumbo points back at him, grinning with self-pleasure.

"Folks, come on now, you know I love you," Atwell says. "I am so excited about this program and what it can do for you and your families. If you haven't enrolled, or if you just want to talk VLE with someone, Sadie Wilkerson and her people are in the back waiting to answer your questions."

People like Sunny Takamoto don't get invited to parties like this. Maybe one day, years from now, she will. I know she'd kill to get on that VivaLong waiting list. Me? I'm not buying anything Atwell's selling.

Recorded: 15 Oct 2101

Stone Heights sits on a plateau in the middle of a vast plain, like an outpost in an uncharted territory of a long-ago era. Being here for any length of time, you could easily trick yourself into thinking nothing or anyone of importance exists outside these walls. Atwell claims he built Stone Heights to last ten-thousand years. I think he believes he'll be around then, in one form or another.

The compound, which contains over a hundred suites and apartments, is powered by solar energy-harvesting satellites. Geothermal heat pumps provide heating and cooling. Other amenities include deep piped-in water, built-in waste disposal and recycling systems, subterranean levels stocked with food, nonperishable goods, supplies, parts and equipment, an enclosed ten-acre garden cultivated and maintained by a crew of edenbots, a state-of-the-art communications center, a landing deck for up to a dozen hoveroos, multiple gyms, indoor pools, observation decks, and facilities designed to keep the body and mind active. Security is guaranteed by a platoon of sentinelbots and a fleet of surveillance drones.

"There was something you wanted to tell me," I say when Atwell finishes his pitch. He leans forward. His smiling face draws close to my brow. The smell of moonsap on his breath is stronger now, and for an awful moment, I think he's going to kiss my cheek. He pulls back and gazes at me, grinning.

"Starling Sayer said the world's going to end this year," I say. "It's October. Do you believe him?"

Atwell goes from giddy to grave in a heartbeat.

"Let me tell you something important, Merlin. You need to stay ahead of the monsters."

"The monsters, huh?"

He shakes his head, puts up a hand and squints at me.

"We do what we have to do."

He tells me about an Old World zombie film he saw as a kid that features hundreds of undead suddenly appearing out of nowhere at twilight and surrounding a group of hapless wanderers. He pauses for a moment before describing how the screams of a man being eaten alive kept him up all night.

"A stupid premise," he says. "How do hundreds of slow-as-shit zombies surprise anybody? Regardless, that dubious scenario did teach me a lesson. It's my responsibility to have a contingency plan. I'm not waiting on others to provide one. The monsters always come back, so you better be ready."

For a while, I stop hearing his voice. I'm looking at his eyes, only his eyes, and I'm thinking, what if I find the boy who was so scared he couldn't sleep? If I find that frightened child, maybe all that's wrong between us gets made right.

But not today. I hear Atwell say, "You've played it out in your head, decided beforehand who it's going to be. You shoot to cripple, not to kill. You want the bloodcurdling screams and the mindless terror, the special brand of fear that draws the zombie mob irresistibly to a single soul. Done the right way, one human dies. Everybody else goes home."

How do you respond to that? I look for Pearl, but spot Mother instead. Lovely Runa is surrounded by her entourage like an Athenian queen, crowned with a tiara, and draped in long, immaculate white. The swanky group are paused before holographic figures promoting the latest VivaBody products.

One of the surreal figures, a naked old man, is examining pigment-compatible floating hands, arms, legs, feet, torsos, necks and heads. The man twists off his swollen, discolored left foot and replaces it with a new foot of his choosing. The refurbishing continues until he performs one last sensational act. He twists off his head and replaces it with a brand new one. The man now looks like a Greek god.

The spectators ooh and ahh. In seconds the refurbished man disappears, giving way to the original broken-down old man. The cycle begins again, left foot and so on.

It's a dazzling, disconcertingly realistic display, the work of Ventidius, the new sensation in Dense Arts Holography. He's also the recent prized addition to the Stone-TH Marketing Department, known more for his provocative DAH works than marketing skills. Father steps away to introduce him to the crowd.

The artist delivers a series of rehearsed platitudes, which don't disappoint. Mother and her companions applaud with disproportionate zeal. *Bravo! Bravo, Ventidius!* reverberates throughout the great dome. Ventidius bows and leaves Stone Heights with a stunning nonbin dressed in black leather from ankle to neck.

Father always looks for new ways to do things. He built Stone TransHumanix from nothing into a Big Six corporation. The company's growing revenues and profits reflect its breakthroughs in genetic engineering, nanotechnology, robotics and artificial intelligence.

"Is that Grandfather Stone?" I say half seriously when Atwell gets back.

"Okay, Merlin."

"I see a definite resemblance."

"Only you see your grandfather there. The rest of us see an aging Ord availing himself of a remarkable opportunity to live longer and better."

Atwell walks away. He won't show it, but I know I've irked him. I wonder if he'll have Chief Cheng fire me when I get to work Monday morning. I watch him cut inside a circle of guests. He says something that triggers laughter.

To see people's reactions, you would think Father is the funniest man on the planet. He's not oblivious to insincerity, though. He regards these folks with special interest. When the laughter tapers off, he extends his hand and draws from the group the spryest female. They dance cheek-to-cheek, in the ancient manner, eliciting applause and laughter.

I wonder what's going on behind Atwell's cold brow as he swings his partner with a flourish and leans her back onto his arm. Her white teeth show suddenly in a frozen smile, and for a moment I imagine the dancers are an ice sculpture.

Recorded: 16 Oct 2101

Through the curved glass wall of the dome, I look east. I follow the straight private road into darkness. The security lights obscure the stars.

Music and chatter volume are cresting. Behind me moon-sap flows like a river, and low-level Stone-TH employees in catsuits slip through the crowd balancing trays near their heads. The catsuit was Mother's idea, no doubt. She's always been fond of harlequins and has a heart for the grotesque.

That Pearl might be avoiding me saddens and annoys me. I need to get my mind off her. I should mingle. I scan the crowd. Pick someone. There, two stylish, long-shoed males, both in their late thirties, one of medium height and build, the other big and brawny. I draw near. They're discussing moving averages and market trends. I dive right in. "Hey there, I'm Merlin Stone. You fellas having a good time?"

"Why yes, of course, Mr. Stone," the brawny one says. "Tad Sizemore. Pleasure to finally meet you." He crushes my hand. I manage to keep smiling.

"Mr. Stone, yes indeed, a pleasure. Flick Ridley."

"Call me Merlin, please."

"This is one hell of a production, Merlin," Flick says with a wave of his glass.

"I had nothing to do with it," I say.

They both chuckle. I smile.

"I'd have to disagree," Flick says. "No Merlin, no party." He looks at Tad, and they both laugh.

"We were discussing market reversal paranoia," Tad says.

"Ah," I say, nodding.

"The sky is falling!" Flick cries wild-eyed, hands raised in mock terror, a wave of moonsap flipping into the air.

Tad is watching me with an expectant grin, so I mimic Flick. Tad follows with his own cringe. The three of us have a good laugh.

"Seriously, though, you'd never know the economy was going gangbusters the way the bears see it," Flick says. "I don't have to tell *you*, Merlin. The bull is long and will stay long, barring an unforeseen calamity."

"All things being equal, I see another year of smooth sailing," Tad agrees.

"Smooth sailing, absolutely," I say.

"People like us, Merlin," Tad says, "we make it our business to know what others don't."

"Yep, yep," I say.

"Read the tealeaves," Flick says. "Hindenburg Omen, classic example. Happens on a single day. New highs and new lows each exceeding 2.8% of advances plus declines. Guess what? There is no furping Hindenburg Omen anywhere in sight. Am I deluding myself?"

"I don't believe you are," I say.

"The Titanic Syndrome," Tad says.

"Another classic," I venture.

"Add that to your list of wakeup calls. More 52-week lows than 52-week highs within seven days of an all-time high? When you see that—and we have not—then by all means, pull the trigger. Sell! Sell! Sell!"

"Sell!" I cry.

"Let's hear it for the Dumb Money folks," Flick adds. "Love the way they cut bait too soon or too late."

"A toast to the Dumb Money!" Tad quips.

"A toast," I say, and we all lift our glasses in the air.

"A toast to Merlin, man of the hour!" Tad bellows.

"May the bull run long," I say.

Ching-Ching!

I should probably come clean, tell them I'm more of a Dumb Money kind of guy. We could all have a good laugh about that. Or not. We gulp down our drinks to the last drop and smack our lips in unison. Flick and Tad burst out laughing. Just then, I feel something change inside me, like a light switch going *click!*

I look at their faces, which suddenly seem familiar. My head begins to spin. My mouth goes dry. I frown, concentrate on slowing the spin.

"Now that we've established the bull is long," I say a little breathlessly.

They look at me, grinning, waiting for me to complete the Smart Money witticism. I don't, because I have no Smart Money witticism to impart.

"Mr. Stone, it's been a pleasure," Flick says, checking his watch.

"Mr. Stone? What happened to Merlin?"

"Merlin, of course." He looks at Tad. "We're supposed to meet with, uhm, what's his name, remember?"

"That's right," Tad says. "Good thing you remembered." He looks at me. "You'll have to excuse us, Merlin. You know what a harsh mistress Coin can be."

No bone-crunching handshakes this time, no handshakes at all, in fact. Flick and Tad nod in unison and slip back into the crowd.

Okay, let's just say for argument's sake I put bushy beards on both their faces, darken their complexions, dye their hair black and grow it out several inches. I add thirty pounds to Tad's frame, fifteen to Flick's, and change their eye color from blue and hazel to brown and brown.

Where does that leave me? It leaves me wondering how Atwell manages to find time to do all the things he does.

Recorded: 18 Oct 2101

Now I'm hearing a lot of people talking about space travel, and trips to Mars, in particular. The shift in theme coincides with the band's transition from upbeat techno to deep space enigmatica. The cacophony of cosmic echoes, wave rushes, winds, clangs, drips, and ghostly hums and howls has stirred the imagination and let loose a flock of tongues.

An exceptionally loud group gets the You Eye Sphere's attention. A bright spotlight envelops the group, and they let out a collective shout of delight. One of them starts doing a grotesque solitary dance for the benefit of the crowd. His companions hoot and point at the hologram of themselves projecting from a You Eye Sphere, one of the half-dozen YES units hovering near the dome ceiling. The mirrorlike progression of hologram within a hologram triggers a fresh avalanche of talk-talk and hilarity.

The overriding theme now is trips to Mars and spending time in New Terra City. Atwell's been there twice, and Runa has expressed interest in visiting the red planet. I'm having a hard time visualizing Mother cooped up in an underground Martian suite separated from her rose garden, art collection, groupies and events.

I notice two animated young women coming my way. I look behind me at no one in particular, glance again at the two ladies, and realize I'm the one they're swiftly advancing toward. They stop inches from my face, smiling broadly, and close enough that I can feel their warmth. In that instant, the three of us are bathed in a cone of white light. I look up at the hologram of ourselves looking up at a hologram of ourselves. My new friends laugh and wave. The crowd responds with cheers and applause.

"Do I know you?" I say when we're no longer the center of attention.

"My name is Violet," the taller of the two says.

"Violet. I'm sorry, have we met?"

The women look at each other and laugh.

"I'm Amber," the other one says.

They are both striking, and oddly disorienting, women. Violet, the braided brunette, is wearing a silver satin cut slip dress that highlights her long right leg. Amber has squeezed herself into a plunging V-neck, deep purple, glittery mini-dress. Her hair is short like a boy's and is the color of polished silver, feathered with lavender accents.

"Tell me, what is it like to be Atwell Stone's son?" Amber says. Her Queen's English accent, which I didn't notice until now, surprises me.

"You don't want to know," I reply.

They laugh and compliment me on Father's contributions to humanity, citing the marvelous results being achieved in skin elasticity and muscle tone by the latest enhancements made to the VivaBody line of products.

"Look at Faye McBride," Violet says by way of illustration, and immediately a cone of softened light illumines Faye. Her holographic form appears high above for all to examine. "How old would you say she is?"

Just at that moment, Pearl appears before us holding a tray of drinks.

"Ninety, but she looks half that age, thanks to Viva-Body," Amber responds for me.

"Hi there," I say.

"Hi," says Pearl.

For a sweet moment, it's just me and Pearl in the world. My unsolicited companions whisk glasses off Pearl's tray. I want Pearl to put the tray down and leave with me, go somewhere quiet where we can talk. But Pearl has a job to do. She smiles wistfully, turns around and walks away.

I watch her disappear in the crowd. I can feel Violet and Amber studying me. I wait for questions about the girl in the catsuit. But Pearl isn't at all on their notables list.

Violet says, "I have an idea."

It's then I notice the heart-shaped birthmark between her left pinky and ring finger. I peel my gaze from the birthmark and stare at Amber's face.

"*Our* idea," Amber says.

The perfect teeth and the Queen's English were keeping me from seeing her. But the subtle suggestion of the far East in those lovely eyes is now peeling back Amber's mask.

My heart starts thumping.

Violet equals Serenity equals Cindy Trapp. Amber equals Sunny Takamoto. Flick equals Zorba Papadopoulos equals Mr. Inferno. And Tad equals Heracles.

That's a lot of math.

A new hologram shows Burr Brumbo and the First Lady doing the enigmatica waltz box step to loud cheers.

"What do you say, Merlin?" Violet says. "Are you game?"

"Uh, no, I'm going to have to pass."

The ghost of old weakness again insinuates itself in my bones as I head to the private lavatorio. My feet and knees want to twist and buckle. But they won't, not unless I give them the power. My hand taps along the corridor wall to keep me from falling. The lavatorio door recognizes my face and lets me in. Father is stooped over a large stone basin splashing water on his face. He won't acknowledge my presence, not immediately, anyway. The face washing demands every bit of his attention.

He reaches for a towel and takes his time to dry every pore. He hangs the towel, finally looks at me and says, "There is something I have to tell you. Come with me."

Recorded: 20 Oct 2101

It's cold on the veranda, and I'm feeling kind of numb. Here we are, father and son marking thirty years of, what exactly? He talks, and I suspend belief. It wouldn't be the first time the man has lied to me. But the numbers he's tossing out demand attention.

"Have you been listening?"

I stop counting the zeros and look at him.

"Galactic anomaly, law of averages, cosmic punishment, however you want to put it, it was bound to happen sooner or later. The Chicxulub impactor wiped out the big reptiles sixty-six million years ago. We've come a long way since then. T-Rex and company lacked the wherewithal to foresee and adjust accordingly. They had no contingency plan. We do."

We? Who is we? I must be dense as granite. This is not what I've been hearing. Not here in the States, not in Greece, nor Iceland, nor anywhere.

I go back to the numbers. I'm reading way too many zeros. I'm drowning in zeros.

"This isn't funny," I say with an uneasy smile.

"No, it's not."

He shakes his head and sighs. "There won't be another Bright Star Day. These next twelve weeks are going to pass like the wind. I want you to come with us to New Terra City."

"To Mars? Me?"

"We're leaving the Sunday after Mars Day."

"Okay, have a safe trip."

Atwell gazes at me, disappointed, vexed and pensive, all at once. "I'm going to miss this old planet," he says. "The fall has a beauty all its own."

I can't be sure if by *fall* he means the beauty of autumn or the beauty of impending doom.

"Mars is dreary as a warehouse, despite the first-rate facilities and indoor gardens we've been developing over the past twenty years. I won't lie to you, Merlin, it's going to take a long time to adjust to the shrinking of life."

Atwell rolls his neck, clasps his hands and stretches his arms above his head. "The people in there? Most of them don't know. Your mom thinks she's going on a space cruise."

"My *mom*? You mean *Mother*?"

Atwell sighs. "The planet is going to hell and you decide this is the time to dig up old grievances."

There go my legs. Well, not quite. Almost. I start pacing back and forth on the veranda to keep my legs from failing. I know it makes no sense, a grown man feeling the need to ward off the phantoms of juvenile infirmity and insecurity. I walk back and forth over the stone tiles. I maintain a good pace. I keep the ghost of the purple bear at bay.

"Merlin has something he wants to show you," Dr. Vance announced.

Miss Eileen stretched out her hands to take my crutches. I felt a flash of vertigo as I handed them over to her. That was October 12, 2080, and for roughly half my life, the crutches had been my legs. I concentrated hard to keep myself upright. I glanced at Father and then at Mother. Everything else was a blur. Father's expression was blank. No surprise there. But in Mother's eyes I saw something new. Could it be regret? The possibility jarred me. I couldn't look at either of their faces as I walked toward them. I stopped once to glance back at Miss Eileen. She smiled and raised one of the crutches, as if toasting me.

Father's eyes narrowed as I approached. I detected a flicker of interest. Mother got up from her seat, drew near, and performed an awkward quasi-embrace.

"All right," Father said.

"Merlin has worked very hard these past four years," Miss Eileen said.

"Let this be a starting point," Father said.

He came around his desk and patted my shoulder. "Good work, Merlin." I fought off a smile. "Thank you, sir."

Dr. Vance shook hands with Father and then with me. Miss Eileen hugged me the way a real mother would. She wiped a tear away and gave me back the crutches, told me to keep them as a reminder of the mountain I had climbed.

"You are a brave and resilient boy, Merlin," she said. "There is no obstacle in life you won't be able to overcome."

I don't remember what I did with those crutches. Father followed Miss Eileen and Dr. Vance out the door, and Mother asked me if I would like to have lunch with her.

"Are you looking forward to school?" she said when we had begun to eat.

School?

"Oh, Merlin, what did you think? That you would be tutored here in Stone House the rest of your life? You need to develop social skills. Didn't Miss Eileen tell you?"

Of course, she had. I remained silent. I was wary of school and had no interest in developing social skills.

Mother was pleased to tell me all about a Mixed Media exhibit in Montreal she would be attending with that odd couple that had been appearing at Stone House lately. She was leaving tomorrow morning. She said she was going to miss me, but I didn't believe her. She got up, said something to Liani, and disappeared. Liani put a big bowl of ice cream in front of me and kissed the top of my head. Then she sat down where Mother had been and watched me eat.

Recorded: 22 Oct 2101

"Why are you doing that?" Father says. I stop pacing. For a moment, Atwell looks like a contrived being, his breath rising and fading in the cool evening air. Party music booms and rebounds against the interior walls of the dome, and Stone Heights trembles just a bit.

"Take the night to think it over," he says. He takes a couple of steps toward the entryway and gets stopped by something left unsaid. He turns halfway. "Do you want me to say we could have been better parents?"

Wasn't expecting that, but yes, that would be helpful.

He nods his head. Is that all I get, a nod? And yet, for the first time in my life, Atwell looks somewhat contrite.

"Regret does not become you, Father," I blurt out.

Silence would have been my better response. I watch him wrestle with my lack of sympathy, and then I think, no, he's not wrestling with anything. He's already moved on to something else.

"We prepare, we make tough choices," he says. "If humanity is going to survive and make its mark on the universe, it's going to be because of people like us."

"Seriously?"

He shakes his head, anticipating what I'm about to say. I say it anyway, knowing full well the words are meaningless.

"The Ords have a right to know."

"Of course, they do. Let's inform twelve billion Ords that most of them are going to die before year's end. In what galaxy is that a workable idea, Merlin? Even if we could move that many people, what do you propose we do with them? Drop them off at the nearest interstellar resort? Set up a tent city on a dried-up Martian riverbed? How in stars are they going to breathe? What are they going to eat? Who's going to provide medical care? And who is going to keep them from annihilating one another once they realize there is no hope?"

"RASA has been issuing reports on Apollyon for over a year," I counter, "telling us this so-called space hurricane was going to pass us by. Stock up on food, water, and meds, they said. Board up your windows, buy a generator, and get ready to tough it out for a couple of months. Sure, people were going to die. People always die during earthquakes and tsunamis. But it wasn't supposed to be anything we couldn't bounce back from. And now you're saying—"

"Apollyon is different. It's not like anything we've ever experienced. By the way, the invitation stands. I suggest you sleep on it. You'll have a fresh perspective in the morning."

Maybe it was his cavalier attitude that finally made me say what I could never take back. "What gives people like you the right to decide who lives and who dies?"

I brace myself. He raises his forefinger to his lips and says, "Not a word to anyone."

I'm shaking my head, desperate to find words to drive home my point. But what point would that be?

"What are you going to do, Merlin, hold a protest rally in front of the White House?"

He turns away and steps toward the dilating glass doors. Loud waves of space enigmatica come pouring out of the dimmed interior onto the cool veranda. Sweeping beams of multicolored light slash the new darkness.

The guests are like electric ghosts performing dances of doom. Maybe we're all already dead.

I look up, but the stars are obscured by the artificial lights. Somewhere in that darkness, Apollyon is speeding toward us, indifferent to human enterprise and dreams.

"Words get people killed," Father calls back.

With all that mayhem going on inside the dome, I don't think anyone else heard him.

I raise my voice. I want him to hear me. "Words, Father? You mean, like the truth?"

He looks past me, distracted by something hovering in the darkness, and then vanishes among the electric ghosts.

Recorded: 23 Oct 2101

The best day of my childhood happened when Paloma turned twelve. This was before the tunnel and the purple bear and the nightmarish skirmish in the Montoyas' kitchen. Runa had decided Paloma was old enough to babysit me, which freed up Liani to perform other tasks.

When required, Paloma would sleep in the bedroom next to mine in Stone House. Not that I didn't love Liani, but at age seven I was in full bloom love with her daughter.

One night I woke to a strange noise. I got up out of bed, grabbed my crutches, and hopped next door. Paloma looked like she was wrestling with someone in her sleep as she cried out, "*Dios, Dios, Dios*, help me, help me, help me!"

I shook her until she recognized me. She took a deep breath and started to laugh.

"Merlin, you scared away the body snatcher!"

She touched my face and felt the rounds of my eyes and the curve of my cheeks and lips, pulled on my ears, ran her fingers through my hair. Not that I didn't like her hands all over my face and head. It felt very nice, but a little disturbing too. It was like she was making sure the body snatcher wasn't using my body to trick her. She patted the mattress, and I sat next to her on the bed. We didn't say anything for a long while. For my sake, Paloma made an effort to look calm and happy, but I kept seeing her frightened face beneath that poor smile of hers.

"Paloma?"

"What is it, Merlin?"

"I saw Liani crying."

She stared at the floor for a while, then said, "Sometimes you can be happy and cry."

"I don't think so, Paloma."

"I know a girl who won a prize for writing a beautiful story about her mama. Her teacher gave her a certificate. It said, *First Prize for A Beautiful Story.* Underneath was a picture of a gold trophy, and under the trophy was the name of the story, which was also the mama's name. When the girl got home, she showed her mama the certificate with both their names. The mama started to cry, not because she was sad, but because she was happy and proud."

"That was you?"

She shrugged. "I was just giving you an example."

"I don't think Liani was happy."

Paloma turned away. In the dim nightlight I couldn't tell what she was thinking. She walked me back to my room. I got into bed. She leaned my crutches against the wall and then tucked me in and kissed my forehead.

After she left, I said my first prayer ever: "Please make the Montoyas adopt me." I said it four times, one for each Montoya.

* * *

"Merlin."

"Mother?"

Traces of laughter seep intermittently through the open dome entryway past Runa's clutched figure. The explosive sounds and lights roiling behind her like a small supernova seem reason enough for her to test the night air. How long has she been standing there?

"What are you doing?" she says.

"I didn't hear you, sorry."

Most of her entourage have splintered off. But I can see Cliff and Yelena within striking distance. I have this memory that begins with a homedroid in a tuxedo leading me to a hoveroo where Runa and her two inseparables were waiting.

"Merlin, I'd like you to meet Cliff and Yelena."

Yelena giggled. Cliff extended his glass. "Care for a sip, Big Guy?" Mother slapped his arm in mock rage and burst out laughing as moonsap splashed in the air and landed on Cliff's thigh. Yelena reached over and placed her hand on Mother's bare knee. "You are incorrigible, Runa," she said. The three of them laughed. I didn't know why. I had no idea what *incorrigible* meant.

Mother handed me strawberry-flavored water. "We're going to see the fireworks from the Empire State Building, Merlin. I promised you, didn't I?"

Did she?

A little give on her part might have salvaged whatever mother-child bonding she might have allotted. But Runa's maternal instinct, tenuous to begin with, was conveniently suspended. As the day wore on, I became invisible, a background prop to the threesome's moveable feast.

So now, to mark my thirtieth year, she wants to know what I'm doing standing alone on a veranda in the chill of night? Is it too late to be asking such a question?

I walk up to her and kiss her cheek. I take her icy hand and lead her back inside where it's warm and chaotic. She's telling me about her conversation with Ventidius. I hear every third or fourth word. I don't understand this woman. I don't understand her, not at all. But I nod and make a halfhearted effort to follow her train of thought, and then leave her with Yelena and Cliff.

I drift without focus, though not for long. The flashing beams of colored lights fade away for the moment, and I see them together now, the four of them.

What weird symmetry. I'm not totally surprised. They always seem to be where I can see them. And now the four of them are together, waiting for me, pretending they're not. I feel compelled to comply, so I'll go to them, work out whatever it is that has to be worked out.

That said, I'd rather be with Pearl. I look for her, but of course she's nowhere to be seen. I wonder if she's been sent away or found herself a place to hide. I have to talk to Father about her, but not today.

My mouth is dry. I need another drink. I keep an eye on the four as I sidle over to one of the bars. Some things can't be avoided. The game is calling me by name. It's my turn.

"Solar Sour, please." With drink in hand, I saunter toward the quartet and squeeze myself between the two ladies.

"Well, hello there, stranger!" Violet cries as she hooks my arm with hers.

"We thought you were blowing us off," Amber says.

"This calls for a toast," Tad says.

"To Merlin, man of the hour!"

We lift our glasses and drink as one.

"We were just talking about you," says Flick.

"I want to show you something," I say looking from Violet to Amber. We walk away, arm in arm, the ladies and me, leaving Flick and Tad to reminisce about their Thessaloniki theatrics.

Recorded: 24 Oct 2101

Amber and Violet are chatting up decompression and gravitational pulls as we wander through the Sublevel-2 maze. I admit I wasn't expecting to hear anything resembling techy-talk coming out of those glossy mouths. I don't participate in the discussion. I'm focused on keeping my Solar Sour from spilling. I'm also wondering why in stars I'm taking them to the secret apartment.

It's complicated. At this point it doesn't matter if they admit to being on Atwell's payroll or someone else's. It's beginning to occur to me that what I really want is to introduce them to Willie. I want to watch their faces as they listen to my voice coming out of Willie's mouth. I want to enjoy the moment when each of them realizes I'm talking about them, or to be more precise, about Serenity and Sunny.

Violet is saying she'd love to spacewalk one day when a remote bell begins to toll. A few minutes past midnight we arrive at the magic wall. The space between two tall metal cabinets is actually a camouflaged entryway to a Personal Survivor Place, or secret apartment. Father had it designed and built as a prototype for future PSPs. He showed it to me during my inaugural tour of Stone Heights. The moment I first walked through that wall I had a weird premonition I'd one day find my way back here.

Entry activation requires face and touch recognition. I press my five fingertips against the wall and take a step back. An effervescing lime-green archway that looks like something you might see in a virtual time travel arcade appears on the wall. It lasts for ten seconds before fizzing away and leaving an actual opening you can walk through.

I'm curious to see Amber and Violet's reaction, but they don't react at all. They wait for me to go through, then follow me into a living room and on through to an electric candlelit bedroom. No one speaks. With a faint *whoosh*, the opening turns back into a solid white wall. A cello concerto is playing somewhere faraway.

Amber squeals and flashes an ear-to-ear smile as she leaps before me with her arms extended, inviting me to dance.

"Who knew a Solar Sour could pack such a punch," I say, keeping her at bay with my extended glass.

"Didn't you know that about Solar Sours?" Amber says as she flops herself down on the big bed.

I don't know if it's the concerto or the fake candles or the female company, but the sudden, hard fact is that I'm surprised by how much I suddenly miss Pearl. I want to tell Amber and Violet about our near collisions by the Stone-TH dining hall and Pearl's remarkable balance and grace, and about all the times I've put off asking her to dinner. But each time I'm ready to talk about her, I check myself, as if to speak of Pearl would expose her to a deadly toxin.

Violet is pretending to be scandalized by Amber's mattress maneuverings. She looks me in the eye and says, "Can you believe this little tramp?"

"You are such a hypocrite," Amber says.

Violet turns to me, "You wanted to show us something."

Did I say that? Yes I did. I take it back. I'm keeping Willie out of this. No way I'm telling them about Willie, or Pearl.

"The magic wall," I say. "Wasn't that amazing?"

Violet walks up to me and kisses me lightly on the lips.

"Okay, now," I say awkwardly as the Solar Sour nearly slips from my fingers.

This is Cindy Trapp, after all, the girl who sat next to me in *Deconstructing the Twentieth Century* class back in college, the scholarship kid whose daddy bolted. I straighten up and polish off the rest of my drink. She takes my empty glass and puts it on a nightstand. Then she takes my hand and examines the Three Hares tattoo. She frowns, smiles, strokes and kisses it. Some odd sense of guilt tells me to let her do what she wants with my hand. Then she deep kisses me on the mouth.

"Slut," Amber says.

"You're very good at this, both of you," I say, recovering my senses. I pull away. "Topnotch pros. I'm impressed."

Violet tilts her head, pretending she doesn't understand. Then she reaches for my tattooed hand. I pull it behind my back. She goes into sad face mode and sits down on the edge of the bed.

"How much are they paying you?"

They exchange glances.

"Wait, did you mean pros, as in prostitutes?" Amber says, looking wounded. She slides over the mattress toward Violet.

"Look, I don't care, but can we at least stop pretending?"

"Pretending, Merlin? That we like being with you?"

"I never said you were prostitutes. That was your word. People prostitute themselves in any number of ways and for any number of reasons. Only a tiny number of them would be considered prostitutes, per se."

I sound like an idiot. I blame alcohol, Atwell, myself and whoever thought this existence business was a good idea.

"Merlin, sweetie, what is going on with you?" Violet says.

"I don't blame you, Serenity. I don't blame you, Sunny."

They look at each other and start laughing.

"Ho!" Amber cries.

"Serenity, Sunny, Sunny, Serenity," Violet chants and pauses to reflect. "I like it."

"Don't do that," I plead. "Can't we just deal with reality?"

"But this *is* reality, Merlin," Amber says, reaching for me.

"Stop!" I shout and snatch my hand away.

"Jeez!"

"*This* is not reality," I say. "The end is coming. *That* is reality."

"What's he talking about?" Amber says, turning to Violet. "The end of what?"

"I think he means the space hurricane," Violet says, "Apollo something."

"Apollyon?" Amber says.

"Yes, that's it, Apollyon," Violet says. "Oh, thank the stars. Thank you, thank you, thank you, stars! For a minute you had us going there, Merlin. Believe me, we're well aware of the situation. No reason to go losing your head over it."

"No reason at all, honey," Amber says.

"Twelve billion people are going to die!" I cry.

They stand up together. Amber's hand tries sneaking up on me. I flinch, but then relent. I let her skin settle over mine. It feels soft and warm, and a little on the damp side. It feels good to be touched by another human being, even a professional phony.

"Let's please not ruin your birthday, okay?" she says. She sounds so earnest I'm left speechless. "Merlin, sweetie, let's get into bed together, the three of us."

So, this is how I die? Father warned me to keep my mouth shut. And yet, I feel strangely at peace. Times are rough everywhere. Is sitting in bed between two beautiful assassins so bad? I could have had my throat slit in the Greek hills. I could be sitting in this bed between Flick and Tad.

My deadly guests become suddenly pensive. I become pensive too. I've been in strange situations before. But this is in a class all its own. Before calling it a life, there are things I'd like to know. Like how did Cindy Trapp become Serenity, who became Violet, or vice versa? And what made Sunny Takamoto, Amber, or Amber, Sunny Takamoto?

I grow oddly reflective and sentimental. In an alternate universe, I imagine my two guests could be my sisters, or my friends, or my lovers.

But in *this* universe, they're more likely to be my killers. What delicious irony.

All things considered, this is certainly not the worst way to go, given what's to befall Terra and her children. Two homicidal beauties are kissing my face and hands, caressing my head, uttering sweet nothings, and showering me with motherly affection.

"Here, sweetie," Amber says. "Try one of these."

"I don't think I will."

Amber ignores my remark and patiently demonstrates the proper way to ingest an enormous horse pill. She holds it up between her thumb and forefinger like a 38-caliber bullet, opens her mouth, and deposits the pill lengthwise on her tongue groove, leaving her tongue fully exposed for several instructive seconds before drawing tongue and pill back into her mouth. She then magically produces a golden flask and takes a healthy swig. I watch her smooth throat guide the big horse pill down through her chest.

"My turn," Violet says dreamily.

"But what about Apollyon?"

"Apollyon will always be Apollyon," she explains philosophically. "Why think about Apollyon, which is a grievous waste of time? Close your eyes, Birthday Boy, and enjoy the gorgeous concerto."

"Peace, Merlin," Amber says.

"Shalom, Salaam, Paz, Peace," they say in tandem.

Amber pushes a fresh horse pill against my pressed lips. She pulls back, sighs, takes a deep breath, tries again.

I feel her fingers pry open my lips and slip underneath them. Her fingers tickle my gums. I admit to feeling a little horsey. I have to fight to keep from grinning.

So be it. Let Apollyon be Apollyon.

My jaw relaxes, my teeth give way. The pill pops into my mouth like a tasty treat. Amber passes me the golden nectar. I chuckle like a buffoon before swallowing deep from the flask of oblivion.

Recorded: 27 Oct 2101

02 October 2101

I wake up in a fog and head for the window. Below, city streets are humming, sunrays are beaming off steel and glass everywhere and all around. I think I'm in Merlin's apartment. Wait, I am Merlin. I check my messages.

"Hi Merlin, it's Amber. Wanted to thank you for the most amazing evening. You are the best one!"

Amber?

"Hey, Birthday Boy, it's Violet. Thank you for personally celebrating your big Three-O with us in such a special way!"

"And for giving us fun names."

"I'm telling everyone to call me Serenity."

"Me too! I mean, I'm telling everyone to call me Sunny, ha-ha!"

"What about you, hon? Are you feeling like a new man?"

"For a while you had us going there, sweetie."

"Oh, to see you get so upset like that over such a small thing. It broke our hearts, honey."

"What kind of buddies would we be if we just allowed you to sink into despair on your thirtieth birthday?"

"Anyway, we have to go now. Hope to see you soon, honey. Love and kisses. Shalom, Salaam, Paz, Peace."

I pour myself a glass of water, sit at the kitchen counter. I remember music and lights and lots of people. I remember the big dome. There were flashing rays of colored light and lots of drinking and talk-talk.

Nothing's been lost. I mean my mind, my memory. I don't know how I know, but I know. It's all swirling around in my hyped-up brain. Things are going to slow down and fall into place. I'm certain of it.

How can I be certain? I can't say exactly. I remember a woman's hand in my mouth. I remember listening to a cello concerto. I swallowed a horse pill. We all did, the three of us. And then we all lay down on a big bed and fell asleep. When we woke up, we went back to the party.

Serenity and Sunny led me arm-in-arm to the center of the dome. Hundreds of guests formed a circle around us. Sweeping lights and deep space music made us all sway as if we were sailing on a float boat. Everybody was staring at me and singing one of the ancient hymns, *For he's a jolly good fellow.*

People looked up at the ceiling and saw the three of us in a hologram. Hundreds of guests cheered and clapped. A girl in a catsuit appeared holding a tray of drinks. Her appearance quieted the crowd.

They all watched me stare at the girl. It wasn't the same girl, the one I knew and liked so much, but I still couldn't stop staring at her. Amber took two drinks off the tray and handed me one. The girl turned and disappeared.

I scanned the crowd, and then in a loud voice I cried, *But what about Apollyon?*

Half a minute of eerie silence followed. Then everyone started chanting, *Peace, Merlin. Shalom, Salaam, Paz, Peace.*

How can I feel peace?

I need to talk to Atwell Stone, my employer, who's also my father. And Runa is my mother. And now I remember her name, the other girl in the catsuit. I need to talk to Atwell about Pearl.

Recorded: 30 Oct 2101

04 October 2101

Atwell comes out of a meeting with a group of Biotech engineers and immediately splinters off. When he sees me, he doesn't slow down at all. I could be an anonymous IT guy. I follow him to his office and close the door behind me. He sits down at his desk and studies his visipad. He doesn't say a word, doesn't even look at me.

Over the past two days, I've recovered large swaths of memory, both long and short-term, including the details of my New Life Plan. If I can't present Atwell my NLP specs after the end times craziness of my birthday party, when will I ever?

"At Stone Heights we had too much to drink," I say.

He ignores me. Not a glance, not a nod, not a word.

"I was with these two women," I say, raising my voice. "I said some things."

"What you do in private is your business."

"No, that's not what I mean. I've seen those women before. I'd just like to know what's going on. And what you said about the space hurricane and all those people dying."

He stands up and leans forward, spreading his hands over the wide desk.

"There are those who say drinking Dinkum Distillery Moonsap is a transcendent experience. I wouldn't go that far, but it does have a propensity to liven up the gray matter. And you never, ever mix DDM with a Solar Sour. But that's minor stuff. Presently, what you most need to concern yourself with is this: a whole lot of people are going to die before Bright Star Day. The offer still stands, by the way."

"The offer?" I feel sick all over again.

"Come with us to Mars."

"No, thank you, but no. I won't be going to Mars."

Father sits back down, fiddles with his visipad. A six-foot wide hologram appears between us. It depicts a series of low interconnected structures sprawled over a reddish wasteland.

"New Terra City," he says. "An emblematic achievement for humankind. A new vision for new visionaries."

"I need a favor."

"Fine, you can move to Stone Heights after we're gone."

"How did you know?"

"Cities and towns will be reduced to rubble. The stench of death will be everywhere. Survivors will be divided into predators and prey. If you don't get disemboweled by some mutant, we'll likely see each other again."

"You're planning to return one day?"

"Stone Heights is a special place, a timeway to the future. My work there isn't finished."

For a moment I imagine he's talking about time travel, but that would be ridiculous. No, this is about life extension products and post-apocalyptic architecture, right?

"I've got a meeting. Anything else on your mind?"

"Actually, yes. Stone Heights is a huge place. I'm going to need some help there."

I forward specs from my Q-Phone to his visipad. I watch his face as he studies them.

"If you agree, and if possible, I'd want them at least two weeks before Bright Star Day."

Go on, Atwell's eyes seem to indicate.

"We'll need a few days to acclimate ourselves to one another. I want us to be a functional family. I mean, team."

Father looks at me. I can't tell if he's amused or insulted. He takes another look at the specs.

"Is it workable?" I ask.

He eyes me. There's a smile hiding behind those lips.

"I know what you're thinking," I say.

"I said nothing about the Montoyas."

"You didn't have to."

"The specs call for taller specimens, lighter pigmentation. No language or cultural matches to speak of. Father, mother, boy, girl, but other than that, these are not the Montoyas."

"Actually, I did use them as a baseline, but that's all."

"Have you talked to Cheng about this?"

"I wouldn't do that without running it past you first."

Atwell forwards the specs to the Robotics Chief.

"Roscoe, need four Yada-7s, as per specs. Any questions, contact Merlin. Book task under Experimental with delivery to Stone Heights 01 December."

He turns back to me. "That gives you plenty of time to acclimate yourselves. The specs will be modified slightly, in accordance with security requirements."

"Site-specific security, yes, of course."

"I'll be curious to see how it all turns out," Atwell says, looking strangely satisfied.

Is he proud of me? What would it be like if he and Runa took the master suite at Stone Heights? We wouldn't even have to see each other all that much. Wait, what in stars am I thinking? The sentiment passes as quickly as it arrives. It would never work. I'm a new man, and I'm going to have a new family, and their names are Nap, Loretta, Vick, and Pam.

"Before you were born, Cleavon Blinkhorn presented me plans for an android prototype, our first at Stone-TH. You never met Cleavon, did you?"

"No, I don't think so."

"Brilliant guy. Likes keeping people off balance. Retired before you got back from Europe. Cleavon developed the Homie-1 prototype, male and female models. Primitive and clunky by today's standards, First Grade level cognitive and interactive capabilities, lacking the functional suppleness and versatility of the Yada-7. But the H-1 gave us a baseline for developing more accomplished and lifelike models, like the Elara-3, for example."

Why is he telling me this?

"Oh, yeah. I have heard Roscoe talk about Cleavon on occasion. Hey, if you don't mind, there was one other thing I wanted to talk to you about."

"Pearl."

"How did you know?"

"I'm sorry, Merlin, but that would be a No."

"No what?"

"She can't stay with you in Stone Heights."

"Huh? Why not? Is there a rule against me and a woman living in the same place?"

"Stone Heights is a secure, strictly controlled facility."

"I understand, but what does that have to do with Pearl?"

"We're taking Pearl to New Terra City with us."

"I think we're talking about two different people. I'm not talking about a Deo. I mean Pearl from Admin."

"I shortlisted Pearl a year ago. Quiet, sneakily attractive, good worker, personable, respectful, solid upside, a nice asset to bring along with us to Mars."

"A *nice asset*? I'm sure Pearl would love to hear herself described that way. Good stars, is this your way of getting me to go to Mars?"

"The girl has no family, Merlin."

"No family? Okay, and she has no idea what's coming, does she? Did you even consider asking her what she wants?"

Atwell stares at me like I'm the dumbest person ever.

"She likes me a lot," I say. "I'll protect her."

"Her future lies in New Terra City. Pearl wasn't designed to thrive in a broken world."

"Designed, huh?" I laugh. "What is she, one of Cleavon's projects?"

Father seems dimly amused as he whistles an old dreaded tune, the kind that expresses surprise at abject ignorance, just before it delivers a dire pronouncement.

"You don't understand her situation," he says.

"Did something happen to her? Is she ill?"

"She's fine. In fact, she's as fine as she'll ever be. Pearl is one of our top prototypes, a stellar representative of the Elara-3 line."

"That's a sick thing to say."

"We stopped producing the Elaras after Cleavon retired. Simulation-wise, the E-3 is a notch below the Y-7, though quite comparable, nearly equal to the Y-7 but for relatively minor deficiencies in thought processing flexibility. We built on our understanding of the Elara to make the Yada more socially adept. We also amped up Y-7 cognitive complexity and unpredictability levels. Ironically, these enhancements make the Y-7 more capricious than the E-3's, which is to say, more human. Overall, one could say it makes the Y-7 more interesting and appealing."

"Why are you lying?"

He's not lying, but how in stars am I supposed to deal with having my heart ripped out of my chest?

"I thought you and I were making progress," he says.

"Whether what you say is true or not, it should still be Pearl's decision."

"Androids don't decide things, you know that, Merlin. Pearl has as much choice in where she's going to end up as your Mollys do."

"Is this some kind of experiment? Is that what the kidnapping was? An experiment? An entertainment? Have you been collecting psycho-data on me? Am I an asset, Father?"

I stare at him. I give him plenty of time to tell me I'm being melodramatic. He doesn't.

"If Pearl was just like any other ordinary android, you wouldn't care. You'd have no issue letting her stay with me in Stone Heights."

"I tell you what, Merlin. I'm going to have Roscoe build you a Yada-7 that looks and sounds just like Pearl. Mind you, it won't be the Pearl you've come to know. Naturally, the shared world experience, memory compiling and associative networking will be in the embryonic stage.

"But these Sentience-Simulation models offer a special brand of uniqueness and versatility. Call her Ruby, or call her Sapphire, or whatever you like. She'll drastically enhance your quality of life.

"The Y-7 is more durable and will hold up better in the new world than any E-3. She'll be less reserved than Pearl, more daring and demonstrative to compensate for the lack of a shared history between you, and perfectly suited for accelerating the progression of the intimacy quotient. Ruby will surpass Pearl in every single Play and Passion marker. She'll make you forget Pearl. You'll look back and wonder, why the angst? You may even thank me one day for Ruby. Or for Sapphire. You know what? Why not have both? I'd be happy to arrange it. Consider it an early thirty-first birthday present. Sleep on it, Merlin. We'll talk again soon."

I head over to Admin and talk to Tiffany Rosales, who forwards Cleavon Blinkhorn's address in Key West to my Q-Phone.

Recorded: 05 Nov 2101

08 October 2101

Babatunde flies me from Miami to Key West. He is friendly, though shy. I tell him I like his accent. He tells me it's Scots-Nigerian and that I can call him Bob, if I like. He drops me off at Baptist Lane, near Cleavon's cottage. The hovercab lifts several feet and floats in place.

"If you have time, Mr. Stone, you may enjoy a visit to Ernest Hemingway's old residence," he says pointing, "three blocks that way, on Whitehead Street."

"Good to know. Thanks, Bob!"

He waves awkwardly and takes off. I hesitate, then start running after the shrinking hovercab.

"Bob! There's something I should tell you!"

And what would that be? That the world is soon coming to an end and, probably, so is his life?

I walk back toward Cleavon's cottage, wondering if all this is just a waste of time. A jumbo-sized elderly man with coiled white hair and brown skin is planted on the front lawn like an ancient palm tree. He's wearing sandals, Bermuda shorts, and a t-shirt displaying an enormous pineapple.

"Excuse me, I'm looking for Cleavon Blinkhorn."

"What kind of name is that?" the big, strange man says, sounding put out.

"I was informed he lives in that house."

"You making this up?"

"You're Cleavon, aren't you?"

"What did you say to that boy?"

"Nothing."

"Nothing make you go running after him like a crazy man? What did you want from that boy?"

"With all due respect, sir, if you're not Cleavon Blinkhorn, this conversation is over."

"I know who you are. You're Atwell's kid. You hungry? Doesn't matter, I am. Let's take a walk."

We walk three blocks up to Whitehead Street. Blinkhorn stops to point out Hemingway's old Spanish Colonial. A group of Ord tourists have just finished their tour of the house and are lining up to board a Nostalgia Bus. A woman carries a framed vintage photo of the author at his typewriter. A boy is holding up a foot-long scale model of the *Pilar*, Hemingway's fishing boat. Two middle-aged couples are discussing love and death in *For Whom the Bell Tolls*.

The tourists forage the past, leave with slivers of human history that carry the scent of hope. I smell it in the warm breeze of palm and speckled sunlight. I can't help but wonder, will any of these vacationers be left alive to read and hope and talk about love and death after Bright Star Day?

Cleavon and I walk another two blocks and take a left on Duval Street. It's a pleasant walk to Sloppy Joe's. I try to stay in a good frame of mind. But it's hard. I keep thinking of

Bob. I imagine him in the sky when Apollyon strikes, Bob in his hovercab swatted away like a fly.

"I was going to tell him to come back," I say. "I was going to tell him to leave his hovercab job and come live with me in Stone Heights."

Blinkhorn eyes me with suspicion.

"His name is Bob," I say. "Babatunde, actually."

Blinkhorn nods knowingly and grins like a devil.

"What?" I say.

"Who you choose to shack up with is none of my business."

"That's funny, Cleavon. By the way, what's with the pineapple t-shirt?"

He frowns, tries to ward off hilarity for as long as he can before exploding in waves of laughter. We both enjoy a good gut laugh. I watch his big belly rock and roll. I point to the dancing pineapple but refrain from commenting.

Blinkhorn stops laughing and doesn't say another word until we get to Sloppy Joe's. He swings open the door and waves me through. "After you, Funny Man."

"Why did you ask me about the hovercab guy?" I say after we've been served.

"Amazing sandwich," Blinkhorn says with a full mouth. "Transcendent might be the better word." He wipes the spicy brown sauce from the corner of his mouth. "I was breaking the ice, man, that's all."

"Okay, so now you can tell me how you and Atwell met."

He stares at me and shrugs his big round shoulders.

"I was working at a Biotech startup back in 2054 when I got the call. By the time I got to the hospital, my Helena was dead. The baby was two months early. Doctor said baby was going to be okay, but what was I going to do with a preemie? I had a cousin who couldn't have kids, so she and her man took Jenny and raised her as their own. I made them swear they'd never tell her about me or Helena.

"I spent a lot of time staring long and hard at life through a dark lens, actually put off killing myself a couple of times. I admit to being oddly intrigued by my mind's ability to rouse itself now and again, lively as a hummingbird, and to set grief aside for a while. I'd been dabbling in android evolution well before Helena passed, and had come up with some compelling ideas. Be a shame to let it all go to waste, I told myself. A dereliction of duty. But there were also plenty of times it seemed to me ambition was the wrong reason to go on living. But I did go on living, one day at a time.

"The Biotech I was working at went bankrupt. One day I heard a blogcast by this twenty-three-year-old whiz kid out of MDIT who was talking about the progression of genetics, senolytics and cell reprogramming, nanotechnology, neural networks, robotics, and spacetime theory.

"The science establishment kept pushing back the goal-posts—twenty years before we get to X, thirty years before we get to Y—but your daddy was saying seven years to get to X, eleven years to get to Y, and giving reasons why. Nobody took him seriously, but I liked how his mind worked.

"One day I'm listening to your daddy quote this forgotten dude who theorized about what he called *mechanistic* life way back in the nineteenth century. Samuel Butler was talking about how we're creating our own successors, supplying them with *self-regulating, self-acting power which will be to them what intellect has been to the human race.* He was talking about machines becoming more, and humans becoming less. The servant becoming the master, so to speak. So, there's your old man quoting some guy no one remembers, keeping the thread of human genius and imagination from snapping. Atwell said we were on the trajectory Butler was talking about, but it wasn't inevitable. How it all turns out is up to us, he insisted. That's how your daddy was back then.

"I went to the Bronx warehouse he was working out of, told his secretary, a bot named Roy, that I wanted to see the boss. Roy said if I wanted to meet with Mr. Stone, I was welcome to make an appointment and come back another time. Or I could sit on a plastic chair for seventy-five minutes. I flipped through decades' old copies of *Wired* and *Popular Science* and cursed under my breath at the one-hour mark for not getting my ass up off that chair and leaving.

"Atwell showed up seventy-four minutes after Roy pinged him, told me he didn't have time to waste, and I said I didn't either. I got right to the point. I told him I'd been developing some ideas for a sentience-capable android and gave him just enough of a taste of what I was talking about so he'd know I was legit. He wanted to know more. I said no and got up to leave.

"He said, 'Mister Blinkhorn, geniuses like us have to work together for the common good. How much are you willing to take to work for me?' I gave him a number. He tried to lowball me. I came down ten percent, but no more. I started walking away. 'Cleavon, welcome to Stone TransHumanix,' he said. Your daddy shook my hand, and told me to be there at six sharp the next morning.

"When I met the rest of the team the next day, there were only four other employees. Later I learned your daddy had fired three of his people right after he met with me so he could afford me. That told me a lot about the kind of man Atwell Stone is. I didn't lose a wink of sleep over the three individuals who lost their jobs because of me. We were all about the Big Picture, your daddy and me."

He pauses to gaze at me, to see if I'm judging him.

"Your daddy kept pushing me to get on the VivaLong program. I said no. One day I told him I was retiring to Florida. He said fine, and then wouldn't talk to me for a long time. We're good now. He never asked me why I left. He didn't have to. He knew I didn't like the direction we were heading in and who we were dealing with."

"Like who, exactly?"

Cleavon grins and shakes his head.

"If your daddy wanted you to know, he'd have told you."

"I understand. Hey, will you be heading over to New Terra City?"

"There's nothing up there for me. I like my gravity just the way it is down here."

"You're staying in Key West?"

"Yes, sir. And you're not leaving here without having a *mano-a-mano* staring contest with the six-toed cats."

"It's likely you'll die here."

"More than likely, but I won't die alone. There's someone I want you to meet after we pay our respects to the cats."

"Why don't you come to Stone Heights? Bring your companion. You know how big that place is, probably the closest thing to indestructible on the planet. We wouldn't have to see each other much if you didn't want. It's going to be just me and four Yada-7s."

"Not six?"

"Atwell told you about our conversation?"

"Uh-huh."

"And about Pearl?"

He nods.

"You wanted her to be unique," I say.

He stares at me with sad eyes.

"Why did you want Pearl to be special?"

"She was designed and manufactured off a rigorous set of specs, same as every other Elara-3. Do yourself a favor, tell your daddy you'll take the extra two Yada-7s. The Molly situation is going to get old sooner than you'd want to believe. A thirty-year old man like you is going to want to have someone around to help take the edge off. Ruby and Sapphire are guaranteed to keep you happily occupied. I've got one at home. Margarite is my sweetheart."

"You modelled Pearl after a real person, didn't you? Someone you know, someone dear to you."

Cleavon smiles and shakes his head.

"Let's not order that third beer. Margarite is going to want you to stay for dinner and spend the night. She's awfully loving, you know, great maternal instincts. She'll treat you like a son. We've got a large spare bedroom upstairs. You can spend the night. We'll have a nice, big breakfast in the morning. Then you and I get on a boat and go fishing in the bay reef for a few hours."

Cleavon and I walk back to Hemingway's old place and move quietly through its light and shadows, and have staring contests with the polydactyl cats. I carve for myself a sliver of human history and store it away in my brain.

Dinner with Cleavon and Margarite is an exercise in audacious gluttony, with a *Last Meal Ever* feel to it. Margarite is just as Cleavon described her, sweet and lovely as can be. But I can't stay the night. She squeezes me a lot harder than I anticipated, plants a big juicy kiss on my cheek and, sweetly sad-faced, waves goodbye from the front door.

Cleavon walks me to the corner. His voice rises above the hum of the idling hovercab: "Don't ever again forget Willie."

I smile uncertainly. I wonder what he's getting at. I keep waiting for his downturned mouth to spring into big round laughter. I want our time together to end on an ascending note.

"You keep Willie close, you hear?"

He stares at me, waiting.

"I won't forget Willie, Cleavon. Don't worry. I'll always keep him close."

He nods and walks back to the cottage.

On the flight back, I spend time thinking about Cleavon and Margarite, and about people and machines and how quickly a human life and an entire planet can change.

But mostly I think about Pearl, the flesh and blood Pearl who surely must exist somewhere in the world.

Recorded: 13 Nov 2101

03 March 2104

Loretta doesn't like it one bit when Nap and I go out on surveillance flights. We went on our first flight a few days after Apollyon. We started flying out once a week, then twice a week. Three years later, we fly every other day, sometimes two days in a row. We tell her the flights are necessary. In a post-apocalyptic world, security is paramount. She's skeptical, still occasionally complains. "So what the heck are the drones for?" We tell her the drones are a nice bonus, good to have, like an insurance policy, but they can't do what we do.

They can, actually, and better. Our two dozen drones cover a perimeter one-hundred miles out in every direction, the monitored area divided into six zones with drone pairs auto-launched every four hours on a rotating basis. The drones perform the same surveillance tasks as Nap and me, though a lot more efficiently.

The truth is, Nap and I like getting out. Being cooped up in this state-of-the-art, impenetrable, dead-world fortress for too long dulls the mind and spirit. Nap and I have different dispositions, but we both share a fondness for floating high

138

up where silence is so pure you don't care that you can't remember much of what happened before Death Day, which is what Nap used to call it until Loretta told him to stop. So Nap came up with Apo Day, which Loretta insists on pronouncing as Apple Day. No one has tried to correct her.

Loretta is Nap's wife. She's eleven years younger than Nap and pretends to be my mom, though she's just three years older than me. I call her Mom because she likes it. Despite my occasional misgivings, I do appreciate Loretta's maternal overtures, gestures, hugs, and kisses.

To anyone outside these walls, this arrangement may seem inappropriate, or even borderline perverse. But to me and the Mollys? Well, it's very simple. We're all about being a tightknit family, and we don't get all hung up on what might seem to others random irregularities, not that anyone knows we're here, or that we even exist.

I'm lucky to have the Mollys and grateful for their whole-hearted acceptance and support. I feel a unique tenderness toward Nap, Loretta and their children, Vick and Pam. I can't imagine feeling more tenderness toward, say, actual genetic progenitors and blood siblings, though to be fair, I have no basis of comparison given the gaping hole in my memory.

Over the past couple of months, I've become increasingly concerned about Loretta. She hasn't been herself. I trace it back to New Dawn Day, but I may have missed subtle signs of unhappiness prior to that. New Dawn Day has always been her favorite day of the year, an annual reminder of our happy family life lived in peace, harmony, and uber comfort. New Dawn Day also comes with the promise that more of the same is to come for years on end.

Loretta's not the kind of person who makes a habit of harboring negative thoughts, so when I see her downcast, I sidle up next to her. And because I'm the good quasi-son, I give her a hug, a kiss on the cheek, and a casual *I love you*. That's usually enough to snap her out of her funk.

But the tedium of confined living can degrade even the peppiest temperament. I haven't noticed comparable signs of discontent in Nap or Pam, and we're all accustomed to Vick's mood swings, which we attribute to ordinary teenage male misery.

That said, I have a confession to make. Whatever is ailing Loretta has begun to creep into my own daily disposition. The novelty of family life with the Mollys has lost a bit of its luster. I don't blame them, not at all. It wouldn't be fair. But I do find myself wondering too often, is this all there is?

Having the first thirty years of my life erased from memory doesn't help. I too often crave deep sleep, moonsap binging and hoveroo getaways. I manage the best I can. I do my utmost to put on a brave face for the benefit of the family.

Recorded: 03 Apr 2104

06 March 2104

Loretta takes a turn for the worse during dinner when Pam, who turned fourteen on New Dawn Day, says, "Something's been on my mind lately."

It's worth noting we were all being lulled nearly to sleep from consuming too much Just-Like Chuck Roast Stew and lunar grog before Pam opened her mouth. Pam sounds all grown up suddenly, and her confident tone gets everybody's attention.

"I'm sure there are people out there who could use our help," she says, pointing at the far wall to indicate where *out there* is.

Sweet, thoughtful Pam and her uncanny timing. *Uncanny,* because of what happened this morning during hoveroo surveillance duty.

Over the past several outings, Nap and I have started seeing tiny signs of new life that suggest the planet is stirring from its coma. Small but unmistakable details, like specks of color here and there, intimations of sunlight and so on. Pam's remark has me and Nap exchanging cautionary glances. I'm tempted to pry the topic wide open but restrain myself for fear of upsetting Loretta.

This is such a rare opportunity, though, and it would be a shame to let it pass. I peer at Nap, hoping for a nod of assent. Instead, his incredulous blue eyes knock me back. He can't believe I would even consider it. If eyes were mouths, Nap's would be shouting, *Are you out of your furping mind?*

Hate to admit it, but he's right. Given Loretta's extremely delicate condition, we should keep our mouths shut and hope Pam doesn't press us for feedback.

What Nap and I saw from high in the drifts this morning looked like a bug crawling over gray dirt. The hoveroo descended in Stealth mode, and we hovered undetected within the colorless effluvium. A closer look revealed a human with a backpack, the first person we'd spotted outside Stone Heights since Terra nearly died three years ago.

We glanced at each other but said nothing. The hologram appeared above the hoveroo console like a hand-sized ghost. A ragged, middle-aged male was heading northwest at a normal pace, about ten miles outside the hundred-mile radius alert zone Nap and I had established.

We made no contact with the subject. Nap marked the time, location, and the subject's trajectory. Preliminary data in hand, we flew back to Stone Heights. Nap named the refugee *Coronado* because of his long walk across the desert, though he didn't say anything about him—and I didn't ask— until we were well on our way home.

No-Contact Protocol was established early on. That was Nap's idea. I'd been okay with it until today. On the flight home, I considered suggesting we amend the protocol and reconfigure how we're going to engage survivors in this new emerging world. I couldn't bring myself to say anything. I tell myself Nap and I are going to have an earnest discussion on the matter, sooner rather than later.

Meanwhile, Loretta is responding to Pam's suggestion with a mix of disbelief and disgust. "People *out there* who could really use our help?"

Technically, she's responding to what Pam said, but she's looking directly at me.

"So, all this talk about *security is paramount* is nothing but poppycock?" she adds raising her voice while still locking me down with that look of incredulity.

Poppycock is as close as Loretta's ever going to get to cursing, and now this thing started by young Pam is careening toward emotional chaos. Loretta's eyes are still punishing mine even though Nap is the one who said, *In a post-apocalyptic world, security is paramount.*

"Have we lost our minds?" she wails suddenly, her face contorting. "You would jeopardize the safety of our family?"

She snaps her head and stares at Nap for a few seconds, then glances at poor Vick. She never even looks at Pam, who got this whole thing rolling.

"Because you're bored?" she says with special emphasis after zooming back to me.

Pam treats her mom's emotional response and outburst as if they are useful building blocks for her transition to womanhood. She isn't at all perturbed by Loretta's loss of composure. She excuses herself, gets up and walks away.

I wish I could do that, but I know better than to try. Vick is waiting for an opportunity to bolt, and Nap looks tight as a block of ice. I make small talk, grin a little, casually point out how the sky won't be gray much longer, but all that does is make Loretta tense up even more, and Nap want to bite my head off.

But there's more to Nap's gaze than ordinary quasi-dad reproach. His icy silence is also telling me he has no intention of bringing Coronado inside our walls under any circumstances, and no interest in hearing about any pie-in-the-sky rescue mission plans Pam or I might be contemplating.

Recorded: 04 Apr 2104

07 March 2104

I love Nap but he gets on my nerves sometimes. I can't imagine the turmoil he stirs up in poor Vick's teenaged brain.

Don't get me wrong, Nap's smarter than me and far more competent when it comes to dealing with the unprecedented technical and physical challenges of a post-apocalyptic world. I'm awed by his discipline, skill set, loyalty, and resourcefulness, but he's one stubborn, narrowminded individual. I hate to say it, but the man lacks depth.

Take this collective amnesia situation, for example. It doesn't bother him one bit that he, Loretta, and the kids have no memory of anything that happened before their flight to Stone Heights on 01 December 2101.

We live pampered, carefree lives in a resort-like fortress, are healthy as can be and lack for nothing. The moment the Mollys got to Stone Heights, Nap became convinced that no one in his right mind would change a single thing when everything was perfect just the way it was.

Of course, *perfect* means different things to different people, but you can't tell Nap that.

"Don't you think forgetting who you once were is like dying a little?" I once asked him. After giving me a ten-second blank stare, he guffawed and spit out two words, "You're hilarious," which is just one illustration of what I mean when I say my quasi-dad lacks depth.

Nap calls our collective amnesia, Brain Eat, says it's a condition resulting from the Apollyon Effect, which has spread across the planet afflicting all life forms, but mainly humans, and some more adversely than others. Like me, for instance. I know it gives Nap pleasure to know he remembers more than I do.

When I asked him how he knew about Brain Eat and the Apollyon Effect, he said, "Obviously, that knowledge was in my brain before the shit hit the fan."

I said that seemed unlikely. He waved off my skepticism, got very serious, and told me I really needed to trust him.

Nap enjoys recalling the day we met, an encounter that remains remarkably vivid in his mind, and which he loves repeating.

The Mollys arrived by hoveroo. They watched me walk out onto the landing deck to greet them. Loretta ran to me and threw herself into my arms, nearly knocking me over. She couldn't stop hugging and kissing me like I was the prodigal son who was once lost and has now been found. Vick and Pam kept looking at Nap like there was something wrong with their mom. Why would he allow Mom to so fervently kiss and hug this man they didn't know? Stars above, how he'd laughed his head off. Every time Nap repeats the story, he laughs his head off. All four of the Mollys have a vivid memory of that encounter. I do not.

* * *

Nap and I don't usually go out two mornings in a row, but the unexpected appearance of Coronado yesterday morning leaves us no choice. Loretta stages a protest by shutting down Roz, the kitchenbot, and assuming all of Roz's normal duties, including needlessly scouring a blackened frying pan with her own small hands in what is clearly an act of self-mortification. Her intent is to shame us. Me, in particular.

We fly northeast below thinning drifts to get a cleaner look at the countryside. The land is ashen, but less so, with specks of ochre, sienna, umber, and green showing here and there. In spots, the splotchy gray sky is tinted faintly yellow.

"I don't remember what the sun feels like," I say wistfully.

Nap stares straight ahead, his pained expression denoting forbearance rather than annoyance.

"I've been running air quality tests the last few days," he says after a long silence. "The yellow you're seeing in the sky isn't obscured sunlight. Furp me, Merlin, don't I wish it were. I hate to say it, but it's nothing more than a tease, an illusion caused by a new toxin that's making its way across the continent. I didn't have the heart to tell you, Bubba, but since you've brought it up. Well, it just didn't seem right to keep you in the dark any longer."

The hazy sky whizzes past and Nap is as gloomy as I've ever seen him. After all the death and destruction, after Brain Eat, after three years of isolation and the recent family travails, just when we're glimpsing a beam of hope, we have to contend with a spanking brand-new toxin? I would slam my head against the hoveroo console if it would do any good.

"Just kidding," Nap says and gives me a playful shove.

"Lookie there, quick, a ray of sunshine!" he shouts.

The beam of sunlight appears and vanishes. I saw it, I did. I glance over at Nap. His teeth do all the smiling. It's not the mouth, lips, eyes or cheeks, or body language. It's his teeth that draw the eye, oversized teeth, white as fresh snow.

The hoveroo tilts left as we draw nearer to Coronado, arcing around in Stealth mode to ensure we're not seen. Based on Nap's upbeat mood, though, I'm feeling hopeful we can make some preliminary contact. I packed a couple of protein loaves and power drinks in the drop bag without telling him.

Nap slams the hoveroo to a sudden midair stop, shifting it back into Standard mode to preserve energy. We float in place where the haze is thinning. Down below, Coronado's backpack lies on the gray surface like a small black rock. We descend slowly and follow the foot trail. Not quite a mile northwest of the backpack we find Coronado lying faceup on a red blanket.

Nap summons a hologram and preview-floats Coronado. That's no blanket. Nap rotates the 3D image to get the best angle from which to explore the damage, then blows it up by three-hundred percent, the size of a toddler. Coronado has been split open throat to groin, his eyes fixed on a hint of sunlight. His exposed ribs have been picked clean. There's a terrible dark hole where his organs once were.

Quasi-dad examines the image for a full two minutes before gauging my reaction. I offer a clinical nod but avoid eye contact. Nap keeps staring at the side of my face. Reluctantly, I make an effort to scrutinize the eviscerated man in earnest so that I can offer a credible opinion. I try to keep my eyes from dancing with the console lights flickering behind the carnage and tell myself that's not a human body down there, it's a livestock carcass. Nothing works. I gag once, regain control, gag twice and fight like all stars to keep Loretta's breakfast from projecting onto the console.

Nap clicks off the hologram and gazes at me with fatherly forbearance. He pats me on the shoulder. Without words, we agree to keep Coronado and his grisly fate from Loretta and the kids.

Recorded: 07 Apr 2104

15 March 2104

The following week Nap points at four figures moving over the gray plain to his left. He summons a hand-sized hologram and triples it in size. For a disorienting moment, the refugees are the Mollys twenty years from now, only with suntans and bad clothes.

"What are you doing?"

"What do you think I'm doing?" Nap says, astonished.

"I don't know."

"What is wrong with you?"

"Huh?"

"Dang, Merlin, how about paying attention."

Loretta, Pam, and Vick are back at Stone Heights, Nap is sitting to my left, so—

"Merlin!"

"I'm tracking," I say. "Two men and two women heading northwest."

They're not the Mollys, not now, nor ever, but I have this eerie feeling those four people have been wandering inside my head for a long time, trying to get out.

"Descend seventy feet, ten feet per second," Nap says. "Let's take a naked eye look at those creatures." The hoveroo drops into Stealth mode through the thinning effluvium. We're behind the refugees, in the drifts, soundless as a tomb. "Descend twenty-five feet, five feet per second."

My eyes sting at the sight of an old man and two women being led across the wasteland by a rangy male in his thirties who looks the way I imagine Vick might look twenty years from now.

"Uncanny, don't you think?" I quip.

Nap gets super focused and stares at the four a long time before speaking.

"I know what you're doing, Bubba, and it ain't funny."

Nap and I are sitting side by side in the surveillance office. We're going over plans for the day when he says, "I've been thinking about Loretta. Considering what you and I have witnessed in recent days, and before things go spiraling out of control, I've decided we need to be proactive."

"What are you suggesting?"

"The old gal needs to get properly inoculated."

"I'm not tracking."

"Social inoculation to reduce fear of outsiders. I'm talking after-dinner Saturday night extravaganza, a high-definition, AudiVisi simulation executed in the controlled, nonthreatening environment of the Family Time Room. The girls can observe those four sad sack refugees from a discreet distance or mingle, as they see fit, free and easy, and unencumbered by social or civic obligation."

"I don't get it."

"The key to maximizing simulation pleasure is scale, make those folks one-hundred percent life size. We want to create an environment that offers safe and playful pretend interaction."

"I was hoping we could go a little further than simulation pleasure."

"Never underestimate the emotive power of true-to-life-size simulation, Merlin. Independent studies have shown that one-hundred-percent scale makes hologram figures more relatable. Life-size simulation has also been proven to increase blood flow to the brain, spark the imagination, and increase the appetite. We need a morale boost in the worst way. And you and I both know that a happy Loretta equals a happy family."

"I want to boost family morale and ease Loretta's concerns too, and I don't have any issue with life size simulation in and of itself, but—"

"But, but, but. But what, Merlin?"

"I was hoping we could engage in something more meaningful than simulation pleasure, that's all. I don't mean that we should go rushing into anything. Maybe we can start by having a family discussion about what Pam said."

"What Pam said? What did Pam say?"

"You know, at dinner last week. She said—"

"Forget what Pam said. She's just a kid. Answer me this. You think Loretta mingling with those holographic humans wouldn't be meaningful? Broaden your mind, son, come on."

"It's a matter of degree, Nap. Look, I am trying to keep an open mind."

"If you want, we can pipe in wind noise to maximize authenticity."

"I don't care about maximizing authenticity. It just feels like what we do or don't do is always determined by fear."

"Fear, my ass. There's a huge difference between being scared and being prudent."

"This place is big enough and has enough resources to house and feed a couple of hundred people for at least fifty years."

"Whoa! Whoa! Whoa! Hold your horses, cowboy! Are you out of your furping mind?"

Whenever Nap does a sudden head twist to show me how outraged he is, I always get the weird feeling that his head is going to snap right off his neck and fall on the floor. As much as he drives me nuts, I don't want him to hurt himself.

"Take it easy, Nap."

"Nobody ever told me we were in the furping hotel business."

Both of us remain silent for several minutes. Nap is pretending to check atmospheric data on a screen.

"Nap, you ever wonder how or why we ended up here?"

"None of it matters. Only now matters."

"Those refugees are people too. They're like us."

"Uh-uh, no sir."

Nap shoots me a look of suspicion, grins, and starts slapping my thigh rhythmically, as if it were a bongo.

"Would you stop doing that?"

He laughs it off, then turns serious again. "For the life of me, I can't figure why anyone of sound mind would object to using AudiVisi technology to boost morale and build family cohesion."

Why do I bother? Nap is Nap, He's always going to be Nap, a man with a mind like a rusted steel trap.

"We could have saved Coronado's life," I say.

"I know."

What? I barely recognize Nap's voice. I look at him as if he were a stranger.

"Are you saying you agree that maybe we should do whatever we can so that what happened to Coronado doesn't happen to someone else?"

"Slow down, I'm not agreeing to anything. I'm preaching patience, prudence, and responsible timing."

I'm not feeling patient, nor prudent, but I check myself because this feels like progress, however slight. Nap is trying to meet me, if not halfway, maybe a tenth of the way.

"I have the feeling Pam's going to point out a certain resemblance between the four of you and the refugees. Loretta won't like that. She'll think Pam is trying to guilt her into helping them, but she won't blame Pam, she'll blame us. Then what you and I are trying to accomplish—that is, if I'm understanding you, Nap—is going to get crushed before it even gets started."

"No worries, Bubba. I talked to Pam after last week's hubbub. She'll keep her mouth shut. Let me handle Loretta, okay? I'll prep her up, make sure she's in the right frame of mind."

Why do I feel like we're talking in different languages about different things? Nap eyes me for a few seconds, nods and walks out of the surveillance office.

After we get back from our surveillance flight, Loretta spots me in the kitchen chewing on a protein loaf. The *old gal* sidles up next to me without uttering a word and puts her arms around my waist. I lay my chin on her curly red head. We're locked in a tender, wordless state for an uncomfortably long time, me munching on the protein loaf, Loretta adjusting her hug pressure every few seconds.

When she's finished hugging me, she reaches up and musses my hair. The last bit of protein loaf goes down my throat like a billiard ball as I watch my quasi-mom waltz off happy as a bride on the way to her honeymoon.

I don't know what Nap said to her. I wouldn't get a straight answer from him anyway. I love the Mollys, but I'm having trouble seeing how this arrangement can end well.

Recorded: 11 Apr 2104

"That lady looks like me."

"Oh, Pammy, you silly child," Loretta says. "She looks nothing like you."

"I mean like me in the future."

"What nonsense," Loretta says. "Her skin is much darker than yours."

"And the old lady looks like you, Mom," Pam says.

"Oh, for the love of stars," Loretta says, and shoots me a curious glance.

"I mean, you in the future," Pam clarifies.

The refugees don't look all that much like the Mollys, I realize, but Pam is intent on playing that game.

Loretta glances at Nap. "Dear husband, are you going to let your daughter get away with that?"

Nap is all business during family festivities.

"I need you both to go stand next to those refugee gals," he says. "Go on, get over there. How am I supposed to make a meaningful determination when you're standing thirty feet apart?"

Nap winks at me as the two Molly gals prance toward the hologram and place themselves next to their counterparts. Pam starts marching in place, keeping pace with the refugees, and Loretta soon follows suit.

"Well, Dad, what do you say?" Pam says.

"For the love of stars, dear husband, will you please make a determination?" Loretta says.

Nap likes to milk situations like this. He knows his wife is pretending to lose her patience with him. Everyone knows Loretta's having a ball. It's moments like these, precious and disturbing at once, that remind me why I love the Mollys and why they make me lose sleep. Nap is happy in an understated way because Loretta is happy, which seems to please Pam (not sure about Vick), and which has always made me happy too, regardless of the lurking challenges and the potential for chaos to erupt at any moment.

"Mom, that charm bracelet looks like one of yours," Pam says. "See the silver panda bear?"

"How odd, Pammy. It sure does look like one of mine."

Loretta's eyebrows arch with excitement as she turns her attention back to her big old shifty uncooperative husband.

"Napoleon Molly!" she shouts. "For starsake, can we please have a determination?"

156

Nap clears his throat. "Everyone, listen up. I see before me four distinct generations of women. Furthermore, I am estimating a twenty to thirty-year gap between you gals and your respective counterparts. This I can say with a high level of confidence. However, I've been tasked with determining whether or not I see a corresponding resemblance between you and these female refugees. I'm afraid I am not able to offer a meaningful determination at this time, based on conflict of interest, me being a spouse to one of the parties, and all. Unfortunately, I'll have to defer to Merlin."

Oh, come on.

Loretta moves her pale face right up against the old woman's dark lined face.

"You'll have to come closer, Merly," Loretta says with a come-hither gesture. "All that nonsense about conflict of interest. Please, don't make me laugh. Nap doesn't want to do it because he's strange that way. Does it surprise you? It's okay, you're more than qualified, Merly. This is all about having family fun, anyway."

I stride forward. My stomach sings a high C note that trails off in a poignant fade. Vick, roused from his couch coma, gives me a distracted look as Pam giggles.

"Quiet as a Jupiter moon," Nap says.

"Who, me?" I say.

Nap motions with his head, indicating Vick, who's staring at the brown-skinned, thirty-something year old man.

"You know, I'm not qualified to do this either," I say. "I'm going to have to defer to Vick."

"Oh, so your stomach made a funny noise," Loretta says. "Who cares? You're going to use that as an excuse to not play? And do you think you're going to hurt my feelings if you suggest I look like a beaten down old woman?"

"She's really not that old, Mom," Pam says. "And is it just me, or did anyone else notice how the young man could be Vicky with a tan twenty years from now?"

"Please shut up, and stop calling me Vicky!"

Vick gets up off the couch and walks to within an arm's length of the hologram.

"I think Pam has a point," Loretta says.

"Who cares if we do or don't look like them?" Vick says as he stares at each of the holographic refugees. "Who cares about anything? We just stay in this place day after day and keep doing the same things over and over, so who cares?"

Nap gives Vick a quick and dirty look, but neither he nor Loretta say a word to him. I feel for the kid. Even Pam looks a little sad as she reaches out to hold the old man's elusive holographic hand.

"Well, I'll be darned if they don't look a little bit like us in some sorry-ass, generic, broken-down sort of way," Nap concedes.

I amble back toward the couch, sit down and lean my head back.

"Nap, please turn off the AudiVisi," Loretta says, looking concerned. "What's the matter, Merly? Tell Mommy."

"It's nothing."

"Migraine?"

"Yes," I lie.

"Let's see," she says. She makes some internal calculation and starts massaging my temples with both hands. She works her way around my ears, down my neck, and then back up to the crown of my head. Her strong, nimble, little fingers penetrate deep, releasing waves of heat that ripple down my neck and make my head tingle.

"Feel better?"

I roll my neck. "I do. Thank you, Mom."

"I wish you wouldn't worry so much, Merly. We're never going to be helpless and dirty and unhappy like those people. Stars forbid it."

She rests her hand on my forehead, checks for fever, and follows up with a reassuring smile and a big wet kiss on my cheek.

"There, feeling all better?" she says, stroking my head.

"Yes, Mom, all better. Thank you."

"Pam, let's get these boys some dessert," she says.

I watch the Molly girls mosey across the Family Time Room arm in arm. From the corner of one eye, I see Vick sprawled on the couch, both eyes shut. From the corner of my other eye, I see Nap pacing to-and-fro, staring at his feet.

And me? I'm stuck in a terrible paradox, ravaged by love and horror in equal measure.

Recorded: 15 Apr 2104

It's just me and Nap and Vick now. I close my eyes and think of cold, creamy, tasty slush slide-melting off a big spoon into my mouth and sliding down my fevered esophagus.

"Can I go?" Vick says, breaking the spell.

"Is that all you have to say?" Nap snaps.

"Uhm, can I *please* go?"

"After you finish your ice cream."

"I don't want ice cream."

"I said you can go after you finish your ice cream!" Nap roars.

I launch Nap a pro-Vick look. He shakes his head in disgust, but I can see he's reconsidering. "All right, get out of here. You have your brother to thank."

Vick stands up and starts striding away.

"I said you have your brother to thank!" Nap shouts.

Vick stops, turns around, tosses me an obligatory glance, then looks at the floor as he says, "Thank you, Merlin."

"Who passes up ice cream?" I say after Vick leaves.

"Weird kid," Nap agrees.

"I wish I could remember what that's like, being sixteen."

"You don't want to remember."

"I don't?"

"Teen years are a foretaste of hell. Vick and Pam give me and Loretta all the teen drama we can stomach. I tell you what, Merlin, the last thing a teenager needs is a Mr. Softy Ass for a daddy."

"I tell you what, Nap, you are no Mr. Softy Ass."

Nap stands up and slaps his butt cheeks, three times each. "Sound soft to you?"

"Nope."

"I said! Does it sound soft to you?"

"No, sir!"

We share a laugh. With ice cream on the way, and the Vick drama set aside for now, we're both feeling giddy. It's good to be back on relatively good terms with my quasi-dad. He pulls up a chair and sits in front of me.

"What's got you so spooked about those refugees that your stomach goes rogue and your head starts hurting? Is this about Dream People?"

"You mean people I dreamed of?"

"Next time we go out on surveillance, I'll introduce you to my Dream People Theory."

"I know it sounds crazy, Nap, but it feels like I've met them before."

"Dad, mom, two kids, two males, two females? Uncanny? Maybe. Crazy? Nah. Makes sense you would think that. I wouldn't worry about it. Something else on your mind, son?"

"No. Well, yes, actually. I know you're very protective of Loretta. Me too, and with good reason. But maybe we're underestimating her. She's a sweet, loving woman, and a cheerful extrovert by nature. Her adjustment to other people may go a lot more smoothly than we think."

"I'm going to ask you to stop right there, sir."

"Nap, come on. Living as if there's no one else in the world isn't going to help Loretta or anybody. The kids need to meet other kids. I'm really worried about Vick. I think it would be good for him, for all of us, even you, Nap, to interact with other real flesh and blood people."

Nap is shaking his head the whole time I'm talking. "Tell me something, Bubba, you aiming to steal the Biggest Pain in Nap Molly's Ass Award from Vick?"

"Earlier, for a moment, I thought we were getting closer to being on the same page. I guess I'm not all that clear on the specifics."

"The specifics are *maybe* we do something. And if we do anything, we do it *only* when the time is right."

"How many dead is it going to take for the time to be right, Nap?"

Nap has been doing this annoying thing with his nose lately, like there's a sudden stink in the air.

"We don't know squat about those refugees," he says. "For all we know, they jump at the first chance to cut our throats and take over Stone Heights. And even if they're not violently inclined, who's to say they're not infected with some communicable disease. When do we find *that* out? When we're gasping for air? And let's not forget Coronado. Do *you* know who or what gobbled up that man's innards? I don't believe you do, so there's that too. And one other thing. Who's to say these so-called refugees aren't shapeshifters? How do we know body snatchers didn't get sprinkled all over Terra on Apo Day? We wouldn't have a furping clue about that until it was too late."

"And what if, right now, I'm not talking to Nap Molly? What if I'm talking to a body snatcher pretending to be Nap Molly?"

"What the hell are you saying, boy?"

"I'm trying to make a point, Nap. You can always come up with arbitrary reasons to justify not doing the right thing."

"And I'm trying to make a point, Merlin, that what I'm doing is the right thing to do because you can't rule out any reasons you naïvely call arbitrary until you've ruled them out one-thousand percent, which would require the kind of irrational commitment of time and energy we simply can't afford."

I stare at Nap in disbelief. Loretta and Pam reappear arm in arm, with Roz, the kitchenbot, right behind them pushing a cart stocked with bowls piled high with ice cream. Loretta doesn't at all mention Vick's absence. She's more than happy to scoop half of Vick's portion onto my immense bowl, the other half onto Nap's.

I get right to it, spooning ice cream down my throat with a steady hand and feeling amply compensated as I distance myself from Vick's unhappiness, Nap's hard headedness, and Loretta's bipolar tendencies.

At one point my spoon-bearing hand pauses in midair. I stare at Loretta and Pam's bright, happy faces, their machine-like hands shoveling enormous quantities of ice cream into their shapely little mouths, their red tongues clicking and licking the cold creamy sweetness from their shiny lips.

I check to see how Nap's doing. For the moment, at least, he's content to be in his own special world, working the ice cream in his big old mouth as if it were meat.

Recorded: 17 Apr 2104

16 March 2104

Sleep is no option due to sugar overdose and agitated mind. I walk the long perimeter corridor toward Stone's Eden, an enclosed ten-acre sanctuary built by someone with amazing foresight and a surplus of Coin. I go there seeking peace.

The flower beds, shrubs and fruit trees are real and surprisingly lush. During the warmer daylight hours, the bee and butterfly bots are busy sounding and looking real and being soothingly efficient pollinators.

The gorgeous, reddish-gold chickens look real too, but they're not, though they do produce edible fake eggs. During the day they come out and wander about the garden, pecking and bobbing their tiny heads. Sometimes I stop to talk to them. They don't speak, but often pause to lend an ear. They make far better listeners than the short, sturdy edenbots who maintain Stone's Eden and are possessed of a work ethic and single-minded diligence that is second to none.

When twilight comes, the bees and butterflies hide away, the chickens go back to their state-of-the-art coop, and the edenbots return to their cool, clean shed.

At a distance of about a hundred yards from the main entrance I'm surprised to see Vick coming out of the garden. He's heading back to his rooms the long way, which means he probably saw me before I saw him. It's after midnight, way past his curfew. By Nap's draconian standards, he should be in bed sleeping. There's no way I'm telling Nap about this.

Night in Stone's Eden is always twilight. I'm greeted by the fragrance of rose, jasmine, and gardenia as I enter. Within moments I'm feeling a wonderful high. Who can blame Vick for coming here, for wanting to feel the way I'm feeling now? Why does Nap have to be such a hard ass?

Hey, what was that?

I saw it in the corner of my eye, a flash of movement. My body tenses as I turn and scan the area. Nothing but brain-teasing stillness and complete silence. Did I imagine it? No, I don't think so. What in stars was that kid up to? Should I call Nap? No, no, no. Not if I can avoid it.

I grab a gardener's shovel and make my way through the garden. I check behind every tree and shrub as I advance. The edenbots' shed entrance dilates on my approach. I peer inside at the twelve edenbots lined up in Sleep mode, formal as cadets, their green and red indicator lights flickering lazily, noting my preapproved presence. Inside the state-of-the-art coop, the two dozen chicken bots are settled in sleepy repose on the roost.

At the sound of scampering feet, I swing around and catch a glimpse of a dim form disappearing behind a cluster of rose bushes. I close in, concentrate on my breathing, try to slow down my racing heart. I pause to consider what I'm about to do, realize it may be the last thing I ever do.

I'm tempted to whack the rose bushes with the shovel, but I limit myself to gently nudging the thorny stems forward.

"Ouch!"

A soft and vulnerable young woman's voice, one I find faintly familiar. Not a fearless voice, but not fearful either. I would say she sounds embarrassed more than anything else.

I get sucked right in. The part of me that would suspect dark and sinister forces at work bows to the gentle voice. I place the shovel down on the ground.

"That's not a good place to hide," I say.

Thirty seconds of tense silence later, I reinterpret the situation and reach for the shovel.

"No, not a good place to hide at all," comes the reply.

Where have I heard this voice before?

"It's alright. You can come out. No one's going to hurt you, I promise."

A young woman with scratches on her face and hands comes out from behind the thorny bushes.

"Who are you?"

"It's me, Merlin. Pearl."

Recorded: 20 Apr 2104

Don't be a dumbass, Bubba.

"Are you going to hit me with that shovel?" she says, both hands shielding her face.

The shovel looks barbaric extending from my half-raised hand. I lay it down on the ground.

"How do you know my name?"

She looks as confused as I feel.

"From work."

"What do you mean, work?"

"Stone TransHumanix, Central Offices. I don't mean to imply we did the same kind of work. You had a much more important job than I. We would often run into each other and wave. Sometimes we'd talk a little."

"Stone TransHumanix," I say.

"Do you remember now?"

"No."

"Oh, for a moment I thought—"

"I have no memory of Stone TransHumanix or you."

She frowns and lowers her head. The gesture has an unexpected effect on me, makes me feel oddly nostalgic, and worst of all, conflicted. If the Apollyon Effect erases human memory, as Nap contends, why didn't it erase hers? Because shapeshifters are good at manipulating the human heart and the human mind, according to Nap.

I take a step back to get a better look at her. She's wearing turquoise sneakers, gray sweatpants, and a yellow t-shirt with a square robot head floating above block-lettered words that say, ARE WE SQUARE NOW?

Her moist dark eyes are disarmingly familiar. My heart begins to race again, but for a different reason.

"How do I know you're not a shapeshifter?"

She seems to want to respond, but doesn't know how.

"Prove to me that you're not," I insist.

"How am I supposed to do that?"

"I don't know. Never mind. How did you get in here? Was it the boy?"

She shakes her head.

"Have you spoken to him?"

"I have, but he's not the reason I'm here."

"Well, are you going to tell me, or what?"

"I have so much to tell you, Merlin. You don't remember the secret apartment, do you?"

"The secret apartment," I say with skepticism written all over my face. "The one here, in Stone Heights."

"Two levels down," she says.

"Oh, that one."

She sighs.

"Look, Miss, Nap and I have reviewed all the construction diagrams. We've visited every inch of this compound. There are no secret apartments in Stone Heights, unless by *secret* you mean secret because you've been hiding in some nook without anyone knowing."

"Your father threw you a big thirtieth birthday party in the dome. There were over six-hundred guests, including President Brumbo and Rodolfus Barnesby."

I give her a good stare. She doesn't flinch. The words sound crazy coming out of her mouth, but settle in my brain as if they belong there.

"A birthday party, here, in the dome."

"Yes."

"You know my father?"

"Everybody knows your father, Atwell Stone. He built Stone TransHumanix."

"Stone, as in Stone Heights, Stone's Eden."

"Yes."

"So, I'm Merlin Stone."

"Yes."

"Interesting. What else do you have to tell me?"

"You don't remember the catsuits?"

"I don't."

"There were about thirty of us in catsuits carrying trays with drinks and hors d'oeuvres. Nothing, huh?"

"You haven't answered my question. How did you get in here?"

"I'm trying, Merlin. I saw you with two beautiful women. We said hello to each other. I was very uncomfortable with the situation, so I went to the lavatorio to take a break. When I came out, you were walking past with the two women, one on each arm. I don't know what got into me. I followed you down to Sublevel-2 through a maze of corridors to a large storage area. Somehow you made part of the back wall disappear. The three of you went through the opening. I caught a glimpse of a sofa, some chairs, and a coffee table before the opening closed and became a solid wall again.

"I tried heading back to the dome but kept losing my way. I managed to double back to the apartment. I hid in the storage area behind one of the cabinets. I told myself I would just follow you back to the dome when you were finished doing whatever you were doing in there."

She looks down at the floor, embarrassed. I have no idea what she's talking about.

"I fell asleep and woke when I heard your voices. The three of you passed by and didn't see me. Yes, I was going to follow you back upstairs, but I had to take a quick look inside. I don't know why. I just did. Then the opening closed, and I couldn't find a way to get out. I was convinced you would return after the party to spend the night there. I didn't care if

I got caught. What was the worst thing that could happen? We would both have a good laugh?

"Hours passed. I fell asleep on the couch. When I woke up, I realized I had no means of communicating with anyone. A second day passed, and no one came. I started to think I might die imprisoned in that apartment.

"Luckily, I discovered the place was designed to keep a person alive for years. It had everything I needed. Power, temperature control, an auto-food generator, filtered air and water, a waste disposal system, and thousands of books, auditory tracts and holographic materials. There's even a small gym, and other interesting surprises." She stares wistfully at me. "You don't remember any of this, do you?"

I don't, and yet I find that I can no longer say I don't, because somehow it all feels true.

"I'm not making this up, Merlin."

"You've been inside these walls since 2101."

"Yes, since your thirtieth birthday party."

"And, obviously, you discovered the way to exit the apartment."

"I told you, everything I needed was inside."

"Including directions on how to get out."

"Yes, actually. Once I learned how to get out and get back in, I began to make tiny excursions. Every day I'd wander a little farther. It took me a few days to summon the courage to find my way to Sublevel-1, and another week before I made it to the main level.

"Eventually, I found the garden. It was there I first saw Nap. He was working on one of the edenbots. He didn't see me, but I began to limit my outings. One morning I saw you with him. You were heading toward the hoveroo deck. I wanted so much to call your name, but I was afraid."

"Why would you be afraid?"

She shakes her head. "Nap."

"Nap? He's harmless, all bark and no bite. What about the boy, Vick?"

"I got careless one day. I sometimes visit the garden late on Sundays. That seemed the safest time. Some months ago, Vick saw me coming out of there. He followed me down to the apartment right into the living room. 'Hello, Miss,' he said, and I jumped. He nearly gave me a heart attack. He wasn't menacing in any way. He was curious, that's all, and a little confused by my reaction."

"What else did he say?"

"He was looking at everything, his eyes big with wonder. You would think he had just stumbled on a treasure. When the doorway closed behind him, he seemed upset. I told him not to worry, that he could leave any time, and that it might be a good idea if he left soon. He said I was lucky no one checked the surveillance videos, that I'd be in a lot of trouble if they did. I was worried he might tell Nap about me. He said he wouldn't tell anyone and wondered if he could come by to see me once in a while. What was I supposed to say? Every Sunday evening he comes by, and we walk to the garden together. He warned me to be careful, to not let anyone see me, because something bad could happen to me."

"Nothing bad is going to happen to you. Vick is a lonely kid. He's got no friends, just Mom and Dad, a kid sister, and me. And now he has you. He doesn't want to share you with anyone. What else did he say?"

She lowers her head.

"You can tell me."

"He said Nap would consider me an intruder and a threat if he found out I was here and would hunt me down, torture me for information, and then kill me."

"Oh, he did, did he?" I don't know whether to laugh or kick the little punk's ass. "I'm sorry he frightened you. Maybe if I explain a couple of things, you won't be too worried. First of all, Vick and his dad don't get along. That doesn't make Nap heartless or cruel. I don't believe he's capable of hurting anyone, other than with his words. But he's too hard on the kid, and that distorts how Vick sees him and what he imagines his father is capable of doing."

"Even if Nap doesn't hurt me, he won't be happy about me living in Stone Heights for over three years."

"No, you're right, he won't like that, but not because he won't like you. He will and it won't take long, trust me. It's just that Nap wants to be in total control. He likes to think he knows everything. The existence of that secret apartment without his knowledge will irk him to the end of his days. I'm curious about it myself. Like I said, according to all the schematics, the place doesn't exist."

"And yet it does," she says with an insistent gaze.

I am starting to believe her. What kind of friends were we before, I wonder?

Pearl's expression softens as she studies me. I'm feeling a little exposed. I wish she would say something. She doesn't, so I do.

"Nap is a rare bird. He does take some getting used to. But Loretta is a sweetheart."

In fact, Pearl could be just what Loretta needs. I'm not worried about Nap. He'll be a solid, if at times maddening, quasi-dad to Pearl. And Pam's going to be the perfect little quasi-sister.

Vick won't be happy about losing exclusive rights to Pearl, or the prospect of me and Pearl forming a relationship, which is beginning to feel inevitable. It's going to take a little time and effort to win him over.

I need to keep him informed, treat him more like an adult. I'll tell him how we're going to build a community, and how he's going to have lots of opportunities to meet people his own age.

"Everything's going to be fine," I say.

Pearl doesn't say a word. Her eyes have stopped blinking.

"Nap and I have been talking. Slowly but surely, we've been narrowing the gap on how we should deal with other survivors. We're looking beyond these walls, beyond the here and now. We're going to build a community. I want you to be a part of that."

Did I say something wrong?

"Pearl?"

There, I said it. The ease with which her name spilled from my mouth surprises me. She blinks, and her eyes come alive and settle over mine.

"So, can I introduce you to the Mollys?"

She nods. "But before you do, there are other things you should know."

"What other things?"

"Come with me."

Recorded: 22 Apr 2104

According to Nap, I had been living at Stone Heights for three weeks when the Mollys arrived on 01 December 2101. He said he was certain about that, and Loretta confirmed what her husband said when I asked her about it.

They later admitted that other details leading up to their flight were somewhat sketchy. In fact, most of what went on before their move to Stone Heights remains a mystery. And yet, the void represented by all those missing years doesn't seem to bother either of them one bit. Nap says the memory loss is probably temporary, but doesn't care one way or the other.

Pam's description of the day the Mollys arrived at Stone Heights is a little more evocative than her father's. She mentions how cold and windy it was, and how I was struggling to zip my coat as I walked out onto the hoveroo deck to greet them. Pam said Loretta looked like an Eskimo all bundled up as she rushed toward me to give me that famous hug. The wind blew her furry hood back exposing all that curly red hair. Pam said my coat was flapping like a cape because I never did get it zipped up.

By all accounts, it was quite a memorable encounter, but hard as I try, I have no memory of it.

I do remember Apo Day, 22 December 2101, and how I woke up in the midst of a loud, sustained howl, and noticed a pile of chocolate chip cookies trembling on a plate, and milk moving around inside a glass, and the coffee table they were on shaking. I was lying on a leather couch in a spacious room, which I later came to find out was the Stone Heights Family Time Room. The world felt like a tortured giant, and I was sure the building I was in would soon collapse.

The glass tipped over, and milk spilled onto the Persian rug under the coffee table. I heard a woman groan. She had red hair and was sitting on a sofa chair with a young girl. She stopped twirling the girl's long hair and gazed at the spilled milk and then at me. A man across the way held his hand against a wall of curved glass and stared intently out at the roiling darkness. On the other side of the room, a teenaged boy scrawled strange figures on a whiteboard with black and red markers.

I examined my hands, limbs and feet. I touched my face. I seemed to be made of flesh. I thought I must be alive, but it didn't feel good to be alive under the circumstances.

The worst of it passed after a few hours. The tremors and howling continued for days, but with waning intensity. All the Mollys, but Vick, were astounded that I had no idea who they were. It wasn't until after the tremors stopped that I began to consider that what they were telling me might be true.

Conveniently, the basics of human functionality continued to operate on autopilot, immune to my memory loss. I knew how to eat, drink, and vacate without help. After our first Apo Day meal, a useful image of myself brushing my teeth popped into my head. I went to a lavatorio and brushed without issue. No one had to teach me how to walk, talk, or climb into bed. Being a human animal was no problem. Being a human person proved far more difficult. For days I wrestled with the details of my current condition and my relationship with the Mollys. Identity and relationship were elusive and mysterious things.

I discovered that I also retained the more refined skills of my forgotten life: reading, writing, performing mathematical calculations, posing reasonable questions, drawing rational conclusions, and behaving in a more or less civilized way. Further boosting my hopes of a full recovery, I also found that I remembered the essentials of human history up to Apo Day. High impact people, places and events began to multiply in my fertile memory banks.

The idea of human civilization in a world now effectively stripped bare of it would persist in my mind. But that fateful day, when Apollyon nearly eradicated humanity, I woke as if I had been ejected from a black hole, with only the Mollys present to assure me I existed.

Nap Molly has been my primary source of information regarding everything related to the past three plus years. *This is Stone Heights. This is Stone's Eden. This is the Eat Room. This is the Family Time Room.* And so on.

Just as I once had guided him, Nap guided me around the compound, determined to overwhelm me with technical minutiae. But the first time he took me to the dome, he got really quiet. After a while, I hardly noticed he was there. I stood in the center of that large open space, looked straight up, and thought I heard a voice say, *You've been here before.*

It wasn't a real voice, but I told Nap about it. He chuckled dismissively and started spewing nonsense in a weird, echoey dome voice: "You've been here before, Bubba, of course you have, reason being you're Bubba Molly." He continued in this vein, half-serious, half-joking. It wasn't funny, and I'm not sure why I let him go on for as long as he did, but I finally made him stop. He frowned and got analytical. He explained that the dome was stirring up my subconscious, and that was a very positive thing.

On our way back to my rooms, he started reciting a series of mind-numbing facts and figures about the dome: light-sensitivity, temperature and humidity controls, refraction and filtering factors, cubic footage, and other particulars I don't recall. My mind wandered a bit, and that annoyed him, but by the time we got to my suite, he seemed over it.

He playfully shoved me and reminded me tomorrow was Bright Star Day. He told me to get a good night's rest because we were going on our first post-Apollyon surveillance flight in the morning. Being in a hoveroo high up in the air, even in a gray sky, would do us both good, he said.

"What's my real name?" I said as he was turning to leave.

"Bubba… Nah, I'm messing with you. Your real name is Merlin."

"No, I mean my surname."

He thought about it for a few seconds, and said, "Molly. You're Merlin Molly."

"No, come on, Nap. What's my real family name?"

"You're as much a Molly as Vick or Pam."

"I'm flattered, Nap, and I appreciate your saying that, but logic says that's not possible."

He stared at me in that disquieting blank way of his, which has since become a bit irritating.

"Loretta is three years older than me," I reminded him.

"That doesn't mean she's not your mom. That doesn't mean you're not a Molly, damn it."

His eyes weren't even pretending to engage mine. They were fixed on my nose, or the space between my nose and upper lip.

"What are you looking at?"

"Does *Quasi-Mom* work better for you? How about we call you Merlin Quasi-Molly?"

I must have looked hopelessly dazed because Nap flashed his big-toothed grin and shoved me again, a lot harder this time, knocking me off balance. He said he had to go run some maintenance checks on Hoveroo-A and told me to take a sleep pill.

Tomorrow was going to be a historic milestone, he said with his chest puffed out, our first venture outside the walls of Stone Heights since Terra got crushed by Apollyon.

Pearl and I step out of the float shaft onto Sublevel-2. She leads me through a maze of dimly lit hallways and nodes to a terminal point showing three closed entryways. I watch her pace like a ballerina toward the middle one, which opens as she nears.

I'm disappointed when we walk into Warehouse S-2B, which is essentially our junk repository. "Here?" I say staring at the forgotten tables, cabinets, and shelves loaded with miscellaneous hardware, spare parts, and equipment. "Where's the sofa and coffee table?"

She smiles and motions for me to follow her to a row of tall metal cabinets lined along the back wall. She stops before a bare section of wall and presses her fingertips against it, holding them in place for a few seconds.

Before I can ask her what she's doing, she steps back, spreads her hands like a magician, and says, "Watch this."

A green line appears at the bottom of the wall. It thickens and rises like liquid poured into a bottle, filling out what appears to be an archway. The lime-green filling then begins to fizz, burning away the wall and revealing what looks like a living room with a coffee table, sofa, and two lit lamps.

"This has been my home for the past three years," she says, reaching for my hand.

Recorded: 24 Apr 2104

The stacked bookshelves are colorful and alluring. They feel like a living thing. Faintly familiar names and phrases trigger a maddening brain buzz: The Iliad and the Odyssey, The Divine Comedy, The Works of Shakespeare, Don Quixote, War and Peace, Crime and Punishment, Moby Dick, Pride and Prejudice, Les Misérables, Bleak House, Huckleberry Finn, The Lord of the Rings, One Hundred Years of Solitude, Beloved…

I almost forget where I am and who I'm with. Pearl slips between me and the books. She smiles, and I smile back.

"There's more," she says and walks toward a closed door.

"How did you do that? Make the wall disappear."

"Oh, that? Willie taught me."

"Who in stars is Willie?"

Pearl is surprised by the edge in my voice. So am I. Her features soften. "It's okay, really."

Is it? The door slides open. Pearl turns around and extends her hand. "Come on, Merlin."

She pulls me into a circular white room, clean and stark as a monk's dormitory. White unadorned walls, a round white table and chair in the center, and atop the table, a turquoise rabbit. I stare at the inanimate rabbit for a few seconds before doing a preliminary 360-degree scan of the room. Then I start sniffing around. Pearl watches patiently as I check for secret doors, closets, and compartments along every inch of wall, floor and ceiling. I find no sign anywhere of hidden openings or concealed humans.

Pearl points at the rabbit, flashes me a knowing look, and walks to the far end of the room.

"So, this is about a toy rabbit?"

She stops before what looks indistinguishable from any other part of the white wall, shifts her feet, and fixes her gaze on something I'm not seeing. Suddenly, part of the wall begins to roll gently. Within moments all movement stops, and then, as if a pebble were dropped in its center, waves of concentric liquid light ripple outward, fade, and vanish, leaving behind a four-foot-diameter circle of blueish smoke.

Pearl turns toward me and says, "This is a timeway."

Her words don't register, I guess because I'm having trouble understanding what I'm seeing. How come the blue smoke isn't drifting into the room?

"You don't remember, do you?" she says.

"I, uh..."

"It's a timeway for others to come through."

"What are you talking about? What others?"

"The ones from the future."

"Oh, yeah," I say nodding and, of course, I'm thinking Apollyon Effect. I walk over to her, my eyes fixed on that circle of blue smoke. I try to be diplomatic.

"I don't know how you learned to do these things. Totally amazing, really, but what I do know is the Apollyon Effect hits us all in different ways. Me? Well, you know about my memory issues. Others suffer from distorted perceptions, an inability to grasp reality. It's important we keep each other grounded."

Pearl is listening to me the way a nice person patiently listens to an idiot.

On an impulse, I reach into the circle of smoke.

Pearl shouts "No!" as my arm disappears. She grabs me around the waist and pulls me back.

I feel a little dizzy, but I'm relieved to see that my arm remains attached and intact.

"What was that?"

"We're not meant to go that way, Merlin."

"What is this thing?"

"I told you, it's a timeway, and one day people from the future are going to come through it."

"Come here, to Stone Heights? How did you come up with all this?"

"I didn't come up with anything, Merlin. Willie told me."

I stare at the agitated smoke with new respect, then glance back at the turquoise rabbit.

"I take it that's Willie."

"Okay, look, I know this sounds totally insane, and I don't pretend to understand it. What I do know is that Willie told me this is a timeway, and people from the future are going to come through it, and I believe him."

"Come to do what?"

"I don't know. Something important. Look, Merlin."

The smoke thins out to reveal a cave, and for an instant, I see in the background what appears to be a pool of water.

"They'll come out of the water," she says, pointing.

"Is that what Willie told you?"

Pearl nods, and the dynamic we witnessed reverses itself. The blue smoke changes into waves of concentric liquid light that ripple inward toward the center point of the circle, which becomes transformed into a rolling mass that gradually hardens into the solid wall that was there minutes ago.

"You need to talk to Willie," she says.

I go, I sit, and I stare at the turquoise rabbit.

"Hello, Merlin!"

The greeting startles me. The voice is echoey, part feral, kind of human, and faintly familiar.

"Merlin, old friend, how good it is to be reunited!"

Willie's eyes brighten, and a turquoise and gold image of *The Three Hares* projects from its eyes onto the top of the white table. "A token of our enduring friendship," Willie says.

The image is identical to the tattoo on my hand, which I have no memory of acquiring. The image fades away. I don't know what to make of this talking rabbit. I reach out and touch its head. Its ears bend back. It closes its eyes.

"How long have you known me?"

"We go back a long way, Merlin. You were a boy living in Stone House with your parents. You had little to do with me then. We shared but one brief session, which was hardly a success. When you were no longer a child, you rediscovered me and began to understand my usefulness and purpose."

"Willie, you know who my parents are."

"Atwell and Runa Stone. The Notes will also help you remember other people and places and things."

"The notes?"

"You returned from Europe a motivated twenty-nine-year-old man and began organizing and further developing notes you composed during your years abroad, including thoughts, observations and reflections regarding private and public matters. You began dictating these notes to me 08 July 2101 AD. These now form a living oral history you've titled, *Notes to Unknown Survivor.*"

"A *living* oral history?"

"Yes, *living* in the sense that they are not finished. Soon you will want to resume developing and dictating the Notes as you did before this interruption."

"Are you sure you're not thinking of someone else?"

"Your identity has been confirmed and verified by my vocal and facial recognition functionalities, which were tested for accuracy and reliability seven-hundred times in the Stone-TH Robotics Lab before my release and delivery to Stone House when you were a child. Lab results confirmed one hundred percent accuracy in both modes. I would be pleased to review with you the results of those tests, if you wish."

"That won't be necessary, Willie."

"And yet, you remain skeptical."

"Everything you've said sounds highly improbable."

"I would not reveal such information to anyone but you, Merlin Stone, the indisputable author and voice of *Notes to Unknown Survivor.*"

"The Apollyon Effect has stolen my memory, Willie."

"I am the de facto guardian of your notes. When you hear them, you will know that what I have told you is true. Be advised, however, there is no evidence to suggest this so-called Apollyon Effect was the cause of your memory loss."

"Nap Molly says Brain Eat is one of the symptoms of the Apollyon Effect, which in addition to memory loss includes delusion, reality distortion, and other mental failures."

"A scan of extant data shows zero references to memory loss vis-à-vis the term *Apollyon Effect*. However, memory loss pertaining to the colloquial term, *Brain Eat*, are available, though said data are strictly anecdotal and pertain primarily to pre-Apollyon schoolyard, locker room, and warehouse lingo. I would be happy to summon specific examples."

"No need, Willie, but thank you. I just want to know who I am."

"What better way than to listen to the one best equipped to help you remember?"

For a moment, Willie's rabbit mouth looks almost human as it moves in response to a new voice that hits me like a splash of cold water.

I hear myself talking to myself, and the walls of forgetfulness come crashing down, one after another.

Recorded: 25 Apr 2104

30 March 2104

Pearl knows a lot about me, but she knows very little about herself. She's totally unaware of her artificial consciousness and biosynthetic constitution. She doesn't know she was programmed to think she's a human being. She smiles like a human, sounds like a human, walks and stubs her toe and cries out like a human. She eats and sleeps and relieves herself like one, even bleeds a synthetic fluid that looks and smells like human blood.

All standard fare for Elara-3s and other comparable high-level android models.

Having listened to my dictations every day for the past three years, Pearl is able to recall details with astonishing precision. She knows me better than she knows herself. Credit for authoring this irony goes to Cleavon Blinkhorn, who programmed Willie to conceal all android-sensitive content about Pearl from Pearl.

For the second time in my life, I've learned that the person I most cherish in the world is not a human being but a machine. Adjusting to this double-shock has been quite the challenge. Sometimes I lower my expectations and tell myself this artificial Pearl is all the Pearl I could ever want or need.

But how long can a rational being keep pretending things are what they are not?

The revelation about the Mollys is far less emotionally exhausting. They exist only because I chose them to exist. They were built from my specs, with a few added site-specific security modifications Atwell said were a required formality. Those last second mods might explain a few unexpected glitches, particularly in Nap and Loretta, and why I should have reviewed them when I had the chance.

Despite my rough encounter with the past, rediscovering Pearl and Willie has proven to be liberating and empowering. I was hopeful, yes, but I never expected Nap to fully endorse my vision of a community. At best, I thought we might reach a somewhat acceptable compromise.

I now see the opportunity this awkward development has presented me. I won't have to answer to Nap or Loretta any longer. I'm the Technical Administrator of Stone Heights, not Nap. I can rein in the Mollys any time I want by invoking my Admin privileges. I have the power to manipulate facility and asset controls, settings, and protocols, as I see fit.

But I don't want to overreact. Our conflicting views on the kind of planet we want to live in notwithstanding, I'm still very fond of Nap and Loretta, though in a different, more detached way. I also wonder now about Pearl's precise role in this android melodrama. Should I tell her the truth about the Mollys? Would she begin to question herself?

From the beginning, the Mollys have treated me like a son. Even now, with all I know, I feel oddly indebted to them.

Such a complicated thing, the human heart. Why should I feel melancholy when recalling that first encounter with the Mollys? I see them clearly now, the four Yada-7s stepping out of the hoveroo, oldest to youngest. Nap, age 44, Loretta, age 33, Vick and Pam, ages 15 and 13.

Loretta did come charging toward me, just as Nap and Pam had said, and she did nearly knock me off my feet. Nap followed with an iron grip handshake and a series of brutish backslaps. Then came a tentative hug from sweet, little Pam and a glum nod from Vick.

Perfect, I had thought at the time. My New Life Plan was off to a great start. I felt happy and fulfilled inviting my new family inside the walls of our invincible fortress. How many people do you know get to handpick their family?

Then came the Notes and my eyepopping wakeup. For a couple of days after my meeting with her and Willie, Pearl remained a secret to everyone but Vick and me.

We were eating ice cream in the Family Time Room when Loretta said, "Oh, Nap, why do you always feel the need to contradict me?"

She was so happy, and though she was addressing Nap, her blue eyes—as was too often the case—were fixed on me. "Come here you. Give Mommy a big hug!"

Like the good quasi-son I'd always been, I got up and gave Loretta a hug. I'd given her many hugs before, but this one felt different. Programmed and squishy would be one way to describe it.

I haven't been down to see Pearl since our first and only meeting. I'm afraid of what might happen when she takes my hand. What if her hand feels programmed and squishy?

I remember Pearl most vividly when I'm alone with Willie. Like a fool, I relive those tenderly awkward moments at Stone-TH, the sweet, almost adolescent, tension we felt whenever our paths would cross. It does me no good to relive those moments, but I do it anyway, and before I descend too deeply into gloom, Willie starts shooting off song titles.

Can a human fall in love with an android?

Pearl never dropped from a woman's womb. She never wailed to announce her arrival. She was assembled in a lab and programmed under the cold light of science. She has no heart, no soul, no dreams.

So what gives?

I tell Willie to stop with the song titles and suggest he slip into Sleep mode. I keep an eye on him until he does, and I think strange thoughts, and I ask strange questions.

Here's one: Can the essence of what it means to be profoundly human—which is unique across the frozen wastes and blazing deserts of the universe—somehow, as by some outlandish edict or cosmic miracle, find its way into the synthetic neural networking of a machine?

I try to sleep but fail miserably. I get out of bed with Pearl's lovely smile carved on the front of my brain. What kind of weird grief is this? What am I supposed to do with this ridiculous aching heart of mine?

The only thing I can think to do is sit at my desk and bleed words onto paper for a few hours. When I've bled enough, I wake up Willie and tell him I need to dictate some new material.

Recorded: 26 Apr 2104

01 April 2104

Vick never talks to me. I try to be the good big brother, but he doesn't buy into it, never has. At first, I thought it was just a case of random teen resentment. That could still be true, but there's another layer to this, I realize. He's known Pearl for a few months and kept the secret of her existence to himself. The poor kid sees me as competition.

Pearl told me Vick doesn't know anything about the Notes or Willie. She didn't think it was a good idea to tell him. I'm glad she didn't.

I hear a knock on the door of my suite. It's Vick. He looks troubled. It's the first time I can remember him coming to my rooms.

"So I know you know about Pearl," he says in almost a whisper.

Easy now, take a couple of seconds to formulate the right response. No way he's talking about me knowing Pearl is an android, right? There would be no way for him to know this.

"Are you angry with me, Vick?"

"How could you abandon her like that?"

189

I can barely hear him. I need to get this right.

"I messed up. Two weeks is too long. I should have gone down to see her the day after we met. You know, I just think I was a little nervous about seeing her again."

I watch the mix of confusion and anger dissolve from Vick's face. I have to remind myself he's not human.

"I will fix this, I promise. You're right, Pearl should not be left alone down in Sublevel-2 like some forgotten spare part. I'm going to introduce her to Mom and Dad, and I don't want you to worry. It's going to take them a little while to adjust to her presence. But you know what, Vick? When they get to know her—and it won't take that long—they're going to love her too."

I take a moment to think about what I just said. *They're going to love her too.* Vick looks away, a little embarrassed, and still a little worried.

"It's going to be fine, you'll see. We're all going to have someone new to talk to, share meals with, and have fun with in the Family Time Room."

He looks at me uncertainly, like he's trying to balance fun with Pearl and the likelihood of a Merlin-Pearl adult relationship.

"There's something else I've been meaning to tell you. We are not going to stay trapped inside Stone Heights too much longer. One day soon we're going to go outside these walls and meet new people and make new friends. One day you're going to meet a special someone, and you'll—"

I stop right there to take a cold, hard look at myself. Vick thinks he's human like me, and I'm using that fallacy to secure his cooperation. Sometimes the time I spent refining my New

Life Plan and developing the Molly specs feels like a pro-tracted exercise in self-deception. Sometimes I feel a bit like Dr. Frankenstein.

I'm stunned to feel a tear welling up in my right eye and threatening to roll down my cheek. I wipe it away quickly, hoping Vick won't notice.

He does, though, and the strange sight appears to distress him. When he comes up to me and puts his arms around me, I'm the one caught off guard. I respond with a quick hard hug and then I give him a gentle push.

"I'm glad you came by, Vick. I'm going to see Pearl tomorrow, okay? I'm going to bring her up to meet the rest of the family."

Vick is unable to suppress a smile. He strides out into the corridor. I go to the door to watch him. He's walking away fast, arms swinging and pace denoting rare optimism and resolve. He stops suddenly, turns around and yells, "I'll tell her to meet you in the garden by the rose bushes."

This is not the way I envisioned it, but there's nothing gained by nixing Vick's idea of how this pivotal moment should play out.

"Okay!" I shout back. "Tell her to meet me in the after-noon at two o'clock."

He doesn't move. Is he waiting for an invite? I don't really want him there when I talk to her. I would like to have a few minutes alone with her. But how can I can tell him that?

"Okay, I'll see you there!" I yell.

Recorded: 27 Apr 2104

02 April 2104

When I get to Stone's Eden, Vick and Pearl are standing by the rose bushes chatting away. Can't say I'm not a little disappointed.

What kind of special moment was I anticipating with Pearl anyway? And what do androids talk about when no human is around to hear them?

On the way back we catch Pam coming out of her rooms. She's almost too easy, instantly brightening up at the sight of Pearl. Thoughts of shapeshifters and body snatchers are the furthest things from her programmed teenaged mind. Pearl fits the big sister part to a T, and that's good enough for Pam.

I have allies. Now, if we can just hook Loretta, Nap will go down without a fight.

Vick goes on ahead, looking anxious as we approach the threshold of the Family Time Room. Loretta is standing at the big oak work table in the arts and crafts section of the FTR. She's painting a ceramic vase. Her skill is undeniable, if overly technical, as one might expect. She's focused on the task at hand and seems unaware of us.

Vick turns and gazes at me doubtfully. Pearl is standing between me and Pam, who hasn't let go of Pearl's hand since their happy encounter. Now, on the edge of a potential family debacle, I have to admit I'm okay with Vick being the one to break the news to Loretta.

"What did you say, Vicky boy?" Loretta says without looking up.

"I said Pearl's here."

"You sweet boy, you brought Mommy pearls?"

Loretta isn't paying attention, obviously. It's all about the vase and the thin horizontal looping brush stroke she's winding round the vase's neck, contorting her body, the tip of her tongue poking out between her ruby red lips.

"Not pearls, Mom, a lady named Pearl."

Loretta's head twitches as she pulls the brush into the air to avoid marring her work. I've seen her produce this birdlike tic before, and I've always attributed it to an unexpected encounter with displeasure. That was before I remembered she was an android, which makes me marvel at the level of detail her creators insisted on bringing to her design. Loretta still won't look at us. She goes on to finish that last tapering brush stroke.

The timebomb element too often present in family life is ticking loudly in my head. Vick turns and waves us into the Family Time Room. I walk ahead of Pearl and Pam, offering myself as a shield. Loretta puts her brush down on the table, straightens her back and turns around. She looks past Vick and me and locks eyes with Pearl.

What follows is not what I had anticipated. In fact, nothing happens for a long while. No one says a word, no one moves. Loretta is as expressionless as an edenbot. The five of us are frozen, literally, locked in a *System Down* type scenario. There's a glitch in the system, and the glitch is Pearl.

Then, without warning, Loretta roars, "I'm going to kill somebody!" She storms past Vick. My right hand reaches for her, but she shoves it aside. Pam, the last defense, slips in front of Pearl. Before I can move another muscle, Loretta has positioned herself before Pam and Pearl, and all I can do is stand down.

"I'm so confused," Pam cries. "Who are you going to kill, Mom? Surely, not Pearl!"

Loretta ignores her. She's looking over Pam's shoulder at Pearl. She can't peel her eyes from the young stranger.

"I'm not going to bite her head off, Pammy, so be a good girl and please step aside."

Pam hesitates but relents and moves a few feet away.

To my surprise, I detect no hostility or fear in either Loretta or Pearl. When Loretta raises her hand suddenly, I make a panicky coughing sound. But I've totally misread the situation. With mystifying gentleness, Loretta touches Pearl's cheek and leaves her hand there awhile.

"Have you had something to eat today, hon?" she says.

"Yes, I have, but thank you very much."

"Tell me, darling, was it my dear husband who brought you to Stone Heights?"

Pearl shakes her head as Nap barges into the Family Time Room shouting, "Brought who into Stone Heights?"

Despite the sound and fury, Nap's reaction to Pearl is similar to Loretta's. His eyes go right to the newcomer. Pearl bears Nap's scrutiny calmly, without worry or fear.

"Vicky brought me a Pearl today," Loretta says cheerfully.

My big brother instincts are triggered, and I blurt out, "Actually, I'm the one who found Pearl in the garden."

No way I'm going to let Nap badger the kid for the next several days. I send a quick warning glance Vick's way. His intense frown indicates he understands why I'm taking responsibility, but he's also peeved that I've stolen from him an occasion of questionable glory.

"Before you all arrived in Stone Heights," I say, "someone locked Pearl down in a Sublevel-2 apartment and left her there. We don't know who or why. Eventually, she found a way to get out and started to look around. One day she saw us, but she was afraid to approach. She thought we wouldn't believe her story. She was worried we would think she was an evil intruder and that we'd torture her to get the truth out of her. She was scared, so she kept out of sight and remained hidden and all alone."

"Oh, for starsake!" Loretta cries. "Pearl, you poor dear, why would you ever think we would do such a thing?"

Loretta and Pam hook theirs arms into Pearl's, protecting her flanks. Nap remains frozen. Did Pearl unwittingly trigger a glitch in Nap's social programming?

"Nap, are you okay?"

He takes two steps forward, shakes his head.

"Sublevel-2? I've checked every corridor, room, closet and cabinet in this facility. Every nook and cranny. What apartment are you talking about? There's no apartment down there, and there's never been any sign of undocumented occupancy anywhere onsite, ever."

"She's been living in a secret apartment behind the back wall of Warehouse S-2B."

"Come on, Bubba, use your noodle. There's no secret apartment in Stone Heights. You know that as well as I do."

"Well, actually, there is. I saw it with my own eyes. You won't find it on standard construction diagrams because, guess what, Nap, it's secret."

Nap looks confused. That's a first.

"Show me," he says.

I glance at Pearl, and then at Loretta.

"Oh, go on," Loretta says. "Show your Dad that secret mystery apartment so he doesn't drive me crazy all night. While you're gone, Pam and I are going to show Pearl her rooms. And take Vicky with you too, so he doesn't feel left out. When you all get back, we'll have a celebratory dinner to welcome Pearly into the Molly family."

Could things have gone any better? Probably not, at least not much better. So why do I feel queasy?

Recorded: 28 Apr 2104

196

16 April 2104

Pearl's seamless integration into the family over the past couple of weeks seems to have softened up Nap. But I know better than to test my assumption. I say as little as possible on the subject of refugees and community-building.

I let Pam do the heavy lifting. Her remarks are less threatening and offensive to Nap. He scrunches his face and stares at her but doesn't say a harsh word back.

Meanwhile, Loretta looks cool as melting ice chuckling over Pam's social responsibility concerns. Often, after one of Pammy's remarks, Loretta will look at Pearl to measure her reaction.

During these exchanges, Pearl always maintains a serene silence. She's discerned the inflammatory nature of the subject and steers wide of it. I mean to talk to her about that in private, but I keep putting it off. I know she's picked up on my reluctance to be alone with her, but she seems hesitant or unwilling to bring it up.

The harder I try to act normal around her, the more awkward things get between us. I've caught her staring at me a couple of times, drilling down to the unreachable heart of someone with whom she thought she was destined to build a life. Both times she turned away, embarrassed, and seemed to be looking for someone. I think she was looking for Vick.

That has me wondering. Does she think Vick's the reason I'm being distant? It's a convenient premise, one I can use to my advantage. I can tell Pearl that for Vick's sake it's better we not spend time together, at least not until he's had an opportunity to meet someone his own age. But being dishonest is exhausting, even with androids.

Actually, Vick is pretty happy, the happiest I've ever seen him. Sure, Pearl's presence has something to do with it, but I think the prospect of making friends, and maybe one day meeting someone he can form a special connection with, has kindled in him some version of hope that had no chance of existing in the xenophobic world created by his parents.

Today before breakfast, Vick tells me he wants to go with us on surveillance. The kid hasn't been outside Stone Heights since the Molly arrival over three years ago.

In the middle of buckwheat pancakes, strawberries and cream, I say, "Hey, Nap, I was just thinking. How about we take Vick with us today? Weather conditions look perfect. It would be a great learning experience for the kid."

Everyone but Vick stops chewing.

Nap is giving me that new scrunched-up look he's developed since Pearl came on the scene, the one usually employed whenever Pam opens her social duty mouth.

"What about me?" Pam cries. "Why can't I go?"

Nap throws his hands up in the air, but brings them down softly onto the table. I've got one eye on Loretta, the other on Nap. I think Loretta's trying to picture Nap and me up front in the HA, Vick and Pam seated behind us. I detect no visible twitch this time, no trace of displeasure. I'm fairly confident Loretta is okay with this.

"Ahh," Nap moans, looking aggrieved.

Pearl's fork pings her plate. She leans forward on the table, smiles and says, "What a great idea! That would be such a wonderful learning opportunity for both Vick and Pam, wouldn't it, Nap?"

The confidence with which Pearl now addresses someone who once frightened her is what is most stunning to me. We all know what Nap's going to say before he says it.

"Yep, I don't see why not."

Nap's voice sounds oddly distant, a little disembodied. I stare at Pearl, proud of how quickly and easily she's become a force for good in the family.

After breakfast, when Nap and the kids are heading up to the hoveroo deck, I pull her aside, out of Loretta's range. "I want you to help me convince Nap and Loretta that we should start making direct contact with survivors."

She smiles. "I would love to help you, Merlin."

For the first time in weeks, I think I've reminded her of the pre-Apollyon Merlin. I think I should kiss her. I do. It's our first kiss ever, I realize, and in a moment of dizzy wonder I think, how can these lips not be real?

"Okay, great, thanks," I say awkwardly, and rush up to the hoveroo deck with a caution light flashing in my brain: *This doesn't make me crazy, does it?*

* * *

199

For the sake of the kids, we avoid the Trail of Misery as much as possible. That's what Nap calls the northwest passage traveled by Coronado and other doomed refugees. We fly northeast, over a hundred miles past our security perimeter. It's the farthest we've ever gone.

A splash of yellow in the distance draws us. We descend, hover over a large field of dandelions. I remember dandelions. I never thought they could be so beautiful. Vick and Pam start chirping about wanting to get out so they could run through the yellow and green. Nap ignores their requests, but lowers the hoveroo to within a few feet of the ground, which is the next best thing. I'm tempted to leave the cockpit and leap into the dandelions. That would force Nap to land the HA, and we could all spend a few minutes feeling the earth beneath our feet and plucking tiny yellow flowers.

But undermining Nap in front of his kids would be wrong, as well as counterproductive. Nap did agree to bring them, after all. Sure, it was under slight duress, but he did agree, and that's progress.

All the way back Nap hardly says a word. Vick and Pam are talking excitedly about this amazing world they're beginning to discover. The sad truth is no one at Stone Heights has ever had any reason to get excited about anything until now, Loretta's Family Time Room fun projects and games notwithstanding.

I can't wait to see Pearl. I can't wait to tell her about the dandelions and my plan for rebuilding Terra, one unknown survivor at a time.

Recorded: 29 Apr 2104

30 April 2104

Vick has devoured an entire Just-Like chicken and a bowl of mashed potatoes soaked in spicy brown gravy. Like most teens, Vick consumes staggering amounts of food. But that hasn't always been the case. Since Pearl's integration into the family, Vick's appetite has soared.

I try to not obsess over the gastrointestinal prowess of others, though the Mollys and Pearl make it hard. Heartburn, indigestion, constipation, hemorrhoids? Not on their register. They eat what they want, when they want, and in whatever quantities they want, without dire consequences, ever.

It can be disheartening to repeatedly be reminded of such digestive excellence. I don't recall including the consumption and vacating of digested food and drink on my specs (why would I?), suggesting the simulation of human digestion is standard for Yada-7s and Elara-3s. Again, I try to not dwell on such things, but the mind is its own master, and the mind can be a harsh companion.

Loretta has four kitchenbots preparing and serving meals, drinks and treats around the clock. Occasionally, she'll keep the bots on standby when she's in the mood to bake cookies and pies, which she's been doing with greater frequency since Pearl joined the family.

Thoughts about artificial digestion can be unsettling for some, but what can be worse than to ponder the crushing of dreams? Another two weeks have passed, and the progress I thought I saw in Nap has come to a dead stop. There may even be some regression. He seems more than content to waddle in the status quo for the next millennium. And, more ominously, Loretta may be trending in that same direction.

Vick doesn't feel it's his place to make suggestions. And Pam's observations and recommendations have become no more than harmless background chatter during our obscenely gluttonous, ever-lengthening meals.

It's on me to get things back on track. I talked to Pearl earlier today. I asked her if she would be comfortable raising the possibility of the six of us taking a ride on the Hoveroo Bus. She said she would be glad to do it.

Dinner seems to be the best time to discuss change. When the moment is right, I catch Pearl's attention and wink three times, left eye first, then right eye, then left, as agreed. On cue she smiles and leans slightly forward over the table, this time looking directly at Loretta but tossing a respectful glance Nap's way.

"I was just thinking, Mom, why don't we have a special family event? Something we've never done before. You know, something that will be both exciting and lots of fun."

"Oh, I love the way you think, Pearly!" Loretta exclaims, somewhat surprisingly. "Family fun and excitement are so very important!"

"Pearl, tell us!" Pam cries.

Pearl shoots a smile at Nap and then turns her head to speak directly to Loretta.

"What I have in mind is going to be amazing," she says.

"What is it?" Pam says.

"Shush, Pammy! Go ahead, Pearl, tell us what's going to be amazing."

"Let's all go see the dandelions. All of us, together, as a family."

Vick immediately follows up with, "We'll have to go in the Hoveroo Bus."

A heavy silence follows. You would think Vick was talking about the six of us mounting a fire-breathing dragon and flying across the continent. I toss Nap a glance. He looks detached and guarded. He's washed his hands of the affair. It's all up to Loretta now. Her face sparkles with joy.

"Stars above! What a nifty idea, Pearl! Don't you think so, Nap?"

"Uhm."

Everybody's chattering away, except for me and Nap. I have to admit, part of me feels sad about my quasi-dad being knocked off his lofty perch. But you could see it coming the moment Loretta touched Pearl's cheek. Thanks to Pearl, Loretta has increased and Nap has decreased. The poor guy never stood a chance.

"The H-Bus hasn't been flown in over three years," Nap warns.

"All the more reason to use it, Dad," Pam says.

Nap winces, takes a reluctant breath and says, "I'll run tests and do maintenance checks."

"Okay, everybody," I say. "This sounds like it could be a lot of fun, but Dad has to be sure the H-Bus is in optimal operational condition. He'll give it a good look and see if it's safe to use. A thorough check takes time, though."

Nap looks like a statue.

"I'll help Dad with the tech prep and the maintenance checks," I add. "When he says it's okay, you guys can come help wipe down and clean up the H-Bus so that it looks, feels and smells brand new. Assuming everything checks out, the soonest we can go on this family expedition is, what, day after tomorrow, Nap?"

"Weather permitting."

"Right, of course. We're taking no chances. If it's not Friday, it'll be some other day, but only if and when Dad says the H-Bus is ready to go."

"I can't wait to pluck dandelion flowers," Pam pipes. "I can't wait to see the natural wonders of the new world!"

"Ha-ha-ha, isn't Pammy something else?" Loretta says. "Wonders of the new world, oh my!"

Loretta reaches over and pats Pam's face.

"Just look at my two girls, will you?" Loretta says, and dabs the corner of her eye with the side of her pinky.

Nap gets up and starts heading out.

"Where are you going?" Loretta calls out. "What about ice cream?"

"Uhm, yeah, no. No more room in here," Nap says, squeezing his belly with both hands. "I'm gonna take a peek inside the H-Bus, make sure there are no stowaways or critters hiding in there, ha-ha."

"I'll go with you, Nap," I say.

After a few preliminary checks on the H-Bus, we sit in the cockpit. For a long while, neither of us speaks. Then Nap says, "The years are like tumbleweed, Merlin, the way they roll by one after the other. Who knew life would be a wind-swept plain of rolling tumbleweed?"

I sneak a sympathy glance, observe a dispirited android thoughtfully assessing the swift passage of time, mimicking the human drama, asking himself the same old human questions filtered through an artificial brain: Who am I? What is this place? Is there a God?

True, he only *seems* to be asking himself those questions. That doesn't keep me from putting my hand on his shoulder the way he so many times has put his hand on mine.

That doesn't make me crazy, does it? No, that just makes me someone who's desperate to hold on to anything even remotely close to what's human in this upside-down world.

"I'll see you in the morning, Nap," I say.

I go looking for Pearl. We walk down to Stone's Eden. Without speaking, we drift over to where I found her. The roses smell especially beguiling. I tell her how amazing she is, and I kiss her again. This time, to my surprise, she kisses me back, igniting a quiver deep within me. I pull away.

"Did you hear that?" I say self-consciously. "I thought I heard a beebot."

She stares at me, confused. Then she draws close again.

I force a yawn, tell her I'm tired, busy day tomorrow, need to get some rest. Before she can again lift her chin to kiss me, I jerk my head away and start coughing.

I'm a bad actor and the worst liar, but I press on with the charade, make myself as unappealing as I can. The look on

Pearl's face pains me. I offer a vague apology and walk her back to her rooms. We observe a cruel silence the entire way there.

Recorded: 01 May 2104

02 May 2104

Because the H-Bus can accommodate up to twelve, Loretta decides to bring along two kitchenbots, four sentinelbots, enough food to feed forty teenagers, flex chairs with expandable table, and a lithium-ion battery-powered grill.

Pearl and I are watching a pair of sentinelbots lug the grill onto the H-Bus when she tells me she planted the picnic seed with Loretta a couple of days before I even asked her to help. Both of us are pretending our botched intimacy session never happened.

"Oh, you did? That explains why she was so agreeable."

"I said, 'Mom, how nice would it be to have a family picnic out in the fresh air and sun? Wouldn't that be the best?' She locked up for about a minute, then changed the subject. I know what that's like. It happens to me sometimes. It takes me a moment to process things I'm not expecting to hear. Or to get past things I would like to hear but never do."

She gives me a half-tease, half-reprimand kind of look, but quickly moves on. "Loretta and I are different, but we're alike in some ways too."

"I should go help with the loading," I say and nearly collide with a sentinelbot carrying a crate filled with Just-Like meats. Pearl starts laughing. I laugh too. And there I go again, wanting to kiss her, though this time I'm able to control myself.

The flight is smooth and wonderful. We spot a recovering poplar grove, which offers some shade. It's the ideal spot to set up camp. I recommend we land near the trees, but Loretta rejects the idea outright. She wants us in the sundrenched field of dandelions, about a twenty-minute walk from the grove. It's the same dandelion field Nap and I discovered when we flew out with Vick and Pam.

We mark off a three-hundred by three-hundred-foot zone. Working shoulder to shoulder with the sentinelbots, we all chip in to set up the picnic area in the center of the square. For Loretta's peace of mind, we post a sentinelbot on each corner of our secured area.

After hours of eating and drinking, I propose we all go on a fun walk to the poplar grove. Loretta flatly rejects my suggestion. If I want to walk, I can do it inside the secured area. It would be foolish to take unnecessary risks, wouldn't it, Merly? So, we amble about like inmates on free time, twice setting off shrill warnings from the sentinelbots.

All in all, though, other than my flirting with heat stroke from hours exposed to the midday sun, the outing is a huge success. Animated repartee and smiling faces—except for Nap—make for a swift and happy return home. My head is filled with dreams of better things to come.

On sighting Stone Heights, Loretta says, "Merly loves trees. Next time we should go to a place with more trees. And with a stream. We should find a stream with lots and lots of trees, isn't that right, Merly?"

"Yes, Mom, we should. There are beautiful trees and streams, and skies that are blue."

And people too, I want to add. Instead, I say, "What do you think, Nap, where's the best place to go to enjoy beautiful trees and a beautiful stream?"

"I'll have to look into it."

Loretta's expression turns mawkish. "Oh, would you just look at me?" she says, pressing the fleshy pad of her palm against her right eye. "Who could have imagined so much excitement and fun at my age?"

She's three years older than me, remember?

"This was wonderful, Mom," Pam says, and her cadence suggests this is a prelude to some ruinous declaration. I hold my breath, waiting for the *but* to come. Pam meets my eye, winks her left eye, right eye, left eye and says, "And, by the way, Mom, it's okay to get emotional."

That's it. That's all she says. I exhale.

We talk about trees and streams. We talk about woodland creatures. We talk squirrel, rabbit, woodchuck, chipmunk, fox, raccoon, possum, bear, lizards, turtles and birds. But not humans.

We don't talk humans, not yet.

At the next picnic, everyone but Nap has a blast. We go thigh-deep into the stream. We talk about new colors springing up all around, buds and seedlings and flowers. We lounge in the shade of resurrected maples.

I go easy on the Just-Like pork and try to stay out of the sun as much as possible. Positive momentum continues to build. On our return to Stone Heights, Loretta is already thinking about the next picnic.

"Garlic butter on Just-Like lamb chops, couscous and tomato sauce," I hear her chanting to herself.

Days pass quickly. Another picnic, this time on a hill. The scent of Just-Like lamb chops on the grill makes my mouth water. Busy kitchenbots cook and serve us. Stalwart sentinel-bots have our backs. A hawk soars near the sun. And a week later, our splendid little life in Stone Heights comes crashing down.

Recorded: 21 May 2104

09 May 2104

How long am I supposed to wait to speak my mind? Another month? A year?

The picnic outings have given the Mollys a false sense of accomplishment. Even Pam and Vick have become content. I've grown complacent myself, and my dream of building a community of human beings is on the verge of imploding.

There are times when it's easy to forget that the people I share my life with are composed of synthetic flesh and electronic circuitry and governed by algorithms. It's a choice I make, a temptation I choose to indulge now and then, a lonely man's consolation.

The family outings have progressively made my returns to reality less appealing. I tempt madness. I ask myself, what harm is there in pretending the Mollys and Pearl are human beings? Why would it matter to anyone, anyway?

And yet, it does. It matters to me. If I were the last living human in the universe, madness might be a blessing. But I'm not the last one. There are others, and I can't pretend they don't exist.

Today everything is going to change. It has to. I can use my Admin privileges anytime to tame Nap and Loretta, if I choose. I can make them less exasperating and more accommodating. If I want, I can strip them completely of their decision-making capabilities.

I'd rather not. As maddening as things can sometimes get, and as imperfect as these androids are, they are still the closest thing I have to human companionship. I may sound like a fool, but I hope I can still find common ground with Nap and Loretta.

We all stand up after dinner. We stretch, yawn, and saunter lazily from the Eat Room to the Family Time Room. Kitchenbots trail behind, bearing cannisters of ice cream and flasks of moonsap. We sit, we settle in, we sigh, and we are served. The kitchenbots bow respectfully as they drift into the background.

Unlike other foods, ice cream tends to keep talk-talk to a minimum. Ice cream-hungry extroverts become introverts, talkers become listeners. Today, I am acutely aware of the gurgles and slurps that form our familiar gluttonous concerto. But I won't be seduced. Not this time.

"We've had some amazing picnics," I say, licking my lips.

All eyes are on me now. I seize the moment, place my ice cream bowl down on the coffee table and stand up.

"Amazing, wonderful, and exciting experiences."

My legs start to tingle, so I pace about.

"We've never been closer as a family. Have you noticed? It's because we've shared these incredible adventures."

I try to avoid Nap, but our eyes meet all the same. I'm wondering if he knows I've been sneaking up to the hangar the last couple of nights to run diagnostics and perform maintenance prep on Hoveroo-B. Yes, of course, he knows, but he's not going to let on. That would be un-Nap-like.

"I wouldn't exactly call a picnic an adventure," he says.

"Oh, Nap, don't be such a fuddy-duddy," Loretta says. "Go on, Merly. What else did you want to say?"

That was Nap's first complete spoken sentence in days, at least in my presence. I try not to make too much of it.

"Merly? Go on, hon."

"Oh, yes, thank you, Mom. I was just saying…"

"You were talking about family adventures," Pam says.

"Yes, Pam, I was. These family adventures just keep getting better and better, don't they? Who could forget the field of dandelions? And our second picnic by a stream on the edge of a maple grove. And just a couple of days ago, there we all were on a hilltop gazing at this amazing planet of ours that's coming back from the dead."

"It was so cool," Pam says. "We could see for miles and miles with the naked eye."

"A hundred miles, at least," Vick chimes in. "Probably two-hundred."

"Amazing and exciting, yes indeed," Loretta agrees. "What else would you like to say, Merly?"

I feel Nap staring at me. I shouldn't do it, but I do. I turn my head and stare back at him for several seconds.

Nap straightens his back, places his ice cream bowl on the coffee table, and leans forward, hands on knees, his head wrenched in my direction.

Undeterred, I say, "Terra is alive. We can see it with our own eyes. The sky is blue. We see and feel the sun. We pick flowers, sit in the shade of trees. We hear the birds sing. From the hilltops we see birds of prey soaring and gliding across the blue sky. And from the H-Bus, when we fly low, we can see a rabbit dashing across a field, a loping coyote, a cougar climbing a rocky hillside."

I scan all the faces except Nap's. *Go on*, Pam and Vick's faces are telling me.

"But the most amazing thing we've seen, by far, is human beings."

Suddenly, everybody but Nap is talking.

"Shush! Shush everybody!" Loretta cries. Her head does that little twitch thing. Bad sign. She makes an effort to compose herself. Nap sinks back into the couch. It's me and Loretta now, one on one, quasi-mom versus quasi-son, a pair of reluctant duelists.

"Merlin, dear, you'll have to clarify what you said so that everyone can calm down. You meant the most amazing thing *would be to see* human beings walking out there, not the most amazing thing *we saw* was human beings. That makes it sound like we actually saw people, when, in reality, we did not. Tell everyone we did not see people, but that you meant it would be amazing if we did, though I am not so sure it would be."

Her smile is not fooling me.

"Nap and I saw a dozen people heading northwest."

"Stars above," Nap chuckles. "Sounds like Bubba-boy has had a bit more moonsap than he's accustomed to."

"I should have said something then. I should have pointed them out to you."

"Alcohol level through the roof," Nap says standing up. "A dirty dozen, no less, good stars!"

I wish Nap would sit down and shut up. Loretta looks distraught and confused. I wish Pearl would go to her, take her hand, speak a word of assurance. She glances at me. I start doing the left eye right eye left eye blink routine, but that just seems to confuse her. She turns her attention to Loretta and stares at her with dewy-eyed sympathy.

I kneel before Loretta and take her cold hands in mine. I'm surprised she doesn't pull them away.

On our way back from the hilltop picnic, Nap and I detected the ant-sized refugees. Neither of us said a word. Nap veered away from them just enough to make them disappear before anyone else could notice them.

Nap picks up his bowl, gets right behind me, and starts shoveling ice cream down his throat at a feverish pace. Everybody stands up. Does anyone else think he's going to bring that bowl down on my head?

"Mom, Dad and I decided to keep it a secret because we were afraid to upset you. But I've been thinking a lot about this. Everything is changing. You've seen for yourself how someone we would have considered an outsider has become so important to us. Look at her, Mom. Look at Pearl. Can you imagine your life without her?"

Loretta gently pulls her hands away and stands up.

"What do you want from me, Merlin?" she says.

Her simple cold directness takes me by surprise. Pearl draws nearer. She stands beside Loretta, but is careful not to make physical contact with her.

"Mom, life is more than just having family picnics. It's time to help the ones out there."

"Oh, is that right?"

I reach for her hand, but she pulls it away.

"Don't you dare!" she snaps.

"How can we justify spending the rest of our lives pretending no one else exists?"

Loretta closes her eyes and rubs her temples.

"I need to lie down," she says, and walks out of the Family Time Room.

I watch the impression of Loretta's bottom rise from the sofa cushion. I drag myself up and turn around to face Nap.

"I tell you what, Bubba," he says, his head rocking from side to side. "Don't count on any Molly taking part in any of your bleeding-heart mercy expeditions. No sir, not a one!"

"But, Dad," Pam moans.

Nap snaps his head in Pam's direction and slams his forefinger to his lips.

"Not a single Molly," he repeats, grinding his teeth.

"You needn't worry, Nap," I say. "I won't be taking a Molly with me. I will be taking the HB, though. And Pearl. I mean, if she wants to go with me."

"You go ahead. You do that. You take the HB and you take Pearl with you too."

I nod grimly. There's no turning back now.

Just as Pearl and I are about to leave, Nap starts pacing. He looks upset, possibly remorseful.

Nap's not the type of man to own up to his own poor judgment or mistakes. He'll want and expect me to be the one that bends. He'll want me to utter some conciliatory bunk so that he can issue a meaningless retort that will lift him back up onto some imaginary high ground where he can manage our disagreements more conveniently.

No, I'm not going to make things easier for you this time, Nap. I'm done kissing your Yada-7 ass.

Pearl and I watch Nap pace back and forth for nearly two minutes. How much longer are we supposed to wait? I touch her elbow and we start heading out. Before exiting the Family Time Room, I stop and glance back. Nap is ignoring us, but his pace has slowed significantly. He looks exhausted. Vick and Pam avoid my gaze. I feel awful.

I walk Pearl to her rooms. "I don't think we should have breakfast here tomorrow," I say as she opens the door to her suite. "I'll bring Fake Eggs and Just-Like bacon, coffee and vita-fluids. We can eat in transit. I don't want a morning faceoff with either Nap or Loretta."

Pearl nods. Her mouth opens, and I'm thinking she's going to say something poignant. Instead, her lips do this little vibrating thing that takes her a few seconds to get under control. She looks suddenly tired and dispirited. I haven't given much thought to how this level of family discord might be affecting her.

"Pearl, I'm sorry, I just assumed... Look, you don't have to come with me. Stay, spend some time with Loretta. I can do this by myself."

Now that I think of it, that would probably be best. A Merlin and Pearl versus the Mollys situation isn't going to help matters. I've miscalculated, and I feel sick about it.

"I'm going with you," she says.

"Are you sure?"

"Yes, what time?"

"I'll be here at seven to pick you up."

She smiles wearily and disappears behind the closed door.

* * *

I'm too wound up to sleep, so I head up to the hangar. Exiting the lift, the first thing I see is Hoveroo-A occupying center stage on the vast deck, its outline dramatic against the setting sun. Five-hundred feet away, on the eastern half of the deck, sits the TransHumanix RE Collector, the jewel of Stone-TH's Renewable Energy Division.

The first time Nap explained T-REC, I drowned in a sea of techy-talk. I didn't even try to pretend to understand. After Nap wrapped up his lengthy exposition, I asked him to start all over again, but this time maybe he could just tell me the two or three most important points I should know in simple layman's terms.

Turns out, our lives at Stone Heights are dependent on T-REC, which powers everything from toasters to edenbots to hoveroos. Androids too, I'm realizing. The Stone Heights master plan called for dedicated collector satellites situated outside the Terran atmosphere. The collectors convert solar energy into electrical energy, which powers laser emitters that transmit the energy to the T-REC, which distributes power throughout Stone Heights, keeping me alive and the Yada-7s and Elara-3 functioning.

I try not to stare too long at T-REC, but on nights like this it's hard not to. On the cusp of the most important day, possibly in my entire life, my weary brain is telling me that every artificial thing is charged with its own brand of life and will, and is just waiting to spring into action to derail human enterprise and hope. I tell my brain to relax.

The hangar lights are on, meaning Nap's inside doing something. I was hoping to avoid him, at least until after our return tomorrow. The HB hatch is open. Nap is bent over inside the cockpit. He doesn't hear my steps as I approach, or he's pretending he doesn't.

"I already ran the diagnostics," I say.

"I know you did."

"I made a few tweaks. Everything looks good to go."

"It doesn't hurt to have a second set of eyes."

"Look, Nap, I know it's my first time up there without you. But you don't have to worry. You taught me well."

"Damn right I did."

I let him have the last word. I head back to my rooms, take a sleep pill, and endure a series of nasty dream bits, one of which produces an overpowering sensation that bears the icy feel of eternity: me and my body floating in the infinite weightlessness of space.

I'm glad to wake up on a mattress. As I reorient myself to the here and now, I remember how I left Willie all alone for years in the back of a closet, and I get a guilt chill. I don't know who or what Pearl and I are going to find beyond the walls of Stone Heights. What I do know is, Willie's coming with us.

Recorded: 26 May 2104

10 May 2104

My internal clock tells me it's time to start heading back. We've cruised well past our security perimeter. No sign of refugees anywhere along the way. After yesterday's family dramatics, I welcome the ordinariness of today.

Pearl seems recovered from yesterday's drama and starts talking about our time together at Stone-TH. We go back and forth, we laugh, I lean over and kiss her cheek. She recoils in a funny way and giggles. There's no awkward tension between us this time. It seems that getting away from Stone Heights and the Mollys for a little while was the best thing for both of us.

I'm cautiously optimistic. Maybe our family squabble has given us all an opportunity to rethink things. My encounter with Nap last night, though brief, was encouraging. I'm glad we were able to end the day on a positive note. I'm hoping that, in time, Nap and Loretta will come to understand that, long-term, the positives of community building far outweigh the negatives. I can't mess this up. I have to make a concerted effort to always be patient with them and show due respect.

"Merlin, look," Pearl says as I'm setting our course back to Stone Heights.

I actually saw it before she did, another dead animal. Not the first, nor the last. No reason to extend our trip. But Pearl won't stop staring at me, like she expects me to say or do something. I redirect the HB toward the carcass and we begin our descent. I don't want to alarm her with a gruesome in-your-face video or hologram, so I lower the HB carefully, gradually gathering naked eye data as we descend.

"Looks like a wolf," I say.

"It's a dog. See the collar?"

She's right. A German Shepherd, a big old boy, badly mutilated.

"That dog's a hero," I say. "I bet it saved a human being today, maybe an entire family."

We fly low, follow a blood trail leading northwest. About a mile up we spot another dead creature. A man? No, not a man, something else. I warn Pearl before summoning the hologram.

The figure floats before us over the dashboard. Pearl looks away. A large repulsive manlike creature with a big jaw and tiny eyes appears inches from our faces. Looks like it bled to death, probably after finishing off the dog.

We continue following the trajectory. Three miles later we spot four survivors, two women and two men. When they see us, they burst forward in flight, but only for a few steps before their escape attempt turns into a slow-motion slog.

It would be comical if it weren't so damn sad. I feel bad about terrifying them, but these are the kinds of people we need to be helping, even if we briefly have to scare them.

As the HB draws closer, the old man falls and kicks up a cloud of dust. The old woman drops to her knees beside him and pleads with the sky. Her snow-white hair flows down to her waist. The young woman shields the elders with her body as the young man positions himself before the trio wielding a knife.

We land, and I walk toward them, my open hands raised in the air. For an instant I imagine the guy has a laser pistol tucked behind inside his belt, but that monster probably doesn't get anywhere near them if he does.

"We're here to help. We bring *ayuda*, okay? Help, *ayuda*."

"We think you kill us," the young woman says.

It takes me a moment to understand she means, "We thought you were going to kill us," not, "We think you are going to kill us."

"No, no," I assure her. "We're here to help you. *Ayuda, comprende?*"

Pearl is right behind me, like an offering of flowers.

The old man's left calf is wrapped in a bloody rag. Pearl gives him analgesics and water. She tries to examine the wound but he slaps her hand. Pearl tells the young woman we have food and water and shelter where we live, and that we can treat the old man's wound properly there.

The young man whispers to the young woman. They go back and forth in Spanish.

"We saw a dead German Shepherd. Did the monster do that?" I say, pointing to the old man's calf.

The old woman covers her head with her hands. Her electric hair obscures her face and mutes her peculiar sobs.

The young woman nods.

"Vigo and Paco save Papa," she says.

"Vigo, the dog?"

"No, Vigo is my husband."

"Oh, sorry." I glance at Vigo and nod. "We saw Paco's body. What a brave dog. We followed a trail of blood and found the monster a couple of miles from here. He bled to death. We didn't stop. We thought we would find people in need of help if we continued, and we found you."

"In Stone Heights we have a medical room with lots of supplies and medicines," Pearl says, "including antibiotics, everything *Papa* needs to get well."

The young woman says something only Vigo can hear. He lowers his head and says nothing. We all board the HB.

Ten miles from Stone Heights a drone appears. It heads directly toward us, buzzing hysterically. About thirty feet from the nose of the HB, the drone veers right and loops around to our other side, repeatedly feinting suicidal strikes and repelling back just in time to avoid colliding with us.

Nap says the drones are Stone Heights' immune system. They react aggressively to anything they identify as a threat to the compound, even if the unknown agent is harmless. Any suspect element larger than a finch can trigger an aggressive response, depending on the drone's threat sensitivity settings. The detection of four strangers inside the HB has put this drone on high alert.

Behind us the passengers shift and murmur.

"There's no reason to be alarmed," I assure them. "The drone is doing what it's supposed to do, though a little too enthusiastically. Not a problem. We'll correct that when we get to Stone Heights."

My words sail right over our passengers' heads and are clearly of no comfort to them. Their murmuring soon gives way to a doomsday silence. They're probably wishing they had never laid eyes on us.

"Drones like this keep us safe," I tell them.

Hearing no response, I turn to see if the young woman understands what I've said. She nods, but doesn't translate my words to the others.

"I'm sorry," I say glancing back again, "I don't think we ever mentioned our names. My name is Merlin. This is Pearl. I know Vigo's name, but what is your name?"

"I am Paloma."

Good stars, another Paloma? What are the odds? I stare at the wasteland below. Pearl senses my unease. She places her hand on my forearm. It's light as a sparrow. Paloma is not that unusual a name, I remind myself.

"That's a pretty name," I say.

"What about Papa and Mama?" Pearl says. "What are their names?"

"We don't know," Paloma says. "We find them on the side of the road near a ghost town. Mama pretend she can't talk. And Papa, he sometimes say strange things, like that his name is Mister Lincoln."

"They have no identification?"

"Nothing, only what you see."

"They don't survive without your help," I say.

"We do what we must," Vigo says, his English taking me by surprise.

I turn my head toward him and nod in agreement.

"What is a ghost town?" Pearl says.

"No people, only strange noises, like voices of the dead," Paloma says.

A second drone comes speeding toward us. It gets closer than the first, veers right and darts around to the other side at the last instant. The two drones work in tandem now, alternately provoking us with near collisions, their Buzz feature activated and set to max volume.

Four more drones appear in succession, seconds apart, each more aggressive than its predecessor. The six drones whirl about us like angry wasps, lurching menacingly and withdrawing just in time to avoid crashing. An aura of doom permeates the HB, and the loud, relentless buzzing makes it hard to think clearly.

I ping Nap but he doesn't acknowledge. A minute later I ping again, and then a third time. No response, so I ping Pam.

"Merlin," she whimpers. Her tiny hologram floats before me like a miniature doll.

"Pam, sweetie, where's Dad?"

"He's not happy with you, Merlin."

"Is that right? What did he say?"

"I'm not supposed to be talking to you. I'm sorry."

Pam fizzes and vanishes. I glance at Pearl, whose eyes are bigger than I remember.

"Everything's going to be all right," I announce to everyone in a loud voice.

I try Nap again but get no response. So annoying, but this is no time to be losing my head. I have a contingency plan. When I get back to the Control Room, I'll reclaim my Stealth Admin privileges and execute the plan. A clear set of commands appears in my head, and I begin to whisper them to myself: *1) Login as Stealth Admin; 2) Activate Android Control Mode; 3) Select Yada-7; 4) Select Nap Molly; 5) Select Obedience; 6) Select Total and Unquestioned; 7) Click Execute.*

Quick and easy. Repeat for Loretta, but only if necessary.

Mr. Know-It-All Napoleon Molly knows nothing about *Stealth Admin* privileges. How would he? These concepts don't exist in android consciousness. If they did, what would keep androids from running the world?

I don't want to overreact, but I won't hesitate to do whatever I have to. Sure, I'm fond of Nap and Loretta, even now, and I wish we could have avoided this ugliness, but the fact is, they are not human. They are not Paloma, Vigo, Mama nor Mister Lincoln.

When we're half a mile from the landing deck, another half-dozen drones come speeding toward us like launched missiles. They repeat the same threatening maneuvers as their predecessors and swarm over us as we approach the landing deck. They do their best to impede our descent, thumping against the HB's belly and sending tremors throughout the vessel. Mama unleashes a series of terrible moans, and Mister Lincoln pounds a side window with his open hand.

When we're about thirty feet above the deck, sentinelbots come jogging from all directions armed with laser rifles. They form a wide circle around our targeted landing spot even as the drones wait to the last instant to squirt out from beneath us, then rise silently and circle above us like vultures.

"They're going to kill us," Vigo says as we touch down.

"No one is going to kill anyone," I say.

Nap is still nowhere to be seen. I ping him again. No response. I ping Pam. No response.

"Stay here, please, all of you."

I open the hatch, leap onto the deck, and immediately get pinged. Nap's holographic face floats before me, small as an orange.

"Looks to me like we're having a problem accepting reality," Nap says in an unusual tinny voice. "For starsake, son, reality dictates that people like *them* don't belong with people like *us* in places like *this*."

The tiny face maintains a three-foot distance from me as I advance toward the hangar. One of the sentinelbots shoots off a warning beam that ricochets off the deck a few feet to my left. A piece of the composite deck surface chips off and stings my outer calf.

The pain is surprisingly sharp and penetrating. I pause, expecting to see blood on my pant leg but it's all clear. I limp forward, the blossoming pain stoking my anger. Four sentinelbots rush together to form an impenetrable barrier. I try to bull my way through them but they stiffen like a wall and toss me back onto the ground.

The hoveroo hatch opens and slams shut. Pearl comes running. She kneels beside me, presses her hands against my chest to protect and restrain me at once.

"Dang it, Pearl!" Nap's voice is large now. The tiny Nap face puffs into nothingness. The big voice reverberates with Olympian authority. "Pearl, you come inside now, you hear? Mom's preparing you a delicious Just-Like salmon dish with yummy brown sugar glaze and her special brand of sweet and sour soup."

"Stop playing games, Nap. Come on out here. Let's have a real discussion, father to son."

"Pearl, you come on inside, hon," Nap says. "Mom's worried sick about you. You can make fifty percent of her worry disappear in a heartbeat just by coming inside."

Pearl gives me a *Nap is right* look. I understand and resign myself to losing her. But then she says, "I'm not leaving you, Merlin," and I'm struck by a pathetic desire to hold her in my arms and pretend I don't know she's an android.

"Now see what you've done," Nap says. "This is totally on you, Bubba."

Pearl won't take her eyes off me. "I'm with you, whatever happens," she says.

"Good stars, girl," Nap sighs. "I can't force you to stay, hon. Well, actually, I can, but… Look, Merlin, this goes one of two ways. You take those refugees back to where they came from, and then you and Pearl return home. We all pick up where we left off and get back to being a tightknit, happy family. Better yet, you and Pearl come inside and let Mom feed you some fresh Just-Like salmon. Me and the bots will take care of everything else."

"This isn't you, Nap."

"What in stars does that mean, Bubba? If this isn't me, who is it?"

"For starters, when did you decide hiding your face was the best way to communicate with your son?"

"Now see what you've done?"

"What are you talking about?"

I turn just as Vigo is leaping onto the deck.

"Get back in the hoveroo!" I cry too late.

A stream of beam blasts knocks Vigo to the ground.

"Nap! You sick, twisted monster!"

"You trying to slice me open, Merlin? Well, son, you have succeeded. My heart is bleeding, even as I speak these words. You show me no respect, gratitude, or love. But I tell you what, mine is a big, forgiving heart, and I know you didn't truly believe I'm a… Good galaxies, son, I can't bring myself to repeat what you just called me. It's not your fault, though, you being afflicted with a severe case of Brain Eat, and such."

Miraculously, Vigo stands up, holding his hand against his bloody cheek.

"No harm done, see," Nap says. "Be forewarned, though. Next time these boys won't be so forgiving."

I keep expecting to see Nap's triumphant face appear in the sky, enormous, terrible and godlike. But he chooses to remain hidden. The sentinelbots lower their rifles but remain on alert.

Pearl and I walk back to the hoveroo. I take Vigo's arm, look him in the eye, and say, "I'm going to need you, Vigo. Do you understand me?"

I'm not sure he does, but he nods anyway.

Pearl boards first, followed by Vigo. I hesitate, watch half the drones glide back to the hangar and half the sentinelbots march back to their regular posts.

Nap's voice fills the HB now. "Just so you know, Bubba, I took the liberty to turn off T-REC Auto-Recharge for the HB, meaning you'll have just enough juice to drop the refugees off where you found them and to make it back home, but no more than that. I want you to know how I feel about you and Pearl, and to understand that the two of you belong here in Stone Heights with your family. You know, Merlin, I'm not a young man anymore, and frankly, this family discord has exacted a heavy toll on me. You heard that right. The once indestructible Napoleon Molly is feeling a tad mortal these days. I tell you truly, I'll be as happy as Loretta to put this dark chapter behind us. I want us to go back to having good times like the ones we used to have, you and me floating up above in the HA and then flying home for some quality family time. Yes, sir, the six of us sitting down eating ice cream and planning our next family outing. What's better than that?"

I don't think Nap wants those things. It's Loretta who wants them. Does that make Nap a good husband, or a liar?

Six drones escort us east for a couple of miles before splintering off one by one and flying back to Stone Heights.

Recorded: 03 Jun 2104

Paloma, Vigo, Mama and Mister Lincoln know what Pearl and I are up against, how we've put ourselves on the line for them. They won't judge us, whatever we do.

During the flight, I keep an eye on the electro-charge gauge. Seems Nap didn't lie. We have enough juice to leave the four some sixty miles closer to their destination and still make it back to Stone Heights. They'll be that much closer to what Paloma calls the Haven.

This is the first I've heard of the Haven. I imagine that's where Coronado and all the others were trying to get to. How did we not know about this place?

"Paloma, what is the Haven?" I ask her after we land.

"*Los desperados* go there to be saved."

"*Desperados*, the desperate people?"

"Yes, the desperate people."

"I know of no such city or town."

"It is a place, not a city, not a town."

"How far away is this place?"

"Far away, but maybe not too far away."

Should I express my doubts about the Haven? What good would come of that? Sadness overshadows me.

I watch Pearl, med kit at her side, cleaning and stitching up Mister Lincoln's wound, working through his squirms and yelps and curses. She is methodical, precise, and single-minded. When she is finished with the bandaging, she helps him up. She draws a folding cane from the kit and shows Mister Lincoln how to use it.

I pull emergency food packs and fluids from the HB as Pearl explains the purpose of each item in the med kit to Paloma and Vigo. I show them the survival bags.

"Food and drink, enough for a month," I say.

"You are leaving," Vigo says, his eyes fixed on mine. "I understand."

"We have to go back. There is enough power in the HB to return to Stone Heights, but no more."

Paloma stares at me without blinking.

"You go," Vigo says. "I will protect them."

"Listen to me, we're not going to abandon you. As we were flying here my thoughts became very clear. Pearl and I must first go back so that we can return for you."

"I don't understand," Paloma says.

"Nap will allow us back into Stone Heights. Our quarrel will be forgotten. You will be forgotten. We'll eat and talk as a family, as if nothing has changed. When everyone has gone to sleep, I'll go to the Control Room and—"

I see their troubled faces and stop. *Control Room?* How can those two words bring comfort to a refugee?

"I'm sorry. I didn't mean to confuse you. I have a plan to make everything better. I'll come back for you, I promise. You'll have nothing to fear then."

Despite my efforts, I feel Paloma and Vigo emotionally distancing themselves. Only a sense of inbred courtesy keeps them from turning their backs on me and walking away.

They saw what happened, how I was knocked to the ground, how I had no *control* over anything. They don't know Nap is a machine and that I have the power to neutralize him, the sentinelbots and the drones.

"I will not abandon you," I repeat.

They remain politely expressionless.

"What if Stone Heights is the Haven?" I say, the possibility, however outlandish, suddenly occurring to me.

"Yes, maybe," Vigo offers graciously.

I'm only making things worse, so I nod to Vigo and say, "Pearl, it's best we leave now."

"I'm going to stay," she says.

My impulse is to reject her proposal, but I check myself. She's right. And just like that, I see hope again in Paloma and Vigo's eyes. In their minds, there's no question now that I'll be coming back for them.

I go in the HB and draw from the copilot compartment a laser pistol. Vigo has never used one. I show him the safety, instruct him in the pistol's use, put it in his hand.

He stares at the pistol, then at me. "Okay, thank you."

I climb back into the HB cockpit. "If all goes according to plan, I'll be back tomorrow before sunset."

When the HB lifts to ninety feet, it meets resistance and can rise no higher. Nor can it advance laterally. The hoveroo is repelled each time it attempts to penetrate an invisible ceiling.

Well before the HB runs out of juice and initiates its slow descent, I have a distinct picture of Nap in the hangar fiddling around in the HB's cockpit. Why was I so eager to believe his intentions were honorable? It's obvious he tampered with the electro-charge gauge, and who knows what else.

I land the HB. Paloma tries to hide a smile, but fails. Vigo looks invigorated, ready to take on whatever monsters come our way. Pearl gazes at me with sympathy. Mister Lincoln sounds like he's reciting the Gettysburg Address while Mama tugs on his arm like a little girl.

How long will the food and drink last now, I wonder? Pearl and I go back inside the HB and dig around for hidden resources. We discover another laser pistol and a backpack filled with packets of nuts and seeds.

I remember there's a secret compartment in the HB's tail. There we find a lithium-ion battery-powered four-wheel fold-cart, cooling suits, blankets, an expandable temperature-control tent kit and other survival tools and supplies, as well as additional food and fluids.

Vigo and Paloma help us unload. Their spirits are lifted by our newly discovered bounty and my forced change of plan. I try to share their optimism, try not to think too much about what awaits us. Food and supplies should last us a while, an ironic testament to Nap's cruel mercy.

233

The sun slow-dips into darkness. We set up the temp-control tent within sight of the HB on one side and the woods on the other. When everyone is asleep, I sneak off to the HB and, with Willie keeping watch, I write down what's in my head, so that nothing will be forgotten.

Recorded: 15 Jun 2104

31 July 2104

The new world shimmers under the blazing sun, content to watch us wither. Pearl, our resident nurse and family unifier, hasn't smiled in weeks. No one says much anymore. The spoken word is a thief that robs us of precious energy. I can't remember the last time I spoke to Willie. He stays in my backpack, still and quiet.

For the sake of the others, I keep all my doubts and fears to myself. What would be the point of telling Paloma and Vigo there is no Haven?

The heat is a different kind of monster. Each day at dawn we put on our cooling suits, light as spider silk. Our eyes patrol widely, seeking signs of potential danger.

We travel twice a day, early and late, to mitigate the punishment dispensed by the indifferent sun. We trod northwest. We follow the edge of recovering woods when possible, our legs heavy as in a dream. I try to imagine the river Paloma is certain exists. We stop to eat and rest, and then walk again until it's too dark to see. I watch our rations and fluids dwindle day by day.

We load Mama and Mister Lincoln into the cart. They recline without protest, like groggy children. One day the cart battery dies. Vigo and I drag the cart like oxen, our cooling suits sticking like wax to our skin.

In the distance, we see the dead. We stop. The others rest while Vigo and I go examine the damage. Most of these have been slow deaths, unlike the quick mutilations visited upon Coronado, Paco the German Shepherd, and others.

What is the best way to die? In a flash of brutal finality? Or in conscious lingering agony? Which would I choose? I change my mind from day to day and from corpse to corpse.

We march on. Nearly two days without fluids now. Does water have a scent? I smell something, and through the twilight haze I see a river not far away. An illusion, I suspect, the fabrication of a withering brain. I call no one's attention to it, for what purpose would words of madness serve?

And yet, I lead my little group in the direction of that illusion. They follow, their heads bowed like penitents. No one speaks a word. See, I was right. There is no scent of water because there is no river. My desperate mind has conjured the river, endowed it with odor and hope.

Where else can we go? What other option is there? What choice do we have but to pursue the mercy of imagination?

Vigo remains steady at my side. He's physically stronger than I am and will be the last one to die. I don't envy him the loneliness that awaits him.

"The Haven is not far from the river," he says.

His words are made of dust. I turn my head and gaze at him. He glances at me, waits for a response. These are the first words any of us has spoken today.

I stop and raise my hand. Everyone is staring at me.

"Am I crazy, or is that a river over there?"

I point toward a hazy, indistinct stretch of land. The words coming out of my mouth sound unreal. I touch my cracked lips to keep them from falling to the ground.

"If it is not a river, Merlin, then I too am crazy," Vigo says with a dry smile.

Our pace quickens, but within minutes we stop again at the sight of death. This time I go alone. The detached heads lie neatly side by side in the dirt, a young woman, a young man, eyes stretched with terror, limbs strewn about, torsos split open, organs confiscated.

I rejoin the others and keep the details to a minimum as we slog toward the river. We bypass stagnant pools thick with cattail, sedge and marsh grass and drink where the water runs freely. We fill pouches with water for Mama and Mister Lincoln and watch them drink greedily. We set up camp beneath a small cluster of oaks near a riverbend. Vigo, invigorated, climbs a tree. From there he can see the river loop north and east for a short distance before winding west and north again.

"This river will take us to the Haven," he proclaims when he comes down from the tree.

Maybe.

We divide the last couple of packets of nuts and seeds. Paloma holds court before the freshly hydrated elders. Mama and Mister Lincoln are mesmerized by Paloma's happy reports and her animated body language. Vigo gazes at the river with refreshed eyes. I wonder if he is contemplating his own New Life Plan.

I sit next to Pearl outside the tent. We stare at the glittering, moving waters. Behind us, I hear Paloma explain to the elders, *"Es el Río Haven."*

Pearl places her hand on my forearm. "Are you alright, Pearl?" She nods.

I ache to hear her voice, but she has to preserve her energy. Nap once told me T-REC powers all things, and T-REC is far away.

Tonight, I pull first shift guard duty. I sit in a folding chair with my back to the river. I watch every shadow, laser pistol balanced on my thigh.

"I'm going to kill the monster," I say to the night, "and then we're going to eat him."

Recorded: 01 Aug 2104

02 August 2104

We follow the river north and west. Our diet of minnows, salamanders, eel, bugs and river water, though challenging to the palate, endows the group with a false sense of security. For two days now, I'm convinced we're being followed by a predator or two.

I disguise my anxiety to the best of my ability. I can't let my fear infect the group. Tonight, I'm down for second watch, but I can't sleep, so I relieve Vigo two hours early. He protests with half a heart, yawns and crawls back into the tent. A small kindling fire and laser pistol keep me company.

Behind me the river. The immediate rear area is clear and free of flora that might conceal predators. Before me, fifty yards away, lies a thicket of wild shrubs backed by clusters of oak. What seemed a congenial nod from nature just before twilight has turned ominous. Every chirp, brush, rasp, and creak sets me on edge.

A rough swishing noise gets me up on my feet. I pace slowly toward the thicket, laser pistol at the ready.

Come on in, turd boy. Come get some.

How did that get in my head?

A rustling noise now, louder and more provocative. Dark foliage sways from side to side. I approach, pause at the edge of the thicket, pistol raised. My eyes peel the darkness. All is still and quiet now. I let a minute pass, two minutes.

Let it be a frightened animal. Or better yet, let it be my treacherous imagination.

I glance back at the tent. All seems peaceful there. I hear a cricket chirp. Its lazy refrain doesn't fool me. My eyes grow accustomed to the moonlight. I won't be caught off guard. If there's a monster in the bushes, I'll kill it.

Other crickets start chirping. I enter the thicket slowly, one hand raised against the branches, the other looking to shoot. I glance back in the direction of the tent, but it's become obscured by the dark mass of shrubbery.

A sudden rustling sound rattles my heart. I squeeze the trigger and listen to the disheartening *zip-zip!* of burnt foliage. I shoot again into the darkness and nearly fall as I twist to face a loud commotion on my right that almost immediately goes silent. I feel my mind nearly slip away as I flinch at a faint movement behind me. I whirl, seeking certainty, and nearly lose my balance. I've lost all sense of direction as I imagine the monster slithering toward me over the too soft ground, silent as a snake, positioning itself to tear off my leg and bring me down.

My heart pounds as I strain to hear the sound of water. The river is behind me, yes. I back away toward it. When I'm nearly out of the thicket, I hear screaming. I turn in the direction of the tent, and the shrubbery behind me explodes. I swing my arm toward the oncoming force and shoot. The creature's head flies off its neck, and its propelled body knocks me onto my back.

I drag myself out from beneath the decapitated mass and stagger to the tent. Another monster lies dead inside. Paloma is holding Mama in her arms, stroking her electric white hair.

"Something woke me," Vigo explains, his voice as grave as a prophet's. "I couldn't sleep. I saw you going into the bushes. Then I heard noises, and shooting, and I ran to help you. But on my way, I felt something behind me. I turned and saw a shadow enter the tent. I ran back as fast as I could. I shot the monster in the back, high, near the shoulder. It turned around. I shot it again, this time in the heart, and it fell dead."

"We were lucky tonight, Vigo."

"Yes, we were lucky."

"In the morning we'll have a barbecue."

Vigo and I drag the carcass out of the tent. At dawn we skin the monster and cut steaks to eat.

Recorded: 06 Aug 2104

10 August 2104

Fear drifts alongside us like a ghost. I hear its presence in the turning of the cart wheels, in the shuffle of our weary feet. I see it in the troubled faces of Paloma and Vigo.

"Do you smell that?" I ask Vigo.

"River rot?"

"No, something else."

I won't say what I'm thinking. I won't tell them I smell monsters. I could be wrong.

The Apollyon Effect has many manifestations. We may imagine things that are not. What we see, hear, smell, taste, or feel may have no connection to reality. There may be things we remember that never were. Things we think are true are false. And things we think are false are true.

Vigo frowns. He looks behind us and then across the open field to the west, but makes no further comment.

Mama and Mister Lincoln are reclined against inflatable pillows in the cart. They look like tired children in their cooling suits and, for hours at a time, remain silent. Pearl and Paloma flank the cart on either side, forming a security detail.

"Paloma, do you smell that?"

"Do I smell what?"

Every word now comes at a cost, but we have to talk. "There is a different odor in the air today," I say. "Maybe I'm imagining it."

Eight nights ago, we killed two monsters. Paloma came out of the tent to speak to us the following morning. We were cutting slabs of breast, thigh and flank. "We shouldn't eat that, best to leave it for the vultures," she advised.

I lifted my shirt, showed her my protruding ribs and hip bones, explained our dire need of protein. We'd disposed of the unusable remains, and Vigo and I had put in a good deal of work preparing the meat for safe consumption.

I told her I would take what she said under consideration and make a final decision after the meat was thoroughly cooked and sampled. She shook her head without saying another word and walked back to the tent.

Of course, the smell of cooked meat always makes the hungry mouth water. That's what I was counting on. Mama and Mister Lincoln seemed to come more fully alive at the prospect of sinking their teeth into a juicy steak.

I folded a slab of monster meat and shoved it into my mouth. Much tougher than I had imagined. I chewed until my jaws ached. I swallowed three or four mouthfuls of the fibrous mass before giving up. Within minutes, I knew I had committed a serious blunder. It was too late to warn Vigo, who was chewing away. I got up and loped downriver to purge in the tall marshland grasses.

I returned with my insides sore and hollowed out. Paloma was standing a few feet from her gagging, doubled-over husband. She gave me a *told you so* look, and didn't seem at all interested in dispensing words of consolation to either of us. Vigo willed his way upright and went hobbling downriver.

Later, Vigo and I moved fifty pounds of cooked meat downriver and left it for the scavengers. We battled stomach cramps and bouts of diarrhea for several days.

As far as today goes, no one admits it, but we're all thinking the same thing. There are more monsters out there. We can all smell them now. And we know they'll keep coming. They'll torment us, and when they've worn us out, they'll eat our organs.

Paloma no longer mentions the Haven. Rio Haven has become the river that has no end. Its only purpose now, I think, is to mark our march toward horrible deaths.

Our morning trek is nearing its end. A half mile ahead, concealing the river's bend, I spot a grove. We'll rest there, in the shade of oak trees.

"Look!" Pearl cries.

Her unexpected shout gives us all a start. The singular effort drains her already dwindling energy reserves. She falls to her knees, her hand pressed against the side of the cart.

"Is that Nap?" I say, astonished.

Hoveroo-A glides toward us and slowly descends. My heart races as I consider the possibilities. Could it be Loretta and Nap have changed their minds? I can almost hear Loretta saying to Nap, *If you absolutely have to, then bring the darn refugees too, but only if you have to, you hear?*

The HA swoops down close, rises and then recedes, halting about thirty feet away and hovering in place thirty feet up. Nap appears to be alone. The HA seats six normally, and with Nap, that would make seven. That's why he didn't bring Vick along. We can make this work. Though the HA is designed for six, it can accommodate seven in a pinch. There's a pulldown shelf in the rear by the storage compartment that turns into an emergency seventh seat, which me or Vigo can strap ourselves onto.

"I've got a Porta T-REC onboard," Nap says, his voice loud and clear through the H-speakers. "It'll give Pearl a temporary boost, enough to get her back to Stone Heights in decent shape. Loretta's worried sick about her, given the girl's particularities. That's on you, Merlin. You thought we didn't know about Pearl? You think I wouldn't know such a thing? There's a lot you don't know that I know."

Pearl looks at me. "What particularities? What is he talking about?"

How can he know about Pearl? "That's just Nap trying to be funny," I tell her. No, he doesn't know. He's just trying to get inside my head. "Okay, so you and Loretta talked, and she said she wants us back."

"*Us* meaning you and Pearl, no one else."

"That's nice, but Loretta knows the only way we're going back is with Paloma, Vigo, Mama and Mister Lincoln."

"Mister Lincoln, huh? Don't see the resemblance, but I'll take your word for it."

"You knew this would be nonnegotiable. Loretta knows it too. Come on, land that thing and let's all get out of here. I can't wait to give Mom a big hug and introduce these good people to her. She's going to love them, Nap. So are you."

"Whoa, that was fast," Nap says, his eyes fixed on his dashboard.

"What are you looking at?"

"I started seeing them a few weeks ago, traveling in pairs and small groups, then in larger groups. Too many to ignore. Sent me straight to the SH Archives, where I did my due diligence. They're called Chimera. Kim, for short. These bad boys are human-ape hybrids first generated in military labs a hundred years ago. Their existence was supposed to be Top Secret, but it got leaked, which started a whole confounding hoo-hah over ethical concerns. Once smart folks started seeing the Kim as versatile assets with huge profit potential in the commercial realm, those concerns got relegated to obscurity. A few Kim were illegally released—no one knows by whom—and started multiplying in the wild. Apparently, these monsters are better equipped to handle the rigors of an apocalypse than the rest of us. You can't make this stuff up, Bubba."

I stare across the field to the west while Nap continues talking. I notice a faint discoloration in the lower sky, possibly caused by dust displacement. And the odor I thought I was imagining earlier keeps getting stronger.

"You're going to get an up close and personal look at them real soon," Nap says. "This particular group of about forty is some kind of vanguard. You go farther south and you can see hundreds of them grouped in herds, thousands all told. Seems to me they're seeking cooler pastures, what with the heat and all. Looks like they're heading northwest to the Haven."

"The Haven? What do you know about the Haven?"

"Let me tell you something. Too much knowledge is a heavy burden to keep to oneself. Oh, to be blissfully ignorant.

How I wish it sometimes. I could have unburdened myself with you countless times. A whole lot of hard things I could have told you, but you weren't ready for them. Maybe now you are, but this isn't the time for a father-son talk-talk. The Kim are coming, and they're coming pronto."

"You led them here, didn't you?"

"You mean intentionally?"

"That's exactly what I mean."

"Don't you go condemning me for doing whatever it takes to keep my family together. You can pretend all you want that we're not family, but that won't make you right. So, if you and Pearl would just say your goodbyes, I'll get you both back to Stone Heights where you belong. Pam's dying to see you both. Vick, well, you know the kid, he won't say it, but he's just as giddy as Pam over the prospect. And Loretta? Well, I don't have to tell you about Loretta's feelings for both of you."

"Pearl, go with Nap," I say. "The Mollys will take good care of you."

She gives me what feels like a look of pity, or maybe it's her unit's diminishing charge taking a toll on her social response function.

"I'm staying," she says.

"Stars almighty!" Nap shouts. "Look what you've done to that poor girl!"

"I'm not leaving these people to die."

"Now, that's the dumbest thing I ever heard. Of course, you can leave them to die. By my calculation, you've got less than five minutes to get on board and save your moonstruck asses. Less than two minutes if you insist on bye-bye hugs."

I see them now, small as ants, advancing toward us. The cloud of dust keeps expanding above them.

"Pearl, it's okay. Go with Nap."

Pearl ignores me and waves the HA away.

The hoveroo shifts slightly so that glare flashes over the windshield, obscuring Nap's face, leaving a blank sheet of reflected nothing. HA floats for a few seconds, faceless and silent, then rotates and heads back the way it came.

Pearl and Paloma go inside the tent. Vigo and I stay outside. I'm no field commander, but I can see how this is going to play out. There's no place to run or hide. The Kim will spread out and approach our flanks as far as we'll permit. Some will split off north and south and double back along the riverbank and try to attack us from the rear.

At about a hundred and fifty yards, the Kim halt their advance and spread out in a wide semicircle. They'll be wary of the lasers. They'll test our threat capacity and our resolve. Every laser beam we shoot is going to have to count.

The Kim don't strike me as suicidal. If they deem the price too high, I'm willing to bet they draw back, reassess, and wait for reinforcements.

Recorded: 16 Aug 2104

Most likely, you're going to die today, so try not to crap your pants.

It's not so much a matter of devising a plan of action as just doing what's right in front of you. See the Kim, kill the Kim. See another Kim, kill another Kim. Keep doing that until you can't. That's where my head's at as the hours pass

248

and the planet swallows the blushing sun. Darkness falls and we die? Is that all that remains?

The laser pistol has a nocturnal scope that projects a cone of light a hundred yards, offering a degree of deterrence. We have to stay sharp, kill with cool efficiency, take ownership of the nightmare. Vigo and I have to go full-blown warrior mentality and be focused one-hundred percent on crushing the enemy's resolve and filling the air with the scent of burnt monster meat.

Is that all? Our backs are to the river. There are too few of us, too many of them. They can wait us out for as long as they want. Just remember, try not to crap your pants.

Surprisingly, we survive the night without incident. But the Kim aren't going anywhere. Their patience grows more terrifying by the hour. Starvation won't do us in, exhaustion will. When we're blinded by fatigue, they'll come running from every angle and overwhelm us. They won't wait for us to die. Live human flesh seems to be their meal of choice. They'll split us open, throat to groin, and we'll watch in horror as they pluck and eat our organs.

What will they do with Pearl? Toss her in the river? Leave her to melt in the blazing sun?

The steaming daylight hours pass, and my spirit is heavy with remorse. If I'd listened to Nap, I would have saved Pearl and myself. Death would have come for four, not six. Our return to Stone Heights would have been greeted with hugs and kisses from Loretta, a grand feast, bottomless ice cream and excited talk-talk about the next family outing.

Returning to Stone Heights with Nap would have been the sensible thing to do, and the better math. Four dead, not six. Four that would probably already be dead if not for me and Pearl anyway.

In a couple of hours, the sun will set again. Odds of surviving another night? Slim to none. My mind slips away in search of an alternate reality, one where Hoveroo-B has enough juice to take me and Pearl back to Stone Heights, where I reconfigure Nap and the sentinelbots and the drones, where Pearl gets optimally recharged by T-REC without ever noticing she's a machine, where my synthetic angel configured of circuits, microchips and silicone loves me the way a real woman might.

In this alternate reality we don't forget our friends, we don't leave anyone behind. Refreshed and recharged, we fly back in a souped-up, weaponized hoveroo, pick off Kim one by one on our way, save Paloma, Vigo, Mama and Mister Lincoln and bring them home to Stone Heights, which, it turns out, is the Haven.

A lovely fairy tale. If I could live in that fairy tale and draw the others into it, what would we have to fear? Dying without fear would almost be like not dying at all. It would be like moving from here to there, A to B.

Against a pale orange horizon, I see silhouettes of riders on horses galloping across the dusty plain, their lasers blasting. My body tenses, and my pistol rises up and is ready. The stallions are kicking up clods of dirt.

Vigo is shouting, "Mother of all stars, the cavalry's here!" I rub my eyes and when the blur dispels, I see that what Vigo has shouted is true.

The Kim are in disarray, scrambling in every direction. The clash of howls and the cries of agony and triumph sound almost too theatrical to believe.

Recorded: 17 Aug 2104

We're being transported in an open-air, horse-drawn wagon. Half a dozen Dread Squad horsemen lead the way. Close behind us, Ding Stoker is riding a gorgeous white stallion, and to his left rides Lenguo Piper. Behind them, surrounded by another forty or so riders, four Kim tramp in single file. Tooth-edged steel collars, linked in sequence by metal rods, cut into their thick bushy necks. I try unsuccessfully to ignore their whimpers, moans and musky scent.

Ding has brazenly been eyeing Paloma. I'm really worried about Vigo, what he might say or do. Our rescuers don't appear to be the warmest folks, but they haven't collared us yet, nor subjected us to a forced death march. With any luck, we'll be fed and allowed to rest for a day or two.

Stoker is getting nowhere with Paloma. He tries prying into Pearl's world, no success there either.

I wonder if Pearl registers his interest. I take her hand and gaze steadily at Ding with a nonthreatening, bland expression until he yawns and loses interest. He shoots a glance back at the Kim, looks up, and says to the sky, "Pueblo Town, you've got guests tonight."

The Kim gingerly roll their heads and shoulders, seeking lesser agonies, but there is no escaping the sharp steel teeth. I rub my own neck and suppress stirrings of pity.

"Hey, you, what's your name?" Ding says.

Paloma ignores him. Vigo delivers a warning glare that makes me wonder if we'll all survive this dismal journey.

"Pueblo Town," I say. "Big town?"

Ding studies me, and just when I'm convinced he won't answer my question, he replies, "Old World theme park. Dirt plaza, saloon, wooden church, houses, corral, stable."

"Just wondering, how do you power such a place?"

He looks at me like I'm stupid and bares his teeth, wolf-like, before trotting to the front of the wagon. Not that any random REC would save Pearl anyway. My heart tells me to let her go. I release her hand and pretend she's no longer there, and once again remind myself she's not a human being.

Warm light and noise spill out of the saloon and the wooden houses as we enter Pueblo Town. The dirt plaza is illumined by oil lanterns just bright enough to obscure half the stars in the night sky. Town folk begin to appear as the riders dismount and hand the reins over to stable boys and girls who lead the horses away.

Delvin Stoker materializes in our midst. He looks us over, introduces himself, then says something to Ding I can't make out. He checks the prisoners and exchanges a few words with Lenguo Piper. The Kim are led to the center of the square, where they're chained to a stone obelisk the height of twelve tall men, one captive bound to each of the four sides.

A woman with a radiant smile walks up to us. She's followed by a small group of women and men. She says her name is Bess Stoker, asks if we're hungry, and then directs her assistants to carry our belongings to one of the wooden houses. I hand over my backpack with Willie in it. There's no keeping these strangers from going through our belongings if they want. But I don't anticipate a toy rabbit in Sleep mode, or anything else they find in our bags, will set off alarms.

A generous supper of cabbage and potato soup with real meat bits, bread, and homebrewed ale lifts our spirits. Within a half-hour of sitting down to eat in the noisy saloon, Paloma and Vigo are looking livelier and more optimistic than I've seen them in weeks. Mama and Mister Lincoln seem content and are showing rare interest in their surroundings. Even Pearl's demise appears to be on hold, or slightly reversed, as if the atmosphere of optimism permeating the place were somehow reviving her circuitry.

"We've got a lot to talk about, Merlin," Bess says as she leads us to our rooms. "But that can wait till tomorrow. What you folks need more than anything else right now is a full night's rest followed by a robust breakfast. Sleep tight now, you all, and we'll see you in the morning."

The others fall asleep quickly. The euphoria of the saloon soon dissipates in the darkness, and I find myself wide awake. What do the Stokers want from us? Is Ding going to be a problem? And what's his old man, Delvin, going to do with those wretched prisoners?

Recorded: 24 Aug 2104

12 August 2104

An explosion of bugles and drums wakes us. I'm the first out the door.

The Kim are gone! Riders are scrambling, flinging themselves onto horses and racing over the dirt square and out the front gate.

"What happened?" I say grabbing one of the stable boys by the arm.

"Someone freed the Kim," he says pointing to the blood-stained obelisk.

Bess is shaking her head as she approaches me. "I keep telling Delvin torture doesn't sit well with everybody. We're over two-thousand strong here, and not everyone shares the same inclinations."

"Any idea who did it?"

She gives me a long look, then grins. "Sure, I have an idea. We all have our ideas. I'm no proponent of torture myself, not even for savages. It's no secret. Delvin knows where I stand on the issue."

Pearl, Paloma and Vigo join us.

"Those creatures can't help who they are any more than we can help who we are," Bess says. "Doesn't make any sense to increase suffering in the world willy-nilly. There's more than enough of it to go around even on the best of days."

I wonder if she's testing me. I decide to keep my thoughts to myself.

"You have to understand," she says, "Delvin is special."

She pauses, studies me.

"You see, the Angel Centauri has given Delvin deep knowledge of the Kim. He's instructed Delvin to bleed and burn them alive so that the demons governing them get expelled. The Angel Centauri has instructed Delvin to perform each exorcism in public as an act of mercy and to build up the faith of the righteous."

I scan her face for hints of skepticism or mockery, but Bess Stoker looks as clinically detached as a psychoanalyst.

"I instructed Ding to put the fugitives out of their misery wherever they find them, and leave their bodies for the scavengers," she says. "There's no explaining some kinds of mercy to the children, and we've got our share of young ones here."

"Will there be an investigation?"

"Of course. There's always an investigation, and a trial. And then we move on."

"A trial?"

"If a suspect is identified, yes, a trial."

"And if no suspect is identified?"

"Delvin takes his cues from the Angel Centauri," she says and walks away.

* * *

Toward the end of our afternoon meal in the saloon, Lenguo Piper appears and tells me Delvin wants to speak to me. I follow him to a table where Delvin, Ding and a couple of other Dread Squad riders are having drinks.

"Have a seat," Delvin says. He stares at me for a long minute. "What do you have for me?"

I don't like the sound of that, but I don't want that showing on my face. "I have a temp control tent and some cooling suits."

Delvin shakes his head. "I don't need things, I need information."

"What kind of information would you like?"

"Everything you know."

"You mean, what I know about out there?" I say, pointing to the saloon's swing doors.

He waits.

"I'll tell you the most important thing I know right now about what's going on out there. The Kim are moving north, and they're coming in big numbers."

"Is that right?"

I'm not inclined to disclose the existence of the Mollys or Stone Heights, so I lie.

"I could see them from above."

"No kidding."

"From high up in a hoveroo, I could see them grouped in herds of hundreds, thousands all told."

"You and those others saw thousands of Kim."

"No, not those others. I meant me and Howie, who's dead now."

"Howie's dead. Who the furp is Howie?"

"We worked together."

"Where's the hoveroo?"

"Had to leave it. Engine malfunction forced us to make a landing several miles from the river. We followed the river northwest on foot for weeks."

I gaze at Delvin. He knows I'm lying, or highly suspects it. I don't have the luxury of changing my story at this point, so I pile on.

"One morning I went downriver to relieve myself. The sun was just starting to rise. I sat under a tree and watched. It was beautiful. I lost track of time. When I started back, I saw two figures crouching in front of our tent. From a distance, they looked like a couple of refugees having breakfast. That's what I wanted them to be. Howie had a big heart, but he was too damn trusting for his own good. I used to tell him that. I cursed myself for not having taken my laser pistol with me. I drew closer and hid behind some bushes to get a better look. One of them lifted its bloodied jaws to the sky, and I knew it was too late to do anything. I stayed hidden for over an hour, until the Kim left. I went back and buried what was left of Howie. A few days later I ran into those other people. We followed the river northwest for two months. A week and a half ago, we survived an attack. And if not for the timely intervention of your Dread Squad, I'm not sitting here talking to you."

"How many Kim did you say you saw?"

"From above, all told, at least four-thousand. We spotted several herds heading north, like I said, seeking relief from the heat, I imagine. I'm concerned at least one of those herds is going to stumble upon Pueblo Town."

Delvin closes his eyes for several seconds. I get the feeling he's being counseled by the Angel Centauri. He stands up and leaves the saloon without saying another word.

Recorded: 26 Aug 2104

31 August 2104

It's the end of August, and we're still in Pueblo Town. In retrospect, I got a little carried away during my Delvin interrogation. Shouldn't have said anything about the Kim coming our way. Don't know what got into me. The Stoker Squads have reported no sightings of herds within a hundred miles, which makes me look bad.

The Kim presence within the general area is more of the aimless and scattered, rather than big herd, variety. But aimless and scattered is still good enough to limber up the horses and keep the cavalry sharp. At least twice a week, Stoker horsemen catch the occasional monster and chain it to the obelisk.

The traitor who released the original four captives remains unknown, at least officially. No one talks about it anymore, and no further seditious acts have been reported since our first day here.

Midmorning, Delvin Stoker calls an assembly of the entire population of Pueblo Town in the big dirt square and reveals the Angel Centauri's new command: get the children directly involved in the public exorcisms through the ancient practice of stoning.

Later that day, over a hundred kids hurl rocks at a bound and wounded Kim until they kill it. The disfigured body is dragged by a pair of horses a couple of hundred yards outside the walls and burned in the Purification Pit.

When I tell Vigo we have to get out of this place, he goes silent on me. I press him, and he tells me he's going to be a daddy. Paloma is beginning to show, haven't I noticed?

Naturally, she wants to stay, at least until after the baby is old enough to survive the rigors of travel in this unpredictable and dangerous world. Or they can stay in Pueblo Town forever, who knows? Vigo tells me Paloma is beginning to think Pueblo Town might be the Haven.

Bess Stoker does seem to like the young couple. She picked up quickly on Paloma's condition and assured her that mother and child would receive the best possible care.

Since meeting the Stoker matriarch, they've had no issues with Ding Stoker or anyone else. Vigo also tells me he had a dream in which Bess wrests control of Pueblo Town from Delvin, who everyone knows has lost his mind. Vigo tells me he puts great stock in dreams.

Inwardly, I entertain the possibility of just me and Pearl leaving, or me alone, but my responsibility to the others weighs on me, and I dismiss the temptation.

Pearl conserves her diminishing energies for her mornings with Paloma. They often sit side by side in the saloon kitchen peeling potatoes and shucking corn. Sometimes I see them gathering eggs in the chicken coops and feeding the hogs.

Vigo and I have been receiving horsemanship lessons. We've begun to accompany Stoker Squads on limited surveillance duty. Some field labor and livestock tending await us down the road, but for now, the relatively safe environs of Pueblo Town afford me time to think, plan and even write and dictate notes to Willie. And there is no quieter place in Pueblo Town to do that than the old wooden church.

The first time they saw me, the cats froze mid-stretch, mid-step, mid-lick. They all stared at me with the focus of a single creature, totally absorbed by my seemingly miraculous presence. When was the last time any human had entered this place, I wondered?

Willie and I sit at a table in a room off the altar called the sacristy. The cats assemble around us. In their world, the talking rabbit—who was at first an object of terror, then of intrigue—has evolved into a kind of deformed cat.

The cats like to hop onto a mahogany stand pushed up against the wall. They exit and enter the church through a barred window in the sacristy. Today, while I'm in mid-dictation, several of them come dashing into the sacristy and leap through the iron bars out the window. I have just enough time to hide Willie in my backpack before Lenguo Piper saunters in.

The large silver cobra head belt buckle seems more prominent than usual. I say nothing. Lenguo waits for me to speak. I don't.

"What are you doing?" he says.

I'm tempted to tell him to go furp himself, but I hold my tongue. He eyes the backpack lying on the floor against a table leg.

"Something I can help you with, Lenguo?"

"Help me? Nah, just came by to make sure you and the cats aren't lacking for anything."

Lenguo Piper's laughter continues to echo inside the church walls long after he's gone.

Recorded: 01 Sep 2104

07-08 September 2104

Two more Kim are dragged into the town square and chained to the obelisk. They squirm and moan and whimper, and are left to bleed and bake in the sun all day long. Just before dawn, Pueblo Town wakes to another round of bugle blasts and thundering drums. It's happened again! Someone has released the Kim prisoners!

Vigo is assigned to the Dread Squad, but this time, with no reason given, I'm not summoned for duty. Before leaving, Vigo says, "Should anything happen to me, promise you'll take care of Paloma and the baby."

The Dread Squad is a strong, disciplined, heavily weaponized force, far superior to any random assembly of savages. What could possibly happen to Vigo? And yet, I keep hearing Lenguo's terrible laughter. Vigo repeats his request in a soft, almost desperate, voice. He mistakes my failure to respond immediately as ambivalence.

"Of course, Vigo. How can you even ask such a thing?" I smile to reassure him. "The Dread Squad is strong. Nothing is going to happen to you. In your absence, I'll make sure

Paloma and the baby are safe and well taken care of, I promise."

"Keep an eye on Ding, okay?"

"He's not going?"

Vigo shakes his head. "No, Lenguo Piper is leading the Dread Squad today."

"Okay, listen, you do your job. Don't let your guard down. And don't worry, I'll make sure Ding doesn't go anywhere near Paloma."

"And if he does?"

"It's not going to happen, okay? I'm going to talk to Bess."

Vigo stares at me. "Okay, Merlin, I trust you."

I pat him on the shoulder. To my relief he says nothing more and mounts his horse. I watch him trot away with the other riders. I'm suddenly very tired. I wonder if my fatigue is that obvious to others, if it's the reason I wasn't called to ride with the Dread Squad.

I find Pearl and Paloma in the saloon kitchen. Paloma is whispering something to Pearl, who appears to be listening, or at least mimicking the act of listening. I interrupt Paloma, tell her I need to speak to Pearl. Paloma leaves, one hand on her belly.

"Maybe we should start thinking about leaving Pueblo Town," I say. "Things aren't right here. I'm very concerned. When Vigo returns, I'll try to convince him we'll all be better off away from here. Pearl, can you talk to Paloma, try to convince her we should leave this place?"

She studies me. Why do I hurt so? Is it because I imagine love in those eyes? Her hand rises and reaches for my lips. I watch the warmth of her eyes cool to a glaze and her fingers lock in space, inches from my mouth.

"Oh, Pearl."

Somehow, I manage to abort the cry rising to my throat. I swallow my grief whole, its power leaving me nearly breathless.

Pearl's demise is a perplexing and devastating blow to the others. Paloma is disconsolate. Vigo, back from a failed search mission, is confused and troubled by what's happened. Mama insists on touching every inch of Pearl's face before she's formally buried in the Pueblo Town Cemetery, and Mister Lincoln paces to exhaustion before sitting on the dirt.

"How mysterious and terrible," Vigo says. "Someone so young and kind, to die suddenly, and for no clear reason."

I can't tell them Pearl was an Elara-3. It would stain their memory of her forever.

"Her beautiful heart stopped," I say. "We don't know the reason. A mysterious illness, perhaps a virus, maybe something to do with the Apollyon Effect."

The next morning, Vigo rides off again with the Dread Squad. I go to the church with Willie. The cats sense my grief and gather around me. After a couple of hours, they begin to stir, but not one leaps out through the barred window. I hide Willie anyway. Paloma enters the sacristy and tells me she has cried enough to fill a barrel with tears.

This is the time, I realize. I reach for the backpack and introduce Paloma to Willie. He pronounces her name perfectly and registers her face and voice. She is astonished. I tell her about the Notes.

Then, in a chilling moment, I find myself echoing Vigo.

"Should anything happen to me, Paloma, I want you to take Willie and talk to him, so that nothing is forgotten."

She nods, though she doesn't fully understand. For now, it's enough that she is willing. When the time comes, Willie will help her, and she'll know what to do.

Later, I see Ding in the plaza talking to a woman named Roxie. The woman looks to be upset about something. He's listening, frowning, and questioning her. The exchange feels like a performance. Something bad is going to happen, and I need to figure out what that is.

Recorded: 09 Sep 2104

08 September 2104

Paloma wakes me at one in the morning, tells me the Dread Squad has returned, but Vigo is not with them. I calm her down, tell her I'll go find out what's going on. As is always the case, the noise pouring out past the saloon swing doors after a hunt is always rowdy and crude.

I walk in, order an ale and stand at the bar. Unlike most of the drinkers, Ding, Lenguo Piper, and others are having a quiet discussion. I catch bits and pieces, something about predawn patrol and the Winch twins. Then I hear his name.

"Where is he?" I demand as I approach the table. "Where is Vigo?"

Lenguo looks at Ding and pretends to be shocked by my outburst. "Why, he's in church, isn't he?" he says, looking concerned. He glances at the other riders. "Last I heard, he was in church."

Head-nodding and mumbled affirmations follow.

"The boy must have had a strong need of prayer," Lenguo adds with a straight face. He chugs down ale and spits out a mouthful as he bursts into laughter.

Ding is not amused. He stands up and says, "Your *compadre* is being held on suspicion of treason and awaits trial."

"What are you talking about, treason?" I shout.

Ding asks one of the other riders something that has nothing to do with Vigo, and they all go back to talking and laughing about other things.

I storm out of the saloon.

"It's no lie. Your friend is being held in the church."

I turn around, see someone leaning up against the saloon front. The lighting's bad, so it takes me a moment to figure out who it is. One of the Dread Squad riders, an anvil-faced guy named Hammertuss. I had never heard this guy utter a single word until now. Why should I believe him? And why would they stick Vigo in a church sacristy when they could hold him in a jail cell? No, I don't think I'll stick around to hear another rider have a good laugh at our expense.

I head back to the guest house and stand at the front door. What do I say to Paloma? I don't say anything, not yet. What if Hammertuss was telling the truth?

I turn around and head over to the church. A dim golden glow emits from the wide-open front doors. The inside is illumined by dozens of candles. The smell of paraffin is strong as I march up the center aisle. Slouched over the presider's chair on the altar is a big, burly armed guard. I stop at the foot of the altar.

"What do you want?" I hear to my left.

On the front pew, a second guard is sitting up from a prone position.

"Is Vigo in there?" I say pointing to the sacristy.

"He's not going anywhere," the burly guy says from the altar.

"I need five minutes to talk to him."

"Best you move on," the skinny guard says. "If you don't, things are going to get complicated."

"Five minutes is really not that complicated," I reply.

The big guy stands up, rolls his shoulders, cracks his neck, and says, "Are we going to have a problem?"

I don't wait for him to come down off the altar. I turn and walk out of the church without saying another word. I stop at the Stoker house and stand motionless before the front door. I need to talk to Bess really bad. But what seems more likely to happen is an ugly encounter with Delvin Stoker and the Angel Centauri, maybe an appearance by overly aggressive guards who knock me around for a while before sending me off with a bloody nose and dire warnings echoing in my ears.

What is the Stoker penalty for treason, anyway?

I knock, softly at first, then a little louder. I wait. With any luck, Delvin's in the woods talking to Centauri and Bess is alone. I bang on the door a third time, and it opens with a lingering creak. She's not pleased to see me, but doesn't say a word. She listens to what I have to say and leads me back to the church. She instructs the guards to give me ten minutes with Vigo.

"It's crazy," Vigo says. "This woman named Roxie told Ding Stoker I said filthy things to her. She accused me of lusting after her."

"That's why you're being held?"

"She's lying."

"Obviously, but Ding told me you were being charged with treason. How is lusting an act of treason?"

"I wasn't lusting after her or speaking filth. She's a liar."

"I know she is. Look, I'll talk to Bess tomorrow. We'll get this all straightened out, but you'll have to sit tight for a few hours, okay?"

"They're saying I'm the traitor who freed the Kim."

"Wait, what?"

"They say they have witnesses."

"Good stars. Like I said, I'm going to talk to Bess."

"Bess knows all about it."

"Oh? She didn't say a word to me. But I wouldn't read too much into that. She made it possible for me to see you, didn't she? By the way, who are these so-called witnesses?"

"Roxie's brothers."

"Her brothers claim they saw you free the Kim?"

"The skinny guard, Carl, he was in the saloon. He heard the whole thing."

"Carl talked to you about this?"

"He doesn't believe them either. He said he tries to be fair-minded, but fairness isn't always a consideration in Pueblo Town."

"Carl, the guard that was lying on the front pew?"

"Yes, the skinny one, not the big guy."

"When Paloma told me you never made it to the house, I walked over to the saloon. I heard Ding, Lenguo and some of the others talking about the Winch twins."

"That's them, Roxie's brothers. After we rode out the second morning to track down the Kim, Carl said the Winch twins showed up at the saloon. They said they needed to talk to Ding. Carl was there. He heard everything. The twins claimed they saw me walking back to the house just before four, on the morning the Kim escaped. They said I must have passed out drunk somewhere and had just woken up, so they didn't think much about it at the time. When their shift was over, they went to sleep. About an hour later they woke up to the bugles and drums."

"So they decided, based on no evidence, that you were the traitor?"

"Carl said they confessed to having been drinking on duty and dozing off. One of them claimed he had walked over to the obelisk at three-thirty and found the prisoners asleep and securely bound. They said they should have come forward sooner and expressed deep remorse."

"This whole thing is laughable, ridiculous."

"They're being fined for sleeping on the job, and I'm being charged with treason."

"No, they're being rewarded for lying. The Stokers are covering up for the real culprit. And Roxie's accusations are meant to turn the town folk against you."

I won't say it out loud, but I strongly suspect Bess is the traitor. I'm willing to bet she gave the order to free the captives. Thing is, you can't have the town's matriarch charged with treason, so blame one of the newcomers, someone Ding Stoker would be happy to see put away.

"Carl told me I have the right to legal representation. He said Delvin would assign someone if I had no one to speak for me."

"I'll represent you. Did they say when the trial begins?"

"Thursday."

271

"Okay, that gives us a couple of days to prepare."

Carl opens the sacristy door, tells us to wrap it up. I tell Vigo I'll talk to Paloma, try to ease her concerns. I take his face in my hands and kiss his forehead. I feel a father's love for him, though I'm only a few years older. Carl pretends not to notice, then accompanies me past the altar while the other guard remains slumped like a whale in the presider's chair. Out in the steamy night, Carl grabs my arm.

"Nothing you can say, no evidence you can produce, no reason you can appeal to, is going to change the outcome," he says.

"Is that so?"

"Your friend is going to be convicted of treason."

"The Winches are liars. All three of them. I'll prove it."

He nods. "Yeah, the Winches come from a long line of liars. Everybody knows it."

"You're telling me truth won't matter at all?"

"Not in Pueblo Town, no sir. And besides, the obelisk was scrubbed clean today."

"What does that have to do with anything?"

Carl shakes his head and walks back into the church. I touch my neck. I can almost feel the sharp steel teeth tearing into my own flesh, and blisters erupting across my face, shoulders and chest. I can almost hear Ding Stoker and Lenguo Piper shouting encouragements to the child executioners, and the terrible thudding of stone against flesh.

Oh, Pearl, where are you? I look at the stars. She's everywhere and nowhere.

I'll talk to Bess in the morning, but Paloma is waiting for me. The walk back to the wooden house is long, and my legs grow heavier with each step. I don't want to do this. Right now I'm just not strong enough to bear the fear in Paloma's eyes or to summon up words of encouragement that are sure to fall flat. I'm tired.

When I go inside, I see they're all asleep. Amazingly, even Paloma. I lie down, grateful for small mercies.

Recorded: 09 Sep 2104

10 September 2104

Dear unknown survivor, my name is Paloma Gutierrez.

One day Merlin talked to me about Vigo. He said everything going to be okay. I said, "Merlin, don't you lie to me. I see your eyes and they say everything not going to be okay. So, you tell me the truth."

He said, "Paloma, things are going to be hard, but we are going to do our best to make everything okay. Come, let's go eat breakfast."

In the saloon we ate eggs and pork roll and drank coffee, but Merlin didn't talk about Vigo. Then we went to the wood house and Merlin looked concerned and it made me nervous. He said, don't worry. He said he only had to put his thoughts in proper order. He went in the room and closed the door.

I know my nerves made Mama nervous. She started moaning, so I took her and Mister Lincoln to the plaza. We sat on a bench and watched the children play kick ball and splash water on their face because it was so hot.

Mister Lincoln drew trees in the dirt with his finger, and Mama used a fan like a *señorita* to cool her neck. But she was not happy. She dropped the fan on the ground and got up. Me and Mister Lincoln followed her. When Mama got to the front gate, she started to run, but it was easy to catch her.

"Mama, where you going?" I said, holding her arm. She slapped my hand away and walked back to the house.

I gave Mama a glass of water and knocked on the door where Merlin was but no answer. I went inside the room and Merlin was sleeping, so I touch his arm. He sat up and said, "I have a new plan, Paloma, better than the old plan."

But Merlin never told me the old plan. He got up and said, "Wait here, don't go anywhere."

I waited three hours for him. When he came back, he told me the new plan. Somebody—he did not say who or how—was going to free Vigo from the church when Pueblo Town was sleeping. We were going to leave before everybody wake up and meet with Vigo in some place.

I asked him how is this possible? He said he talked to Bess Stoker and she was going to help us. He said Bess had many followers who think Delvin is a lunatic and the Angel Centauri is a demon from hell.

I was worried, so I said to him, "But Merlin, what if Bess Stoker is playing a trick on us?"

Merlin could not answer my question, because it was an idea that never came into his head. I thought, oh my God, we are all going to die.

So how could I sleep even one hour?

Merlin was sitting on the couch by himself. I sat next to him. Only noise I could hear was Mister Lincoln snoring. Then there was knock on the door, like noise made by a small child. Merlin opened the door, and I saw a little man.

The little man talked to Merlin. Then Merlin said to me, "Go wake up Mama and Mister Lincoln. We have to go."

The little man was Romo. He stayed next to the window, looking very hard at the night. Then we all went outside into the plaza and began walking. I didn't see the guards, and thought, okay, maybe it is true that Bess is helping us. We walked in the shadows and went out through the gate.

After one hour walking, we saw the trees, and three men and one woman standing there. One man walked out of the shadows. "Oh my God, Vigo!" I cried and he kissed my tears. There were beautiful horses and two wagons waiting for us near that place. My heart began to fly like a bird.

One horseman went in front of the first wagon, one behind the second wagon. Mirembe drove the first wagon. She was a very nice lady, but not a good talker. I don't know what happened to Bess Stoker, or how Vigo got free. I don't want to know anything that takes away my happiness.

I was happy, but Merlin was sad. I knew how much he missed Pearl. When possible, I visited him in the other wagon. Every time, I gave him a big hug, and said nice things to make him smile, but he didn't remember how to smile.

One time I think Merlin's sadness was on my face, because Mirembe looked at me and said, "What does *Paloma* mean?" I said, "Dove, and what does *Mirembe* mean?" She said, "Peace." And we both smiled, and we talked about nice things, like babies and flowers.

Romo said we were going to a place to begin a new life. He didn't say it was the Haven, but I thought, yes, of course, it is the Haven. We were going to be okay, I thought, just like Merlin promised.

Maybe one day Merlin finds happiness again, I thought. I had so much to be happy for. I had my baby inside me, and Vigo, Mama, Mister Lincoln and Merlin. And now I also had Mirembe, Romo, Carl, Hammertuss, and Lars, all of them beautiful people with beautiful names. Together we made a beautiful family.

Recorded: 25 Sep 2104

20 September 2104

Reality won't let you hide or forget what you don't like. We want to remember good things only, but bad things come like bandits and steal our happiness. We want nice surprises, but too many times we get bad ones. To die is no surprise. But when and how? Who can say?

In dream I saw Pearl in front of the trees. She waved to me. The two wagons were stuck in the sand. I told Vigo, but he was talking with Romo and didn't notice. I started walking across the desert to talk to Pearl. Maybe she could help us. But a tornado came and blew sand everywhere. I couldn't see, and I couldn't breathe.

The fear in my heart was like an arrow, and the sharp pain woke me up. I saw the sun rising on the river, and little purple and yellow flowers all around. I heard Romo say Merlin was dying. We went to the other wagon. Merlin looked at me like I was a stranger. I covered my mouth to not cry.

"Merlin, you not feeling too good today?"

Who is this woman, he was thinking?

I said to Romo, "Why is he like this?"

Romo shook his head and looked confused.

I touched Merlin's cheek. It was cold like ice.

"Merlin, come walk with me," I said. "The baby wants you to walk with us. Come see the pretty flowers."

I tried to help him get up, but his eyes said no. I looked at Vigo, and he shook his head. So, I got on my knees. I don't know why, I just did. Maybe my heart was too heavy and I had no strength left to stand.

When I looked at poor Merlin, I remembered a story from the Old World about a king and a kneeling man. The king touched the man's shoulders with a sword, and the man became a knight. And the knight had a special purpose, which was to always fight for what is good and true.

Merlin tried to touch my mouth, but his hand stopped in the air. His hands and eyes and breath, and everything that was Merlin, stopped.

After we buried him, I said, "But Willie, I have no expertise to dictate Notes. And Vigo, his English is much better."

Willie said, "Correct, Vigo's English is much better and he has expertise, but you have something Vigo does not have. You have new life inside you."

"Yes, okay, I have new life inside me. A baby, and so?"

Willie said, "Merlin explicitly instructed me to tell you that when he goes away, he wants you, Paloma Gutierrez, to keep and continue the Notes."

Explicitly, he said, okay? So how could I say no?

We rode the next day until the sun went down. I fell asleep and had another bad dream. It was like a painting of horses jumping and crying, their big teeth cracking like glass. I woke up. It was dark, and we were under attack by the Kim!

The lights from laser pistols showed Kim holding rocks and clubs, which was a surprise, but they had no chance against lasers. Vigo killed four Kim, maybe more. The attack was ten minutes, then Kim retreat. When light came, Romo counted nineteen dead Kim. But Carl, Lars and Mirembe were dead. And seven horses dead. One wagon had broken wheel that could not be fixed, and other wagon could not move because of dead horses.

Romo rode out to see the situation. Vigo and Hammertuss worked to free wagon from dead horses and arrange new team, then to dig graves for Carl, Lars and Mirembe.

When Romo came back, he said the Kim were gone, but he saw big dust cloud made by large Kim herd coming from the west. Another cloud from the south was made by Stoker squad, so there was no time to bury our poor friends.

Romo said Delvin Stoker going to murder us right where we are if we stay, except Vigo. He wants him alive for stoning purification in Pueblo Town. Hammertuss said Delvin Stoker is a crazy, bloodthirsty monster and maybe he listen to Angel Centauri instead of common sense and waste his time killing many Kim before chasing after us.

I got up and took Carl's laser pistol and showed to Romo. I said to him, "I know how to use laser, okay? So you go help Hammertuss and Vigo get wagon ready to go. I do watch."

Romo hesitated, but he knew I was right. I sat on ground with my back against the broken wheel. Romo was gone one minute when I get a surprise from two Kim who came from nowhere. I fired and missed my first two shots. But I kept my nerve. When they got too close, I shot one in the chest, and he fell dead, and the other I get in the arm. He tried to run away. I shot him in the back. He fell and rolled in the ground making horrible screams.

"Paloma!"

It was Vigo. I said, "We okay. You finish what you doing so we can get out of here."

I walked to the wounded Kim and pointed laser pistol at its head and pulled trigger to end its misery. I was dizzy when I went back to the wagon. I sat down on the ground and put my head between my knees. When the blood came back to my head, I looked up and saw hundreds of Kim coming from west and Stoker squad coming from south.

Vigo came for me and we all got in the good wagon. Hammertuss shouted to the horses, "Let's ride!" and we started to move slowly over the rough land, but then faster and faster.

Romo rode up next to us and said in a loud voice, "If something happens to me, remember what I told you. Follow the river north, always. Late tomorrow you'll see the river bend to the west. You can make camp there for a couple of hours only. Then keep going north and west. Just before sunset you'll see the forest. Go there, to the trees!"

"We are all going to the trees, Romo," Vigo said. "You and Hammertuss too! We all go!"

"Remember what I told you!" Romo shouted. Then he took his horse, named Apollo, and he rode watch behind us.

From far away, the Kim herd and the Stoker squad looked like two armies of ants preparing to fight. Hundreds of Kim were going to die today. How many Stokers were going to die? Even if one died, it would be too much. Romo was right when he said the Angel Centauri was Delvin Stoker's demon master.

He was also right what he said about the forest, and after many more hours riding, we could finally see the trees far away, and no more signs of Kim or Stokers. But then the other ones appeared, and we knew we had to face one more attack. This time no Kim, no Stokers. This time the enemy was other humans that looked like us, with wagons and horses. They shot two of our horses, and they fell dead and made the wagon stop. Romo and Hammertuss put Vigo and me on Apollo. They said they would protect Mama and Mister Lincoln. But I knew they were all going to die.

I wanted to protest, but Vigo touched my lips and shook his head. Romo slapped the horse on the back, and Apollo raced over the plain. Vigo told me to hold tight. I held him tight and did not look back. For a time, we heard shooting, and then we heard nothing.

We had no words left to speak.

After the long ride, Apollo walked into the forest. We saw no more attackers. I thought, this is the Haven. I remembered Merlin and Pearl. I remembered Mama and Mister Lincoln, Romo and the others, and I began to cry.

And then I heard one bird singing.

Recorded: 30 Sep 2104

Birdsong

2094 - 4844

An Ord, a Deo and a Xeno walk into a Greek bar...

- Doctor Marny Blue

One

That's me in the Cloud, a female of indeterminate age. That's me scrolling life bits, bloodlines, twisted histories, Merlin's *Notes to Unknown Survivor*, and yes, Krol's *The Human Show*.

That's me up there behind a virtual blue desk gathering the lost pieces, sorting, editing, manifesting here and there with a poke or a prompt and looking exactly the way you might imagine.

I wasn't always like this. I had a *before*, when Topper and I floated in the waters of new life. The blood mystery of Mama's joys and sorrows seeped down to us, worked its way inside us. We grew eyes and ears. Then came the surprise of her voice.

August 31, 4090, Topper slipped out into the cold, blinding whiteness, screaming like I didn't know he could. And me? I was gone, watching and listening from the Cloud.

Mama lay awake in bed grieving and sore, her breast leaking while Topper slept. Then I heard a voice like living water say, "Gather the lost pieces, Lola, and sing them in the Key of Blue."

And so I do.

I watched the Xeno hook their first big fish two-thousand years ago. I'll start there. How did they do it? It was easier than you might expect.

I'll give you the short version, and then we'll move on. It goes something like this:

New Year's Day, 2094 AD, Burr Brumbo tightens the knot of his diamond-studded tie, gazes at his puffy face in the lavatorio mirror, and chirps, "And why the hecky-ho not?"

Pin streams of air whistle out both his ears and anal cavity.

Hmm, what's this, he wonders?

Lightheaded, he totters back to his gilded highhub, hand tapping along the pearly wall. He steadies himself, loosens his tie, notes air streams flowing up his nostrils—faintly scented of beef bouillon—and starts to feel more like himself.

Air going out, air coming in. A peculiar sensation, to be sure, though not entirely unpleasant. No, not at all.

What should he have expected? Being head honcho of Brumbo Luxury Enterprises and Uber Six Tycoon is one thing. Making a run at the presidency of the Reconstituted States is quite another.

No doubt, something or someone says.

Huh?

Don't get me wrong, POTRS is fine. Why, it's more than fine, but while you're at it, why not elevate to Master of the Universe?

What in stars?

Brumbo creeps back to the lavatorio, splashes cold water on his face, dabs his eyes, cheeks and chin with a fluff towel, and scrutinizes his flushed face in the mirror. The curious vacate-refill exchange has, for the moment, been suspended. He narrows his eyes, bends his neck left and right, and draws his face closer to the mirror.

And then, like magic, there it is! The old Brumbo smile!

He likes what he sees, yes sir! A face like gold bullion, hair hanging in damp, silvery-pink-blond sickles over his forehead and whatnot.

"Let's do this!" he cries.

Brumbo faints. His head bounces off the gilded floor tiles. The vacate-refill dynamic resumes at the speed of light. The process completes in a snap, and he's back at his highhub scripting in his refilled head what he's going to say at his first town hall rally.

Two

It takes Ava Blue a moment to orient herself. Okay, so she's back in Apartment D55-12, in Collective 64, Six Four City. The year is 4104, and her sib, Marny, is deep-sleeping in the other bed.

She tiptoes out of the bedroom and pauses before Mya and Fyo's door to confirm they're asleep. Outside, in the hallway, the voices of the Lagooms go silent. Ava listens to the soft patter of their footsteps. They stop just outside the Blues' apartment door.

Pela whispers something to Len, who whispers something back to Pela. Ava listens carefully but can't make out what they're saying. They sound like aliens, though, and that gets her heart racing. She presses her fist against her teeth as she waits for the dreaded knock on the door, the demand that she wake up her progens, and the delivery of catastrophic news.

But there's no knock on the door. The Lagooms don't even know she's standing inches away fretting and thinking her entire life is about to be turned upside down. They stop whispering and resume their walk down the hallway toward the lift.

The Lagooms are even-keeled, mundane folk, typical empty nest Ord progens. Ava visualizes their hushed fifty-five story descent to the ground floor. They'll exit the tower, each carrying an essentials bag, and walk to the ordporter station, their blank faces ghostly white under the night lights. An eight-hour ride will leave them at TransHub-1, outside Midway City, where they'll board a skycruiser to…

Magnificent Paradeo?

Ava removes her fist from her mouth and softly pounds her hip to chase away the bits of nightmare that have left her brain feeling unsynchronized.

She tries to collect herself, notes that it's just after 3:00 AM, which means the Lagooms' night walk is but one more instance of Protracted Elevation Reassignment in action.

PER happens like clockwork every night somewhere in Six Four City. No intrigue, no alien tongues, no catastrophic revelations, just PER doing its thing, in accordance with Article 2 of the Ord Elevation Initiative: *Protracted Elevation Reassignment ensures the generational vitality and continuity of the Collective and safeguards the inalienable right of Ords to prosper beyond their Call Date.*

Ava is annoyed with herself for succumbing to crippling anxiety. She's no longer a child, after all. She's fifteen and has recently discovered she has a mind of her own. No longer is she willing to accept anyone's word *just because*. Especially Miss Glinty's. And that includes everything the Keepers have been teaching her about elevated thinking, *The Rights of Ords*, truth talks, and so on.

But bad habits die hard. She works through Article 2 and feels her heartbeat slow down as she reaches the end: … *secure better living and elevation fulfillment upon completion of transfer to the Ord's final destination, Magnificent Paradeo.*

Miss Glinty says memorization and regular recitation of truth talks is the best way for Ords to keep their heads perfectly balanced. Maybe there's something to that. Ava knows recitation of familiar words and dictums does help disperse brain fog and restore personal equilibrium. But couldn't she get the same result reciting Mya's bucknut pie recipe? Probably, but her brain hasn't been saturated with Mya's recipes, it's been saturated with truth talks.

Ava shoots a guilt glance at the K-Eye, and for a moment feels exposed. The K-Eye can't read her thoughts, can it? The silver and black thing hovers like a shrunken one-eyed head a few feet away, inches from the ceiling. It regards Ava the way a sleepy-eyed dog might, with no particular expectation or discernible malice, just mere curiosity. Still, Ava would like to pluck it from the air, stick it in her backpack, take it out into the barrens, and stomp on it.

Of course, that wouldn't be a good idea because everybody knows an abducted K-Eye shifts into Distress mode and transmits a signal back to Midway City. Within seconds, Receive and React Drones would be launched from the tower tops of Six Four to remedy the situation.

Remedy how? No one knows. No one has ever tried to abduct a K-Eye, that Ava is aware of. Plenty of Ords think K-Eye scrutiny is a good thing and feel it is responsible for abolishing most Ord-on-Ord crime. It has been said that within a generation of K-Eye implementation throughout Six

Four, every conceivable type of Ord Downer—killer, rapist, thief, huckster, rebel, pimp, pusher, et al—has been identified and transferred to distant rehab camps, never to be heard from again.

Many Ords view Keeper Deliverance Day as a sign of cosmic mercy. Three centuries after Apollyon, the Keepers appeared throughout the wounded planet wearing eye-catching pressurized suits and projecting flashy holograms promising stability and prosperity for the hapless Ords.

The Keeper as Savior sentiment grew as Eon Reconstruction went into full swing. COW, the Center for Ord Welfare, ensured that no Ord would ever lack for food, shelter, work, healthcare, an education, and wholesome pleasures.

These and other quality of life assurances are delineated, amplified, and secured by COW's seminal document, *The Rights of Ords*. This lifechanging text includes the standout Progen Elevation Enhancement Amendment with its celebrated Never Alone Algorithm, which identifies and assigns perfect cohabitation and reproduction matches for Ords who have come of age, effectively eliminating the scourge of Ord loneliness.

What bunk.

Ava sneaks another glance at the K-Eye, then crawls into bed. The K-Eye, as is its custom, hovers in the doorway observing her. She turns onto her stomach and remains motionless until a wisp of air movement tells her the K-Eye has nothing further to gain by remaining and has drifted back to its ceiling port. Ava closes her eyes and tries to sleep, but she can't stop thinking about the Lagooms and what their journey to Magnificent Paradeo might really mean.

Three

Ava has seen her fill of colorful life views. Up until recently, she has produced a few of her own indifferent renderings. All these works, with some variation, feature sparkling waterways and lawnpools, golden buttressed coastlines and rolling green hills, leaping multicolored petbots and harlequin androids, semitransparent skycruisers gliding beneath a pale sun in a forever silver-blue sky, and many other wonders.

But for the skycruisers, which spirit Keeper culturalists, engineers and civil guardians between the cities of Midway and Six Four, no Ord enrolled at the Elevated Thinking Academy, or at any of the Collective Local schools, has ever actually seen or experienced the wonder and beauty that is said to abound in the vast spaces and intimate nooks and crannies of Magnificent Paradeo.

Other than in virtual format.

Despite this, Ord cadets are periodically required to produce impressions, or life views, of their alleged ultimate destination. This time Ava has departed from the norm. Her new life view is so provocative and disturbing, it forces Miss

Glinty to summon Mya and Fyo Blue, via K-Eye voice mail, to Midway for a consultation.

Ava's progens get on an ordporter at dawn the next morning and arrive at their destination, ET Academy in Midway City, nine hours later.

For the benefit of Fyo and Mya, Miss Glinty pauses in the tunnel gallery and summons a life view produced by one of Ava's fellow cadets. Miss Glinty offers a brief positive commentary on the rendering as it hovers in front of her guests before releasing it back to its preset on the curved white wall. She shows them several other life views strikingly similar to the first.

"What these renderings have in common is a forward-thinking, elevated perspective," she points out. "These life views all demonstrate a healthy outlook regarding oneself and one's relation to others and the planet. By contrast... Well, it's best that I show, rather than tell you, what I mean. Please follow me."

Poor Fyo, poor Mya, so painfully out of their element. They follow the silver and gold culturalist back to her office. Ava stops and imagines Fyo and Mya a few years from now on their Call Date, floating high above Midway in a skycruiser on their way to Magnificent Paradeo, their unhappy faces pressed against the glass.

She remembers another time that now seems very distant. Fyo and Mya were standing at the Collective 64 rail stop in the gray dawn as an ordporter began to squeak over rusted tracks. Ava, all of five, was on her way to Midway City to begin her indoctrination at ET Academy. Through the cabin window she could see Fyo gazing in her direction, but he didn't appear to recognize her. Mya was rubbing her right eye and standing several feet behind Fyo, her face partly turned away in an attitude of *morbid discontent*, a condition Miss Glinty often mentions.

Did Mya's morbid discontent affect Ava that day? She did feel a bruising sensation in her chest, but that soon went away. The unfolding wasteland with its rock outcroppings, wild flowers, forgotten ashtowns and imaginary beings kept her young developing mind occupied.

Ava rushes to catch up with Miss Glinty, Mya and Fyo before they notice her absence. The four sit together in Miss Glinty's office in form-shifting chairs arranged in a small intimate square.

With a wave of her hand Miss Glinty summons one more life view, which she floats before Fyo and Mya. Ava's progens make a concerted effort to remain composed. No pretty lawnpools, petbots, android harlequins, skycruisers, nor pale suns are depicted.

"Who are these men?" says Miss Glinty. With a flick of her forefinger, she realigns the image so that it faces Ava.

Ava hesitates. "I don't know."

Miss Glinty crosses her long golden legs, the pointy tip of her silver high-heeled shoe grazing Fyo's shin. Fyo shifts a little too abruptly, making the moment all the more awkward.

"Would you like a better view?" Miss Glinty asks Fyo.

"I, uh…"

"Of course, you would," Miss Glinty says. "Why don't we try this?"

Miss Glinty realigns the life view so that it settles evenly between Mya and Fyo. Her hand dances in the air and the image becomes three-dimensional and enlarged by a hundred percent.

"Is that better?"

Fyo sneaks a glance at Mya, and says, "Yes, thank you."

But is better, *better*?

Two ghastly figures float before them. They could be versions of a single being, or perhaps a prey figure and its predator. The prey figure is falling forward, its head colorless and empty. The predator's crimson face is turned craftily toward the viewer. From its mouth projects a snake that stretches and coils, its jaws glomming onto the base of its prey's skull.

This image, in all its ghastly detail, has issued from their firstborn offee's developing mind. Ava's unsettling life view suggests a failure of progen oversight and a dereliction of progen duty.

"A most curious life view!" Miss Glinty announces in a peppy voice. She gazes at Fyo as if expecting an explanation from him, and then glances for just an instant at Mya.

"Ava, let's talk about this," Miss Glinty says. "Is it that you are attempting to show two conflicting sides of a single person? For example, the conflict between the desires of the mind and the desires of the flesh?"

Ava sees herself twice in Miss Glinty's glossy pink-framed spectacles. The DermaGold-treated skin of Miss Glinty's face seems to be glowing more than usual today.

"These figures," Ava begins, "yes, they could represent two sides of the same person, or..."

"Yes, Ava? Or?"

"Or two distinct entities."

"Two distinct *entities!*" Miss Glinty exclaims. "How interesting!"

"I mean, no, that's not what I meant to say. I meant two sides of one *person*, not two *entities*. I got mixed up, sorry."

Miss Glinty takes off her glasses and opens her violet eyes wide to attract as much light to her irises as possible. She draws closer and says, "Why do you suppose you constructed such an unpleasant life view, Ava?"

"As I told you before, Miss Glinty, it was a dream."

"And when did you have this dream?"

"During our most recent provisional leave, while I was in Six Four."

"In Six Four City," Miss Glinty says and nods. She glances at Fyo with a knowing smile and repeats, "In Six Four City, of course. So, tell us, Ava, what do you really think this life view represents?"

Ava stares at Miss Glinty's jewel-like eyes. Opticolor eye treatments are all the rage lately and are being marketed throughout Midway as the perfect complement to Derma-Gold-treated skin.

Miss Glinty blinks several times, and for an instant Ava imagines she has detected a faint electronic lag, like a microsecond reset.

"I had a dream, Miss Glinty," Ava says. "One person or two persons? I don't know. It was just a dream."

Miss Glinty frowns. "But Ava, the more closely I examine this, the more it seems to me you did mean to show two distinct *entities*, not two sides of one *person*, nor two *persons* in the traditional sense. Clearly, one is a predator, the other is its prey. Were you perhaps trying to depict a body snatcher?"

Miss Glinty's big smile goes unreciprocated.

"A what?" Ava replies. "I don't know anything about body snatchers or what they might be or look like, or if they even exist, but I think the predator and prey here may really represent one and the same person. Now that I think of it, maybe the dream is trying to teach me that people sometimes can be their own worst enemy."

Ava stares at Miss Glinty, hoping to dispel any suspicions she might have that Ava knows more about the world than she is letting on.

"I know I'm my own worst enemy sometimes," Ava says, "so I really have to be careful. I have to work hard to learn all my ET lessons inside out. I don't want to get out of balance and become unsynchronized. Isn't it possible that's what the dream truly represents, Miss Glinty, me being my own worst enemy?"

Miss Glinty crosses her arms and stares at Ava for an uncomfortably long time.

"Yes, it is possible, I suppose."

"You once said Ords my age—"

"Yes, yes, young Ords are occasionally prone to irrational flights of fancy and wayward imaginings."

Mya, who has been stroking her right eyebrow all the while Ava has been trying to dig herself out of trouble, stands up and excuses herself. Fyo leans forward, as if preparing to stand, but he remains seated. They all watch Mya walk out of Miss Glinty's office into the hallway.

"A minute in the oxygen booth could be of benefit," Miss Glinty says to Fyo. "There is one right down the hall."

Fyo, embarrassed, looks down at the floor.

"Mister Blue, numerous COW studies indicate that Ava's aberrant behavior is particular to Ord children. The good news is that the condition afflicts a small percentage of the most exceptional cadets. Overly inventive offees endure a Chaos of Perception period while the imagination struggles to adjust to the reality of the universe during what for some becomes a quite trying maturation process. If COP happens, it usually does so between the thirteenth and sixteenth year, as in Ava's case. More often than not, once correctly addressed, the condition resolves in a couple of weeks, or even days. Of course, there are exceptions where special measures are necessitated."

"What do you mean, special measures, Miss Glinty? What special measures?"

Miss Glinty leans forward, silver bracelets jingling, and places her long golden fingers over Fyo's knuckles. She gazes into his eyes with kaleidoscopic intensity for several seconds before speaking.

"No need to be alarmed, Mister Blue. Special measures are taken only in extreme cases, those involving multiple variables, including certain hereditary factors. These make up less than one percent of all related instances. We should be encouraged that Ava has already demonstrated positive signs of ET Resynchronization. The tour through the viewing tunnel, our productive little talk, and your presence here have all contributed to the beginnings of Ava's recovery, I'm sure. I expect to soon see Ava composing dazzling vistas, petbots at play in lustrous meadows, skycruisers filled with bright, smiling faces, and many untold marvels. I would not be too concerned, at least not about Ava."

Miss Glinty glances at the open doorway through which Mya exited, then turns her attention back to Fyo, her glossy lips parted, her violet eyes smiling inquisitively.

Fyo carefully slips his hand out from under Miss Glinty's as he stands up.

"Thank you, Miss Glinty. We've already taken up too much of your time. It is a long way back to Six Four City."

"Not at all, Mister Blue. Thank you for coming, and please know I am always happy to set aside a few minutes if you would like to continue our conversation."

Miss Glinty stands up and slides her hands down her snug silver body wrap, smoothing away nonexistent wrinkles. She extends a limp hand toward Fyo, who hesitates before touching it.

Four

After a nine-month absence, Derelok Yoreasy reappears in the games court in the exact spot where the transfer cadet surprised Ava with a passing kiss on the cheek, a wink and a winning smile.

The moment had taken her breath away, and she had wondered excitedly, what in stars were the odds that the Progen Elevation Enhancement Amendment's Never Alone Algorithm would identify modest Ava Blue and this dashing newcomer to be a perfect match?

The thrill didn't last long. Moments after striding past Ava, Yoreasy stopped to talk to Bryno Palink. The two leaned back against the climbing wall and did a lot of laughing and observing. Occasionally, they'd glance Ava's way. It soon became clear to her, and to the many others who were paying attention, that she had been singled out by Yoreasy and Palink to be the day's object of mockery.

Ava wouldn't be the sole target of Yoreasy's sophomoric abuse over the days that followed. She watched him perform cruel stunts on other vulnerable cadets, each time sharing his pleasure with Palink. Then one day, without explanation, the two bullies disappeared.

Rumors began to circulate. LeBoris Silky, a respected L-12 and soon-to-be graduate, believed Yoreasy was not a biological being in the strictest sense.

LeBoris posited that because Yoreasy was disruptive and antagonistic only during recess, and otherwise well adjusted, he had probably been inserted into the cadets' unstructured and unsupervised recess sessions as an agent of agitation, the catalyst for a social adversity experiment. The experiment was used to generate useful data for Keeper behavioralists, who were secretly monitoring every cadet's word and act. This data, LeBoris explained, would be distilled and used to refine Elevated Thinking curricula and training algorithms. The experiment's ultimate goal, he suggested, was to perfect ET cadet formation.

Ava, who was present during Silky's theorizing, has since suspected that LeBoris himself is not a biological being in the strictest sense either. But that's for another time to ponder. As much as she tries telling herself she is no longer the naïve L-10 cadet who was publicly humiliated by Yoreasy, she is dismayed to find her nerves getting the best of her yet again. She resists the temptation to press her fist against her teeth, and instead sends her mind racing across her *Rights of Ords* memory banks in search of pulse-lowering words to recite to herself.

But this time it doesn't work because she doesn't want it to. She takes a good look at Yoreasy as he walks directly toward her and notes the stupid grin that once seemed to her dreamy and enticing.

"You once thought him spectacular, but look again, has there ever been a dumber Ord?" she whispers to herself. Yoreasy doesn't hear her, but the words are like magic, producing within Ava a surge of self-confidence.

"My oh my, it's Ava Blue!" Yoreasy shouts. "Long time no see!"

In anticipation of another ugly spectacle, cadets have already begun migrating toward the pair. Yoreasy waits a few moments for the numbers to build.

"I've been meaning to talk to you about those space vamps," he says, "the ones that made Miss Glinty blush?"

How would he know about that, Ava wonders as she catches a glimpse of Bryno Palink assuming his old position at the climbing wall?

"I think it's important for everyone here to understand that space vamps are suckers," Yoreasy says. He takes note of the undivided attention, and delivers the punch line, "Suckers of brains, that is, like the one Ava Blue once had."

He scans the crowd, but the response remains tepid and unsatisfying. The few strained chuckles irritate, rather than please, Yoreasy.

"Derelok, some say you're not a biological being in the strictest sense," Ava counters. "If so, why not come clean and confess you're a closet brain sucker?"

"Ha-ha, that is hilarious," Yoreasy replies, annoyed by the crowd's laughter.

"I don't know if you're a closet brain sucker, Derelok, but you are, hands-down, the dumbest Ord ever."

Yoreasy does a doubletake. Is this the same girl he abused last term?

Palink shuffles through the crowd, whispers in Yoreasy's ear, and retreats back to the climbing wall.

"First of all? It's so lame to suggest I'm a closet brain sucker," Yoreasy says. "Nobody's going to believe that. And second of all, ha-ha, it's even lamer to say I'm the dumbest Ord ever." He slaps his face, grabs his chin and wags his head. "Is this the face of the dumbest Ord ever?" he says, turning to the crowd. "By the way, the only space vamps I know of are the ones living in Ava Blue's dementalized head."

That should have got the crowd going, but nothing is working. Yoreasy is bewildered. Before he can make things worse, Bryno Palink raises both hands in the air and starts to clap. Three or four others join in, but the modest outbreak fizzles out in seconds.

Ava knows she can walk away now, having elevated her image and restored a measure of self-respect. She even takes a few steps indicating the skirmish has ended, and there's nothing Yoreasy and Palink can do about it.

The problem lies in that irksome phrase, *Ava Blue's dementalized head*. She just can't bring herself to let Yoreasy have the last word.

"Derelok Yoreasy, I take back what I said. You are even dumber than the dumbest Ord ever, and dumber than your dumb name would suggest."

Yoreasy's face contorts with incomprehension. Then some self-preservation instinct kicks in, and he shoots a needy, dog-grin glance at Palink. His mouth starts to fidget as it tries to articulate unwieldy sentiments. He's incapable of putting together the right set of words required to unleash the collective laughter of vindication he desperately craves.

"This is bald-faced character assassination!" Palink cries out as he rushes forward. "I demand CC Resolution Restitution!"

"CC Resolution Restitution?" a skeptic cries out. Another voice in the crowd, curiously familiar, adds, "But you are not the aggrieved. You have no right to demand CCRR."

He's right. Bryno Palink is *not* the aggrieved. Immediately recognizing his blunder, Palink sidles up next to Yoreasy and whispers in his ear.

"I demand CC Resolution Restitution!" Yoreasy shouts.

For a moment, Ava thought Palink's blunder had voided the demand. But the procedural faux pax was remedied within the prescribed thirty-second period.

Why couldn't that big-mouth cadet keep his trap shut? Wait, was that LeBoris Silky?

The Conflict Circle Resolution Restitution Act was instituted during the early days of Eon Reconstruction as a means of resolving disputes among Ords in a quick, decisive, and cost-effective manner. Bowing to mounting criticism, the Council of Deciders passed the Conflict Circle Resolution Restitution Act Discontinuation Order just in the past year, effectively overturning the act on the grounds that it is *a primitive and questionable practice that could be perceived as being contrary to the spirit of elevation.*

Regrettably, though the order officially banned CCRR, it failed to eliminate its practice, as the Discontinuation Order lacks clear enforcement directives and punitive guidelines. By all accounts, the CCRR continues to be performed throughout Six Four City, and not a single violator of the act's Discontinuation Order has been punished, nor reprimanded.

Ava shakes off a faint spell of dizziness. She notes with dismay how Yoreasy's body has not only lengthened significantly since their last encounter, but has packed on additional meat and muscle and must now outweigh her by a hundred and fifty pounds.

The one-sided nature of the conflict is blatantly obvious, yet no cadet has invoked the Obscenely Disparate Clause on her behalf within the prescribed period. She watches the cadets form a six-deep circle around her and Yoreasy, who initiates the affair by circling to Ava's left in an exaggerated crouch. Ava sighs and suppresses a shudder. Her eyes begin to burn. The thought of crying in front of her fellow cadets startles her, and on an impulse, she jumps straight up into the air as high as she can. And then she jumps again, and again, confusing everyone.

She doesn't care what anyone thinks. The tension that has been accumulating in her bones and muscles begins to ease a bit. Cadets exchange comments and theorize about Ava's peculiar strategy. Even Yoreasy stops circling. He stands up straight and stares at Ava in abject bewilderment.

Would reciting aloud *The Rights of Ords* help, she wonders? For how can someone in the middle of reciting truth talks be attacked? It's not possible, it is forbidden, and totally contrary to Elevated Thinking. In theory, she can stop jumping and begin reciting Article 1, Paragraph 1, and so on, until recess comes to an end, or until the bored crowd disperses, or until Yoreasy gives up and walks away.

But she can no longer publicly recite lies, she realizes as she continues jumping. She's done with that. No more spreading Keeper lies!

Yoreasy crouches and resumes his prowl. Ava, running out of steam, stops jumping and steels herself in anticipation of the beating of her life. She narrows her eyes and counters Yoreasy's every movement, turning with him, keeping pace, squaring her shoulders so that Yoreasy is always directly in front of her.

What happens next seems incomprehensible. Ava's fear spikes, causing her to leap straight up as high as she ever has. As she reaches her high point, she feels a sudden adrenaline rush and rocketing dopamine levels that sharpen her mind, making her thought processing superfast. As her feet touch ground, she experiences a strange exhilaration fueled by two convictions: she is infinitely smarter than Yoreasy, and she likes having a brain.

She finds consolation in pondering the mysteries buried within the gray folds, all those incredible things percolating in the cranial shadows, waiting to be released and refined, half-formed notions on the cusp of blossoming into fertile ideas that make living better.

Given all that, what will a physical beating matter when she is so much more than flesh and bone?

Sure, sounds great, but Yoreasy is gigantic. She's never noticed his fists before, clenched like that, each as big as her head. She endures a delicate wave of nausea and marshals untapped resources of concentration. The surest thing right now is that she doesn't want either of those fists hitting her in the face.

Her mind races ahead of her fear, and she recalls a grimly compromising assertion from the Conflict Circle Resolution Restitution Act: ... *a knockout by vicious strike to the head is deemed a satisfactory means of restitution for the Aggrieved and provides an immediate end to the proceedings…*

Not what she's looking for, necessarily. In desperation, she scampers through her CCRRA memory bank, locates a tricky but doable escape clause, and replays it in her mind verbatim: *If the Alleged Offender is no longer able to remain upright—not voluntarily having lowered self to the ground but having been forced to the ground by the Aggrieved while still in a conscious state—the Alleged Offender may curl self's body into the fetal position, cover self's head with two hands, and speak loudly enough for at least three verifiable witnesses to hear the words, "I invoke the Faller's Mercy Rule," whereupon such a pronouncement would instantly prohibit the Aggrieved from further striking, or in any way punishing, the Alleged Offender, thereby bringing the proceedings to a just and immediate close in favor of the Aggrieved.*

Theoretically, a less painful path, but one requiring a high level of coordination and agility that may presently elude her. The element of surprise, however, might give her a puncher's chance. She envisions lowering her head and bull rushing Yoreasy, driving her shoulder hard below his diaphragm, listening to him grunt in surprise as she wraps her arms around his waist and holds on for dear life as he raises her up into the air and hurls her to the ground, whereupon she'll immediately assume the fetal position, cover her head with two hands, and invoke the Faller's Mercy Rule, if she has the breath to do it.

But it's too late! Ava is assailed by the sickening realization that Yoreasy has been recalling the exact same lines from the CCRRA and has moved to neutralize her plan of action with a bull rush of his own.

Then everything stops!

A loud noise like a clash of cymbals brings Yoreasy's bull rush to a skidding halt, inches from Ava's face. Both Ava and Yoreasy watch the Conflict Circle split open. And there, standing in the opening like a supernatural being, the sun shining at his back, is an L-10.

It takes Ava a moment to recognize the cadet. It's Topper Birdsong, one of those background figures that moves quietly and largely unnoticed through the halls and parlors of ET Academy. Ava studies Topper, sees no good end for either him or her. He's dwarfed by both Yoreasy and Palink, but his small, slender frame doesn't keep him from walking right up to Yoreasy.

It is an amazing development, an unfolding paradox of tremendous proportion. Topper's graceful entry into the fray places him directly in the mouth of the beast, so to speak, captivating Ava and the entire crowd of cadets like nothing they've ever seen.

Topper extends both hands and flips them over a couple of times, displaying his palms so the crowd can see his hands are empty. Then he waves his right hand in an S-shaped motion beneath Yoreasy's nose, producing the day's loudest laughter.

"Asinine L-10!" Palink shouts as he takes two tentative steps forward.

"You all know, you *should* know," Topper proclaims in a clear voice, "that the Conflict Circle Resolution Restitution Act was banned on the first of May, 4103 AD, by the Council of Deciders with the passing of the CCRRA Discontinuation Order."

He speaks with such authority that no one thinks to point out that since the order's passing, CCRR continues to be practiced at large, and every known breach of the order—lacking any enforcement procedures or punishment protocols—has been ignored by Keeper law enforcement.

Topper moves his cupped right hand beneath Yoreasy's chin, in the manner someone might approach a wary dog. Yoreasy stands stone still, for he is as curious as anyone to see what Topper is going to do.

Yoreasy's face contorts, his mouth opens. He looks as if he is about to vomit. A roar erupts from the crowd as a bluebird ejects from his mouth. The bird lets out a quick, brisk song as it flies straight up and disappears in a cloud. A small blue feather floats down from the sky. Ava catches it.

"What is going on here?" demands Mr. Polaris.

For a Keeper, Mr. Polaris always looks unkempt in his silver wrapping. He is followed out of the Relax Wing of the ET Building by Miss Glinty, Miss Lapelle and several other culturalists.

"This," Ava says as she twirls the blue feather between her thumb and forefinger, but not everyone hears her.

The culturalists glance with little interest at Ava and her feather. They make tired hand motions to indicate recess is over. Yoreasy and Palink vanish before everyone else begins moving toward the training wing doors to resume the rigors of ET formation.

"The birdsong is what's going on," Ava says to herself as she stares at the feather. She looks up just in time to receive Topper's magical smile before he disappears.

Five

The ordporter slows to half speed as it approaches the ruins. Ordporters always slow down when nearing an ashtown. Ava once believed it was out of respect for the billions of Ords who perished during The Great Purge, as some like to call the Apollyon catastrophe.

She no longer believes that. She thinks the ordporters slow down to remind Ords what their world would look like if the Keepers had not come to their rescue.

It wasn't long ago the nine-hour rides went quickly. For most cadets on their way home for provisional leave, they still do, thanks to standard-issue visipads preloaded with interactive ET Adventure games produced by the Wired for Ord Elevation Company.

By far the most popular game, for as long as Ava can remember, is Forever Tower Quest.

FTQ Phase Alpha randomly assigns players to sixteen Elevation Force platoons that are pitted against one another in a no-holds-barred race to the Forever Tower. The Tower is perched atop Galaxy Peak, the highest elevation point in

BENEATH AN ALIEN SUN

the Milky Way. Select competitions are made available on any compatible view screen to an ever-growing number of non-playing viewers for a nominal fee. FTQ enthusiasts watch and place bets on which platoon they believe will cross the drawbridge to the Forever Tower. Crossing accomplished, the drawbridge rises, preventing all rival platoons from advancing. Viewers are then granted the option of leaping directly to FTQ Phase Omega or lingering awhile to observe the unhappy fate of the losers, which begins with the sudden paralysis of their lower limbs, continues with an impromptu lagoon skirmish with hundreds of snakes, and ends with a firestorm that cooks both human and snake alike.

With the screams of former adversaries still ringing in their ears, the victorious survivors, and onetime platoon mates, become pitted against one another in a harrowing climb to the Forever Tower's golden spire, thus offering non-playing viewers a second opportunity to place a winning bet. Who will be the first to touch the Golden Brain? And with that touch, the Master of the Golden Brain is proclaimed and all other finalists immediately begin to explode sequentially like a series of celebratory fireworks.

No one playing games on a visipad ever burns or is torn to pieces. It's true that the excitement of Forever Tower Quest can be exhilarating and intoxicating. But recently, Ava has discerned a troubling contradiction in the game's design. On the one hand, FTQ Phase Alpha promotes the idea that working together in the interest of achieving a common goal—however questionable the means—is a good in and of itself. But FTQ Phase Omega reveals that the ultimate prize is only won through the single-minded pursuit of self-interest, no matter how appalling the damage inflicted on everyone else. Which makes Ava wonder, is it in the Keepers' best interests that every Ord grow to regard every other Ord as a natural enemy?

She glances about the ordporter cabin in a casual manner, checking for monitoring devices and probers. None that she can detect, but that doesn't mean anything. She knows she has to be careful.

Ava leans back against the cushioned seat and closes her eyes. Sometimes she wishes she could go back to losing herself in ET Adventure games. Thinking about Keeper secrets and motives is exhausting. What benefit is there in thinking too much anyway? In a Keeper-dominated world, too much thinking induces anxiety and loneliness.

Topper Birdsong quietly strolls into her thoughts wearing that indefinable smile that is like a gateway to a better place. She would like to sit down with him, ask him a few questions. Like, where did the bluebird come from? What does he think about Miss Glinty? Does he believe what the Keepers teach about Eon Reconstruction and Magnificent Paradeo?

The ordporter is less than an hour from Six Four City, and she has yet to see him. She has walked up and down the center aisle several times, moving from cabin to cabin, observing hundreds of enthralled ET Adventure enthusiasts, their noses buried in standard-issue visipads. Is Topper's nose buried so deeply in one he's become invisible to her?

On her way back to her seat after one last long walk, she toys with the idea she made it all up, the grim Conflict Circle encounter with Derelok Yoreasy, Topper's intervention, and the magical flight of the singing bluebird. Then she draws the blue feather from her pocket, places it over her upper lip, and inhales its magic. Back in her cabin, she finds Topper sitting in her seat.

"Are you following me around?" she says, hiding her surprise and pretending to be annoyed.

Topper looks up at her. "I don't know when," he replies.

What does that mean? She studies him. He isn't much bigger than Marny, she realizes when he stands up. They stand eye to eye. He's a tad taller than her, but just barely.

"You don't know when what?" Ava says.

"When to tell you everything."

She would have said something clever just then, if anything had occurred to her. Instead, she laughs, and because she hasn't had much practice, the laughter comes out wrong.

What is he seeing in her eyes?

"Ava," he says.

"I'm sorry, I didn't mean to—"

She stops talking when Topper lifts his hand. He moves it toward her chin, the way he did with Yoreasy. Will a bluebird fly out of her mouth too?

No bluebird this time, a turquoise rose. He gives it to her, a real, aromatic, utterly astonishing rose. When has she ever seen a rose of any color anywhere near Six Four City?

"How did you do that?" she says as she sniffs the petals.

"Ava, listen."

She stares at him, mystified, her mouth partly opened.

"Our destinies are intertwined," he says as a statement of fact. "I'll say more about that another day."

Should she press him to be more specific? No, not today. She sits down in her seat, and he sits in the empty seat next to her. He leans his head back against the seat cushion and closes his eyes. She does the same. Neither of them speaks again until Topper stands up a short while later.

"I have to go," he says.

The ordporter comes to a stop and Ava watches Topper hop off with his backpack onto the Collective 01 station platform. He pauses, turns, and waves. She watches him through the cabin window. It doesn't occur to her to wave back until he's already disappeared in the crowd of walkers. He doesn't see her do it, but she waves anyway.

Six

The puzzle box depicts a classic Magnificent Paradeo scene. Rainbow-colored dolphins leap out of glittering lake waters into the air against a backdrop of purple, silver and white mountains. Amid pink and yellow cumulus clouds float sky-boats packed with wide-eyed children who are amazed by the wonders that surround them.

Fyo informs Ava the puzzle was distributed free of charge over the past week to all Collective households in time for the current provisional leave, compliments of a private philanthropy group called Keepers for Ords, which is headquartered in the Midway financial district. Fyo has taken the time to identify and arrange several pieces corresponding to the corners and borders of the puzzle so that Marny won't get overwhelmed and discouraged.

Ava walks into the small bedroom she and Marny share when she's home. He is sitting on the floor between the twin beds holding a carving knife and a small piece of wood.

"Marny, would you help me do this puzzle? Fyo says maybe you would enjoy helping me."

Marny ignores his sib and keeps whittling away at the wood. Ava places the puzzle on the floor.

When Marny was four, and well into his chronically aloof childhood, Fyo took him to the Brain Center in Midway, where a specialist diagnosed him with Conflicted Brain Disorder, or CBD. The brain specialist explained to Fyo that Marny, for the most part, was an extraordinarily dull boy, with a less than adequate attention span and staggeringly low levels of comprehension.

Of course, the CBD diagnosis automatically disqualified Marny from being considered for admission to Midway's elite ET Academy. Disqualification came as no surprise to either Fyo or Mya, given the Academy's high admission standards, CBD or not. During an average school year, only one of every five-hundred age-eligible Ords, or less than 0.2%, qualifies for ET Academy enrollment.

Fyo did not dispute the specialist's observations, but he did inform her there were instances when Marny gave the impression he was quite gifted. At such times his gaze made him look highly intelligent, and for a minute or two he would articulate marvelous-sounding observations and sentiments. Granted, these were voiced in a language neither he nor Mya could understand, but all the sounds coming out of Marny's mouth sounded surprisingly elevated.

The specialist nodded and pointed out how these bizarre manifestations were a common symptom of CBD. What they heard coming out of Marny's mouth at those moments was gibberish, nothing more. The specialist recommended they ensure that Marny complete all his Collective Local 64 training as prescribed and, when not in school, that he always be kept occupied with ET Adventure games, puzzles and approved hobbies.

The care and attention with which Marny carves wood makes Ava wonder if Conflicted Brain Disorder is uniformly misunderstood. Could CBD possess some less than obvious benefits? What if unintelligible languages aren't gibberish at all, but real languages spoken in other real places, at other real times, and meant for other real ears?

Marny has delivered spontaneous CBD discourses seven times during his young life. Ava remembers the last and most troubling of these. It happened two years ago in the same bedroom she and Marny have shared since his birth.

Ava was asleep, dreaming of a glittering lake much like the puzzle image Fyo got started for Marny. In the dream, gold and silver swans glided over the waters, and bright-eyed children ran about playing Giant Butterfly.

She heard the sky testify in a loud, commanding voice, but she couldn't understand a single word. The intensity of the voice roused her from sleep. On waking, she was astonished to find that she could still hear that voice coming out of eleven-year-old Marny's mouth!

"Marny!" she shouted, but the sky voice ignored her and continued to deliver critical information. Or that's what it sounded like to Ava.

The strange, unremitting discourse prompted Ava to leap out of bed and throw herself at Marny. She buried her face in his bony chest and held him tight, protecting him from the dangers of too much knowledge. Her desperate sobs made the sky voice go away.

"Stop it, Ava!" Marny cried as he shoved her off the bed.

It was Marny's voice now, not the sky's. Ava spent a long time staring at the strange boy she was bonded to by blood. She was afraid to touch him or to say anything more.

That episode seems like ancient history now. Marny is a lot bigger, though no less enigmatic. Ava watches him on the bedroom floor working the piece of wood with Fyo's carving knife. Then, as if scales have been removed from her eyes, she sees emerging from the wood a bird spreading its wings.

"Marny, you have such a gift!"

Marny misunderstands her and misreads her intent.

No, no, no! No gift for you!

He doesn't have to say it for her to hear it. Marny flattens the carving knife against the wooden bird and pulls both bird and knife flat against his belly, drawing up his knees and turning his shoulder to block her out.

"I'm not going to take it from you, I promise," Ava says above a whisper, but Marny fortifies his defensive posture.

She lets it go. No point getting upset with Marny. He can't help who he is. She's too restless anyway, can't see herself picking through puzzle pieces for hours with her gloomy, uncommunicative sib.

Under the circumstances, convincing Marny to let her have the HF two-wheel for the day becomes a snap. He nods curtly, happy to be rid of her. On her way out, she tells Mya she is going foraging. Maybe she'll find a curio Mya can swap at the convenience store for something useful.

On the northwest corner of Six Four City, Ava stops and passes a wide gaze over the flat, gray wasteland beyond. The rock outcroppings will emerge gradually, like blistered earth. She'll be surprised by sudden bursts of purple and yellow flowers growing in the most unlikely places. She'll come across a new ashtown, no doubt, and maybe she'll find something there that's been untouched for centuries.

She walks the HF2 over the ordporter track that encircles the sixty-four collectives and rides west on an old paved road that ends abruptly a mile from the city limits. The barrens stretch to the horizon and beyond.

She's happy, but always a little nervous to go where she hasn't gone before.

Seven

Some Ords believe that if you wander deep enough into the wasteland, you'll eventually cross into another world and never find your way back. There are different theories as to why that is. The most persistent of these is the idea that the ancient Kim rise from Terra's bowels at midnight. They sniff the air with their highly developed olfactory sense, and precisely locate their next meal, that being the nearest Ord.

Centuries of cautionary tales told by Keeper culturalists have produced a rich history of nightmares among Ord young. The stories are essentially one story. It goes something like this: Delso, Morvina and Tink are between the ages of 13 and 16, that jumbled stage of life when Ords are most vulnerable to Downer tendencies. The most common of these is the obnoxious habit of raising questions that have no relevance to the Need-to-Know Elevated Thinking compendium of knowledge. Another is the propensity to display boredom or displeasure with curriculum content and training strategies. One less obvious, but equally unfortunate Downer tendency, is the failure to eagerly participate in discussions about critical formative subjects such as the Path to Elevation and Magnificent Paradeo.

Delso, Morvina and Tink are a lot like Ava. They persist in their aberrant thinking and self-destructive behavior. During a highly anticipated three-day provisional leave, one of our young Ords—we'll say Delso—wanders off into the wasteland. He rides on his HF 2-wheel well beyond city drone surveillance. Several hours out, he stops to rest a while in the shadows of a remote ashtown. He closes his eyes and, without intending to, falls asleep.

On waking, Delso is shocked to see the stars of night. It is, in fact, the Kim Hour. The monsters wake from their slumber, rise from the earth, shake off the dirt, and sniff the midnight air for Ord meat. This is the point in the story where the specter of the Kim becomes permanently lodged in the fertile folds of the young Ord brain.

A roused Kim follows Delso's scent, sights Delso, pursues him, and within seconds has him clasped in its claws. Delso's brief struggle leaves him with broken limbs and shattered ribs. Delso goes into shock, whereupon, as Miss Glinty once described, "The Kim swats and tosses the foolish cadet about, the way a cat might swat and toss a crippled mouse, and then, when it has tired of play, the Kim devours its prey alive."

These monstrous creatures were nearly exterminated by the Keeper Life Guardian Force during the early stages of Eon Reconstruction—if one is to believe the official Keeper accounts of that period—but isolated instances of sightings in the distant barrens are still reported. Ava thinks this is a lie, but she remains wary nonetheless.

After riding north a few hours, she spots a gray plateau in the distance. This is the farthest she's ever gone, but there's still plenty of daylight before curfew.

The HF2 responds to her increased pedaling, and accelerates exponentially. Soon Ava finds herself at the foot of the plateau. She straddles the HF2 partway up a shallow slope, leans it against a boulder, and continues her climb.

It takes her longer to get to the top than she expected, but the effort is well worth it. She stops to take a deep breath and to gaze. There was a town up here once. She wonders if seeing the world each day from a higher place might make you feel closer to the stars.

In such a place, there must be many interesting and tradeable objects. At first glance, nothing stands out. She walks among the ruins to a pile of rubble, removes Fyo's trowel from her backpack and begins to prod and jab and dig through a shifting mass of wreckage. Gnarled and grimy artifacts, plastics, chunks of concrete, shards of metal and glass slide to the ground. But despite her focused energy, the pile offers nothing of interest.

Ava finds another pile, and digs some more. She moves methodically among the ruins, laboring at each new pile with pace and purpose. The random bones she uncovers slow her work a bit. She sets the bones aside on the ground in neat rows and continues to prod and dig.

After three hours of this, she has nothing to show for her efforts. Her limited time in Six Four City would have been better spent sitting on the floor watching Marny coax a bird from a chunk of wood. Maybe she'd see the wooden bird flap its wings and fly away.

She wags her sore arm and drags her feet through the dust and sand. From the corner of her eye, she detects a flicker of light that leads her to a large half-buried object. With her elbow and fingernails, she rubs away a layer of dust and crusted filth. A small weary face marred by dust and soot and crowned with spiked chestnut hair stares back at her from a faded mirror. She frowns and sticks her tongue out to confirm it's her own face she sees, and presses her fingers against the reflection of her lips.

Clouds pass overhead, darkening her mood. It's almost time to leave, and she has nothing to give Mya, nothing to show for all her work. It's a long way back to Collective 64. She sits on the ground, leans back against the ancient wardrobe and closes her eyes.

"Just ten minutes," she whispers.

A ray of sunlight splits the clouds as she wakes from her nap. She gets up and walks toward the illusion of movement caused by the sunbeam and notices a golden object buried in the pile of rubble. She grasps one of its handles and pulls, dislodging the object and stumbling backwards with a large cup swinging from her hand. Displaced sand and dirt slide to the ground with a hiss.

She wipes the dust and grime from the cup, and stares at the image of a smiling girl engraved on the faded chrome. The girl has a ponytail and she's kicking a ball. The words inscribed beneath her image read, *Pearl Hart, MVP, Hopetown Rockets, County Champs, Spring 2090.*

Ava studies the engraved figure and rubs the girl's face with her fingertips to see her better. What does MVP mean? Could it mean Miss Very Pretty?

Ava wonders if Pearl Hart's bones were among those she dug up and set on the ground in neat rows. She also wonders what Ords were like two-thousand years ago. A passage from *The Ords of Terra*, long ago committed to memory, presents itself almost involuntarily.

The destiny of the Ords of Terra is Infinite Elevation. Elevated Thinking, which delineates the Path to Elevation, was introduced to the Ords by Keeper rescuers, whose timely intervention eliminated the growing threat of Ord self-destruction. Keeper vision and ingenuity restored order and stability to Terra during the post-Apollyon period by putting an end to barbarities such as Ord cannibalism, which is a breach of Cosmic Law. There are reasons to believe the widespread practice of Ord cannibalism, in the decades prior to Apollyon, provoked the galactic wrath that resulted in the near obliteration of Terra and its inhabitants.

Pearl Hart hardly looks like a cannibal. Ava stares at the scratched, discolored image of a girl her own age kicking a ball. Or is that a head she's kicking? Ava examines the cup more closely. The sphere is scratched and worn, but no, that is not a head, it is a ball.

More sand slides down the pile, hissing like a snake. Two nubs rise from the rubble and extend up into the air. A turquoise rabbit head pokes up from the pile, its eyes blinking away grains of sand. It takes the rabbit a few seconds to adjust to the light and its surroundings. After spitting sand out of its little mouth, the rabbit says, "Why, hello there!"

At the sound of the rabbit's voice—part machine, part creature—Ava decides she has not woken from her nap, after all, but has transitioned to a new phase of her dream. For this can only be a dream, right? And though the dream possesses a curiously thrilling charm, she knows it will soon end, and she'll wake up and ride back to Collective 64, and in two days, she'll be seated on an ordporter on her way to ET Academy and the likes of Miss Glinty and Derelok Yoreasy.

"My name is Willie."

Willie waits politely for a response. When he gets none, he says, "What is your name and would you like to be my friend?"

"Oh, I'm sorry, I didn't mean to… Hello, Willie. I'm Ava. I would like to be your friend."

"How marvelous, Ava! Thank you for being my friend! Now that I know your face, voice, and name, I will be able to tell you many things. Would you like me to continue?"

"Yes, please."

"I have something that will be of special interest to you."

Without warning, the rabbit's hybrid voice gives way to a man's voice.

"What are the odds of any one of us existing? About 400 trillion to one… I need a moment to think about that, Willie."

Ava whirls around. The man's voice is clear, immediate, and oddly intimate. She looks in every direction, sees only ruins and rubble.

"09 October 2101. The day I turned thirty, Atwell threw me a birthday party in a big dome packed with wealthy Deos and informed me the world was going to end before Bright Star Day. Three days later, he told me the woman I was falling in love with wasn't who I thought she was…"

Birthday parties, the Deo exodus, Mars and the moons of Jupiter, songs of the Old World, all of it confusing, but also—

"Ava, because you and I are now friends, you can ask me things."

She stares at the talking rabbit, awestruck. If at all possible, she would like to remain in the dream a bit longer.

"For example, you can say, 'Repeat Note,' or, 'Willie, go to 31 August 2104,' or, 'Willie, initiate Sleep mode,' or you can say whatever you like, and I will respond accordingly."

Receiving no reply, Willie says, "Ava, unless otherwise directed, I will proceed with the next Note: 'Athens proved too busy for my liking. Thessaloniki seemed the better fit. That's where I've been living for the past few months. I spend most of my evenings in a bar called Taverna Momos. The regulars drink the house tsipouro and eat olives and peanuts off small porcelain trays.'"

"Willie, please stop."

"Can I help you with anything else, Ava?"

"Maybe we can talk later?"

"Yes, of course."

Willie's long ears draw back into a relaxed position as Ava runs her sand-roughened fingertips over his head, which is smooth as velvet and hard as titanium.

"Thank you, Willie."

"My pleasure, Ava. Goodbye for now."

Willie's charm and air of permanence broaden Ava's mind with new possibilities. She starts to laugh and wakes from her dream. Only it's not a dream! Willie is still there, half-buried in the pile of rubble.

She digs him out and places him inside her backpack. She also packs the Pearl Hart MVP cup and a chunk of petrified wood for Marny. The HF2's estimator displays the minimum pace she will have to maintain to make it back to Collective 64 before sundown.

On the way to Six Four, her head is filled with the sounds of singing bluebirds, talking rabbits, and the voice of a man named Merlin Stone, who seems as alive today as he was two-thousand years ago.

She can't wait to tell Topper about all the amazing things she's discovered. The HF2's engine hums as Ava pedals with new energy and a heightened sense of purpose.

Ava imagines the unimaginable, and every now and then, she trembles with excitement. The sun is just touching the horizon when she rolls into Six Four City.

Eight

Fyo is gone when Ava gets back. Mya describes how the K-Eye congratulated Fyo for being selected to participate in the newly instituted Ord Elevation Accelerator program, and how Fyo is one of eight-hundred Ords specially selected to dig a tunnel. The K-Eye provided boarding instructions and other pertinent details. Estimated time for project completion is sixteen months, with quarterly three-day provisional leave beginning in eighty-eight days.

"Where are they sending him?" Ava says.

"Southwest, far away," Mya says, shaking her head.

"Why would anyone need a tunnel down there?"

Mya blinks, pretends she has something in her eye, rubs it, walks to the sink, runs water.

"There's nothing down there but wasteland," Ava insists.

Mya splashes water on her eye and takes a deep breath.

Ava checks in on Marny. For now, Marny's content to be sitting on the bedroom floor working Fyo's puzzle. But it's not Marny Ava is worried about. Since the meeting with Miss Glinty, Mya has been in a state of mourning.

Ava pulls her backpack out of the closet. She touches Willie's smooth, hard and reassuringly permanent head. The sight of the turquoise rabbit would surely distract, and maybe even enchant, Mya.

But she can't risk it, not with the K-Eye snooping around. She'd love to pluck the obnoxious little intruder from the air and drown it in the toilet. But that's not going to happen. Instead of Willie, Ava presents Mya the Pearl Hart MVP cup. A glimmer of life returns to her progen's eyes.

"With any luck, this may fetch us a flask of Fyo's favorite moonsap," Mya says.

"Blue Star," Ava replies with a smile.

Mya is thinking she'll have to wait eighty-eight days to give Fyo his gift. Even at her tender age, Ava understands eighty-eight days can pass in a flash like a desert rain, or linger like a killer drought. How it plays out depends entirely on one's circumstances. For Mya, the next eighty-eight days are going to be like eight-hundred and eighty-eight days.

On her second morning of leave, Ava suggests they bake bucknut pies. After some hesitation, Mya reluctantly agrees, and they begin gathering ingredients and cooking materials.

Ava scrapes the sweet powder off the bucknut pods onto a plate and pops the bucknuts from their pods into bowls. Mya's eyes and hands come to life as she mashes the nuts and works the collection of rare ingredients into sweet and tart bucknut pies under the watchful gaze of the K-Eye.

While the pies are still warm, they carry them, along with the Pearl Hart MVP cup, down to Paco Cruz's convenience store on the ground level of Tower 64D. They exchange the half dozen pies for oat milk, bucknut bread, fake egg-bacon wraps, and super soap. The Pearl Hart MVP cup gets Mya a flask of Blue Star Moonsap, just as she had hoped. She hides the moonsap in an old chest in her bedroom closet when they get back to the apartment.

Ava swaps the chunk of petrified wood in exchange for another day's use of Marny's HF2. She rides west this time, wearing a hoodie and goggles because of the surging winds and the dust.

She stops at a massive rock outcropping some sixty miles from Collective 64, climbs to the top and lowers herself into a knobby depression that looks and feels like a pair of cupped hands. She peers over the rock at the surrounding wasteland. The strong wind blows back her hood and whips her spiked hair nearly flat.

Satisfied no one is near, she settles herself in the smooth curve of rock and removes her goggles. She listens to the wind whistling above her head and says, "Willie, wake up, please. Can we start from the beginning?"

Nine

Ava gives Marny a translucent quartz crystal she found at the base of the outcropping where she listened to Merlin's Notes. The crystal gets her Marny's HF2 for a third consecutive day.

She rides east on Eon Mainway, crossing the entire length of Six Four City. The twelve-lane thruway splits the city of 1.5 million evenly into two parallel rows of collectives, thirty-two to the north, thirty-two to the south.

The collectives are marked by four 64-story apartment towers situated on the corners of immense concrete plazas. On a clear day the towers can be seen by the naked eye from seventy miles away. Tall stone obelisks rise from the center point of each plaza. Engraved in the smooth, polished stone of each obelisk are reminders of Keeper Deliverance Day and the glories of Eon Reconstruction. Mosaics commemorating KDD and ER, as well as other Keeper achievements, are also displayed in the lobby of each tower.

Mornings on Eon Mainway are always the same. A parade of slow-moving carriages, sky taxies and pedestrians, ever-present drones circulating above the city like drowsy flies, holograms of Magnificent Paradeo and commercial products flicking on and off along the broad mainway median at alternating heights, flashing vibrant, colorful images upon the dull, gray machinery of everyday life in Six Four City.

Ava shoots a glance down a side street. The first time she saw the grim donut-shaped structures she was almost five and sitting in an ordporter cabin with Fyo on their way to an ET Academy prequalification session in Midway City. Fyo noted Ava's troubled little face. He told her not to worry and assured her the nuclear fusion reactors were guardians of the city. They made sure everybody had light, cool air and water.

After the stressful, exhausting trip to Midway City, Ava was happy to see the NFRs arranged before the city like a welcoming committee, but that safe feeling went away when they entered the lobby of Tower 64D. Fyo stopped before the big wall mosaic, which depicted high-spirited Ords and shiny-eyed robots working side by side building an apartment tower under the watchful gaze of Keeper supervisors.

When Fyo failed to respond to Ava's hand tug, she asked him why he was upset. He glanced at her with a funny look, as if he'd been presented a riddle. Ava looked for the answer in the mosaic and noticed X's slashed over the faces of the Keepers. Fyo smiled, said it was nothing to worry about.

That evening Ava played Robot Warriors on the kitchen floor with Marny. She'd been tuning in and out of Fyo and Mya's murmurings when Marny let a robot warrior drop from his hand onto the floor and shifted his full attention to their progens' conversation.

Marny's focused gaze gave the impression he was understanding everything Fyo and Mya were saying, though, of course, that was not possible because Marny was a toddler and not all that interested in anything he couldn't hold in his hands.

Then Fyo said something that frightened her: "Jaybo Gil disappeared."

It wasn't so much what he said that made her afraid, but how he said it, and the look of intense concern on his face, which was similar to the way he looked when he had stared at the defaced mosaic.

Ava lay awake that night wondering where Jaybo Gil had disappeared to. She also realized for the first time ever how much he looked like Fyo. The thought obsessed her to such a degree that she got up every hour to make sure Fyo and Mya were still in bed and Marny hadn't turned into an alien.

Consumed by bad thoughts, Ava nearly collides with another HF2. In that moment, her decision to cross the entire length of Six Four City to find Topper seems foolish. What if Willie fails to respond to her voice and plays dead in front of Topper? And whatever did happen to Jaybo Gil?

No reason she can't swing the HF2 around and go back to Collective 64. Would it be so bad to spend her final hours of leave dabbling with Fyo's puzzle, or watching Marny carve wood, or lying down in bed with her eyes open or shut and her mind comfortably blank?

But her legs won't stop pedaling. Her doubts and the mystery of Jaybo Gil fade away as she covers the last stretch of Eon Mainway and enters Collective 01. She slows down, turns right at the corner, and rides up First Street. She circles the plaza and its four apartment towers a couple of times, hoping Topper will magically appear.

He doesn't. It's a bad plan. Pretty embarrassing, actually. She's glad no one is paying attention to her.

After the third time circling the collective, she stops at the southeast corner of the city and gets off the HF2. The barrens stretch for miles and miles. She takes it all in, tries to balance the thrill of the unknown with her fear of it. She opens her backpack to make sure Willie is still there. A drone slowly descends and sizes her up as she places her hand on the wobot's hard little head.

Ava challenges the drone. "What are you compared to a bird?" In response, the drone sways from side to side.

The image of the bluebird springing from Derelok Yoreasy's mouth revisits her. Its effect is nearly as surprising and satisfying as its original appearance. She straps on the backpack and mounts the HF2. No more drones or K-Eyes allowed to dwell in her head, no more truth talks that are lies.

What she wants is singing bluebirds and talking rabbits, unimaginable things becoming imagined, the impossible becoming possible. Yes, those things, and maybe a friend too.

Ava spots a shadowy plateau in the distance, the Six Four City landfill. Why, she wonders as she rides toward it, would any sensible person visit such a wretched place? But her legs feel right pedaling toward the repulsive site. Thirteen miles later, there she is, sniffing the edge of a rising, rolling landscape of pungent waste, wondering when she's ever smelled anything so foul.

Despite the nasty stench, she rides all the way around to the opposite side of the landfill and stops upwind where the stink is still bad, but not quite so bad. Out over the open land she is struck by the silver-green creeping mass that looks destined to one day overrun the landfill. She's imagining what that might look like one day in the distant future when she hears a familiar voice behind her say, "Bucknuts."

Ten

"Those are bucknut vines, in case you were wondering."

Ava turns around. "Is that what they are?"

"Follow me," Topper says and heads back toward the garbage hill he came out of. To Ava's dismay, he lowers his head and disappears through a hole.

Ava draws closer. This is not what she wants to do.

"Smells bad, I know, but it won't collapse," she hears him say in a strange fading voice, "and the smell goes away after a while. Leave the two-wheel there with the others."

The others? What is going on here? She enters the hole grudgingly and leaves Marny's HF2 leaning against the buttressed trash wall among several other two-wheels. Topper waves a lumen stick that provides her enough light to keep pace with his dim figure as they jog through a maze of tunnels. The stench fades the deeper they go, just as he said, and the tunnels are wide enough to keep her grim thoughts from suffocating her. But fifteen minutes later, Ava stops at a fork and wonders, do I go left or right?

"Topper?"

So what did happen to Jaybo Gil?

"Topper?"

"I'm here."

She hears his footsteps.

"Did you ask me what happened to Jaybo Gil?" she says.

"Who?"

"He's… Never mind. Where are we going?"

"We're almost there. Here, take my hand."

A minute later she's relieved to enter a large dimly lit cavern.

"We're here," Topper announces, either to her or to the figures gathering before them. "Ava, meet your friends."

What an odd thing to say. Her friends?

"Hi Ava, remember me? I'm Gabi Cruz, your neighbor from 64D."

"Floriah Mills here."

"I'm Winka."

"My name is Rahim."

"Paxto, at your service."

"And Lola also says hi," Topper says.

Ava looks around.

"My twin sib. She's up in the Cloud. That's why you can't see her."

Ava smiles. "Okay?"

She glances at the others, realizes Topper's not joking.

"What are these tunnels for?" is all she can think to say.

"We were hoping you could tell us," Gabi says.

"Me?"

"We've all had the dreams," Floriah says, staring at Ava.

"The space vamps," Paxto says.

For an instant Ava thinks the big, burly fellow is having a little fun at her expense. But everyone looks far too serious for it to be a joke. They're waiting for her to respond, she realizes. She nods uncertainly, caught between surprise and relief. So, she's not the only one who knows?

"What sensible Ord would freely choose to visit this horrible place?" Gabi says.

"And yet, seven of us have come together here in the past couple of hours," says Floriah.

"There has to be a reason," Gabi says.

"Topper was the first," Paxto says.

"Then Paxto, and then the rest of us, one after another," says Gabi.

"Last night I dreamed of seven bluebirds," Winka says.

Ava gazes at the tall, thin girl. Was she there in the games court when Topper did his magic? Were the others there?

"You're the seventh one," Winka says solemnly, and then smiles broadly. Her eyes are like those of a child who has just received a wonderful gift, and the gift is Ava.

Ava's own eyes have adjusted to the dim cavern lighting. She is struck by how different from one another they all are. What a peculiar group of individuals.

Maybe she is the most peculiar of them all, she thinks. She takes a deep breath as she slips off her backpack.

"There's a talking rabbit in there," she says pointing. "I found him in the barrens. His name is Willie."

She doesn't want to look up, but she does. No one is laughing, nor even smiling. They're all listening intently.

"His voice takes a little getting used to. But then a man's voice comes out of that little mouth, and that voice is so clear, it sounds like someone standing right beside you. His name is Merlin Stone, and he lived two-thousand years ago."

The group's silence persists. She imagines herself among them, evaluating the bizarre claim issued from the lips of this spikey-haired stranger.

How would she react to such madness? Why, she'd either laugh or remain politely silent.

"Merlin tells a story like none I've ever heard," she says. "For one thing, it rings truer than any Keeper truth talk we've been subjected to. But what's most engaging about his story, at least to me, is that it's our story too. And somehow, two-thousand years later, it's found its way to us."

The ground begins to shake. Did her words do that?

Rocks and dust rain down from the cavern's ceiling. A deep crackling blast follows. The cavern lurches forward and back, tossing Ava to the ground.

Eleven

She jumps back up onto her feet and dashes through the maze of smoky tunnels into the harsh light of a gray morning wondering how in stars it took Topper so long to cover the same distance on the way in.

The HF2 is right where she left it. She races back to Six Four City, aiming the two-wheel toward the black clouds and the sharp smell of life being burnt away.

She covers the thirteen miles in a ridiculously short time, and finds herself stuck in the middle of a dense, slow-moving crowd that's heading west toward the disaster. The Collective 64 towers are in flames!

"Twenty-four thousand dead!"

Who said that? She can't decide which of the many men surrounding her said twenty-four thousand were dead.

"And what will happen to us if the wind shifts?" a woman to her left says.

Ava squints at her, the simmering air burning her eyes. "Then the entire city will burn," Ava replies, but the woman ignores her and keeps repeating the question.

Hundreds of thousands of Ords continue to pour out of the towers, filling Eon Mainway and every side street. A man stumbles against Marny's HF2, knocking Ava onto the hard pavement. Her elbow cracks like a walnut and she lets out a cry. The edge of the HF2 pedal bar gouges her calf. Flames of pain shoot up through her body.

She gasps for air as she tries to untangle herself from the HF2 and other people's limbs. Two progens with two offees pick their way over her as if she were someone's spilled trash. The youngest, a boy Marny's age, pauses to study her face. His eyes expand with awful wonder as she stares back at him.

Ava drags herself up off the pavement and limps toward the fiery towers, squeezing herself and Marny's HF2 through the crowd. Coughs and groans shape a communal discourse. People keep looking at the sky.

"Why are you looking at the sky?" Ava cries. "That's not where the dead are!"

Her shouts draw one or two glances. No one challenges her assertion that the dead are not in the sky. The choking masses continue pressing forward toward the four burning towers of Collective 64.

Ava rubs her eyes and, for an instant, the chemical world around her brightens to an unnatural degree. A wild thought enters her mind: Apollyon has returned to finish what it started two-thousand years ago!

A hand grabs her arm from behind. She shakes it off and continues pressing forward. But again, the same greedy hand clutches at her shattered elbow. She yelps in pain and wheels around with her other hand raised and ready to strike.

"Winka, what are you doing here?"

"We're being called," Winka says. "Director X is going to appear in the sky very soon, and he'll tell us what to do."

Ava shakes her head, and moves on, but Winka won't leave her alone. She's out of control, spouting nonsense, her head rolling and bobbing emphatically.

"He'll wear hats and have big wings. He'll be here soon to tell us things we should know. Director X will soon be in the sky to provide guidance."

Winka groans as she falls to the ground. Ava drops to her knees beside her and takes her hand. Someone's knee rams into her shoulder, knocking her off balance. An impish boy appears out of thin air, hops onto Marny's HF2 and takes off. The crowd splits open, allowing him passage.

He's got her backpack! He's got Willie! "Hey, you creep! Come back here!"

She scrambles to her feet, but her path is blocked by the thief's collaborators. "You can't do this! He stole my HF2! Someone, please stop him!"

The boy swivels his head a horrifying hundred-and-eighty degrees and flashes a bright toothy smile. Then everything comes to a sudden stop and turns fuzzy.

"Ava, are you alright?" Topper says as he helps her up.

Gabi hands her a water bottle.

"Drink, you're dehydrated," she says.

Ava stares in amazement at Gabi, then at Topper. Winka and the others are there too, everyone there in the large cavern, just as they were before she went on that nightmare ride to Six Four City.

"Twenty-four thousand dead," Ava murmurs. "Mya and Marny."

Gabi glances at Topper. "You fainted," she says as she brushes dust off Ava's hair and shoulders. "Oxygen levels in here are low to begin with. Plus, you've been riding all morning and are dehydrated. You lost your balance and fell during the tremors, bumped your head on the ground."

"Where's Willie?" Ava says.

"In your backpack, right?" Gabi says. "You were telling us about Merlin Stone when the ground started to shake."

"How long was I out?"

"Not long, a few seconds."

Another tremor, more restrained this time, like a warning.

"We have to get out of here," Topper says. "I'll take your backpack, Ava."

The others start moving in the opposite direction from which they all came.

"Marny's two-wheel," Ava says.

"We have to leave the two-wheels," Topper says.

"But—"

"We can't go back that way."

"I bet Miss Glinty has something to do with this."

"I'm not so sure. I have a feeling the Keepers are going to be the least of our worries."

"You don't know Marny," Ava says. "I have to go back."

A steel beam and chunks of concrete crash to the ground several feet in front of them, shooting up a cloud of dust.

"We have to go," Topper says between coughs. "You're no good to Marny or anyone if you're dead."

"I know, but…"

She hears her voice, and it sounds small and ridiculous against the roar of a collapsing world.

Topper's right. She nods and starts jogging after the others. Grief runs alongside her, making her legs weak. But why grieve? In all likelihood, Collective 64 is just the way she left it. And Mya and Marny are just the way she left them.

She glances back. Topper is right behind, wiping dust from his tongue.

Twelve

There are so many turns it makes her dizzy. After what seems longer than ten minutes, they stumble into another cavern.

"Twenty-four thousand dead," Winka says.

"It was a dream," Ava replies.

"What about Director X?" Winka says.

"Who's Director X?" Floriah says. She looks from Winka to Ava and back to Winka. "What's going on?"

"Listen," Topper says. A low murmur, like the beginnings of a growl, puts everyone on alert. "Everybody, grab a hand and let's get out of here."

Topper takes Ava's hand and leads the group through a side tunnel.

"Topper?" Ava says a short while later.

"I know, it's getting louder. It seems counterintuitive, but I'm sure this is the way we have to go."

To Ava, the counterintuitive jog through the tunnel feels like a prelude to mass suicide. A short while later they come to a sudden halt before a wall of compacted earth, and Ava's fears appear to be amply justified.

It doesn't help that Topper is looking uncharacteristically hesitant and uncertain. He releases Ava's hand and goes to the wall. "There is a way out," he says, glancing back. "Wait there, all of you. I want to check something."

Topper disappears. If she hadn't witnessed the miracle of the bluebird, Ava would be assuming the worst, that maybe Topper had just been consumed by the wall, or vaporized.

She dismisses her fears and feels a sudden invisible pull, too powerful to ignore. She releases Gabi's hand and walks over to the wall on her left. Her hands feel along the cool, craggy surface. The wall offers no encouragement, but she now believes Topper's decision to come this way was correct. She runs her fingers over the wall, then stops and tilts her head, as if she were listening to a voice. But there is no voice.

Her hand slips into a small gap that seemed not to be there an instant ago. A shudder courses through her body as she inhales the thin hybrid air of the widening hole. She inserts her head and arms into it, feels the paved surface, estimates a diameter of four feet, and who knows how long?

It seems this is the way out, but rather than relief, she feels dread. The prospect of crawling through a narrow tunnel for who knows how long makes her lightheaded. She pulls herself out of the hole panting and slides down to her knees, her vision clouded.

Gabi touches her shoulder, apparently triggering a series of deafening discharges. Confused, Ava twists around and sees the others stumbling about. Behind them Topper is being chased by plumes of dense white smoke.

Without saying a word, Topper climbs into the hole. The others, though anxious to follow, defer to Ava.

"I don't know that I can," she says.

"You have to," Gabi says. "We have no choice."

No one says another word. Ava climbs up into the hole and begins to crawl after Topper.

"It's going to be okay," she hears him say, and a moment later Topper's lumen stick goes out.

"The lumens are all out," she hears Floriah say behind them.

"It's okay, it's going to be okay," Topper says.

But okay is relative. She'll crawl, but how far? And now she'll have to do it in total darkness. How long before her claustrophobic mind and body lock down? Then she'll lie in place motionless, her body melding with the tunnel. The others will crawl over her if they want to live. They'll have to, like it or not. They'll have no choice, as Gabi said.

Then she hears it again, not a voice in the usual sense, but a movement, like the movement of blood, silent and serene. Is this Lola's language, she wonders?

Close your eyes. Move through the darkness with slow breaths. Move like a steady river, and let the darkness be your pathway to light.

Topper says, "You found the way out for us. You did it, Ava." He waits for her to respond, but she remains silent.

"Move like a steady river," he says.

"Let the darkness be your pathway to light," Ava replies.

"Yes, let the darkness be your pathway to light," Topper says. "Tell Gabi to pass it back."

The words flow up and down the line, but soon they all fall silent again. The rhythmic brush of hands and knees becomes background music to thoughts of coping and surviving. To Ava, the following minutes feel like hours.

"Topper?"

She scrambles forward, her limbs stiffening with fear.

"Topper!"

"Ava?"

"You're going too fast."

"Oh."

She crawls carefully now, extending her hand until she touches the heel of his shoe.

"Let's take a breather," Topper says. "Three minutes. Pass it back."

"Three-minute breather," Ava says. "Pass it back."

"Is it my imagination, or is it getting easier to breathe?" Topper says.

"Now that you mention it, yes, a little easier," Ava says.

She stares at Topper's blurred silhouette, black against the now minimally lightened background.

"I can see you move," she says. "I couldn't before. That means there's light up ahead."

"There's light at the end of the quantum rabbit hole," Topper says cheerfully. "Pass it back."

"Yes, the quantum rabbit hole," Ava says. "Gabi, there's light at the end of the quantum rabbit hole."

Within moments the words come back to them. "Paxto says there's light at the end of the quantum rabbit hole."

A few minutes later, the rabbit hole takes a precipitous dip. Topper hesitates an instant and then slides down a long steel chute that ends with a loud splash and the sound of his laughter. Ava follows, plunging feet first into the pool. They're all laughing and catching their breath and talking as they come out of the water.

But the celebratory mood quickly dissipates. The strange pale blue light emitting from the far wall of the cave triggers much speculation. And the hole they came out of has sealed itself shut, making it impossible for them to go back to the tunnels even if they wanted to. A quick examination of the cave reveals no obvious exit. And to further dampen spirits, Rahim discovers in a recess the skeletal remains of four humans. The Seven take turns examining the bones and the hollowed-out tomb.

"What were they looking for?" Floriah wonders aloud, but no one ventures a guess.

One by one they engage the blue wall with optimism. They run their fingers over it, press their ears against it. Paxto licks the wall in search of mineral clues. Winka sits for hours before it, asking the wall questions, waiting for a response that never comes.

At the end of the first day, Gabi divvies up the protein loaves she's been carrying in her backpack. The Seven sit on the ground in a semicircle and eat in silence.

Topper points at the blue wall. "That is the way out," he says after swallowing his last morsel. "All we have to do is come up with the how part."

The words offer little comfort. After an extended silence, Ava stands up, takes Willie out of the backpack, and sets him on the ground.

"Willie, these are my friends."

"Hello to one and all!" Willie says.

"Willie, bring us Merlin."

Thirteen

Every day is a dim mirror of the previous day. The water that baptized the Seven into this strange captivity is pooled behind them like an unspoken question: Did we come here to die?

Life in the blue cave becomes grimly ritualistic. The hopeful search for an exit begins each day and soon ends in failure. The obligatory word of encouragement follows faithfully. They take turns keeping hope alive.

Then comes the first morsel of the day, followed by an audience with Willie, the quantum rabbit. They sit for hours on the cave floor facing Willie and listening to Merlin's *Notes to Unknown Survivor*.

They listen day after day, revisiting the joys, sorrows and mysteries of a long-ago time and a long-ago people. And with each listen, they recognize something of themselves in that time and in those people. And they find to be true what they've known all along in their blood, that to be human is far more interesting and purposeful than what the Keepers would have them believe. It's also far more dangerous.

After the Notes session, Willie goes into Sleep mode, looking like a disinterested idol, his velvety, turquoise coat enhanced by the blue light emitting from the wall behind him.

The Seven stand and stretch and wander about the cave like caged animals, each lost in memory or weighed down by regret and anxiety. In their worst moments, the skulls and bones of the dead nearby insinuate themselves into their thoughts and nudge them ever closer to despair.

If they didn't fully understand how tricky the art of living can be, they understand it now, and when they feel themselves getting too close to the edge of no return, they offer one another less dire things to consider.

For example, Paxto points to a stalactite hanging from the ceiling and says it reminds him of a sleeping bat. He points to another and a third, but of course, this is of no help.

Floriah follows a more productive path. Whatever happened to Paloma and Vigo after they entered the Haven, she wants to know? The group respond with a number of other provocative questions. Like, what happened to their baby? How did Willie end up in the ruins of an ashtown? And what in stars happened to Merlin anyway?

Ava wonders in silence if the Pearl Hart, whose name was imprinted on the MVP cup, has anything to do with Merlin's Pearl. Another hour passes before anyone speaks again.

"Do androids fall in love?"

The strangeness of Winka's question strikes everyone but Winka. By ET Academy standards, the question is inessential and unnecessarily provocative. It's the kind of question that prompts meetings with progens, followed by strict corrective measures to restore mental synchronization.

"What made you think of that?" Paxto says.

"Androids, or falling in love?" says Winka.

"Both, I mean, androids falling in love."

"I'm curious, that's all. Does anyone know?"

No one does.

Gabi breaks the last of the protein loaf into small pieces, which she distributes to everyone. She appears on the verge of saying something profound, but all she can manage is, "I wish I had packed more food."

"How were we supposed to know this would happen?" Topper says.

"Maybe you packed just the right amount," says Rahim, and they all look at their quiet friend, each pondering what his words could possibly mean.

Ava says, "Merlin's first words to Willie keep popping up in my head. What are the odds of any one of us existing?"

"Virtually zero," Floriah says.

"And yet, here we are," says Topper.

"Here we are," Gabi says, trying to sound upbeat, but her smile is a fleeting thing.

The bones and skulls behind them join the conversation: *How many days can an Ord go without food?*

Paxto initiates a rambling discussion about the adaptive potentiality of androids that soon leads back to Winka's earlier question. Do androids fall in love?

No one claims to be an expert on the subject, and no one commits one way or the other. No one wants to say Pearl, whom they've all grown to love, was herself incapable of giving or receiving love. And no one wants to speculate about what might have happened to Merlin after Pearl expired.

An uneasy silence permeates the cave, and one by one, the Seven recline on the ground and close their eyes.

Ava imagines Mya crumpled in a corner of Apt D55-12, her firstborn swept from existence, like Jaybo Gil. Marny will miss his two-wheel more than he'll miss her. And Fyo? Is Fyo trapped in a hole in the ground and starving, like her?

She drags herself through the exhausting fog of hunger and restless slumber, her brows furrowed with worry, her legs and heart heavy.

Then she hears my voice, which is not a voice in the traditional bio sense, as I've tried to make clear, but a soundless voice that, were it to be heard, would sound something like this:

Okay, Ava, listen carefully. Now is the time to see in a new way. See the barrens and the trees in the distance, see Romo helping you onto Apollo, see yourself galloping across the wasteland to the Haven.

"Wake up, everybody!" Ava cries, jumping to her feet.

"Whoa, what is going on?" Paxto says.

"I dreamed I was riding across the wasteland on Apollo. As we were about to enter the Haven, the blue wall appeared. Apollo huffed and shook his head. He pounded his hoof on the ground three times, then lunged at the wall. The wall gave way as Apollo leaped. When we entered the Haven, I heard the birdsong."

"And then I heard one bird singing!" Winka cries.

"Exactly!" Ava says.

"That's what Paloma said when she and Vigo rode into the Haven on Apollo," Gabi reminds everyone.

"And those were the last words dictated in the Notes," Winka adds, "meaning we've come full circle."

"Full circle, really?" Floriah says. "Can one of you please explain how this dream brings us any closer to getting out of here?"

"But don't you see?" Ava says. "The blue wall isn't just a wall."

"It's a timeway, how did we not see that?" Gabi says.

"Wait a minute," Paxto says.

"The timeway Pearl showed Merlin," Gabi says. "Don't you remember the hole with the silver-blue smoke?"

"The smoke cleared just long enough to reveal a pool of water, remember?" Ava says.

One by one, they all turn their heads. The pool of water that welcomed them to the blue cave is still there.

"Are you suggesting Stone Heights is on the other side of this wall?" Floriah says.

"Yes, I think so," Ava says.

"Stone Heights, like in 2104 AD?" says Paxto.

"Possibly, I don't know," Ava says.

"I'm not totally convinced that's what the dream means," Paxto says. "Like, has anyone considered the possibility the timeway was programmed into Pearl's artificial brain?"

After they've all had a couple of seconds to think about it, Topper says, "Why would anyone go through the trouble of doing that?"

"Gratuitous cruelty?" Paxto replies. "Who knows? And besides, it's not like there's evidence time travel is possible."

"There's no evidence it's not possible," Topper counters. "Let's not rule out the existence of what we don't understand, okay? Time travel? Alternate worlds? Parallel universes? Like you said, Paxto, who knows? We were all in agreement that there's a reason we're here. I think we still believe that. If that's true, we don't get out of here alive, unless maybe—"

"Unless Ava is right, and this blue wall is a timeway," Gabi says.

Topper nods in agreement.

"Or…" Floriah says.

"What?" Gabi says.

"What if we're being manipulated? I agree, I feel like there's a reason we're here, but what if that reason is to serve the Keepers' purposes? If I have to decide which is more likely, time travel, or an experiment by Keeper behavioralists, I'm probably going to lean toward the latter."

"I see your point," says Rahim, "but I also believe dreams sometimes speak truth to us."

"You heard truth?" Floriah says.

"I don't mean just Ava's dream. Just before she woke us, I was dreaming we were floating in outer space. I couldn't tell if we were dead or alive. Then I had this feeling of peace, because I understood we were on our way to some place to do some good thing. A thing far more important than being subjects in a Keeper experiment. Yes, Floriah, I heard truth."

After a long pause, Paxto says, "So all we need is a horse to break down the wall?"

They all start talking at once.

"Everybody, please, this is really important," Topper says and looks at Ava.

"Willie," Ava says.

"Hello everyone!"

"Willie, in the secret apartment Pearl showed Merlin the timeway, and he put his arm through the smoky hole."

"Yes, Note 16 March 2104, recorded 25 April 2104."

"Replay that part of the note again, Willie."

Almost immediately, they hear Merlin's voice:

On an impulse, I reach into the circle of smoke.

Pearl shouts "No!" as my arm disappears. She grabs me around the waist and pulls me back.

I feel a little dizzy, but I'm relieved to see that my arm remains attached and intact.

"What was that?"

"We're not meant to go that way, Merlin."

"What is this thing?"

"I told you, it's a timeway, and one day people from the future are going to come through it."

"Come here, to Stone Heights? How did you come up with all this?"

"I didn't come up with anything, Merlin. Willie told me."

"Willie, stop right there," Ava says. "Just so we're all clear on this, the blue wall behind you is a timeway, right?"

"Correct," Willie says.

She takes a deep breath.

"The same timeway Pearl showed Merlin?"

"Correct, though viewed from the opposite side and two-thousand years of separation; that is, 4104 AD to 2104 AD."

Ava lifts a hand so no one will interrupt her.

"Willie, can you show us how to get to the other side?"

"Of course, Ava."

Willie's casual reply produces a moment of collective stupefaction.

"Willie, why didn't you tell us this before?" she says.

"No one asked me. Also, everything that is happening is happening the way it is supposed to happen."

"Willie, do you know what we'll find on the other side?" Topper says.

Willie stalls for several seconds.

"A spectacle."

"What kind of—?"

"A test."

"Willie, are you alright?" Ava says.

"And wagers."

"What do you mean, wagers?" Topper says.

Willie stalls again, opens his mouth for just a moment and closes it. His ears draw back submissively.

"Willie, what's happening to you?" Ava says.

Willie's ears rise to attention. Suddenly, sounding more like himself, he says, "How about I play you a song, Ava? *We Gotta Get Out of This Place*? *Stop in the Name of Love*? *Help*?

Ava glances at Topper's troubled face.

"Some other time, Willie," she says. "Right now, it's best you show us how to get out of here."

Fourteen

The faint sucking sensation ends with a *poof!* Ava is delivered into dark, silent space. Her arms and legs twitch reflexively. She reaches out, but there's nothing to grab onto. After a few frantic moments, she stops trying and lets herself float.

At a distance, three girls that look like her are chasing one another in a perfect circle. The circle drifts closer, and Ava's heart starts thumping. Good stars, it is her, Ava! Three Ava's! Past Ava chasing present Ava, chasing future Ava, chasing past Ava, her life history rendered in a perpetual circle, its gravitational pull keeping her from tumbling into oblivion.

"Ava?" she calls out, but the three Ava's are too absorbed in their pursuit of one another to notice her. "Ava, it's me!" she shouts. Zilch, no nod, no wave of the hand, nothing.

Maybe this was a bad idea. *This* meaning everything. The questioning of this, that, and the other, the bucknut pies, the gathering in the tunnels, friendship, common purpose, the strict, daily consumption of Merlin's Notes, the timeleap.

Just as she's about to scream, she drops like an arrow. It takes only a second, and she lands softly, feetfirst, on solid ground. Someone's holding her right hand, someone her left. It's too dark to see who they are, and the whole thing is enormously confusing, but holding fleshy, living hands feels good, and suddenly things don't seem quite so bleak.

She wishes Willie were here. He told them he wasn't configured to withstand the rigors of timeleaping and would succumb to fatal error on attempting to cross the threshold. He looked droopy and downcast in an eerily humanlike way as he said this, prompting Topper to assure him they would return for him. But Willie seemed in no mood to be patronized, or at least that was the impression he left her. He played deaf and slipped into Sleep mode.

"Off the charts weird, seeing me chasing myself in space," a distant male voice says.

First words spoken since the timeleap.

"The Timeleaper's Dance," a distant female voice adds.

The new darkness becomes so intense it suppresses all sound and whittles to the bone the hands Ava is holding, grinds them down into cold, little sticks that crumble from her grasp.

And now she's all alone again, perched at the entrance of a windy, echoey vault that seems to be suggesting what she suspects, that yes, life has come to a stop. Oddly, the realization doesn't make her sad, or happy, or anything. In fact, this is the time to find a nook to curl into. Who knows, maybe in the distant future a curio seeker will find her bones and lay them on the ground in neat rows in remembrance of an unknown human.

A funny thought—well, maybe not so funny—occurs to her. Is the Timeleaper's Dance the prelude to every human

359

death? Could that be how we all die, gazing at ourselves chasing ourselves?

Oh, for starsake, now what? Her hands, wrists, arms and shoulders crumble and drop like dust. How is she supposed to curl up into anything in this condition?

"Now what?" Paxto says.

Exactly what I was saying. Hey, wait a minute!

"Paxto?" she cries, and with her suddenly regenerated hand, she swats death away, for the moment anyway.

Good old Paxto and his fresh, bold voice.

Huh, so she is alive. And the others too! She can feel Gabi and Topper's hands in her own hands again, fleshy and alive.

A harsh spotlight explodes upon the Seven to the sound of raucous applause, and a freakishly long figure descends from above wrapped in a cone of soft, sparkling light.

At first glance he appears to be naked, but for an off-white fedora and a flowing purple scarf draped around his neck. His grandiose descent pauses a dozen feet above the ground. He remains suspended in the air for several seconds, hands raised in acknowledgement of the wildly responsive audience. Then he drops to the ground with the grace of a world class gymnast, knees flexing, hands and arms spreading wide like wings.

I say *he*, only because he looks remotely like a man. His long skeletal figure is clad in skintight white satin from neck to caramel-colored crocodile shoes.

He bows as he tips the brim of his hat, and his body remains bent for longer than you would think is necessary. When he resumes an upright posture, the spotlights merge, enveloping the Seven and the stranger in a circle of light.

"Formally, Adjudipredilextragalact for Cosmic Spectacles and Wagers; otherwise, known as Director X, serving at the pleasure of Omega Company."

Director X of the burning towers and the 24,000 dead? Ava's and Winka's eyes lock for a moment.

"What in stars?" Paxto murmurs.

"What in stars, indeed! Why, aren't you the lucky ones? Come to claim center stage in the greatest intergalactic production of all space and time!"

Director X waits for the crowd noise to die down before resuming.

"Given how far we've come, it is almost inconceivable to believe that, not long ago, the central question on the staff's Critical Decisions List was: Does *My Greek Adventure* have the legs to carry the production forward?"

"You mean Merlin's kidnapping?" Ava says.

Director X points at Ava and presses his forefinger over his invisible lips as a warning against further interruptions. He passes a mechanical, silver-eyed gaze over the group before continuing.

"At inception, the collaborator, Atwell Stone—given his innate complexity and disproportionate impact on human vision and enterprise—was deemed the prime candidate to fill the production's role of protagonist. Stone provided a solid foundation that guaranteed a steady, if unspectacular, rise in spectator subscriptions, wagers, and spinoff activity.

"In time, steady but unspectacular proved inadequate, prompting discussions regarding Atwell Stone's own recommendation, the so-called *Absurd Proposal*: Why not make his issue, the one of inferior mind, subpar talents and indolent nature, the new centerpiece of *The Human Show*? Oddly, several markers had already begun to point in that direction. But who in his right mind could have imagined that such an ordinary creature would capture the imagination of an interstellar audience to such a degree that intergalactic real-time entertainment would be driven to record levels of popularity and profit? And yet, that is exactly what Merlin Stone brought to the table! And we have the ratings to prove it!"

Abruptly, Director X's eyes dart about seeking the source of his sudden vague displeasure. He stops at Topper, whose firm, defiant gaze, though irksome, is sure to come in handy, production-wise. Director X makes a mental note, straightens himself up to his full nine-foot height, and continues what increasingly appears to be a prepared speech.

"The answer to the question, 'Does *My Greek Adventure* have the legs to carry the production forward?' was a resounding yes. Even now, at this late hour, interest in *The Human Show* continues to build. Bingers from distant galaxies such as GN-z11 and UDFj-39546284 have gone to great lengths to bring themselves up to speed in order that they might join the trillions of viewers eager to see how the next chapter of the human paradox resolves in real time."

At that instant, the merged spotlights shut off, leaving all in darkness.

"The human paradox?" Floriah says.

"Please understand, there is no authorized path back to the blue cave," Director X says from above, his voice fading as he rises. "And, in any event, what would you do in such crude lodgings? Watch one another decompose like the four so-called prophets who preceded you?"

A few seconds later, something like daylight displaces the darkness, and the seven timeleapers find themselves in what appears to be an immense dome.

Fifteen

Because there's no going back, because they have no idea of how to go back or where *back* is, or what's going to happen when they get to wherever they're supposed to go, they trod silently across an ever-expanding dome, their thoughts shifting from dark to light and light to dark.

Winka spots what looks like a shiny cube a quarter of a mile away. Without saying a word, she heads toward it. The group follow her. They stop a short distance from a large glass box. Inside the box is a hospital bed and an IV pole with infusion pump and fluids bag hanging from metal hooks. A biosensor monitor displays vital signs data transmitted wirelessly by multiple sensor patches.

The patient's left foot twitches. They all see it twitch. Unable to control himself any longer, Paxto strides toward the box, only to stop when a young woman materializes at the patient's bedside. The woman, who's in her late twenties, shows no sign of being aware of Paxto, or of any of the timeleapers. She seems, in fact, indecisive and unable to bring herself to touch the sleeping man, which may be what she most wants to do. Gripped by inexpressible emotion, she covers her mouth just as the man's right knee pokes up for an instant and then drops flat like a hammer.

"Merlin," she says, and her voice is like a wound inflicted on each of the timeleapers.

"Good stars!" Gabi cries.

Paxto retreats to the group. It doesn't seem that Pearl heard Gabi's cry, nor saw Paxto scampering away. Looks like she has no idea she and Merlin are on public display.

Neither does the peppy physician who appears on the scene accompanied by a female nurse and male attendants. The doctor introduces herself as Doctor Patty and does a quick check of Merlin's vital signs. She nods to the nurse, who peels the sensor patches from Merlin's skin. The two male attendants raise the upper half of the bed and prop up Merlin.

The stranger that is Pearl draws Merlin's attention, demanding all of it. He groans as he lurches away from her and falls off the bed.

The doctor rolls her eyes as she and Pearl watch the attendants lift Merlin up off the floor and settle him back onto the bed. "Muscle atrophy," Doctor Patty explains to Pearl, "along with a healthy dose of brain torpor, ha-ha. Nothing that patience, time and the right elixir won't fix, though. Now Mister Stone, be assured, there is nothing to fear. Your recovery is fully guaranteed."

"Re-cov-ry?" Merlin says.

The nurse, who looks like a larger version of the doctor, hands Merlin a blue flask. "Mister Stone, you will want to drink this custom elixir to accelerate the recovery of your mental faculties," she says. "To reiterate what Doctor Patty said, we guarantee one-hundred percent recovery. Your mind will reclaim your body and memory and make you entirely you again, and sooner than you might expect."

"How long was me, uhm, was I, er, not me?"

"Oh, but you never stopped being you, Mister Stone, stars forbid it," Doctor Patty says. "No, no, no, don't you see what Nurse Pink is trying to tell you? Granted, the matter can seem complicated, but your lovely friend here will fill you in on the details, I'm sure. Go on, be a big boy and drink up now, ha-ha. No, seriously, for your own good, Mister Stone, you will need to consume every last drop if you hope to effectively understand all the marvelous things your friend is going to tell you."

Merlin glances at Doctor Patty, Nurse Pink, and the two male attendants. Then he settles his gaze on Doctor Patty and waits. She hesitates a moment before vanishing from the glass box with her team.

He lifts the flask and takes an exploratory sip, then sneaks a glance at the young woman, more out of curiosity than suspicion now. Pearl takes a step back from the bed, avoiding his gaze.

After several deep trembling breaths, Merlin lifts the flask to his mouth, and the blue fluid gurgles down his throat like a summer drink.

"Who are you?" he says, licking his blue lips.

"I was in a bed like that," she says turning back to face him. "I was hooked up to the same equipment. I woke up one day. Doctor Patty, Nurse Pink, and the same two attendants were present when I awoke. I drank the blue liquid from a flask just like the one you have there. They told me I would soon begin to reclaim my mind and body, just like they told you. I have to say, within minutes of drinking the elixir I did remember you. And then many other things too, like dying and how sad it made you to watch me die."

She frowns the way one might before breaking into tears. Merlin's expression softens.

"But you didn't die," he reminds her.

"I asked Doctor Patty, do you know a man named Merlin Stone? She said you were being cared for in another room. She said you remained *entangled*, and that the condition takes a little while to resolve. She said I myself had woken from a three-year mental entanglement, and that in time, you would also wake up and remember everything."

Merlin lifts the flask and downs the last few drops. He holds the empty flask before him and watches it reshape itself into a small glass ball. The transformation is no surprise to either of them. He doesn't question why an emptied flask would become a glass ball because, do the laws of physics even apply in such a place? He studies the glass ball and sees an ocean inside it. Okay, but what is he failing to see inside this mysteriously pleasant young woman?

Pearl looks down and away again. He sets the glass ball aside on the mattress and with difficulty shifts his hips.

"Help me up," he says.

She wraps her arm around his waist, and he hangs his arm over her shoulder. With her aid he is able to stand, though unsteadily.

"Let's walk," he says. But it takes Merlin nearly two minutes to stabilize his legs enough to take that first step.

Let's say seven minutes to reach the glass wall. Merlin puts his hand against the wall. They stare at the exact spot where the timeleapers are grouped, but they don't see them. After a minute's rest, they head back to the bed. The journey back takes another five minutes. Exhausted, Merlin drops his bottom on the edge of the bed, and Pearl sits beside him, not quite touching him, but close, very close.

"Pearl," he says after taking a deep breath. "You're Pearl, aren't you?"

She smiles and takes his hand.

"What in stars happened?" he says.

"Your father told me some things, but I can't tell you I understood everything he said."

"Atwell... Wait, don't tell me we're on Mars."

"Yes, we're in New Terra City. We were brought here three years ago, after your thirtieth birthday party."

Merlin gets lost in thought. "There were two women, a bed, a horse pill," he says softly. "I fell asleep."

"I was serving drinks at the party, do you remember?"

"I do, you were wearing a—"

"Yes, a catsuit, which I'd rather forget. I saw you leaving the dome with two beautiful women. You were drunk. I was concerned, so I followed you down to Sublevel-2 to a warehouse. A doorway opened in the wall, and the three of you walked into an apartment. I fell asleep on the warehouse floor. A while later, I heard you heading back to the dome. I saw that the wall remained open. I don't know what got into me. I suppose I was curious. I entered the apartment. Just for a moment or two, I told myself. But the opening closed, and I got trapped inside. I couldn't find a way out. I fell asleep on the couch. The next time I saw you was in the garden at Stone Heights three years later."

"But you said we've been here for three years."

"It's complicated. The boy, Vick…"

"You mean Vick Molly? What about him?"

"He walked out of the garden just before you walked in. I panicked. I don't know why. It didn't take you long to find me cowering behind the rose bushes. You didn't recognize me. That was six months ago, March 2104."

"But wait, if I found you in Stone Heights, how can you say we've been here on Mars for three years?"

"Because—"

"Because we were in two places at once?"

"You could say that. Our real bodies have been here on Mars, but at the same time, our android doppelgangers were living out our lives on Terra."

But why? He stares at Pearl and hears Atwell's voice in his head:

I shortlisted Pearl a year ago… wasn't designed to thrive in a broken world… is one of our top prototypes… a stellar representative of the Elara-3 line… has as much choice in where she's going to end up as your Mollys do.

He touches her cheek. "Please tell me you're real."

"I'm real."

"Say it again."

"I am real, I promise you."

"Again."

"Merlin, I am a flesh and blood human being."

"How can I remember things I didn't experience? How can I remember dictating *Notes to Unknown Survivor*, recording events I couldn't possibly have witnessed or been part of while lying asleep in a glass box on Mars?"

"But you did experience all those things, and you did dictate those Notes."

Merlin closes his eyes and rubs his temples. He stares across the clean white room in the direction of the seven timeleapers, but sees only his reflection staring back at him.

"So they uploaded our minds to artificial brains?" he says.

"Yes, soon after we were knocked out, and before our bodies were transferred to Mars."

"The horse pill knocked me out."

"Yes, apparently."

"And you?"

"They must have injected me with something while I was asleep in the apartment."

"You said Atwell talked to you."

"I think he wanted us to know at least some of the things that happened to us."

"How thoughtful of him."

"Are you familiar with quantum entanglement, Merlin?"

"We were quantum entangled with androids?"

"Something like that. Our minds, will, and memory were uploaded to the androids' artificial brains, just like you guessed, and we became mentally entangled with them. Atwell told me to think of my brain and the android's brain as two separate, but specially connected, bottles. You pour liquid out of one bottle, and that poured amount ends up in the other bottle, and vice versa, no matter where the bottles are, even if they happen to be on opposite ends of the universe."

"Okay, so when our minds got poured into those artificial brains, the androids assumed control of our lives."

"No, the androids could only do what we wanted them to do. They had no reason to believe they weren't human. There was no way for them to do anything other than what our human brains wanted them to do."

Merlin studies Pearl's eyes, her mouth, her eyes again. Then he stares at the floor for a long time.

"Are you all right, Merlin?"

"I saw you die."

"I know you did, but remember, it was your Yada-7 that saw my Elara-3 *expire*. That was the moment full mental capacity began shifting back to me here on Mars. It took me a couple of days to wake up. Your Yada-7 expired a few days ago, and here you are awake now, and in recovery mode. Everything our android counterparts experienced remains with us, as if we ourselves were the ones walking around Terra and doing all the things our minds wanted us to do. Nothing was or is lost."

"One-hundred percent recovery?"

"It takes time for our brains to reorganize all the material, but yes, one-hundred percent recovery. Another thing you should know, Merlin. Atwell said android brains can't surpass ninety-four percent mental capacity at any given moment because the induced deep-sleep state we were in maintains at minimum six percent functionality, which is reserved for bio-maintenance and essential brain activity, like dreaming. In rare instances, like when responding to certain stimuli, real brain activity can temporarily spike to up to twelve percent. Limb and head movements and talking can occur during these spikes, though I've been told whatever we might say is unintelligible, sounding more like an alien tongue than any known Terran language."

How unintelligible? Merlin has a picture of Atwell leaning over his deep-sleep body with hand cupped to his ear trying to decipher the gibberish spilling from his son's mouth.

"Okay, let's say that during deep sleep my mental capacity spikes to twelve percent for a minute or so. That means my Yada-7 back on Terra is operating at eighty-eight percent?"

"Rare, from what I understand, but that would be enough to affect the android's ability to function properly. That twelve percent deficiency would likely trigger some disconnect or disorder and may be the reason your android couldn't remember anything before Apollyon. Getting access to the Notes through Willie and listening to your own voice is what gave your android's artificial brain circuitry the boost it needed to restore the misplaced data."

"And that's why I couldn't remember who you were when I, I mean, my Yada-7, saw you, that is, your Elara-3, in Stone's Eden."

"In so many words, yes," she says and laughs.

"I don't get it. Yada-7s, Elara-3s, you and me turned into lab rats. Why us? What's Atwell up to?"

She looks ready to say something, but holds her tongue.

"What else did he say to you, Pearl?"

"Not much else. I get the feeling he has regrets."

"I can think of a few reasons he might feel that way."

Merlin tries to get up to walk, but his legs don't hold up. He flops back down on his rear end. Pearl reaches for his arm. He takes her hand.

"Our android doppelgangers ran out of juice, huh?"

"The farther they got from Stone Heights, the weaker they became. Dying an android death is no picnic."

"The Molly betrayal, the Stoker fiasco, the Kim attacks. It's all coming back to me."

"Bad things," she says smiling.

"And good things too."

She nods her head. "Yes, good things too. Both bad and good."

"What about the people we helped, and the ones who helped us?"

"Mama, Mister Lincoln, Romo, and the others. All dead but for Paloma and Vigo."

A long moment of silence.

"Merlin?"

He searches her eyes, but whatever she meant to say she has decided to keep to herself.

"Did you know Paloma is having a baby?" he says.

Pearl's eyes sparkle as she smiles. "A baby, yes."

"You'd have to be fearless to raise a child in these times."

"Someone once told me fear is what makes bravery possible."

Merlin thinks it over. "I guess you could look at it that way. Fear is either going to make you brave, or it's going to destroy you."

"It has to be that way, doesn't it?"

"Yes, I suppose it has to be that way. One battle, then a new battle, and then another."

"Are you afraid, Merlin?"

"I am."

"Me too." He takes her hand and kisses it.

"One battle at a time, okay?"

From the corner of his eye, he notices movement. A glass box in the distance is winding its way toward them, smooth and silent as water. It slows and adjusts its trajectory, aligning itself to dock with them.

Sixteen

"The universe is an unforgiving place."

At first glance, he looks like a young radical. Untucked black t-shirt, jeans and red hi-tops. On closer inspection, you can see that the long hair and beard are whitish rather than pale blond, as they first thought.

"I know who you are," Merlin says, standing up without Pearl's help.

"We made a terrible mistake," Sayer says, his eyes shiny with exhaustion, "and now we toil beneath an alien sun. The hour draws near. The cosmic wolves have shown no mercy, but I promise you, even now there is a way through."

What in stars is he talking about? And who does he mean by *we*?

Sayer searches Merlin's eyes, settles his gaze on his mouth and takes a deep trembling breath.

Starling Sayer, aka Star Man, was no young buck way back when he was teaching individuals like Atwell ways to stretch the boundaries of human ambition and enterprise at Manifest Destiny Institute of Technology.

That was before his obscenely spectacular run at Gold Unicorn Systems, and before he *turned*, which still means something different to different people, depending on one's perspective.

"I can think of more than one mistake," Merlin says. "Genocides, slavery, persecutions, racism, xenophobia, bad history books, the deification of Coin, WOPAs. And what about the Deo Exodus? Does that qualify?"

"Everything you've cited points back to one core failure," Sayer replies in a thinning voice. He pauses to gather enough strength to release words that threaten to crush his lungs if left unspoken.

"The failure to be human."

Sayer looks over his shoulder as if expecting someone to hit him over the head with a golf club. And then, eyes closed, he says, "Now is the time to think in a new way on who we are meant to be. In a thousand years, or even a hundred years, will there be anyone left to ponder the odds of any one of us existing?"

Merlin is stunned by Sayer's reference to his first dictated words to Willie. He leans forward, anticipating a fuller exposition of his *Notes to Unknown Survivor*. But Star Man fails to deliver, probably never had any intent to follow through, may not even be aware that the words he just spoke were first spoken by the young man he's speaking to.

The old man gasps and presses both hands over his heart. He doubles over and looks like he's about to drop dead. Merlin gets up and lurches toward the glass wall, loses his balance and falls to the floor. He sneaks a glance back at Pearl, who hasn't shifted from the bed's edge and doesn't appear to be paying attention, or she's just being nice and pretending she's unaware of Merlin's inelegance.

"Could you be more specific?" Merlin calls out as Sayer totters over to a back corner. He carefully lowers himself to the floor as Merlin lifts himself up.

"Are you okay?" Merlin says.

Sayer ignores him. Meanwhile, a large, doughy figure wearing a sparkling diamond-studded tie and navy-blue suit materializes where Sayer was standing. Who could forget the ubiquitous face of Burr Brumbo, former president of the RSA?

Brumbo takes a few moments to ogle Pearl before waddling over to Sayer. He mumbles something Merlin can't hear, and waddles back.

"Cosmic wolves, my ass," he says staring at Merlin. "Are we supposed to believe every cockamamie announcement coming out of the mouths of losers like Sayer? Sure, blame all of the RSA's ills on aliens from outer space. Trust me, this SOB has been undermining the Reconstitution twenty-four-seven since he moved to Africa. What do you think he was doing there all that time? Passing out goody bags?"

Brumbo wiggles his right hand in the air and pretends to wince.

"You recognize this? Lingering effects of Hand and Wrist Rot Syndrome sustained from pulling all-nighters and busting my ass signing Executive Orders to protect RSA interests while also writing tremendous books. But I'm not here to toot my horn. I'm here to show you how to achieve lasting happiness."

"Mister President," Sayer warns.

He waves off Sayer and flashes Merlin an ear-to-ear smile. A table piled high with stacks of orange leatherbound books appears. He grabs one and rubs it against his cheek.

"This here is *the* foolproof guide to happiness, containing my patented Reconstituted Happiness Formula with crystal clear guidelines on how to achieve and sustain incredible prosperity and everlasting happiness. I wrote *The Good Things Book* during my amazing 2094 campaign. Needless to say, it was an instant bestseller, with ninety-million copies sold in the first three business days alone. What I do when I get up each morning—and so should you—is open this handy guide to page one and read my own genius words to myself. *Rule 1, Choose Me, not you.* Same applies in the broader context, *Rule 2, Choose Us, not them.* The rest is like water flowing downstream. Embrace Rules 1 and 2, and Rule 3 naturally follows: *Thumbs up to Happiness. Thumbs down to loser unhappiness.*"

"That's enough, Mister President," Sayer says.

Brumbo gazes at him with feigned stupefaction. "Now you listen to me, Sayer."

"Mister President," Sayer says as he limps toward the stacked table. "You never sold ninety-million copies of *The Good Things Book* in one week or in any length of time. Also, you didn't write it. I know who did, and it wasn't you. And now, Mister President, the hour draws near."

Brumbo rolls his eyes.

"Sure, okay, like I didn't write the greatest book ever. Like wow, what rathole did you just crawl out of? And what the hell is *the hour draws near* supposed to mean? Go back down into your rathole, you old perv. I have critical quality of life info to impart to this amazing young couple."

"It's not too late, Burr, even for you. Oddly enough, Mister President, it would be in your own self-interest to come clean. It would also be in the interest of all Americans, and in the interest of the entire human race."

Brumbo sighs. He pushes his nose flat against the glass and warns, "Don't listen to him. The man's a wolf in sheep's clothing, always has been. Drugs, child porn, sex trafficking, baby-eating, you name it. The things I've heard people say about this nasty codger would make your skin crawl."

"Burr, I beseech you, do the right thing for once. We'll do it together, you and me. Redemption is at hand for you and for all who want it, but time is running out."

Brumbo swings around with a violent energy that has no business being generated by someone so innately slow and beefy.

The orange books and table disappear, and a freakishly long thin figure wearing an off-white fedora and a purple scarf appears out of thin air. Sayer goes back and sits on the floor. The newcomer strides past Brumbo through the conjoined glass, briefly glances at Pearl, who is perplexed by his sudden appearance, and stops a couple of feet in front of Merlin. He tips the brim of his hat and bows.

"Formally, Adjudipredilextragalact for Cosmic Spectacles and Wagers; otherwise, known as Director X, serving at the pleasure of Omega Company."

"Are you for real?" Merlin says.

Director X's nostrils flare with displeasure for an instant. "Do what you have to do," he then says to Brumbo.

Brumbo bows solemnly. "Yes, Adjudipredilextragalact. Understood."

Director X turns his attention to Sayer, who is getting up off the floor, hands pressed against his lower back. Before anyone can say another word, Sayer, Brumbo and the glass box they came in disappear.

"I need to talk to Atwell," Merlin says.

Director X studies Merlin in silence for a long moment, then vanishes along with the hospital bed and the medical equipment.

Pearl is now sitting on the edge of a large sumptuous bed staring at a red, white and blue vase containing a bouquet of unusual multicolored flowers. A tantalizing aroma wafts into the spacious candlelit bedroom from an adjacent dining room. A piano nocturne plays softly in the background.

Pearl stands up and walks over to the small round table. She lifts a pair of entangled, long-stemmed flowers, inhales deeply, turns and smiles in a way he's never seen.

"Where were you?" he says.

"I was sitting on the bed, the other bed, the hospital bed."

"I know, but your thoughts were somewhere else."

She turns her head slightly, and nods.

"Did you see them all, Starling Sayer, Burr Brumbo and Director X?" Merlin says.

"I did, but I was very distracted."

She puts the flowers back in the vase and becomes still.

"Pearl, what did you see?"

Because she's standing motionless now, Merlin can observe the vase and the flowers and the table and Pearl as complementary elements of a lovely still life. A beautiful image, however unsettling. He stares at Pearl's right shoulder, at her angled profile, at her fingertips at rest upon the table, and he fears she may no longer be real. Her stillness nips sharply at his eyes, ears, and lips.

Have they done it to him again? He breathes into his hand. The breath and its warmth feel real, the hand absorbing the warmth feels real. He traces the contours of his face with both hands. The face feels real. But it always did feel real, even when it wasn't.

"Pearl, you promised," he whispers and draws closer to her, tentatively, as if a wayward step will drop them both into a bottomless pit. He stops, his heart lodged in his throat. Does he dare touch her? Remember now, fear can destroy you, or it can make you brave. He glances up and all around. He can't see them, but he knows they're there, watching.

"I love you, Pearl," he says and holds his breath.

How miraculous it all seems when she turns around. Her eager response erases all trace of suspicion that this Pearl's passion was scripted in a lab years ago. In the mad blur of kisses, they tip over the vase. It rolls off the table and crashes to the floor.

The ceramic explosion stops their loving, and for a few moments they stare at the chaos of red, white and blue shards and multicolored flowers splattered over the smooth, golden floor. Silently, and with great care, they pick up the pieces and pile them in the center of the table. Then they gather up the flowers and arrange them in a circle around the shards and watch as the vase reconstructs itself. Neither is surprised by the inexplicable physics. Why should they be surprised by anything ever again?

"I saw Cleavon Blinkhorn," Pearl says in her softest voice and begins inserting the flowers back in the vase, one by one.

"He told me he's my grandfather. I didn't know what to think. Why would he tell me that if it wasn't true? I had always thought he was a friendly, if a bit strange, neighbor.

"He came to my father's wake. I remember that day very clearly now. I was terrified that my mother would die too, and I'd be left alone. He sensed my fear and sat next to me. He told me it was okay to be afraid, but for only a little while, not a long time. He said fear always gives us an opportunity to be brave, and that when I came to believe and understand that, all would be well. I didn't believe or understand what he was saying at all, and I wished he would go away. He touched my cheek, smiled sadly and left. But I'm no longer a child. And, Merlin? I'm a human, like you, and I love you."

Waves of cacophonous applause send chills up and down Merlin's spine. "Leave us alone!" he shouts.

The crowd noise stops abruptly. Merlin and Pearl stare at one another.

"Let's eat," she says.

Seventeen

Is someone clapping? They wake. All is white, nothing but cool white. Love nest gone, magically reconstructed vase with flowers, gone. Mouthwatering food, round table, nocturne, garments, all gone. Pearl and Merlin rise to their feet, naked as newborns. Embarrassed, they avoid eyeing one another.

Where in stars are his pants?

"For modesty's sake, put your clothes on," says Director X, appearing suddenly before them.

"But where—?" Merlin begins. The garments materialize at their feet. "What is it you want from us?"

Director X takes his time reading the long flat of his hand before addressing the audience.

"Enrollment in The Human Show What Just Happened Club is growing exponentially, and the League of Inter-galactic Gambling Hubs reports record-setting activity. No surprise there. A skillfully wrought convergence of elements has brought us to this pivotal juncture. And, yes, in case you were all wondering, the female is with child."

"What?" Pearl and Merlin say at once.

Director X stares at Pearl, a smile like a knife cutting across his long pale face.

"Did you just say I'm…?" Pearl begins, mouth open, eyes bigger than ever.

"Pregnant, yes, as of, well, do the math. Or I can check with our production timekeeper for the precise moment."

Merlin, equally stupefied, glances at Pearl.

Director X lifts a long, thin arm, triggering a roar of approval from the invisible audience. He slices the air with a quick cutting motion and silence is restored.

"The production proceeds in an exciting new direction," he says. "Now the question becomes, what are we to do with you and the new entity growing inside you? What might constitute a suitable exit given your heretofore central role in *The Human Show*? Behind the scenes there has been much debate on the matter. One staffer suggested we deposit you in a wasteland, directly in the path of an oncoming Kim herd, with nothing but two bottles of water and a protein loaf."

Long folds of silver light tumble down from above like theater curtains. They spread open to reveal two alternating scenes: Pearl's final moments with Merlin in the Pueblo Town saloon kitchen, and Merlin's silent goodbye to Paloma in the wagon out in the barrens. Merlin and Pearl watch themselves die all over again.

"The proposal was dismissed on the grounds of tedium," Director X explains.

He waves dismissively at the alternating death scenes. "Who wants to see that again? To be frank, the proposal was made in jest. Regardless, be assured your imprint on *The Human Show* will remain long after you are gone."

"What do you mean gone?" Merlin says. "Gone where?" Director X raises a hand to discourage further inquiry. "Our simulation teams are generating thousands of scenarios and feverishly mining the analytics. In the meanwhile, your request remains pending."

"What request?" Merlin says. Director X grimaces and puts a hand to his ear pretending he's hard of hearing. "What request?" Merlin shouts.

"Why, your request to speak to your father, of course. Don't you remember?"

One long hand goes up once more to keep Merlin from interrupting. The other gets read again. "It just so happens that Atwell has this very moment filed a formal request to speak to you. You'll be pleased to know the request has been granted!"

"He wants to speak to me? When?"

"Immediately."

Weakness seeps into Merlin's joints. He wishes he could sit. He eyes the floor longingly, but resists the temptation to drop on all fours.

Remember, the weakness isn't real. It's in your head.

Waves of raucous applause escalate into a monsoon of sound. Pearl closes her eyes, covers her ears, and lowers herself to the floor. Merlin kneels beside her and puts his arms around her trembling figure.

Director X watches with interest as the noise batters the young couple. Then, his face suddenly hardened with boredom, he swings his hand like an axe and vanishes.

Merlin stands and gently lifts Pearl up. She hasn't said a word since the stunning announcement of her pregnancy. He wants to talk to her about it, but Atwell would be sure to interrupt them at the worst possible moment.

Could they reschedule the meeting? Oh, sure, Director X would be happy to accommodate him. Is he out of his mind? The alien would laugh in his face, sigh and remind him the crowd is ready and eager for a Merlin-Atwell showdown. Does he not understand that unresolved issues, resentments, mistrust, secrets and confusion are premium fuel for ratings?

That said, what's taking Atwell so long? Didn't Director X say he'd be here *immediately*? No good reason to believe X, but somehow, what he said about Pearl rings true.

Or is it that he, Merlin, wants it to be true? He revisits their moment of ecstasy, when he and Pearl became one. It seemed to him, then, that perfection had become tangible, and all things had become possible: joy, purpose and new life.

Merlin wonders if Atwell and Runa have been informed that they are going to be grandparents. Does he want them to know?

Speaking of whom, there they come, riding a glass box and standing several feet apart in the rear of their transport. To his surprise, Runa is wearing a pink hoodie and skintight black leather pants.

The glass box slows as it nears and attaches itself with a *cluck!* In those first raw moments, Merlin, Atwell, and Runa are like strangers on a busy city sidewalk avoiding each other's eyes. But soon, Atwell comes forward. This is a different man than the one Merlin remembers, softer, his edges rounder, his once energetic demeanor now gloomy and uncertain.

Is this to be Father's attempt at reconciliation? Would reconciliation, even Atwell style, be such a bad thing? Merlin is skeptical, given their tortured history. But, would it be so bad to live an impossibly long life with Pearl, compliments of VivaLong Plus? And wouldn't Martian grandchildren, or any kind of grandchildren, be a good thing for Runa and Atwell, in the sense that it might make them less self-absorbed?

Atwell's face never brightens, and his lips never move. He turns around without having said a word and walks back to the rear of the glass box.

"You filed a formal request to speak with me, or didn't you?" Merlin shouts.

Atwell sits down on the floor, still and silent as a monk. Runa is scrolling through her Q-Phone and looking annoyed. She squeezes her phone into the back pocket of her pants and sashays like a girl a third her age along the side wall, her long, sparkling, pink nails tapping the glass as she makes her way toward Merlin.

What is up with Mother? The click-clack of her heels is painfully sharp and resonant.

She stops a few feet away and wiggles her fingers at him. What to do with that mystifying smile of hers? Wave back? Yes, Merlin waves back and takes a step toward her.

"I'm not your mother," she says.

He skips a breath. It takes him a few moments to process the declaration. His legs tingle with weakness.

"So, you're telling me you're an android?" he says, his light-hearted tone fooling no one.

"Amanda, you see," Runa says. "Poor Amanda."

"Who's Amanda, Mother?"

"Oh, I don't have time for this. I've tried, Merlin. Good stars, I've tried. Why don't you ask your father, the world-renowned Sir Atwell Stone? He'll tell you. That is, if he can find the guts to do it."

"Wait, please," Merlin calls as Runa walks away. "What is going on?"

Atwell stands up and comes forward, his face seeming to have aged years in the last couple of minutes.

"I should have told you long ago," he says.

In that instant, the glass boxes detach and, ever so slowly, begin to drift apart.

"Where are you going?" Merlin says.

"It's not us, it's you. You're going."

"What?"

"You're the one moving away, not us. We're stuck."

"Who's Amanda?"

"Runa's sister… Your biological mother."

"What are you saying? Mother, what is this? Is that true?"
Runa remains silent.

"She died minutes after you were born," Atwell says.

Merlin swallows hard. He can't take his eyes off Runa's back. Her head is down. Is she weeping? He wishes he could see her face. Maybe he'd see Amanda's face too.

"I'm sorry, Merlin," Atwell says, raising his voice and spreading his hands. "For this. For all of it. For screwing you over. For doing unforgivable things."

Atwell glances back at Runa for a moment. "I'm sorry for what I did to her and Amanda. What I did to the Montoyas, and to others."

"Why are you telling me this now?" Merlin groans.

Atwell takes a deep breath. "Star Man was right. There is a way through, as impossible as it may seem."

Merlin can barely hear him now.

"Tell me what that means!" he shouts.

Atwell winces as he puts both hands on his head. He is like a man encountering despair for the first time. What's left of his voice is a mix of faint, barely recognizable syllables and phantom sounds. Merlin tries futilely to piece together his father's final words as he watches him and Runa shrink until they vanish.

He stares at nothing for a moment or two, then presses himself against the glass wall and slides down like a cracked egg. Pearl kneels on the floor, puts her arms around him, and pushes her face into his neck.

In perfect silence, the timeleapers watch the glass box containing Pearl and Merlin glide away through a receding tunnel of alternating light and darkness until it disappears.

Eighteen

Like drunk dancers, the tangled pair bounce off a wall, stumble together across the glass box, and repel off the opposite wall. Sayer frees an arm and lands an elbow on Rodolfus Barnesby's jaw, knocking him out cold.

Before Sayer can swing around, Brumbo tackles him from behind, and the two roll across the floor. Brumbo secures the command position atop Sayer amid a flurry of fierce hand slaps, grips and grabs.

"The dark arts will only get you so far, old man," Brumbo gloats in premature triumph. With a superhuman effort, Sayer dislodges the larger man and heaves him onto his back with a stiff leg thrust. He leaps into the air like a ninja and comes down with his heel on Brumbo's throat.

"Aw, for furp sake!" Brumbo croaks.

Sayer is panting hard as he points a finger at his adversary's face. "That's enough, Burr!" Brumbo avoids Star Man's gaze and wipes dribble from his chin. Sayer lifts his foot from Brumbo's throat and takes a step back. He observes the timeleapers with bloodshot eyes.

"This is the time," he says.

"The time?" Brumbo says. "The hell you talking about?"

Brumbo lifts his disheveled bulk off the floor, adjusts his tie, and buttons his jacket. He smooths his hair back into its helmet shape as if it were frosting and mutters, "It's time for you to cease and desist spreading pervy donkey dingo. That's what time it is, you old perv."

Star Man limps forward, places a hand on the glass wall to steady himself, and gazes with purpose at the Seven.

"Watch your back," Topper warns.

Sayer turns around. Brumbo halts his sneak attack an arm's length away. His latest scheme thwarted, the former president crosses his arms and hunches his shoulders. And there it is: *The Pout.* The all too familiar image gives Star Man pause. *Things could have been different, Burr*, Sayer's tired eyes seem to say. He shakes his head. There will be no coming back from what is going to happen, he knows, not for Brumbo, nor for Barnesby, nor for himself.

"Know this," he says, turning back to the Seven, "Omega Company will do anything, allow anything—even what may appear to be entirely contrary to their interests—as long as it increases ratings."

"Watch out!"

Sayer turns in time to elude Brumbo's blow. His counter-punch lands squarely on his assailant's left ear. Brumbo totters sideways and falls to the floor like a wounded wildebeest.

"Why did you have to sock me right on the ear, Sayer?" Brumbo cries, squirming and kicking on the floor, his hands pressed against the hot, throbbing earhole. "That wasn't fair, Sayer! You don't go around socking people in the ear!"

"Xeno ghosts like Krol take up residence where the spirit is weak," Sayer continues, while keeping an eye on Brumbo.

Behind Brumbo, Barnesby stirs, and is just now regaining consciousness.

"Are you furping moondaft?" Brumbo cries, rising to his feet, one hand plastered over his ear, the other slashing the air hysterically. "Starsake, Sayer, what are you doing talking about Krol? What I mean is, who in stars is Krol? There is no Krol. Krol? Krol who?"

"Among the ranks of Xeno and Symbiot, there is no answer to the birdsong, no means of silencing the spirit," Star Man says. "Not Krol, with his reality-altering schemes, nor any other of his kind can overcome such power. Know that you are not here by chance."

"Ha-ha-ha, crazy old perv!" Brumbo cries. "He's a liar! Don't listen to him!"

Rodolfus Barnesby stands up just as the glass box detaches. He stumbles and lands hard on his right shoulder. Startled, Brumbo unleashes a series of stunning high-pitched curses as they begin to glide away. Barnesby twists and groans on the floor but makes no further effort to rise.

Sayer extends his left hand toward the timeleapers in what appears to be a farewell gesture. On seeing this, Brumbo drops to his knees, raises his arms and lets out a piteous howl. Then, suddenly, he turns toward Sayer, his hands pressed together and raised in supplication.

"Why, Sayer? For furp sake, what is so wrong with being a little bit us, a little bit them?"

Brumbo's cries have no effect whatsoever on Star Man. His attention is focused on the timeleapers. Sayer clenches his hand into a fist. A cone of light projects from his ring finger, and a turquoise and gold circular image hovers before the Seven.

"It's Merlin's tattoo," Ava says.

"Good stars, *The Three Hares*," says Floriah.

Sayer, Brumbo, Barnesby, and the box they came in explode in a blaze of shimmering glass and streaks of crimson. A pinkish gray mushroom cloud shoots up and out as the dome's ceiling opens wide. The projection of *The Three Hares* persists for a half-minute more before dissipating.

Nineteen

A cosmic dispensation.

I'll go with that, for lack of a better term. How else to explain the miracle of my voice?

"It's me. Lola. Don't ask, okay?"

I hear my own voice, and its sound amazes me. My first time ever speaking the language of Topper and Ava, and Merlin and Pearl, and you, unknown survivor.

"I can't explain my voice. Only, consider this: among the ranks of Xeno and Symbiot, there is no answer to the birdsong, no means of silencing the spirit. Remember Merlin, who imagined you might one day hear his voice. Remember Starling Sayer, Martyr, who on hearing the birdsong, turned. Star Man, who pondered *The Three Hares*, recognized the spirit within you, and promised you a way through."

Astonished, they wait for me to say more. I want to. My mouth moves, but no more words come out.

The way through lies before you.

Topper looks up and locates me through the silence, the sealed dome, the space debris, the vast and endless darkness.

In the silence of endless space and time, the Seven hear the anthem of human blood humming from age to age and generation to generation, from the first ones to these and the ones to come.

The way through lies before you.

Before us.

Topper begins walking across the desert, and the others walk with him.

Twenty

What a minute ago seemed a distant undulating illusion has sprouted heads and limbs and fury. Three Kim herds are closing in on them. The smooth white sand has yellowed and turned thick and sticky for as far as their eyes can see. Their legs grow heavier by the moment.

Ava remembers Miss Glinty's warning: The Kim wake from their slumber, rise from the earth, shake off the dirt, and sniff the midnight air for Ord meat.

But it's not midnight. And they didn't leap two-thousand years back in time to become someone's dinner. What would be the point of discovering Merlin and *Notes to Unknown Survivor* and leaping through a timeway if they were all going to end up being eaten before accomplishing anything?

"Hey, trees!" Winka cries. "Where did they come from?"

"Could that be the Haven?" says Floriah.

Paxto sprints toward the trees to scope out the area. He waves to them. All is clear. On entering the forest, they wipe the cloying sand from their ankles and feet. From beneath the oaks and cedars, the Kim hordes seem to never have existed.

396

"I didn't hear the birdsong," Gabi laments.

No one did. They cover a mile through the forest before anyone speaks again.

"I badly need to hear the bird sing," Winka says.

"But what if *we* are the birdsong?" says Rahim.

"Did you want to elaborate?" Floriah says.

Rahim looks uncertain as he searches for the right words. He shrugs his shoulders and pats his heart.

"I know what he means," Topper says, and pats his own heart. No one presses either of them for an explanation. Why ruin the lovely sentiment with words? They resume their walk, and more quickly than they could have anticipated, they reach the edge of the woods. There, before what appears to be an immense clearing, they stop to rest awhile.

But Winka is restless and has eyes like a hawk. She notices things others don't. The solitary tree standing more than a quarter of a mile away wants to meet with her, she decides. "That tree feels human," she suggests casually, and her words barely register with the others.

What seems a throwaway remark by Winka gets Paxto started on Joe Tree, the tragic protagonist of a two-thousand-year-old legend called *The Brave Forest*.

"Joe Tree was part human, part tree, though no Symbiot, not in the predatory Xeno commandeers human body and mind sense. Joe was the leader of the last standing forest in the universe. One day the tree killers surrounded the brave forest and threatened to cut down every tree unless Joe Tree made a deal with them."

No one is paying attention to Winka as she sets off alone across the clearing toward the humanlike tree.

"Who told you about Joe Tree?" Floriah says.

"If I said a bluebird told me, would you believe me?"

Meanwhile, Winka continues to advance, but soon her pace slows and she comes to a stop.

Gabi stands up to stretch and notices Winka out in the clearing dropping to her knees. She glances at the others, but they are all engaged in different states of distraction, even as Paxto continues to develop his impromptu legend of Joe Tree and *The Brave Forest*.

Without saying a word, Gabi heads across the clearing. She slows down for a moment as she approaches Winka, who points to the tree. Gabi passes Winka and keeps going, wondering what it is that her friend sees that she doesn't.

Fifty strides later she stops to rub her eyes. Wrapped and bound like a cocoon on a massive branch is a big brown man with white curly hair.

Twenty-One

"Is he dead?" Paxto says.

"I don't know, but we have to get him down from that tree," says Topper.

"How exactly are we going to get up there to do that?" Floriah says.

Before anyone can reply, the tree undergoes what appears to be rapid time reversal, its leaves shrinking to vanishing nubs, its branches retracting and disappearing. The coarse surface of the trunk flattens to a shiny smoothness, and its cylindrical form turns sharply pyramidal, becoming a stone obelisk. The man's body contorts and shifts in obedience to the changing configuration. The ropes that held him to the branch have hardened into chains. A steel collar encircles his neck, and steel cuffs bind his wrists. His limp form slides slowly down the steep surface to the ground and settles in the dirt like an oversized, broken mannequin.

The familiar rumbling and shaking of the world seem less a surprise. Two-story wooden buildings break through the earth and rise all around, delineating a large square with the obelisk as its center point. The reconfigured setting looks just like the dirt plaza of Pueblo Town, as described by Merlin in the Notes.

The big brown man wakes and gazes at the Seven. His vacuous eyes pass from face to face, showing no sign of recognition or understanding. The man appears to be totally indifferent to their presence and to his own dire condition. But there are no signs of blood, nor visible wounds anywhere on his person, not the slightest bruise or abrasion.

When he opens his mouth, they all lean forward to hear what he has to say, but rather than words, the man succumbs to a coughing fit, his eyes enlarging and welling with emotionless tears. When he is finally able to stem the hacking, he takes several labored breaths.

"Those buildings," Topper says. "We need a crowbar or an axe, something to break those chains."

"That will not be necessary."

They turn toward the wooden voice and gaze astonished at what appears to be a tree man.

"Joe Tree?" Paxto utters in disbelief.

The invisible audience, whose existence the timeleapers had put out of mind for a time, ooh and ah and cheer in loud waves. The towering figure executes an elegant bow and lifts a leafy branch-arm to temper the audience's enthusiasm.

He looks down at Paxto. "How amusing. There is no Joe Tree, you see. There is only Bigleaf, Harry Bigleaf, Lord of the Arborians." Bigleaf completes a three-hundred and sixty-degree head rotation and quips, "Unlike those destined to die, immortals never lose their heads." He waves to acknowledge the crowd's laughter and shouting.

"Given the choice," Bigleaf continues, "fans will opt for alternate reality over ordinary reality ninety-nine point nine times out of a hundred. The ratings bear it out. Consider, for example, my beheading in *The Fall of Arbor*.

"An absurd premise, no doubt, and yet, an enormously popular one. Imagine, after seven years of relentless pursuit across the universe, the XenoStar-2 finally apprehends the Lord of the Arborians, yours truly.

"With viewer interest at an all-time high, the pressing question for the production staff became, what do we do with Harry? Lock him away? Subject the audience to a tedious, longwinded trial that will invariably land Harry right back in a glass box?

"Stars forbid it! Omega Company is not in the business of promoting mediocrity. Nor does it attempt to predispose the viewer to any given set of expectations. Omega Company refuses to pigeonhole its productions as either fact or fiction, ordinary reality or alternate reality. Stretch the boundaries! To the point, in the pursuit of mind-bending entertainment, Omega Company opted for the unexpected *and* the inexplicable: decapitate an immortal!

"Imagine the debates triggered by this cosmic irregularity! Of all things, the death of an immortal! The shady premise sparked widespread talk-talk regarding the nature of being, mortality versus immortality, alternate realities, and so on.

"Within hours of my so-called decapitation, discussion groups began springing up everywhere in the universe, abuzz with ideas for extending the limits of real time intergalactic entertainment, the genre that seeks to consistently leave the engaged fan wondering, 'What just happened?'

"The Fall of Arbor will come to lay the foundation for productions such as *The Human Show*, where reality-makers, players, and audience are collectively lifted by a surge of self-pleasing energy that translates into robust and profitable wagers and spinoff activities."

Bigleaf places a hand to his ear and the crowd roars. "Listen to them," he says. "They live for this! The curiosities, conundrums, surprises, conjectures and debates, the games and wagers! The fluidity between reality and unreality makes for stimulating and lucrative entertainment."

"Why is this man in chains?" Topper says, as the crowd noise dies down.

"Chains?" says Bigleaf, looking perplexed. "I see no chains."

On cue, the lights go out.

Ava reaches blindly for Topper's arm and slides her hand down to the hand that made a bluebird come out of Derelok Yoreasy's mouth. Topper squeezes back. It's going to be okay, his hand says. Everything's going to be okay.

So why is it so hard for her to breathe?

A narrow spotlight flashes on the now unchained man. The crowd cheers as he gets up off the ground, rubbing his wrists and neck. He grimaces, shakes his head, and says, "Folks, trust me, this'll work a lot better with the lights on."

Twenty-Two

"I didn't want them fooling around with Margarite," he discloses after all the lights are back on. "I told them they could do anything they wanted with me, but I made sure they wouldn't be able to do whatever they wanted with Margarite. My angel, may she rest in peace."

"May she rest in peace," Winka says, even before Cleavon can finish saying it.

He gazes at Winka, and then looks up at the domed ceiling and says, "I can think of a thousand better retirement destinations off the top of my head."

"You're Pearl's grandfather, aren't you?" Ava says. "You made Willie. Merlin's Notes don't get passed down to us without you."

Isolated clapping turns into broad applause that builds to an almost deafening din before cresting and subsiding.

"Let's get out of here," Cleavon says.

They follow Cleavon out of the plaza and stop at an orchard, where a six-horse Conestoga wagon awaits them. After some hesitation, they all board the wagon.

Cleavon takes the reins, glances at Topper riding shotgun, and shoots a look back at his huddled passengers. He gives the reins a good shake and yells, "Let's ride!"

"Where are we going?" Floriah says.

"The Haven," Cleavon says.

"The Haven, again?" Paxto says.

"That wasn't the Haven," Cleavon says, glancing back at them as the wagon rolls forward. "That was just a bunch of trees. I'm taking you where you need to go to do what you have to do and become who you're supposed to be. But let me tell you, the Haven ain't no holiday resort."

"What do you mean?" Floriah says.

"No picnic, no walk in the park," Cleavon clarifies.

"What happens when we get there?" Gabi says.

"You'll decide how it plays out. Didn't Star Man tell you there was a way through?"

The Seven glance at one another.

"Well, didn't he?" Cleavon insists.

"He did," Topper says.

"He was looking right at each of you when he said it. Don't go wasting precious energy worrying about the stuff you can't control."

Moonlight comes more quickly than seems possible. The dry, bumpy barrens recall the wasteland Paloma and her friends crossed. The swaying wagon groans and squeaks as it rolls over an ever-lengthening trail of divots, rocks and holes.

Gabi is the first to speak after a sustained period of silence. "I haven't heard the crowd since we got on the wagon. Does that mean they can't see us anymore?"

Cleavon doesn't answer. No one follows up.

Silence reigns for another stretch. Everyone but Cleavon and Topper doze off.

Some while later, Winka gets up, stretches, and goes to the back of the wagon. She pulls open the rear canvas flap, looks out across the dry land, and says, "Wake up, everyone, it's a new day."

They take turns going to the back of the wagon to see what looks like the sun just as it begins to breach the horizon.

"It doesn't feel like a new day," Paxto says, yawning as he scratches his arm.

"There," Cleavon says, pointing to a low dark mass in the distance.

Winka leans forward between Cleavon and Topper. "Is that the Haven?"

"Listen up," Cleavon says. Before he can utter another word, a fresh coughing fit shakes his big frame. He puts a hand over his chest until he's able to compose himself. He looks at his hands and draws his head back, as if surprised to see them still there. "If something should happen to me, that's where you go."

"Cleavon, you should come back here and rest a while," Floriah says.

"I'll switch places with you," Paxto says.

"I'll rest when I'm dead," Cleavon says. "You think being old and tired stopped Star Man from entering the Haven and doing what he had to do?"

Despite the confusion caused by Cleavon saying Star Man entered the Haven, Topper turns to the others. "Let's focus on being where we're supposed to be, on our way to doing whatever we have to do."

For a couple of minutes, Topper's words appear to pacify the big man, but soon Cleavon begins mumbling to himself.

"Cleavon, are you okay?" Topper says.

"A king with mystical tendencies once dreamed of three hares chasing one another in a perfect circle. Word of the dream spread. Everyone had an opinion about what it meant. The king died, but not the dream. Thinkers of all persuasions pondered the image of the three hares. Most decided it was a symbol of regeneration and hope, but there had to be more to it than that, given the king's mystical nature. That's how the dream as prophecy movement got started. Competing prophecies emerged, but the most popular and enduring became the one about a group of humans from the future going back in time to free humanity from alien oppression."

Cleavon turns his head, the bags under his eyes darker now. "I'll tell you something else. Blood goes where it sees fit. Merlin, Pearl, Paloma, and Vigo? Their blood traveled two-thousand years to find seven youngsters."

His face contorts momentarily, as if he's just bit into a lemon. He turns back to the trail, trains his eye on the closest horse, and says, "I've said too much. They think I'm a crazy old fool, Toby. What about you? You think I'm crazy?"

"You mean us?" says Ava. "Are you saying we're blood descendants of Merlin and Pearl and the others, which would include you too, being that Pearl is your…"

He doesn't respond. After a brief silence, they all start talking over each other. No one, but Topper, notices when Cleavon starts wheezing.

"Cleavon!"

The others stop and crowd forward.

"Crazy as moon dogs," Cleavon says between gasps, "them ghosts letting me tell you a story like that."

Cleavon drops the reins and clutches at his heart with both hands. His eyes roll up into his head. He begins to pitch sideways.

"Paxto, help me!" Topper cries as he grabs Cleavon and keeps him from falling off the wagon. Between the two they manage to stabilize the old man's body and get control of the reins.

Cleavon half-opens his eyes. "Remember the bluebird?" he says to Topper, and his smile becomes a grimace.

"Hang in there, Cleavon," Topper says. "Let's get you to the back so you can lie down and rest."

"Nah, man, I'm good," he whispers.

Cleavon tries to wink, but only gets halfway there.

Twenty-Three

They'll bury him in the Haven, or whatever the place they're going to is. *On our way to doing whatever we have to do.*

Topper peeks back at Cleavon's restless corpse stretched out on the wagon floor. He stifles a groan and closes his eyes for a few seconds. When he opens them, the trees are racing toward them, enlarging at an alarming rate. Just as the wagon is about to smash itself to bits against the tree trunks, the forest opens wide, and the Conestoga rolls unscathed into the Haven. In that instant, day turns to night, and the timeleapers are right back in the dimly lit Pueblo Town plaza. The horses slow their pace and pull the wagon to within thirty feet of the obelisk. There, the horses pause to rest, looking detached and unconcerned.

Rahim closes his eyes as he recites Star Man's declaration: "Among the ranks of Xeno and Symbiot, there is no answer to the birdsong, no means of silencing the spirit."

Topper inhales like a person just saved from drowning.

"I won't lie, those are some of the prettiest, most utterly useless words ever spoken," a voice from above says.

"It's Krol," Topper says. "Director X, Harry Bigleaf, that thing up there. It's always been Krol."

On an impulse, Topper snatches the reins from Paxto and shakes them. "Come on, let's go!" he cries, but the horses won't budge. He tries again. "Let's ride!" The horses pay no attention. They seem to exist in a different dimension.

Topper hops off the wagon and heads for the obelisk. Slowly, one by one, the others climb down and follow him. The chains that once held Cleavon dangle from a triangle of iron rings anchored to the stone. The steel cuffs and collar looped at the ends of the chains lie at rest in the dirt, waiting for new flesh.

Above the rings, engraved words mock the Seven: WHAT JUST HAPPENED?

They hear the creaking of the wooden undercarriage and watch in disbelief as the horses turn the Conestoga around and begin trotting away, taking with them Cleavon's body. Topper runs after the wagon, but comes to an abrupt stop, his face contorted with anxiety.

On his way back to the group, he glances at Ava. *Don't go wasting precious energy worrying about the stuff you can't control,* her eyes remind him, and in his head, he hears Cleavon's voice repeat those words.

The dome ceiling splits open, and white light floods the plaza. Loud cracking and crumbling noises draw the group's attention to the old church. The church, the saloon and every other wooden structure in sight collapse in a chaos of sound and dust.

The ground trembles and rolls, and the plaza appears on the verge of plunging into a giant sinkhole, but somehow it manages to hold and stabilize. Then slowly and deliberately, a circular wall breaks through the ground and the rubble and rises all around, thickening and shaping itself into a massive coliseum. From the gilded decks and balconies usher weird phonetics, an alien symphony of barks, hums, and whistles, a strange mix of mellifluous and discordant sounds produced by what appear to be countless beings of every shape, size, color and texture.

A clear, empty, room-sized glass box materializes before the obelisk, where moments ago the horses had paused to rest. Another glass box, identical to the first, appears to its right, and another to its left, until there are six arranged in an arc, like solemn spectators poised before a memorial.

The ground trembles anew and the lights flicker as Krol, now appearing as the Angel Centauri, materializes before them. He spreads his enormous gray and white wings and lifts his large head to acknowledge the multitude of spectators.

"Why the long face?" he says, turning suddenly toward the Seven. "Is it because Blinkhorn implied you are the fulfilment of *The Three Hares Prophecy*?"

"Why did you kill them?" Gabi says.

"By them, you must mean Sayer and Blinkhorn."

Gabi stares back at him, her heart palpitating.

"Technically, Sayer killed himself. We tried in earnest to work something out, despite age-related concerns harbored by certain staff members. We assured Sayer he still possessed entertainment value and presented him multiple options with generous terms, all of which he declined."

"Multiple options and generous terms?" Floriah says. "In what language would that be?"

410

Krol stares thoughtfully at Floriah, assessing the potential worth of her impertinence.

"Where have you taken Cleavon's body?" Topper says.

Krol raises an eyebrow as he scours the decks and balconies. He flashes a knowing grin.

"You think Blinkhorn is dead. Of course, you do. I have a surprise for you, he's not."

"He died in the wagon," Ava says. "We were with him."

"Nonsense. In the spirit of complete transparency, you should know that it was Cleavon Blinkhorn, in cahoots with Atwell Stone, who first raised the prospect of transporting you here from the future. Spare yourselves the head shaking for a moment. What I am telling you is one-hundred percent verifiable. The dynamic duo submitted a proposal. Given their extensive work on unraveling the mystery of the Stone Heights timeway, Omega Company was willing to listen. A mutually beneficial arrangement, contingent on the delivery of individuals of special interest, was reached. Did I say seven individuals of special interest?"

Krol studies each of the Seven, savoring their fear and confusion.

"You'll be glad to know Blinkhorn is happy and healthy and on his way to his own supersized glass lodging, where he will be provided everything he needs to build himself another Margarite or two."

"We don't believe that for a second," Paxto says.

"Believe what you will. It won't change a thing. There are more important matters to consider now. *The Human Show* is undergoing an epic transition. Be proud to know your faces will forever be associated with the introduction of time travel to real time intergalactic entertainment, marking the beginning of the genre's Platinum Age, if you will. Don't be shy, take a bow. The audience is eager to honor you."

The crowd rise to their feet, but their loud cheers quickly evaporate as the timeleapers limit themselves to gazing helplessly at one another.

"You said we were the fulfillment of the Three Hares Prophecy," Floriah says.

"I said no such thing. I said Blinkhorn implied it. But never mind, what I am about to tell you should alleviate your concerns. Omega Company investigators have looked into this so-called Three Hares Prophecy, also known as A Tale of Three Hares, The Three-Hared Hoax, The Hare I Am Scheme, and any number of other equally juvenile designations.

"What did the OC investigators find? Anecdotal material, for the most part. The occasional fuzzy papyrus scrawling, a few worm-eaten scrolls riddled with unintelligible allusions, numerous sloppy depictions of three rabbits chasing one another in a perpetual circle, and so on. Essentially, they found nothing but a trail of boredom leading nowhere."

"Then why not someone else?" Floriah says. "Why us?"

Krol studies Floriah, and smiles. "Why not you? But let's not waste any more time, shall we? On behalf of Omega Company, I am prepared to offer you a unique opportunity. An opportunity that will allow you to return to the future to resume your curious little lives."

Krol lengthens his wings and points in all directions at the crowd, eliciting a deluge of affirmative shouts.

"And now, finally, the moment is upon us," he says.

The crowd noise rises several decibels. Krol flaps a wing to quell the outburst. Topper shoots a nervous glance at the chains hanging from the obelisk and then does a quick scan of the burnished decks and balconies, pausing at the random sparkle, as if a flicker of light might dispel his fears and grace him with courage. He searches for the living among the aliens and wonders if such an audience is but an awful illusion.

"What do you want from us?" he says to Krol.

The sudden urge to flee assails his limbs, and he feels his body quiver for just an instant. The fear takes him by surprise. It's a warning, he knows. His center must hold, he reminds himself, not only for himself, but for the others.

In the distance, what at first looks like an ice cube, winds its way toward them, growing in size and consequence.

"As you may have guessed, the best opportunities always come with a caveat," Krol says, scratching his temple.

In the glass box they see a young man, a pregnant woman, and a little girl, all three startled by the crowd noise, their eyes darting blindly in every direction, incapable of seeing what is happening around them.

"Paloma," Winka says.

"And Vigo," says Gabi.

"Yes, yes, yes, and the rescued orphan too," Krol says. "Agreed, now let's move on. Pick one. Decide among yourselves which of the three will be your ticket to liberty."

"What are you talking about?" Paxto cries.

"Must I spell it out?"

Krol's words and the group's gradual understanding of what is happening induce sporadic laughter in the decks and balconies.

"This is not rocket science," Krol says. He looks away and rolls his eyes, triggering an explosion of commentary and merriment. "One of the three dies, and you all go free. I don't know how much simpler we can make this."

"What kind of perversion is this?" Paxto says.

"The perversion business we leave to others. At Omega Company, we prioritize opportunity. Did I not tell you the best opportunities come with a caveat?"

Turning to the crowd, Krol shouts, "Did I not tell them?"

The crowd's deafening response is immediate. Startled, Paloma looks up and holds the little girl tightly in her arms. Vigo reaches for a laser pistol that vanishes.

Krol sighs. "Pick one of the three, we don't have all day."

A loud rattling noise draws everyone's attention to sixty-four ground level gates. Thousands of Kim come crawling out from underground coliseum cells, bending and twisting their hairy, muscular bodies and turning their heads to eye the noisy decks and balconies.

Krol observes the Seven with shrewd anticipation, his thin eyes shining like polished silver.

With uncharacteristic restraint, the Kim slouch forward from all sides, advancing toward the timeleapers. At what seems a predetermined distance, they stop to assemble in a circle, surrounding the six glass boxes, the obelisk, and the young Ords who came from the future.

Twenty-Four

It has to be you.

You heard the voice, the one that can't be unheard. What a difficult and wondrous thing it is to be human, to be drawn from the warm haven of the womb into the icy whiteness of Whatever Is to Come.

Brother, if not you, then who?

When Paxto says, "Leave them alone, take me," Topper is not at all surprised. He walks up to Krol and says, "Don't listen to him. I'll give you reasons why you should take me instead."

"Topper, no!" Ava cries. "Please don't."

Krol folds his arms and rests his big chin in his right hand. He scans the murmuring audience as the glass box with Paloma, Vigo and the little girl glides away and vanishes.

"You gamesters out there!" Krol shouts. "How many of you saw this coming?"

A deep loud groan rises, drowning out the few cheers.

"I'm the one who found the quantum rabbit!" Ava blurts out. "I'm the one who found the hole that led us to the timeway. I'm the one who got Willie to show us how to leap through the timeway. If anyone should die—"

"No, Ava, why should anyone die?" Winka cries.

"Of all the scenarios, there has to be one where no one dies, doesn't there?" Gabi says to Krol. "I mean, there must be someone in the universe who placed that bet."

But Krol isn't paying attention. He's checking his long hand for updates. He spreads his enormous wings and thrusts himself high in the air. The coliseum shakes. The spectators are making awful screaming and shouting sounds. Everyone watches the gray angel's winged acrobatics, the sweeping arcs and trails of sparkling silver dust left behind.

The Kim growl and moan as they close in on the time-leapers, but their advance appears to be regulated by some invisible force that keeps them from turning the situation into a full-blown meatfest.

Winka reaches out and the Seven form a circle. Topper gives Winka's hand a perfunctory squeeze before releasing it. He points at the terrible angel and cries out, "Krol, take me!"

Krol circles the coliseum once more before gliding toward the Seven and landing like a feather in front of them.

"Outright refusal to pick one from among the production staff's choice of man, woman and child was not entirely unexpected," Krol concedes.

"However, this second failure to arrive at a consensus will not be tolerated. I invoke the discretionary power vested in me as Adjudipredilextragalact for Cosmic Spectacles and Wagers and duly announce the multiplication and expansion of betting options. Going forward, wagers will no longer be limited to identifying a sacrificial lamb, as it were. Bets can now be placed on any number of factors including, but not limited to, hours languishing, last word spoken, object of final gaze, time of death, and countless other possibilities."

Krol pauses briefly to allow the audience to express their pleasure. "But first things first." An off-white fedora appears in Krol's hand.

"Seven coins with seven faces," he says, and shakes the hat so that everyone can hear the coins clinking. "Go on, pick a coin."

"No, not like this," Topper says.

To everyone's surprise, Rahim steps forward and, without saying a word, picks a coin out of the hat. He looks at it quickly and holds it in his fist. The crowd noise builds. Rahim begins to tremble and drops to his knees. The coin slips from his hand onto the dirt. Before he can retrieve it, Topper snatches it. "It's me," he says.

"Show us," says Krol.

Topper refuses. A dozen Kim advance toward the Seven. Two of them grab Topper while a third rips the coin from his hand and gives it to Krol.

Krol holds up the coin between his thumb and forefinger. A gigantic hologram reveals the image of Rahim's face. The Kim advance toward Rahim, their bodies flexing with barely controlled rage.

"Don't touch him!" Winka cries, and throws herself in front of her friend. The others form a shield around the two. The Kim groan as they await orders.

"Is there a rule stating the Adjudipredilextragalact lacks the power to sentence all of you to death if he so chooses?" Krol sighs.

Getting no response, he paces back and forth, his wings shuddering and flinging droplets of dew from the feathers. He stops and stares at Floriah, anticipating her need to speak.

"You're going to kill us all," she says. "That was your plan from the beginning." She turns to her friends. "That's what he's going to do, he's going to kill us all."

"No, Floriah, he won't," Topper says.

"How can you possibly believe what you just said?"

"Careful, Topper, don't let him get inside your head," Paxto warns.

"He won't kill us all," Topper insists.

"He had us brought here precisely to eliminate us," Floriah says. "Don't you see? The Three Hares Prophecy is our death sentence."

"The prophecy, Floriah?" Topper says. "Don't you know Cleavon made it all up?"

Floriah is momentarily stunned, almost believes what Topper is saying, wants to believe it. "But even if he did make it up," she says, "it doesn't matter now."

"I agree with Topper," Rahim says. "It's going to be okay. One of us has to die so the others can go back. That's my face on the coin. This is how it's supposed to be, okay? Fate has chosen me."

"Merciful stars," Paxto says, tossing his arms in the air.

"What's gotten into you two?" Floriah groans.

Krol motions to the Kim, but their advance toward Rahim is met with resistance. An awkward, one-sided scuffle breaks out. In the midst of punches, grabs and pulls, Topper cries out in a wrenching voice that stuns everyone but Krol, "Stop it! I'm the one the audience wants!"

"Leave him, leave them all," Krol says, his eyes fixed on Topper.

The Kim back off. Topper's suspicion that this is what Krol has been anticipating and wanting all along is confirmed.

"A most curious creature, this one," Krol confides to the teeming decks and balconies. "Tell us, then, why are you so sure you are the one the audience wants?"

"Entertainment currency. I provide greater value. Rahim is frail. He won't last more than a few hours. I'm much stronger, both physically and mentally."

"You must think our production staff a team of amateurs. Do you think them incapable of performing suitable work-arounds to account for your friend's limitations? But go on, tell us more about this entertainment currency."

"None of these others will spark viewer interest and betting activity like I will. My strangeness excites the audience. Check for yourself if you don't believe me."

Krol is reading his hand, monitoring real-time audience response to what Topper is saying. He looks up. "What about this one?" he says, indicating Paxto. "He is the biggest and strongest of your group."

Topper hesitates slightly before replying. "He won't last long either. His mind is weak."

He feels the heat of Paxto's perplexed gaze, but knows he must forge ahead with his proposition. Floriah is right. Krol has no intention of keeping his word and means to kill them all. Topper allows himself the vague comfort of considering that maybe Atwell and Cleavon's roles in Krol's scheme are not as self-serving as they appear to be.

"I have something unique to offer you," Topper says.

"Aside from the strangeness that excites?"

"A secret. I'll reveal it to you in the final moments, but only on the condition that you publicly agree to release these others unharmed back to the future from where they came. Only then will I whisper the secret in your ear, and may the universe be our witness."

Krol stares at Topper, his face expressionless. He is only mildly intrigued by the offer, but when he reads his hand again and listens to the escalating roar of the crowd, he knows what he must do.

"In the final moments, you say? My, how dramatic. Fine, so be it. Agreed. May the universe be our witness."

"And may the universe gasp," Topper replies.

Krol ponders the peculiar remark for a long moment. He passes a wary gaze across the coliseum decks and balconies and then extends both his hands toward Topper in mock applause. "Indeed," he says, "may the universe gasp."

The crowd rises to its feet and stomps the gilded floors with eager anticipation.

•

Twenty-Five

From within her glass box, Ava can look in five directions. Four of those keep her from seeing Topper, the magical boy who once rescued her and is now slumped in the dirt chained to an obelisk, his eyes swollen shut, his body bruised and broken, his young life ebbing away.

She's going to die too. They all are. Floriah was right. The question is when. That's where most of the betting action and fan club chatter are right now. Who dies next? Who dies last? First to laugh cynically? First to cut deal? First to fart audibly? So many ways to win. Separated from one another by glass, friend will watch friend die in scintillating and, for a lucky few, highly profitable fashion.

Could they have done things differently? Could they have dodged this predicament? No, there was no escaping this. The only way out of the blue cave led them here, to this time and place, to this malicious captivity.

But why?

She recalls the moment Topper was led to the obelisk to be chained. When he glanced at her, his eyes seemed to say,

All will be well, as in a happy ending well. Given the way things have gone, it could be she misconstrued. Maybe Topper's eyes were telling her all will be well, as in, *Now look, Ava, we'll soon all be dead, so all will be well.*

To make matters worse, if by some freakish twist of fate, Krol were to keep his word and release the six survivors back to the future, how would they be able to endure the memory of Topper's horrific suffering and death? How would they ever again bear the sight of one another?

It would be better for them to die one at a time, even if it meant dying in unspeakably vicious fashion. Only then, truly, would all be well, fatalistically speaking.

In this nowhere place Cleavon ironically referred to as the Haven, it's always midday now, and the sun is always burning a hole in the world, and the sun is burning away the hours and burning away Topper and burning away her will to live.

How many days has it been? Topper is like a burned and broken doll picked from the ashes of a city in ruins, his young skin blistered and cracked, his eyelids and lips swollen and split. The wild-haired head rests loosely on the chest, the back curls like a sickle against the stone.

Topper? Are you there among the bones?

He gasps. She walks to the unbreakable glass wall, and runs her hands over it, seeking the button that frees them all.

In a sudden burst of rage, she pounds the glass with her fists and cries out the reality-maker's name, "Krol!"

One by one, the other five follow her lead. Several times a day, with ritualistic resolve, they pound the clear glass walls and scream and wail and cry out Krol's name. But the reality-maker is content to make himself scarce.

422

The crowd-pleasing *Human Vignettes*, as Krol calls them, are programmed to happen between the captives' outbursts, when they are drained and listless, like now. A new glass box appears and aligns itself with Ava's, providing her the best possible view. She braces herself for the latest cruelty, a woman and a boy seated on the floor with their backs to her.

It didn't take Ava long to figure out the source material for the *Human Vignettes*. That first day, after the Kim chained Topper to the obelisk, Doctor Patty, Nurse Pink and the two male attendants visited each of the timeleapers, beginning with Paxto and ending with Ava. Doctor Patty joked and offered assurances as Nurse Pink and the attendants hooked up Paxto to a machine.

"We're checking vitals, is all," Doctor Patty had explained with a smile.

The whole routine was repeated five more times. By the time they got to Ava, she had already calculated the entertainment value of a brain scan, the mining and manipulation of memories, emotions, doubts and fears.

The woman and boy are watching a hologram of a vibrant Miss Glinty dressed in a revealing silver V-top, miniskirt and matching stilettos. She is guiding someone through a tunnel at the Elevated Thinking Academy. She talks nonstop and gestures with one hand, then the other, summoning life views depicting luxurious villas for the benefit of her unseen guest. The setting changes, and Miss Glinty and her companion are now standing beneath a grapevine on a terrace. They are surrounded by dozens of potted daylilies, geraniums, and coneflowers. "You have made the right choice, Mister Blue," she says, as she draws her gaze from the gorgeous lake below.

The woman seated on the floor twists away, gasping for air. Though hardly surprised, Ava's heart again nearly stops at the sight of Mya's tortured face. The boy, her sib, Marny, appears unaffected by what he is witnessing and watches Fyo and Miss Glinty embrace and kiss.

"It's a tired lie," Ava says.

Mya and Marny glide away.

"Is it?" Krol says, suddenly appearing. "Mya and Marny? Miss Glinty and Fyo? Was that not they? Are you not you?"

"Fyo would never betray us," Ava says. "How many times must I say it?"

"Wouldn't he? Do you really believe he was sent to dig a tunnel that goes from nowhere to nowhere?"

Ava stares at the large mocking angel face and imagines herself smashing it to pieces with a stone mallet. Just then a dozen Kim from the surrounding encampment begin making their way toward her. The glass wall of her cell flickers and vanishes. The guards grab her by both arms, lead her directly to the chained prisoner, and leave her standing before him. She glances back at her friends. They are all pressed against the glass walls with their hands raised high, like prisoners about to be lasered. She touches the top of Topper's blistered hand and moans.

The Kim yank Topper up off the ground and jerk him around to face Krol, who gives his captive a long, probing look before addressing the many gamblers in the audience. "Had you taken the over on the six and a half, you would have made a fortune."

The remark elicits the isolated cheers of a small number of winners.

"But he's not dead," Ava whispers.

Two Kim guards hold Topper up by the arms. Krol's wings twitch, and the audience begins to stir, thinking he's going to launch himself up into the air to fly a few more awe-inspiring laps. But instead, he quiets the assembly and pauses dramatically.

"Consider this one," he says, indicating Ava. "Notice how she trembles. Is it for herself or for this other that she trembles?"

Krol frowns inquiringly as he scans the murmuring crowd. "Now look at the others. See how they agonize and press against the glass, as if expecting to redefine the narrative. Is it for themselves or for the one about to die that they agonize?"

He goes up to Ava, bends his broad nine-foot body, and tilts his huge head to within a couple of inches of her face. His thin silvery eyes peer deeply into hers. She doesn't flinch, nor turn her eyes away, but she knows that at any moment she might break into howls of fury and grief.

"Mya and Marny need you," Krol says. "Wouldn't you like to go back to Collective 64 to be with them?"

Ava stares at Krol's grotesque countenance. Her gaze is diverted to the stone mallet that suddenly appears in his hand.

"One blow to his head, or as many blows as it takes, for that matter, and the six of you are on your way back to Six Four City."

Liar.

She hesitates a moment but accepts the mallet from Krol's hand and again imagines shattering his face. But Krol won't let that happen, she knows. The mallet is heavier than she expected. She looks at her friends and then at Topper, and lets the mallet drop from her hand.

Krol studies her for several seconds. Then he levitates a few feet above the ground and slowly spins as he scans the multitudes. His gigantic image is projected holographically high above, spinning ever so slowly, his booming voice speaking in circles to an interstellar audience.

"Who in all the universe would seek to add to their own misery? And yet, it is this conundrum that makes *The Human Show* such a beguiling success. We ask ourselves, is time's assault on one's own existence not vicious enough? What benefit is there in freely supplementing one's own misery with the misery of another? And yet, it is not uncommon for humans to do so.

"Oh, you needn't take my word for it. Their chroniclers attest to it. Some go so far as to glorify self-sacrifice to the point of death! Such a skewed existential perspective gives one pause, does it not? In fact, irregularity of this magnitude begs the question: Are humans really that stupid?"

The holograph vanishes and Krol is back on the ground reading his long hand. "I have received notice that, in any case, this one will die within the hour, mallet blow to the head or not. It has been recommended that we proceed without further delay."

A Kim guard restrains Ava as Krol grasps Topper by the throat and lifts his body up like a trophy for all to see. Topper's feet flap helplessly in the air.

"And on the seventh day," Krol resumes in an elegiac tone… He stops in midsentence and watches with interest as Topper struggles to lift his right hand.

Krol turns to the audience. "Ah, the matter of the secret, remember? Even now, this one bequeaths us one final tidbit of entertainment. Very well, then, as agreed, I am all ears. Tell me this secret of yours, while you still have breath to speak."

Topper's lips move, but no words come out. His feet dangle limply now, and his eyes are shut. Krol adjusts his throat hold just enough to allow sufficient airflow to keep Topper from passing out.

The alien's eyebrows arch dramatically as he shoots the crowd a knowing glance. "There, there, did I not give you my word? Yes, your friends will be released back to the future from where they came. Come now, speak in total confidence. I am listening."

He draws his enormous face closer to his captive.

Topper can barely open his eyes. With the last of his strength, he moves his trembling hand toward Krol's chin.

For an instant, Krol becomes immobilized by curiosity and confusion. When he realizes what is happening, it is too late. He releases his grip and Topper falls to the ground.

Krol lurches sideways, his great wings twitching violently, powerless to lift him to safety. He gags, his frown deep and monstrous. His hands claw at his own throat. He falls to his knees, and his mouth opens as if to vomit. His eyes grow enormous as a bluebird ejects out of the gaping hole that is his mouth.

At the sound of the birdsong, the Kim scatter like frightened sheep, fleeing toward the ground level gates from where they first emerged. The six glass boxes flicker and disappear, leaving the astonished timeleapers free to run to their friends.

The bluebird sweeps over the coliseum like a laser beam, burning away Krol's former displays of vanity and power and wreaking havoc in the crowded decks and balconies. When the bluebird flies up to the clouds, the obelisk, the coliseum and the chaotic audience vanish with a cosmic gasp.

Ava cradles Topper in her arms as Krol undergoes irreversible molecular diffusion. Ava watches the quivering limbs, torso and head detach, crumble and rise in colorless vapors that drift and vanish.

Krol's flattened eyes linger, flipping like silver coins for a second or two before going *poof!*

Twenty-Six

For the past forty years Topper has stayed out of the sun. He now spends much of his time sitting in a wheelchair in the covered deck of his home on a hill overlooking Starling City. His gnarled hands rest like chiseled marble on his lap, his eyes see what others don't.

Ava is sitting next to him staring at the night lights in the city below. Now and then she reaches over and places her hand over Topper's once fine, magical hands and wonders if her touch gives him any comfort at all. She tilts her head and peeks at his scarred profile and playfully draws her face closer to his. She's looking for his smile. Sometimes it appears, and when it does, she believes he is remembering who she is.

Other times, like tonight, and for too many nights now, he does not remember her. At times like this, the night lights of the city become a constellation of stars, and Topper is off on a journey across the universe. She is jealous of the stars and of the journey.

What seems a lifetime ago, the Seven leaped through a timeway into another pool of water, a beautiful fountain in a park filled with flowers and Monarch butterflies, and families, and young and old, and grinning dogs running in circles. The dogs and the people stopped what they were doing to watch what seemed impossible. Whatever fear they felt during those first astonishing moments was dispelled by the gentle words and demeanor of the sad and weary young visitors.

The Seven, with their consistent, detailed accounts of their historic travels and encounters, became the talk of the planet, and a catalyst for a concerted reassessment of human history and purpose. In 4819, on the fifteenth anniversary of *The Miracle of Haven Gardens*, a unanimous Terra-wide decision designated Timeleap Day the first official worldwide holiday. It was also on that jubilant occasion, amid countless parades, celebrations, and widespread global optimism, that Ava and Topper's nine-year old twins, like many other young Terrans, took an informal vow to one day become timeleapers.

Could it happen? Several studies of the Haven Gardens Fountain and vicinity had left experts mystified. The appearance of the Seven was deemed a time travel miracle by most Terrans, but where in stars did the timeway go?

The Seven agreed that one day another timeway would be discovered on Terra, and humans would travel to distant places and times, possibly never to return. It was a sobering prospect, one Topper needed to address. There were things he had never said that he wanted to say before his steady decline left him incapable of making himself understood.

After ice cream and coffee, and with Ava sitting by his side, Topper fixed his gaze on the twins and said, "So you want to be timeleapers, huh?" The nine-year-olds nodded in unison and stared at their father, expecting to be challenged.

"It's not just about leaping through actual timeways and floating in space and landing in weird places, okay? That may sound like fun. It's not. There's another type of time travel that won't get you killed or scarred for life. Do you know what I'm talking about?"

"No," the twins answered in one dull voice.

"The human mind is the most awesome timeway ever. It can take you to the past, the future, and back to the present in a matter of seconds. And what makes it extra special is its ability to hear the birdsong, which is the spirit of hope and love. It's the birdsong that endows timeleaping with purpose, takes it to a whole new level. It interweaves memory, under-standing and dream, producing a vision that transcends time and connects every human being to every other human being *in the present moment*. You follow?"

No. How would they? They were nine-year-olds. Ava winced in sympathy when Topper turned to her.

"What Dad means is *just be human*. You know, the things we talk about. Respect, patience, understanding. When you run into a nasty, remember the odds of any one of us existing, and how we're all connected across time and distance. You and me and Dad, nasties, strangers, every human being."

Ava stared at the twins, and the twins stared back at her.

"I know it's not always easy, but that doesn't mean you stop trying. We never stop trying to get it right, right?"

Ava remembers how her words and Topper's failed to tame the twins' ambition to become timeleapers who actually leap through physical timeways and float in space and tumble into the unknown. And yet, despite their clumsy lecturing, Ava believes she and Topper must have planted some good seeds along the way because their daughter and son have grown up to be exceptional human beings. At the moment, they are at the Cleavon Blinkhorn Institute in Starling City attending Doctor Marny Blue's presentation, *The Three Hares Prophecy: Fact or Fantasy?*

Ava rests her head on her husband's shoulder and watches the universe turn. Today is the fortieth anniversary of *The Miracle of Haven Gardens*. The tantalizingly soft, warm breeze prompts her to venture a word, "Sometimes life feels too much like a dream, don't you think, Topper?"

A painful, extended silence follows. She's afraid to speak another word. Afraid of what her voice will sound like. Afraid that, at any moment, Topper will drift up to the Cloud and leave her alone on the deck staring at the city night lights down below.

But fear always presents an opportunity to be brave, remember? No one ever said this was going to be easy. Any of this. So, take a deep breath. Take another. Take one more.

It's alright if Topper never speaks again, she decides. It's okay if he never runs his fingers through her hair or caresses her cheek ever again.

Not ideal, no, not at all. She'll have to make do. Her center will have to hold, for her own sake, and for the sake of the others. That she can rest her head on his shoulder, in the present moment, is enough for now.

The two-hour presentation went as well as he could have hoped on this special day, but as Doctor Marny Blue leaves the podium behind and moves to the front of the stage, he is feeling a tad anxious. Not entirely because of the question-and-answer session that's to follow. This is his favorite part, after all, the back and forth, the give and take with young people.

But it all feels different this time. The bad dreams have been coming more frequently now. He sets his feet, scans the audience of three-thousand, and smiles. For the moment, the bad dreams recede.

After a number of entertaining exchanges regarding *The Three Hares Prophecy*, a young woman stands up and says her name is Lola. She tells him she was named after me! Imagine! Marny has no reason not to believe her and, in fact, suspects I arranged this *serendipitous* encounter.

"With all due respect, Doctor Blue," my namesake says. "I know you've been asked some variation of this question many times before, but I feel compelled to ask it in my own words, if you don't mind."

"Not at all, Lola, I'm interested in what you have to say."

"The Seven have been with us for forty years now. They arrived before many of us were born. We all grew up hearing about Merlin and Pearl and other memorable Terrans and, of course, Willie and Merlin's *Notes to Unknown Survivor*. Some people—granted, a small number—suspect the timeleapers are benevolent aliens, maybe even supernatural beings. I myself believe they are humans just like us, but there are times when…"

"Go on, Lola."

"There are times when the whole thing seems so unlikely, Doctor Blue. The expulsion of the Xeno twenty-seven-hundred years ago changed everything. The ruins of Six Four City

R. GARCIA VAZQUEZ

belong to a different Six Four City, one lacking the direct influence of the Xeno. When the Keepers arrived, the Xeno had been gone for three-hundred years."

"Yes, and?"

"The Seven changed the course of history. They changed everything, how people thought and lived, the circumstances under which they existed. In fact, the parents of the Seven might never have met, or even been born, which means…"

"Which means?"

"Doctor Blue, what's going on? Are we all cuckoo?"

Knowing laughter trickles across the audience of three-thousand.

Marny nods fatalistically. "Indeed we are," he says, before a sneaky grin triggers more laughter. "We're all cuckoo. It's in our human DNA. I see two kinds of cuckoo: Know-It-All Cuckoo and Wish-I-Knew-More Cuckoo. The Know-It-All folks pin themselves to a board. They get nowhere, no matter how hard they wiggle. The Wish-I-Knew-More folks never stop asking questions, always seek to grow in understanding, always hunger for what's true, and always listen for the bird-song. You follow?"

"I do. I get that part, at least."

"As for time travel? Smarter people than me have some-times sounded foolish trying to explain it. And what about the Seven? Are they benevolent aliens? Are they supernatural beings? We have every right to ask those questions. I myself take them at their word. Their humanity speaks to me quite clearly."

He pauses for several seconds, his eyes seeing what others don't.

"I often find myself imagining the timeleap that dropped the Seven in the Haven Gardens fountain. It didn't take them long to realize this was not their home, nor their time. The world had aged seven centuries, though they had aged but days. No loved ones were there to greet them. Every person they encountered was a stranger. What a profound sense of loss and disorientation they must have felt, what sorrow."

Marny pauses again, lost in thought. He forces a smile and continues. "My ancestor, Ava Blue—despite the death certificate stating she died seven-hundred years ago—once asked me if anyone had come up with an explanation for the contradictions of time travel. No, I said, not yet. There are various theories, all of them unsubstantiated. Topper alluded to one of these when the Seven were trapped in the blue cave. Does anyone remember what he said?"

Several hands go up. He points to a young woman.

"And you are?"

"Sophie."

"Tell us, Sophie."

"Topper briefly mentioned the possibility of a parallel universe. Maybe the timeway dropped the Seven into an alternate Terra?"

"An alternate Terra? Is that where we are?"

"I mean, that would be one theory, Doctor Blue."

"A Terra spared thousands of years of Xeno cruelty?"

Sophie hesitates, nods her head. "In theory, Doctor Blue. And yes, we have been spared, whether or not this is the only Terra in the universe, or one of many alternates."

Marny's face darkens. The bad dreams are closing in on him like shadows. The dreams have no right to be here. He tries to smile, but can't. He heads back to the podium, his steps heavy and awkward. Halfway there he turns around and says too harshly, "Spared for now."

His words cast a shadow over the entire hall. The air thickens with uneasy silence as he returns to the podium.

He clings to the wooden lectern to steady himself and passes a weary gaze over the expectant assembly. Unconsciously, he waves his hand at them, as if dismissing them back to their carefree lives. He shakes his head and again tries to smile, but what he really wants is to be home in his old man slippers having a drink and listening to songs of the Old World.

But what a disappointment that would be to these young optimists. He gathers himself, opens his mouth, and hopes for the best.

"We are surrounded by mystery. We ask questions, we try to figure things out, we try to say the right words. But some things can't be explained with words, and reason has often failed to convince. The timeleapers defied the crazy Know-It-All world order, leaped two-thousand years into the past, suffered the unimaginable…"

He winces as he imagines Topper chained to the sun-scorched obelisk in that strange, paradoxical Haven. These Terrans are nowhere near ready to tangle with the unimaginable. There's so much he wants to say to help prepare them, but Marny doesn't trust his voice, nor the words that might come out. Six-thousand eyes are fixed on his face, forming a blazing spotlight.

If he were detached and nimble enough, he would wave goodbye and leave. But he's neither. He stares at his notes and watches his crafted words mingle and swirl like a mixed drink.

A painful minute of silence passes. He looks up finally, and thinks, why not tell a joke and exit to the sound of laughter? An Ord, a Deo and a Xeno walk into a Greek bar…

"And then I heard one bird singing!" a young man cries out.

Heads turn. Who was that?

A second voice repeats the ancient declaration, a female this time, and immediately a third voice follows, and many more. The beloved cry echoes throughout the great hall, and the cheers and applause build and merge into a torrent of affection and affirmation. Doctor Marny Blue, startled and confused by this outburst, gets an unexpected and unwanted standing ovation.

He waves them down and tells them to be seated, his weariness and anxiety lifted for the moment. Oh, they're not yet ready for the unimaginable, but they will be. Some of them, enough of them to move the species forward.

"Doctor Blue?"

"Yes?" Marny says, turning to his left. "Where are you?"

A young man stands up.

"Why, hello there, you wouldn't happen to be Cosimo, the Good Samaritan?" Marny says, managing a smile.

"No sir, ha-ha. My name is John."

"John, yes."

"I listen for the birdsong, sir. That is, when I remember."

A few chuckles of recognition from the audience.

"I'm working on it, Doctor Blue," he continues. "I want the birdsong to live inside me, you know?"

"I'm glad, John."

"I have a question which may sound a little cuckoo."

"I wouldn't expect less than cuckoo."

"Ha-ha, I understand. I've been wondering, sir…"

"Yes, John, go on."

"I was wondering, Doctor Blue, is the birdsong meant for everyone?"

"For everyone. Yes, John, it is."

"I don't mean just humans, sir."

"You mean all creatures."

"Yes, sir."

"I believe so, John, yes, meant for all creatures."

"Are we to take the birdsong to every creature?"

"By we, you mean those of us here in this hall?"

"I mean all of us, sir, the human species. Are we to be the ones who take the birdsong to the ends of the universe?"

Marny, moved by the young man's spirit, and fully aware of the dire cost of such a calling, smiles sadly.

"If not us, John, then who?"

A penetrating silence fills the hall. Should he offer them a word of comfort? No, they are no longer children. Let the word be what it must be.

Marny pats his heart the way Rahim once did. Before he can blow them a parting kiss, three-thousand heads turn stage left. Walking briskly toward Marny is his colleague, Mirembe Sol. She puts her hand on his arm and leans in toward him.

Her words stun Marny. He laughs, wipes his eyes, and takes a deep breath. His expression softens. His gaze passes slowly and tenderly over all the gathered. One can imagine Marny Blue gazing at a meadow and counting wildflowers.

The young humans grow more restless by the moment. Their sparkling energy ripples up onto the stage, enveloping Marny.

"We found him," he says as calmly as he can manage. "What were the odds Willie would still be around?"

Acknowledgments

The gift of kindness, distributed without discrimination or self-interest by ordinary people, is always a cause for celebration. It was these disciples of compassion who inspired me to spend the past three plus years writing *Beneath An Alien Sun*. In my life, these people have included family, friends, neighbors, teachers, classmates, coworkers, and strangers, individuals whose self-giving acts and words remind us in the most simple and beautiful ways what it means to be human.

A huge thank you to my darling wife and best friend, Ana Maria, for evaluating my countless drafts with dogged objectivity, making no effort whatsoever to spare my delicate ego, and liberally pointing out what she hated—but also what she loved—in those hundred-plus thousand words. Being the ever-astute husband and writer, I listened.

Special thanks to my grandson, Sam, for recommending and confirming the inclusion of a romantic element in the novel, and to my grandson, Xavi, for summoning from his fertile young brain the name *Hammertuss*, which became the valiant, if peculiar, Dread Squad horseman.

About the Author

After graduating from Rutgers University, I became many things: a landscaper, factory worker, darkroom manager, security systems technician, college writing instructor, military logistics and communications systems technical writer, sole proprietor, husband, father, grandfather, occasional alien, and wise protector, as my birth name, Ramon, would indicate. Over the years, writing stories has helped me become a more compassionate person, though no less a realist. I was conceived in the gorgeous, bagpipe-loving Celtic region of northwestern Spain known as Galicia, born and raised in Newark, NJ-USA, the firstborn son of Spanish immigrants who taught me how to be human.

Thank you for reading *Beneath An Alien Sun*. If you enjoyed the novel, please take a few minutes to leave a review on Amazon. Your support would mean a lot to me. Knowing I've connected with a reader is always humbling and gratifying.

Author website: rgarciavazquez.com
Facebook: @rgvtimeleaper
Twitter: @rgarciavazquez2

Printed in Great Britain
by Amazon

29030641R00260